Atomic Candy

A NOVEL

Atomic Candy

Phyllis Burke

 The Atlantic Monthly Press, New York

Published simultaneously in Canada
Printed in the United States of America

Library of Congress Cataloging-in-Publication Data

Burke, Phyllis, 1951–
Atomic candy.
I. Title.
PS3552.U7234A95   1989   813'.54   88-7660
ISBN 0-87113-274-5 (hc)
0-87113-364-4 (pb)

The Atlantic Monthly Press
19 Union Square West, New York, NY 10003

FIRST PAPERBACK PRINTING

Acknowledgments

I would like to thank
Cheryl Deaner, Lynn Hendee, and Michael V. W. Crain
for their support.

This book is dedicated to James N. Frey.

FLIRTING WITH DANGER—Last week, at a Saints & Sinners party in Washington, Dick Nixon ran afoul of both at once. ... Seated sourly in a cage at the party was Sheba Sheik, a lion unable to distinguish between Presidential timber and more edible human material. Also in the cage were photographers. ... They yelled at Nixon to come in and pat the beast. Nixon hesitated. "He's afraid," said the host.

—*Life,* June 1953

If that had been JFK, the lion would have licked his hand.

—Kate Kelly Albion, June 1953

SENATOR KENNEDY GOES A-COURTING—The handsomest young member of the U.S. Senate was acting last week like any young man in love.... Mussing the Senator, Jackie tousles his hair, his political trademark. At times Kennedy broke away from fun to get Senatorial work done.

—*Life,* July 1953

There hasn't been anyone like Nixon before because the rest of them at least had souls.

—Marilyn Monroe
Alternate Delegate
Democratic Convention
April 1960

Contents

PART THREE

PART FOUR

PART FIVE

Part One

CHAPTER 1

"You're on the Threshold of a Thousand Thrills"

[Life magazine ad for Buicks]

September 1952

Eight months pregnant, Kate Albion wore three-inch spikes. She never had morning sickness because she didn't believe in it, and nothing was allowed to interfere with the national elections. Kate Albion was a woman with a purpose, working her ward in Boston, Massachusetts, working for Mr. John Fitzgerald Kennedy, contestant in the political beauty pageant for a seat in the United States Senate. She worked for the sake of the nation, and she worked for the sake of JFK's hair, his political trademark.

Kate's jubilant glow was not so much due to her pregnancy as to the fact that the Republican presidential ticket was in trouble. Dwight Eisenhower's vice-presidential running mate, Richard Nixon, had been caught redhanded with $18,000, an enormous sum, in illegal contributions. Richard Nixon was going to be on television tonight, and Kate was certain he would drop off the ticket like badly permed hair from a lady's skull.

Summer had ruptured into an early burst of red and yellow autumn, and the baby in Kate Albion's belly was taking its cues. Not due for several weeks, the infant was still growing its fingernails and dreaming about color and light as Kate walked through Boston like a knife cutting through a piece of cake. Pregnant or not, she gave you the impression that she was fashionably thin. "You can never be too thin or too ruthless," said Kate Albion.

Slicing along in the sunshine toward City Hall and the office of Fatty Finney, the Democratic party boss, Kate Albion was unaware that the umbilical cord was floating around the baby's neck. The baby in Kate Albion's belly scraped its new fingernails along the uterine wall in a fetal Morse code—hot hot flash, hot hot flash—just to let her know it was there. Kate Albion's feet hurt, so she indulged the baby and sat down beside the statue of Benjamin Franklin on the bright green lawn in front of Boston City Hall. The umbilical cord drifted to a safe position.

Kate Albion's heart pumped with pleasure as she stared at the huge curved windows of City Hall. The building conveyed power and privilege and brought tears to her eyes. While her husband was moved by musical extravaganzas, she was moved by pomp and power. Kate Albion envisioned her inauguration as first lady of Boston, hostess of spectacular parties, giver of turkeys to the poor

4

at Thanksgiving, and destroyer of her political enemies. Yes, Boston City Hall brought tears to her eyes because Kate Kelly Albion might have a mean streak, but she was also Irish and therefore sentimental.

Kate grabbed hold of Benjamin Franklin's ankle and pulled herself up. She walked across the bright green grass, up the white granite steps of City Hall, and through the wide mouth of the doorway. She stood in the silent rotunda. The tremendous height of the ceilings and the black-and-white marble of the floors kept the place cool and majestic. The grand staircase of wide marble steps and iron and oak railings led to the chambers on the upper floors, led to the mayor's office. She considered taking the elevator to Fatty Finney's office on the floor below the mayor's but she could not resist the drama of climbing the staircase, surrounded in her imagination by the adoring voting public. The very real baby, however, took the climb as a sign to begin its passage to the threshold and into the world.

A chill cut through Kate's spine as she imperiously climbed the steps, her spikes echoing at each footfall. She stood at the top of the grand staircase and surveyed the rotunda.

Hot hot flash. Hot hot flash.

She thought of her husband, Joe Albion, who was completing his tour of duty at Camp Pendleton in California. Joe Albion's Southern California childhood came to an abrupt end when his widowed mother married New York money. Joe never talked about this because it embarrassed him, and he had fantasies about being a self-made man, like Martin Kelly, Kate's father. Martin Kelly said Joe Albion was a poor-little-rich-boy bastard, but he'd do.

Joe had political possibilities for the Old Man, who could never run for office himself because he had a tragic flaw: he spit.

Kate Albion had great expectations. Perhaps this baby was the boy the Old Man always wanted. For thirty years, every day of Kate's life, he complained that he had been cheated. He said he had risked his immortal soul by bullying and lying his way to power for the sake of his offspring, and then had only one girl to take the reins of power—as if political office were a dangerous horse that could only be ridden by a dangerous man. It was a terrible disappointment.

Kate Kelly Albion did not want to disappoint the Old Man, but not because she was sentimental. The truth was, she wanted power as much as he did. She wanted to walk into the rotunda of City Hall, up the grand staircase, fling open the dark oak door that read PRIVATE—MAYOR'S OFFICE, and walk right in. She imagined herself sitting on the leather couch, beloved of the people, carefully gerrymandering ward boundaries to Democratic advantage, her legs crossed at the knee and one spike-heeled shoe dangling from her toes. Powerful people, noted Kate Albion, move through the world as if they own it.

Today, she didn't own it, so she turned at the top of the grand staircase and walked to Fatty Finney's office. She flung open the door, her long black hair tossing like beautiful snakes, and confronted the fat man wearing red suspenders and seated behind a desk. One low-hanging, green, mushroom-shaped light shade encased one glare-bent bulb that dangled in the air above his head, where cigar smoke undulated.

"Every voter in my ward will be contacted at least

three times," said Kate Albion to Fatty Finney, "and every registered Democrat, dead or alive, will make it to the polls, even if they have to use the absentee ballot. Fatty. There's no shortage of political miracles in Boston, Massachusetts, but even I can't make Adlai Stevenson win the presidency."

Fatty Finney said, "Why the hell not?" The Boston Democratic party boss had a defiant cowlick on the crown of his head that acted like a feeler. Fatty Finney was not a pretty picture as his cowlick twitched toward Kate Albion.

"Adlai sounds too ritzy," said Kate, closing the door behind her and lighting a charcoal-filtered Tareyton. "They could make him a diplomat, or the representative to the United Nations. But if you can't come up with a good jingle with his name in it, forget it."

"What d'ya mean?" asked Fatty Finney, slathering the cigar in his mouth with saliva. "Nixon's blown the Republican ticket."

"Try and say 'Adlai' without taking your cigar out of your mouth," said Kate Albion, blowing smoke to the ceiling.

Fatty Finney rolled the cigar around in his mouth and said, "Adellaid." A drop of saliva slipped from his lips.

"See what I mean? Now try 'Jack.'"

Kate pointed her cigarette at Fatty Finney, who rolled the cigar, clenched it between his teeth, and said a nice clean "Jack."

"Jack Kennedy is destined for great things," said Kate Albion seductively. "Now try 'Joe.'"

"Joe?" asked Fatty Finney. The name passed the political pronunciation test as the cigar rolled from one side of

Fatty Finney's mouth to the other, his hands never touching it, a major qualification for party boss. "There's no Joe running," he said.

"There will be. And don't forget it."

Fatty Finney smiled as he understood that Kate and the Old Man, Kate's father, were planning on running her husband, Joe Albion, for political office.

From the corner of the office, Kate Albion took some campaign posters featuring a picture of JFK and tucked them under her arm. Kate Albion said good-bye to Fatty Finney, whose tongue battled his cigar for eminent domain of his mouth.

With renewed purpose, Kate Kelly Albion descended the staircase in City Hall and walked toward her ward in the Back Bay section of the city. There was still an hour to go before Nixon's televised humiliation. Kate didn't want to miss any of it, and there was just enough time to do a short ward walk. Trees in their autumn colors lined the narrow streets, but they could not compete for Kate's attention with the intricate windows that sparkled in the sunlight and boasted radiant red-white-and-blue Democratic political posters, with a touch of green for every Irish household.

Kate Albion stood at the foot of Marlborough Street. The sedate brick and granite faces of the apartment buildings, with their ornate cast-iron railings, protected her voters from the wind and rain. She walked up Marlborough Street and nailed a JFK FOR U.S. SENATE poster to a tree. She balanced herself on one of the tree roots that had pushed through the bricks in the sidewalk. The baby began to rock and push.

Kate stepped back to admire the poster. She was particularly fond of this picture of John Kennedy. His famous lock of wild hair had been neatly concealed among his obedient hairs, but Kate Albion knew it was there. Kate knew that JFK would win the U.S. Senate seat because he looked at every woman he met as though she were the only woman in the world.

Kate turned and was fury struck at what she saw in the apartment window across from the tree. Her glare could have broken glass as she focused on the I LIKE IKE poster taped in the window.

"What the hell is that *thing* doing in my ward?" she said aloud, trembling with rage. The startled baby opened its eyes inside her womb and kicked. Kate marched up the steps of the Marlborough Street apartment house and rang the bell ten times for the manager.

Kate Albion knew that General Dwight David Eisenhower promised to keep everything in place if elected president. Hup two three four. But this was Kate Kelly Albion's ward, and before the national election, there wouldn't be an I LIKE IKE sign in sight.

The front door flew open and a huge, enraged woman with pin curls and fluffy pink slippers, holding the collar of a furious German shepherd, greeted Kate Albion.

"That 'I Like Ike' sign in the window," said Kate.

"What about it?" asked the manager. The dog strained up to Kate's height and barked like hell, its eyeballs almost white from straining to get her attention, but Kate just pushed his head to the side as if he were a fruit fly, which infuriated him. Kate took a JFK poster, put it in the woman's free hand, and said: "You want garbage service? You want the police to come when you call? You want the SPCA to decide that this dog is not a danger to the community?"

The woman slammed the door shut with her foot, and

Kate walked slowly down to the sidewalk. Nellie Kelly was standing at the foot of the stairs. Nellie Kelly was wearing her emerald green cloche hat, her elegant gray cape slung over her thin shoulders.

"It could be ninety degrees and you'd have on that hat," said Kate, ignoring the judgment in Nellie Kelly's eyes.

"In case I'm struck down, young lady, they'll know I'm of good family and they can't go cutting me up without asking someone about it," said Nellie Kelly. Nellie Kelly was sixty years old, had blue cotton-candy hair, which was the absolute rage for ladies her age, and scented herself with Nights of Araby perfume. She had come from Ireland when Kate's mother died, and she had lived with her brother, Martin Kelly, and Kate on upper Commonwealth Avenue since the day she arrived twenty-five years ago. Nellie Kelly was not particularly impressed with the Old Man. He was, after all, her baby brother. When you've wiped someone's bottom, Nellie Kelly always said, you don't tremble in their presence. Nellie was, in fact, the only one whose presence prevented the Old Man from spitting. She made him wipe it up himself.

Kate walked to the poster of JFK on the tree, and Nellie said, her brogue unusually thick, "There was a little boy, who was a little coy, who had a lock in the middle of his forehead. And when he was good, he was very very good, and when he was bad, he was horrid!"

Kate turned to Nellie Kelly—and knew she had been on one of her excursions to Mrs. Finnegan's in South Boston. Whenever Nellie Kelly returned from Southie, her hair looked a little more blue, her makeup a little bolder. Her behavior indicated the consumption of a large quantity of black tea or sherry, her Irish brogue was thicker, and her predilection for elaborate omen-reading had escalated.

"Aunt Nellie, Aunt Nellie, oh where have you been? Have you been to London to see the queen?" said Kate.

This was Kate's favorite childhood rhyme.

"I've been to Mrs. Finnegan's, and now I'm looking for you, young lady. Come on home for a cup of tea. Do you want to push this baby into the world before its time? Children born before their time have strange fates."

"Oh, Aunt Nellie. Please," said Kate.

"You're in no condition to be nailing posters to trees. You could hire someone for that."

"If you want something done right, you'd better do it yourself," said Kate.

At that moment, Kate saw the apartment manager rip the I LIKE IKE sign from the window and tape the JFK poster in its place. Kate flashed with happiness as the German shepherd barked madly from behind the closed window, and Kate remembered Nixon's television address.

Looking at the poster of John F. Kennedy, Nellie Kelly said, "That boy'd be better off floating in his yacht off Hyannisport. Mark my words."

Kate marked her words as they walked home to the Old Man's house on Commonwealth Avenue, and to the special treat of the televised self-destruction of Richard Nixon.

The thick Oriental rug in the front drawing room was filled with secrets. Visitors, often supplicants to the Old Man for jobs, loans, and references, looked at their feet and planned their speeches in the drawing room, waiting to meet the Old Man. Kate stood on the rug and her feet felt hot.

The Old Man always said, "I hate them if they come in

here sucking up to me just to get something. But if they don't suck up, I won't give them a damn thing." Then he'd spit. Nellie Kelly had seen a legion of housekeepers come and go, unwilling as they were to put up with the Old Man.

Nellie and Kate looked toward the large oak door to the Old Man's sitting room. "I'll get some tea on," said Nellie Kelly. "You go tell His Lordship we're home."

"We have tea for everything around here," said Kate. " 'Are you sick?' 'Have some tea.' 'Are you happy?' 'Have some tea!' 'Are you angry?' 'Are you dead?' 'Have some tea.' It's a wonder the Irish have anything left to their bladders."

"I'll put the kettle down," said Nellie Kelly.

Kate checked her watch, walked the narrow hall that ran the length of the large house, and opened the door to the small garden hidden in the back. There they were: a mass of human-sized sunflowers with tall, coarse green stems, deep black cyclops' eyes, and bursts of bright yellow petals, outstretched and demanding, like the arms of a madman. Nellie Kelly never understood why Kate wanted sunflowers, which were, as any true gardener could see, big weeds. Kate Albion selected one sunflower, walked right up to it, looked it in the eye, then turned her back on it. She left the garden, shutting the door behind her fast and hard. Kate Albion cultivated her mean streak.

Kate walked to the door of the Old Man's sitting room, turned the knob, and entered. The Old Man was sitting in his wheelchair, his plaid afghan across what Kate saw as his bony legs.

"I used to have great legs. Make no mistake," said the Old Man, reading her thoughts. Kate hated this. His little bald head with thin wisps of white hair worked like a radar dish.

Kate Albion noted that the Old Man's latest housekeeper, Molly Finney, had arranged things just as he liked. She had closed the dark green drapes, lit a blazing fire in the fireplace, and turned on the air conditioning. Kate sat across from the Old Man in her favorite seat: a formal black leather chair with carved armrests and legs that ended in claws. She couldn't quite place what she was reminded of in the strange atmosphere of the room. Sunflowers would really flourish in here, she thought, as she waited for Martin Kelly to speak.

"You see Fatty today?" demanded the Old Man, rolling a bit of phlegm at the back of his throat. The flames from the fireplace reflected in the glass of his wire-rimmed spectacles.

"Yes. I did what you said. I told him we were going to run Joe."

"What he say?"

"Said I was just like the Old Man."

"God damn it. If you had balls, you'd be governor."

"Thank you." Oh, if only there were those things that dangle, that go bump in the night, thought Kate.

"Where's that fashion model of yours?" demanded the Old Man.

"He's still at Camp Pendleton."

"When he gets back here, get him ready to run. City council. Then mayor."

"Guess who's giving a speech in a few minutes? Richard Nixon," said Kate Albion.

The Old Man's phlegm picked up momentum in his throat.

Kate smiled. She loved the Old Man. "It's the end of him. You want me to turn your radio on? I'm going to watch it on the television."

The Old Man did not like television. He did not like to

see images of men younger than himself. In fact, he conned himself into thinking that the only difference between him and Joe Albion was that Joe Albion was "whore blond," as he liked to describe it.

The Old Man had a beautiful walnut radio, four feet high, complete with a phonographic turntable on which he periodically played old 78s. Whenever "I've Got a Lovely Bunch of Cocoanuts" was heard, punctuated by a chorus of rolling coughs, you knew the Old Man was celebrating the demise of an enemy, especially if he'd had a good part in it.

"You bet I'll listen to that son of a bitch Nixon confess," said the Old Man. "Turn it on."

Kate Albion turned on the radio and left the Old Man, after she stoked the fire and turned up the air conditioning. As she walked to the door, the potted white lilies in the corner swayed in her wake. Ah yes, she thought. This is the climate of a funeral parlor.

Kate joined Nellie Kelly in the library, where a Revolution-era bookcase had been ripped out of the wall to make room for the television. Nellie was watching the television and sipping her tea. She had placed a cup and saucer near the easy chair for Kate. Books lined the walls, nicely bound editions of the classics, but none of the bindings were so much as bent. The Kelly family read newspapers.

Kate kicked off her black spikes.

"Spikes and a spirited temper give a short woman height, but they can also give her bunions if she's not careful," said Nellie Kelly. "Did you hear about poor Peg Dugan? She exploded. Of course they put 'after a short illness' in the obits, for good taste's sake."

The obits, also known as the Irish sports pages, were the first place Nellie Kelly turned to in the daily papers. Nellie kept Kate posted on wakes that would be politically important to attend.

"Jack Kennedy never goes to a wake unless he knows the deceased," said Kate.

"He won't get elected if he keeps that up," said Nellie Kelly.

Kate had to agree as she propped up her tingling feet. Speedy Alka-Seltzer was dancing on the television screen. He was wearing comfortable white shoes. Boys always do, she thought.

> *Plop plop*
> *Fizz fizz*
> *Oh, what a relief it is!*

Kate's eyelids got heavy as she began to plot Joe Albion's rise to political power. Kate knew that being a marine lieutenant was a great political asset. It didn't matter that he'd never seen action on a battlefield. It was the uniform that was important. The marines agreed with her and had selected Joe Albion as the man you saw on countless recruitment posters. He looked so good that the armed forces didn't want to risk getting him shot to hell. Joe was disappointed that he would never be a battlefield hero, but not disappointed enough to volunteer for combat.

The battlefield foamed with hundreds of Alka-Seltzer tablets as Kate Albion fell into a light sleep. She and the Old Man could sleep anywhere and anytime, which was a sign of a clear conscience, or no conscience at all, according to Nellie Kelly. Kate Albion, in her hypnotic presleep, fantasized Joe Albion campaigning in his sparkling dress-white marine lieutenant's uniform. Joe didn't know a thing about his political ambitions yet, but he'd come around. She was sure. He couldn't refuse her anything. He loved her. Kate knew what was best. After all, Joe Albion was a charmer. He was six foot two, and he had great white teeth and thick, straight blond hair. Hair had a very special place in Kate Albion's politics.

A picture of Richard Nixon intruded on her fantasy; she was infuriated at his image but titillated by his impending demise. Kate Albion had a pathological hatred of Richard Milhous Nixon's hair. It was curly, but it wasn't. It was obedient, but it wasn't. It wasn't being what it was. He had hair that sent double messages. She focused on his eyes, which were small and shifted easily, the eyes which would help to earn him the nickname "Tricky Dick." She studied his eyebrows, those eyebrows that made him look like a used-car salesman. Quite simply, Richard Nixon was not photogenic. But was that a crime in America? Yes! Television made it a crime to be unphotogenic, and if not a crime, a political self-destruct, a Madison Avenue bomb.

Richard Nixon's face came into focus on the television screen.

> **My fellow Americans. I come before you tonight as a candidate for the vice presidency and as a man whose honesty and integrity has been questioned.**

Kate Albion struggled into consciousness. She felt as if the house was on fire, but she could not open her eyes. Behind her eyelids she saw Benjamin Franklin's foot. Her consciousness grabbed hold of it and pulled her up and awake into the library.

"There he is!" said Kate Albion. The baby kicked in her belly.

Wild coughing and muffled shouts could be heard from the Old Man's sitting room.

"Calm down, Kate. He's just a politician," said Nellie. "That baby doesn't need to know about Richard Nixon yet."

I am sure you have read the charge, and you have heard it, that I, Senator Nixon, took eighteen thousand dollars from a group of my supporters. Now, was that wrong?

"Yes!" shouted Kate Albion.

I don't happen to be a rich man. . . . My wife used to teach stenography. . . . I was born in 1913 . . . most of my early life was spent in a store, out in East Whittier. It was a grocery store, one of those family enterprises.

Kate Albion flared into a temper blackout.

"He makes excuses for himself. He tries to make us feel sorry for him," said Kate Albion. "He uses his wife to make us feel sorry for him. That's the most despicable thing a man can do! Women can make you feel sorry for them. That's why there's the applause meter on 'Queen for a Day.' It's a woman's job. But a pathetic man, a whining man, is a man without sex appeal, without guts, and a man like that doesn't deserve to run this great country. Every woman knows this."

"And some men, too," said Nellie Kelly, noting the sound of spitting coming from the Old Man's sitting room. She wasn't going to be the first to go in there after this was over.

I have no life insurance whatever on Pat. . . . I own a 1950 Oldsmobile car. . . . I owe three thousand five hundred dollars to my parents, which I pay regularly, because it is part of the savings they made through the years they were

17

working so hard. .... I should say this. Pat doesn't have a
mink coat. But she does have a respectable Republican
cloth coat, and I always tell her she would look good in
anything.

The baby was pulled down into the birth canal as Kate's
temper flashed and burst.

"He's not quitting! The bastard's not quitting!" shouted
Kate Albion, as Richard Nixon cleared his throat and continued.

Kate Albion was so angry at Richard Nixon's speech that
she went into labor. Her contractions, however, were only
distant thunder against the black-and-white snow job on
the television screen. Kate Albion was not paying attention, and she had no idea that the umbilical cord was
dangerously close to tightening around her baby's neck.

The baby clawed a passionate distress signal onto the
uterine wall:

Hot hot hot. Flash flash flash. Hot hot hot.
Hot hot hot. Flash flash flash. Hot hot hot.

—

Marine First Lieutenant Joe Albion was stationed with
ten thousand other marines at Camp Pendleton, California, on one hundred square miles between Oceanside and
San Clemente near San Diego. The ocean was at one end,
and the hardest dry ground at the other, except when it
rained and the marines were ankle deep in mud. There
was, however, no rain today, and there had been no rain
in a month. Morale was low, but it was on the rise because
the ten thousand marines were preparing for the arrival
of Miss Marilyn Monroe on a mission of mercy. Joe Albion

did not know it, but Marilyn Monroe had the power to absolve him of original sin, the first sin, which brought banishment from the Garden of Eden.

The gold buttons gleamed on Joe Albion's dress-white uniform, with its beltless, tailored jacket and priestlike collar. His white lace-up leather shoes resembled Speedy Alka-Seltzer's, and his hat, his magnificent white hat with gold braid, looked like an Alka-Seltzer tablet.

Thousands of white leather shoes walked across the bone-dry ground, causing little swirls of dust to lift and drop around thousands of white socks. The heat waves rose up from the ground in the distance like a snake charmer's pets.

Drunk with heat, the men marched slowly onto the buses and headed to the sea. Joe Albion was in the passenger seat of a jeep, ahead of the others, leading the strange Exodus: Joe Albion had been chosen for Marilyn Monroe's honor guard.

As his jeep neared the ocean, he saw a hand-drawn sign:

DRIVE CAREFULLY—
THE LIFE YOU SAVE
MAY BE MARILYN MONROE'S

Two young, clear-eyed marines were smiling broadly and holding the sign between them, their caps resting on the backs of their heads as they waved with their free hands to the men driving past. Joe did not return the wave.

The makeshift amphitheater of wooden bleachers, a stage, and a powerful sound system rose into view. It looked to Joe like the kind of place where the Christians got thrown to the lions. He watched the men around him become delirious as they anticipated the arrival of this one woman. As far as Joe Albion was concerned, Marilyn Monroe was just another mirage from Hollywood.

Joe Albion got out of the jeep and walked to the stage entrance at the rear of the amphitheater. He stood at attention. Joe Albion could always be counted on to do his duty. He was not, however, interested in Marilyn Monroe. A woman like that was out to make him vulnerable. He believed she would have power over him by bringing out his desires against his will. She was the poison apple.

The ten thousand men were limp with heat and delirium. No merciful sea breeze roused them from their stupor. Joe Albion thought this was just as well. Keep them sedated. He knew one thing about men: he didn't like them when there weren't any women around. They were all hormone. Their heads were ablaze with the glow of red-light districts, and they didn't care about beauty.

Joe Albion was an angry man, even if he did sparkle in the sunlight.

"Where the hell is she?" The words were expelled softly from between his great white teeth.

Marilyn Monroe was late. Just like a woman. Just like this woman. A piece of raw meat tossed into a lion's cage, but the lion's not supposed to eat it. I hate her, thought Joe Albion.

He hated the men in the amphitheater, too. They were beginning to squirm and the murmuring was rising up, and the smell of sweat was pungent.

Maybe they'll start marking out their territory with their piss, thought Joe Albion.

He wanted to get home to Kate Albion. Now, there was a woman. Kate Albion was civilization. When she sabotaged an enemy, she remained ladylike and made sure that his children had enough to eat. She wasn't like this Monroe, a clinging-vine pathetic air-brain thing you could hurt at any turn. She didn't look at a man's face and see the hairy ape, into a man's heart and see the killer. Kate Albion saw a vote, and power.

Joe Albion did not want a son. Boys are too vulnerable, he thought. He wanted a daughter. No girl of Kate Albion's would turn out like this sex queen Monroe, triggering red-light-district fantasies in men.

The world would be better off without women like this, he thought. Where the hell is she?

Joe Albion did not do well in the heat. Joe Albion was thirsty, but he did not want a drink.

A helicopter hovered over the amphitheater. The men looked up as a shock of blond hair leaned out the open door, and then a full torso in a skin-tight, pale green dress. The copilot had to be holding her by the legs inside the helicopter. Marilyn Monroe blew kisses and waved to the marines as she flew over them, and the marines sent up a cheer that was so loud, God probably heard it. Like invisible fingers, a light sea breeze fluttered across the men's hair as the helicopter landed near the honor guard, behind the stage.

Joe Albion smiled a little. That was pretty gutsy, hanging out of a helicopter like that, he thought. Seven thousand five hundred of the assembled marines lit up cigarettes and laughed as loud as men can laugh. The other 2,500 marines punched each other in the arm, since they didn't smoke.

Joe Albion was disgusted with these men. Don't they have any pride? he thought. Can't they at least appear to be in control? These were the kind of guys who miss the urinals.

Marilyn Monroe stepped out of the landed helicopter and walked toward Joe Albion. She moved in her slow, liquid walk, as if she just might lose her balance maneuvering her splendid body through the world, as if getting from one place to another was an act of God. As Marilyn Monroe closed in on Joe Albion, he fought a compulsion to hold her up, to protect her.

Marilyn Monroe was surrounded by a white light. Marilyn Monroe had walked from the dark side of the moon and onto the grounds of Camp Pendleton.

Joe Albion was mesmerized. He tried to pull himself out of her trance. Poison apple, thought Joe, but he smiled and took a bite as Miss Monroe put her hand on his arm for balance. She took off one spike heel, shook a stone out of it, and put the shoe back on her foot, never looking down, her eyes locked with his eyes.

"Are you a general?" she asked Joe Albion.

"No, ma'am. I'm a lieutenant."

"You look like a general."

Her eyes were full of love. She looked at Joe Albion as if he were the only man in the world, and then she turned and walked up the wooden steps to the backstage area. He watched her breathe. She watched the men backstage breathe. They smiled and were silent. In the amphitheater, the marines who could not yet see her created a distant roar of mantric white noise in the background. Miss Monroe did not seem to be having any thoughts as she looked at the men backstage. Marilyn Monroe was in no hurry, since she was outside of time.

She has no guilt, thought Joe. She's just breathing. She didn't need to take his power from him because she had plenty of her own. She did not draw the beast from Joe Albion; she drew the hero.

Joe Albion felt like a god. Other women could strut, throw their breasts in a man's face, and watch him squirm with desire, but they had no real power of their own. They only had what they stole from men. But Marilyn Monroe moved her body for her own pleasure first, and let men, and even women, watch. All of the stag films he had seen made him feel evil, ashamed of his erection, even though he'd laugh about it with the other men. But the shame was not present now. He looked at this voluptuous blonde with parted lips and enlightened eyes, and saw the ecstatic incarnation of woman: fearless beauty in an evil and dangerous world. It made him proud to be a man. Joe Albion experienced conversion and vowed that he would be willing to die for Marilyn Monroe, as the little wave turned into a big hello in his dress-white uniform.

Miss Monroe walked dreamily onto the stage, as if she could not quite remember where she was or why, as if she could not hear the thousands of male voices cheering. A sea breeze lifted up from the flat ocean, and Joe Albion breathed in the sweet smell of male that curled around the stage.

Marilyn Monroe noticed a microphone and went over to it, as if she were all alone. She looked at the microphone as if she had never seen one before. She tapped it, and the tap triggered a roar. The ten-thousand-headed lion, Sheba Sheik, licked her feet.

She breathed deeply into the microphone, took it into her hands, looked up, and noticed the ten thousand marines for the first time. She looked at them as if she were looking at one man, one man with ten thousand heads.

She turned her back on him, and the band played as

Marilyn Monroe swayed. She turned back to the Marines like a charmed snake, and ripe and sweet, in her small, undulating voice she sang:

Oooooooooooooooh,
Do it again.
I may say,
"No, no, no, no," but . . .
Do it again.

Hot hot hot. Flash flash flash. Hot hot hot.

Small rain clouds formed over the amphitheater.

My lips just ache
To have you take
The kiss that's
Waiting for you.
You know if you do, you
Won't regret it.
Come and get it!

Miss Monroe ran her hands across her exposed neck, and Joe Albion, lifting his white marine's hat, ran his hands through his hair. For a flash, they were Miss Monroe's hands. Joe Albion's powerful body quivered like the applause meter on "Queen for a Day" as he thought, "There's nothing wrong with me. There's nothing wrong with me," and his eyes filled with tears. Hello hello! None of the other marines saw the tears. They were averting their eyes from each other, looking up, up at the stage, the sky, the stage the ground the sky. There was a lot of cigarette smoke in the air. It must have been irritating their eyes.

My mom may scold me,
'Cause she told me
It is naughty, but then,
Oh! Do it again.
Please.
Do it again.

Some of the men began to waltz with each other, others broke ranks, but none broke into the white light that surrounded Marilyn Monroe. The men tossed bright white carnations and yellow daisies onto the stage.

These are good men, thought Joe Albion, and this is a good woman.

Marilyn Monroe held the men in the palm of her hand, pressed them against her heart, and tongue-whipped their ears. The MPs had to link arms to keep the marines from surging onto the stage as Miss Monroe leaned forward and blew them a great big kiss.

Joe Albion experienced a momentary pleasure blackout as Miss Monroe made her way past the honor guard and back to the helicopter.

Joe Albion said, "Miss Monroe."

"Yes, General?"

"You are a great American."

Marilyn Monroe said, "Thanks. Ever so," and kissed his cheek.

Holding her shoes by the heels in one hand, Marilyn Monroe boarded the helicopter, rose up into the air, and flew one last pass over the amphitheater as a light rain began to fall.

For Joe Albion, Marilyn Monroe was now more important than Jesus, because she took his soul to the dark side of the moon and gave it candy. There were a lot of empty candy wrappers on the dark side of the moon, because Marilyn Monroe was pathologically compassionate.

She could save every man, thought Joe Albion, if they'd only surrender to her. Every man. Even Richard Nixon.

—

A man down in Texas heard Pat mention our two young- sters would like to have a dog. . . . It was a little cocker spaniel dog, in a crate . . .

"A dog? He's talking about a dog!" shouted Kate Albion.

. . . black and white, spotted. The six-year-old named it Checkers. And you know, the kids loved the dog, and I just want to say this, right now, that regardless of what they say about it, we are going to keep it.

"Who cares! So you've got a dog named Checkers. It probably cheats. Resign! Checkers has nothing to do with your secret funds!" Kate Albion stormed at the television screen, shaking her fist above her head and holding the bottom of her heavy belly with the other hand as Nellie Kelly led her out of the house and into the yellow-and-black Checker taxicab for the ride to Massachusetts General Hospital.

"Kate. Pay attention. Your water broke," demanded Nellie Kelly, who adjusted her hat on her head. "You're about to give birth."

The Old Man carried on in his sitting room, unaware that he was about to become a grandfather.

The cord lingered near the baby's neck as Nellie Kelly

helped Kate Albion into the taxicab. The cab driver had his radio tuned in to the Nixon speech.

Nellie Kelly studied Kate with alarm. Did Kate have the Kelly affliction of being struck suddenly insane, like a flu—no gradual deterioration, just a surprise event, the payoff and power of teeter-tottering on the edge of reality to get a glimpse into the next world. The Kellys called the affliction "being on tour."

Kate turned to Nellie Kelly and said, "I'm not on tour. Go ahead. Test me. I can name every Democrat running in Boston."

Hot hot hot. Flash flash flash. Hot hot hot.

The taxicab pulled into Massachusetts General Hospital.

Take Communism . . . the danger is great to America.

A gurney was rushed out to the circular drive, and Kate was lifted onto it, Nellie Kelly close behind.

Kate heard the voices of nurses and doctors hurtling through the air, tangling with Richard Nixon's voice. The radio at the nurse's station broadcast Nixon's address, but only Kate Kelly Albion was listening because everyone else was involved in her emergency.

In the Hiss case they got the secrets which enabled them to break the American secret State Department code.

"It's a blue baby. The cord is wrapped around its neck," said a white-light-jumbled voice in a tangle of hands.

"This is Richard Nixon's fault!" shouted Kate Albion.

"That baby can't be blue. That baby's Irish!" said Nellie Kelly with indignation to the nurse.

"No, no. The baby's the blue you get when you hold your breath. Kind of a bruised blue. The baby can't breathe."

They got secrets of the atomic bomb. . . .

"This is Richard Nixon's fault!"

> *Double, double, toil and trouble;*
> *Fire burn and cauldron bubble.*
> *Nose of Nixon, eye of politician,*
> *Liver of blaspheming Republican.*
> *Toe of picket-crossing scab,*
> *Finger of birth-strangled babe.*

Nellie Kelly's hand and heart reached deep into the green light and made a deal with the Banshee. "Get the baby into the world, and I swear she'll have a kind word and a soft moment for the likes of even Richard Nixon. And you can take something old away with you in trade. Your choice. Even me."

> **I say that a man who, like Mr. Stevenson, has pooh-poohed the Communist threat in the United States—he said that they are phantoms among ourselves—**

"Don't push, Mrs. Albion!" ordered the doctor.

"She better keep that Ike sign out of her window, that's all I can say!" shouted Kate.

"She's delirious," said the emergency nurse.

—He has accused us, that have attempted to expose the Communists, of looking for Communists in the Bureau of Fisheries and Wildlife. I say that a man who says that isn't qualified to be president of the United States.

The doctor reached his hands into the green light between Kate Albion's legs and pulled the cord from the baby's neck.

I don't believe I ought to quit, because I am not a quitter. And, incidentally, Pat is not a quitter. After all, her name was Patricia Ryan and she was born on St. Patrick's Day, and you know the Irish never quit.

Kate Albion lost consciousness. Not only did he use his wife, but he invoked St. Patrick.

In the living rooms across America, the applause meter quivered wildly against its upper limit, a kind of saber rattling in support of Richard Nixon that would continue for the next twenty-two years.

"Thanks. Ever so," said Miss Monroe.

Joe Albion repeated these words for the entire flight across the continent to see his new daughter. A daughter. The stewardess brought him a drink, and he said, "Thanks. Ever so." The taxicab driver drove him to the door of Massachusetts General Hospital, and he said, "Thanks. Ever so."

Joe Albion rode the elevator to the maternity ward and walked the green corridor with its exaggerated hospital lighting. He stopped short of room 333 and donned his marine hat, which he knew would please Kate. She loved a military look. He walked slowly, ceremoniously, into her private room.

Kate was bloodless white, nestled in the white linen of the hospital bed, her hair like a puddle of black ink on the pillow. She was not holding the baby. She was holding the newspaper. Nellie Kelly, seated beside her, was holding the baby. Joe Albion winked at Nellie Kelly and motioned for her not to let Kate know he was there. He walked softly toward Kate, lowered the newspaper, and held her hands. He had waited months for this moment, and he felt fulfilled as he put his arms around her and pressed her gently against his chest. He grimaced as something sharp pricked him deeply. He lifted himself away from Kate, still smiling, for he was always brave. He removed the pin which had become lodged in his skin.

"Daddy's Knights of Columbus decoration," said Kate Kelly Albion. "He sent it over before he found out it was a girl." She sighed and said, "I'm sorry."

"I wanted a girl."

"Are you crazy?"

"Are you?"

Joe Albion lifted the little girl in her pink blanket from Nellie Kelly's arms.

"She looks like you spit her out of your mouth," said Nellie Kelly. Joe Albion was pleased with this because it was a high compliment to a man as to his wife's fidelity. Nellie Kelly sighed. She adored this little girl, but she wondered if she were to be exiting soon as part of the bargain with the Banshee.

"The doctor thought she was dead, but a little blarney pulled it off," said Nellie Kelly.

Joe Albion lowered the blanket from around the baby's

neck. "Her neck's a little black and blue, but she'll be all right," he said.

"It's Richard Nixon's fault," said Kate Albion, wiping the newsprint from her hands onto the bed linen and repinning the Knights of Columbus medal to her white nightgown.

"Poor Richard Nixon," said Joe Albion.

"No sympathy for the devil around here, thank you. She's born too early," said Kate Albion. "She's beautiful, but I hope there's nothing wrong with her."

"There's nothing wrong with her," said Joe Albion, rocking the infant girl with great care. He noticed she had a thick tuft of hair for a newborn.

"There's nothing wrong with her," said Joe Albion.

"If there is," said Kate Albion, "it's Richard Nixon's fault."

"She's perfect," said Joe.

"What if she has brain damage?"

"She doesn't have brain damage."

"We'll see."

Joe said, "I know you're frightened, but . . ."

Kate yawned and picked up the newspaper. "JFK is ahead in the polls," she said, the color ripening in her cheeks. "It looks like Massachusetts will have a new United States senator."

Kate Albion closed her eyes and ran imaginary fingers through JFK's hair.

Although he was seated in his den, the Old Man's radar was aimed at the drawing room, picking up the argument between his daughter and son-in-law.

"There are no saints named 'Marilyn,' " said Kate Albion, digging her spikes into the thick Oriental rug in the front drawing room on Commonwealth Avenue. There were one hundred people waiting for the christening to begin at Saint Brigid's, but Kate Albion wasn't moving.

Joe Albion carefully arranged the baby's white lace christening gown and said, "I'm going to name her after Marilyn Monroe."

"A sexpot! A blond bombshell! A whore!" shouted Kate Albion. "You want to name your baby after a whore?"

In the den, the Old Man's blood pressure rose.

"Even the Lord had a whore, Kate," said Joe Albion.

The Old Man chuckled.

"Are you out of your mind?" asked Kate.

"Mary Magda-lyn."

"Don't say that in public, Joe."

"Marilyn Monroe is a great American."

"Marilyn Monroe is a political liability. How can you name your child after her? People will think you're crazy. They won't vote for you."

The Old Man clenched his fists, his wisps of white hair straining to pick up every word.

"I don't need anyone's vote to buy the Blue Lagoon," said Joe Albion, looking only at the little girl in his arms. The Blue Lagoon was an elegant saloon in Scollay Square, the underworld of Boston.

"You can buy anything you want, including a seat on the city council. I haven't worked myself half to death for nothing. I risked that baby's life for your career," said Kate Albion.

"You're damn right," said the Old Man, who had intended to shout, but his thin failing voice was not heard, and his weakness took him by surprise. I'm too mean to die, he thought.

"I'm going to buy the Blue Lagoon," repeated Joe. "And I'm going to laugh and sing."

"You'll get sick of that."

"I'm going to give little Marilyn tap-dancing lessons."

"And you're going to tap-dance your way to a seat on the city council next year, and by 1960 you are going to be mayor of Boston. Do you understand, Joe?" said Kate Albion. "I owe it to my father."

The Old Man's heart opened with a creak. That was the first nice thing anyone had said about him in years. It was almost too much for him to handle emotionally. Someone said something nice about him behind his back!

"The Blue Lagoon. Marilyn, you, and I will own the Blue Lagoon. You'll love it, Kate," said Joe.

"What's wrong with you?"

"There's nothing wrong with me," said Joe Albion, unwrapping a piece of hard peppermint candy with one hand. "I want to name her for Marilyn Monroe."

Kate saw that Joe was intractable. Perhaps the Blue Lagoon could be made to suit her purposes. He was going to do it anyway, so she might as well compromise for something.

"If you run for office, you can name her Marilyn," said Kate Albion.

"Marilyn," said Joe, who didn't mind the idea of becoming a city councilman, or mayor, because his heart was on the dark side of the moon and his fingers were sticky with peppermint candy.

The Old Man dropped dead of ecstasy as his heart filled with joy at the thought of a mayor in the family. The Old Man was not familiar with tenderness, and when his heart had opened upon hearing something good said of him behind his back, the shock was too great. Happy at last, the little white wisps of hair settled to his hard head for the last time, and tomorrow evening Nellie Kelly would feel no guilt at her trade, for Martin Kelly died a happy man with five wide columns in the Irish sports pages.

Kate Albion walked the long hallway past the den and the potted white lilies and entered the kitchen. She dropped two Alka-Seltzer tablets into a tall glass of water and watched them blow up.

> *Plop plop*
> *Fizz fizz*
> *Oh . . . do it again!*

CHAPTER 2

Sputnik Watch

October 1957

City Councilman Joe Albion lifted his five-year-old daughter up onto the thick brass rail of the bar in the Blue Lagoon, as the bartender, Tommy Finney, adjusted the small black-and-white television behind the bar so that the waves stopped rolling across the screen. Marilyn loved the bright red vests that the bartenders and waiters always wore in the Blue Lagoon, and she liked the way Tommy sucked in his cheeks when he smoked his cigarette, how his eyelids drooped as he smiled at her. Marilyn

Albion liked him the way she liked Great Aunt Nellie Kelly, because they were absolutely satisfied with themselves exactly as they were. They were not becoming something else. Whenever she saw them, they would be Tommy Finney and Nellie Kelly. The way Marilyn Albion saw things, they were very nearly saints.

Marilyn liked it inside the Blue Lagoon because the light and temperature were always the same. If it was snowing or blistering hot, the Blue Lagoon was seventy-two degrees, low humidity, and the exotic fish in the built-in tanks along the walls always floated by, full of secrets, forever silent.

The television news anchorman, Walter Cronkite, began to speak.

FLASH

NEWS FLASH

Today, charges of moral decay are being leveled against the Everly Brothers for the lyrics of their number-one hit on the billboard, "Wake Up Little Susie." Charges state that Susie and her boyfriend sleep together, out of wedlock, at the drive-in and in public. Ed Sullivan has signed them on for his Sunday evening show.

In other news . . .

This evening you will be able to see the Russian Sputnik, the first artificial earth satellite, as a gleam of light passing on the horizon. Even though it is night, the sun on the other side of the world will cause a reflection. Here is a drawing to explain it. You can't see the sun, but it's still there. And now for a commercial.

MAKE ROOM FOR DADDY—TONIGHT!

Hello again. The president says there is no need for alarm. The president is not worried about Sputnik. We have the bomb.

However, our rocket and satellite exploded on the ground at Cape Canaveral.

The Russians call it "Sputnik Zemli" which means "traveling companion of the world." It is made of aluminum. Yes. Aluminum! Like your toaster.

Imagine a one-hundred-and-eighty-four-pound toaster twenty-three inches in diameter taking ninety-six point two minutes to orbit the earth.

Joe lifted Marilyn in the air, then gently landed her on the black-and-white tile floor. Hand in hand, they left the Blue Lagoon, as Tommy Finney took another long drag from his cigarette and thought about Sputnik. Standing with Marilyn in the pool of pale blue light cast to the sidewalk by the neon glow, Joe Albion hailed a taxi.

Joe and Marilyn stood in the library doorway and observed Kate Albion as she focused on the television anchorman. From her easy chair, teacup poised, Nellie Kelly watched Kate, as she always watched Kate, for signs of being on tour. But Nellie observed no private conversations with the undead, no glimpses behind the cosmic veil, no unusual choices of nail polish.

There is no need for alarm. Citizens have been expressing their concerns. Citizens have been buying up all of the canned foods for their atomic fallout shelters.

Kate chewed on the inside of her mouth as she studied the television news flash, then she broke the silence. Kate Albion always broke the silence.

"Thank God for Walter Cronkite," she said.

The Philip Morris bellboy tap-danced his way across the television screen, and Joe Albion, briefly and discreetly, imitated him, Marilyn following his lead.

Noticing the suddenly heightened volume of the television, Great Aunt Nellie asked, "Why in the world are commercials always twice as loud as the show?"

Kate observed Joe and Marilyn tap-dancing in the archway to the library.

"So you can tell what's real and what's not," said Kate. Kate turned away from Joe and Marilyn, having an uncanny knack for knowing when to let things slide.

There was no mystery left in the world, living with Kate Albion. There were no unanswered questions. No moments of doubt, introspection, or self-analysis.

Kate Albion believed Walter Cronkite was real. So be it. She loved Walter because Walter had worked out a secret system of eyebrow movements with the American public. If he was reporting something that he did not quite believe but he could not prove untrue, he'd report it as written, but he'd let his right eyebrow rise up and pull on the right corner of his mouth ever so slightly. His eyes twinkling, unnervingly riveted into the camera's heart, Walter Cronkite was a lover letting his beloved in on the private joke. The danger of Walter Cronkite was that he had made such an art of telling the truth, that should he choose to lie, no one would ever know it, except perhaps Kate Albion.

Kate Albion paced the length of the library.

"Thank God for Walter Cronkite," said Marilyn Albion, who entered the room while her father stood in the doorway to watch the drama, which he enjoyed.

Kate paused in her tracks and tossed a catnip smile at Marilyn. "That's Mommy's girl," said Kate, who resumed her pacing, little bits of the high-pile rug flying up as her spike heels drilled the carpet.

Marilyn beamed and went straight for the television set. She arranged the rabbit ears with the same care and tenderness with which she combed her Barbie doll's hair.

Kate Albion said, "Joe. You've got to make a statement about Sputnik."

"I don't think the world is holding its breath to hear what a Boston city councilman has to say about international politics," said Joe, as he prepared a highball.

Marilyn tried to get someone's—anyone's—attention. Nellie Kelly noticed that this seemed to be a fairly full-time occupation for Marilyn Albion. Marilyn was not a neglected child; she was always dressed beautifully, she was always sparkling clean, and she knew exactly what to do in case of an atomic blast. "Duck and cover!" was one of little Marilyn's first complete phrases. However, Kate and Joe had very little understanding that Marilyn Albion also had an internal life that was rather needy for acknowledgment. They did not know that she had a predilection for magical and festive spiritual events.

To this end, Marilyn Albion once tried to fly. She also claimed to have witnessed miraculous visitations in the kindergarten schoolyard. On occasion, she took off her clothes and paraded through the house, declaring herself to be "Marilyn, Queen of Wonderbread." She even tried to establish direct communication with God to petition for the ability to work miracles and heal lepers, should one happen to wander down Commonwealth Avenue. In spite of God's apparent silence concerning these requests, Marilyn Albion knew that someday she would do something so big that no one would ever forget her, something as big and as important as Sputnik, Traveling Companion of the World. Someday, in a sort of American secular canonization, Walter Cronkite would say her name.

Marilyn Albion turned the channel selector knob on the television set as fast as she could. This was very daring, but it was worth getting the effect of one image merging dislocatedly with another. For one brief shining moment, Walter Cronkite hosted "Queen for a Day" from the inside of Flash Gordon's spaceship. And that's the way it was until the knob fell off into Marilyn's hand.

Marilyn trembled and stopped breathing. She broke into a terrible coldness. The knob. It was an accident. She didn't do it on purpose. Kate always said, "There are no accidents." But this was an accident. It couldn't be broken.

Flash. Something strange was going on in Flash Gordon's spaceship. Marilyn saw the evil and beautiful space witch slither through the ship. Marilyn knew she was beautiful and evil because she had blond hair like Marilyn Monroe and shifty eyes like Richard Nixon. She also had a lovely outfit. The space witch tied Flash to a beautiful pillar and began to play enchanted music on her lovely and evil space harp. The music cast a spell on Dale Arden, Flash's girlfriend, who began to dance against her will from the place in her heart where beautiful angry lions lie in wait.

"Sputnik is the greatest of the Commie threats," said

Kate Albion, orbiting the library. "This could be the end of civilization as we know it. And what are we going to do about it? Let the Republicans or the rest of the city council get the glory of challenging the Russians? Joe. Get out there and make some noise."

The evil and beautiful space witch gave Dale Arden a long and dangerous knife, and Dale Arden danced seductively, menacingly toward Flash. It was clear that at the end of her dance, Dale would stab Flash to death. Poor Flash.

Joe Albion had civil-defense-drill–television-pattern eyes as he watched Dale Arden. Joe Albion felt life surge through him, and Kate was a distant thunder, warning about Commie toasters.

"Jesus Christ. She's going to stab him to death," said Joe.

Marilyn Albion rocked from foot to foot to the music of the evil and beautiful space witch.

"Will you stop watching that children's show, Joe, and pay attention?" said Kate.

"He is paying attention, dear," said Nellie Kelly. Nellie Kelly got up and walked slowly toward Marilyn, taking an indirect route so as not to attract Kate's attention.

"The Russians will be orbiting over the country at any time. They are gaining a military advantage, Joe. What if they've got a bomb on that thing? No one's ever come into this country and bombed it. We've never had a war here except for the Civil War when we killed each other. Get out there and say something. You're a city councilman now. Don't you want to be mayor? Don't let them get the jump on you."

Great Aunt Nellie Kelly took the television knob from Marilyn's hand and reattached it to the set. She put her hand on Marilyn's head and stopped the rocking, a task as simple as stopping the metronome from ticking on the polished black piano top in the corner.

Marilyn loved Great Aunt Nellie Kelly.

"Well, Kate," said Nellie, "if they do have a bomb on Sputnik, it won't be able to tell the difference between a Republican and a Democrat."

"Someday they will," said Kate. "They'll even have bombs that'll know the difference between people and buildings."

"Then no one will have to die."

"No, no, no, Aunt Nellie. They'll kill the people and save the buildings."

"You have a deep disregard for humanity, Kate."

"I know the human mind, Aunt Nellie."

"Then what do you think? Will Dale Arden stab Flash Gordon to death?"

"Of course not! This is a children's show," said Kate, who walked at a clip to the television set. Her thin, hard hand slapped the knob and shut up the sound and light, as a low-flying jet from Logan Airport broke the sound barrier. Marilyn Albion marveled at Kate Albion's power, as the sonic boom burst along the invisible line, pouring its vibrations into every house below, rattling the windows, knives, and toasters.

Kate grabbed Marilyn, put her on the floor, and lay down on top of her. Kate shouted, "Duck and cover!" and Marilyn felt loved.

"It's getting to be time for Marilyn's nap," said Great Aunt Nellie. "Lots of fun here, but a nap wouldn't hurt."

Joe Albion had not moved. He was staring, unblinking, at the tiny white light in the center of the screen.

Joe said, "What happened to Flash?"

* * *

The night was perfect for a satellite watch. The Albions and Nellie Kelly sat in green-and-white lawn chairs on top of the roof. The foil was curled back neatly from the edges of their Swanson TV dinners, which were set upon plastic commemorative tray tables bearing the presidential seal.

The Albions waved to their neighbors, who were on their rooftops. "Kate may be active in her husband's political life," the neighbors said, "but she still keeps a nice house, and her daughter is always sparkling clean and knows exactly what to do in case of an atomic blast."

Joe Albion sipped on a highball, his legs gracefully crossed at the knee. He had not eaten his Swanson TV dinner. He was not hungry. There was, instead, a deep look in his eyes, as if he was having a vision or communicating with God. He had been a little frightened of Dale Arden and her hypnotic trance, and now he was a little drunk.

When he had made his Sputnik statement to his constituency, he was amazed that they were more interested in the Hit Parade. The number-one song on the charts had thrown them into a frenzy. Now, his foot tapped to the beat of ". . . Little Susie" as Kate paced at the edge of the roof, her spikes digging into the tar.

Marilyn paced beside Kate, black patent-leather shoes gleaming on her uncomfortable little feet, the thin white lace ankle socks dipping ever so slightly, ever so uncomfortably into the hard polished heel, her bare legs cold. "Looking beautiful hurts," said Marilyn.

Modest even at five years old, Marilyn pressed her small arms against her skirt to keep it from flying up, up! in the bursts of wind that could expose her white panties. Little ladies' panties are never to be exposed, except by acts of God.

Joe Albion watched Marilyn Albion, and he remembered standing in front of the Trans-Lux Theater in Manhattan with a hundred men. They weren't marines this time, but they were there together in honor of Miss Monroe. Yes. Joe Albion remembered the filming of *The Seven-Year Itch*. Yes. The grate Miss Monroe straddled. The giant fans lifting her skirt. He saw her husband, Joe DiMaggio, that night. He hated Joe DiMaggio, and he was glad when DiMaggio walked away. What did he know about taking care of such a woman?

Joe Albion watched Marilyn Albion, and he felt wondrous strange as the image of Monroe superimposed itself upon his daughter. Marilyn Albion's little dress fluttered, and Joe Albion felt a little hello flutter inside of him. Christ, I must be tired, he thought.

Joe looked up to the sky and tried to think of absolutely nothing, white white nothing. Then he looked at his daughter, and he again experienced the little hello. His hand began to shake, as he tried to keep the ice cubes in his glass. He knew he wasn't that kind of man. He was a good man. He was loved by everyone.

Joe Albion caught Nellie Kelly studying him, and he wondered: Could she see it? Did she know it? Can I hide it? He wasn't worried about Kate Albion, who would dismiss it in any case, who always dismissed anything that would take up valuable time.

"Would you be having some sort of vision, now, Joe?" asked Nellie Kelly.

"Just this Sputnik, Aunt Nellie. Terrible nasty thing, this Sputnik," said Joe. Hello. Hello out there. Joe Albion wished that Nellie Kelly would drop dead. Not that he didn't like her. But on occasion she knew what was going on in people's minds. Hello. Hello out there.

Marilyn stood beside Kate Albion, Kate's spikes firmly anchored in the tar roof, her arms folded across her chest. Kate listened for the sound of the enemy rustling in the wind. She watched for the movement of the enemy through the sky. Kate had terrific peripheral vision.

"Did you know," said Kate Albion, "that Russian women have only one shade of nail polish? And it's a yellowish muddy brown the government came up with."

The wind gusted and the empty green-and-white lawn chairs rattled. "Watch your dress, Marilyn! Your dress!" said Kate.

Does Kate know? thought Joe. Oh, God. Women know. They always know. Joe Albion came to life, determined to run interference between his mind and the women.

"And stay away from the edge, dear," Kate added. "It's not safe."

Marilyn raised her arms and moved a little closer to the edge. She prepared for flight. "Marilyn. What's wrong with you?" said Kate. Kate took Marilyn's hand, walked her to the green-and-white lawn chair between Joe and Nellie Kelly, deposited her there, and returned to her post.

"Saved again. Just as well. I'd wager Marilyn's feet hurt," said Nellie Kelly.

Joe relaxed. It must be the highballs. He wanted to amuse his little girl, not be a lecher. He regrouped, leaned toward Marilyn, and softly sang:

> *Well, what are we gonna tell your Mama?*
> *What are we gonna tell your Pa?*
> *What are we gonna tell our friends*
> *when they say . . .*

Marilyn had heard this song many times. Everyone in the entire country and most parts of the civilized world had heard this song. This song had the same meaning to Marilyn as the Catholic mass in Latin. None.

She sang with her father:

> *Ooh la la!*
> *Wake up Little Susie!*

Joe Albion smiled at his daughter, peacefully and with a full heart, but he was overtaken by a startling, unpremeditated hello.

Hello! Oh, Christ, thought Joe Albion, panic frying his nerves.

"There it is!" shouted Joe Albion, jumping from his green-and-white lawn chair. Thank God for Sputnik, thought Joe.

"That's it!" shouted Kate Albion.

Shouts lifted from the rooftops.

"That's Sputnik!"

"No, it's not."

"Yes, it is."

"No."

"Yes!"

"Yes!"

" 'Wake up, little Susie!' " chanted little Marilyn.

The TV dinners flew from their tray tables in a sudden blast of wind. Great Aunt Nellie, nearing the roof's edge, held on to her hat. Marilyn Albion held on to her skirt. Joe Albion held on to his drink. Kate Albion. Well. Kate Albion was neither afraid nor patriotically defiant. The truth was, she was titillated. This made no sense to her but it was true. She was enticed by Sputnik. Treasonously excited.

"There it is! That's it!" said Kate, and she flushed. She felt like a woman whose secret lover has just walked unexpectedly into a room that includes her husband.

Sputnik's delicate reflection shimmered on the horizon, and it appeared to Joe as a tiny diamond on a large, dark woman's hand, sharp enough to cut glass, to sever undesirable emotions from the human heart.

Joe was terrifically tactile.

"Don't worry, Marilyn," he said. "It's just a big toaster. I'll save you from it." "Bastard Russians," he added under his breath. Hello. Kate looked at Joe with admiration. She knew he would rise to the occasion.

Marilyn, however, knew that Sputnik was not a toaster. If Sputnik was a toaster, Flash and Dale and the beautiful and evil space witch would burn up and die inside their spaceship. Why did Daddy say things like that?

Great Aunt Nellie Kelly looked at the shimmering flash and said, "It won't be able to tell the difference between the Reds and the capitalists."

Joe Albion had found a worthy opponent: Sputnik. Joe Albion felt political. Kate Albion was ecstatic. Their eyes met and they couldn't wait to get to bed. They felt part of the human race, because there's nothing like a little adversity coupled with the threat of atomic war to bring people together.

Joe lifted Marilyn on one arm and put his other arm around Kate. He was the white knight, and he was ready to go to war for God and his women. He had no idea that his wife had been seduced, however temporarily, by the power and glamour of the enemy.

"John Kennedy, you've got some work to do," said Kate Albion, her eyes on the heavens.

Joe Albion was sick of John Kennedy.

Nellie Kelly strained to catch a glimpse of the Commie toaster. She leaned so far over the edge of the rooftop that her martian-colored cloche hat tumbled from her head like a little manic flying saucer, lifting and hovering on the peculiar winds, then slamming into the sidewalk.

Hello out there. Hello.

CHAPTER 3

Woolworth's
Fabulous Woolworth's

1959

Led by a solemn nun, the seven-year-old girls and boys, in genderized parallel lines, climbed the thirty wide steps of St. Brigid's Cathedral, where Marilyn Albion had been baptized. The children passed beneath the painted arched ceilings where God and Adam played finger games, and Eve had tea with the snake. Marilyn waited patiently in line to make her first confession. She took pride in the decree that, at seven years, she had reached the age of reason.

She had read about the little girl saint, Saint Theresa of the Roses, and she marveled that roses fell from the sky around Saint Theresa at theatrically perfect times. Her picture book of the event had a thick, glossy blue cover, and the picture of Saint Theresa looked very much like Marilyn Albion, blond and blue-eyed. Saint Theresa did not look vacant for she was in fact inhabited by the Holy Spirit, and Marilyn Albion was ready for inhabitation. Marilyn knew that it is not every little girl who could toss a prayer into the sky and cause roses to tumble from heaven in response, but she had studied and worked very hard and had learned that the way to know if God loves a little girl is if something out of the ordinary happens. A basic miracle. Only through such miracles could little girls be redeemed, because they bore the shame of having tempted Adam with an apple and had gotten them both evicted from the Garden of Eden. Without such a miracle, a girl would have to go through life like Kate Albion, a demanding voice in the wilderness. Lots of fruit, but sinful.

Marilyn entered the confessional booth and knelt in the darkness, supported by the invisible arms of her belief that a great miracle was about to take place. The sliding window snapped open, and Marilyn's heart skipped tra-la my God tra-la. The outline of the priest's head leaned against the wire-mesh grate to listen, but not to look at her. Hairs protruded from his ear like tentacles to search the soul.

"Bless me, Father. This is my first confession."

"My child. You are supposed to say, 'Bless me, Father, for I have sinned. This is my first confession.'"

"I didn't do anything wrong," said Marilyn Albion, believing the priest would be pleased.

"Everyone's done something wrong," said the priest.

"Not me. I'm going to be like Saint Theresa. Roses will fall out of the sky."

"What's this about Saint Theresa?"

"Little Saint Theresa of the Roses. In my blue picture book. After confession, I'm going to be just like her."

"Saint Theresa was a martyr."

"That must be wonderful."

"Do you know what a martyr is?"

"Someone who is loved by everyone."

"Yes. But martyrs like Saint Theresa were tortured until they died."

Invisible arms dropped Marilyn Albion into the darkness, and her plump little heart tumbled inside the heavy air of the confessional booth. Marilyn did not like pain, and even roses falling from the sky with perfect theatrical timing could not seduce her into martyrdom.

"Saint Theresa was a good girl," said the priest.

Marilyn had never before drawn the connection between being good and being tortured.

The priest spoke again. "I suppose if you haven't done anything wrong . . ."

"Bless me, Father, for I have sinned. This is my first confession. I drowned the kitten," said Marilyn.

The priest was silent, and then he spoke. "How did you do this?"

Marilyn was silent. How bad did she have to be in order to avoid becoming a martyred saint?

"I lied," said Marilyn Albion.

"You didn't kill a kitten?"

"No, Father. I haven't killed anything yet."

"That's good," said the priest. "But lying is serious. If we lie, we can lose our eternal souls."

Relief swept over Marilyn Albion. She felt adequately sinful—safe from torture unto death. Marilyn concentrated on the hairs in the priest's ear.

"Is that all, my child?" asked the priest.

"Is that enough?"

"Of course. Recite the Act of Contrition. And do three Hail Marys and three Our Fathers."

The window snapped shut. The ear with the hair in it was gone, and Marilyn felt a deep sadness. Where was this Holy Spirit she was promised? She hunted in the darkness for the doorknob and opened the door. She inhaled the sweet incensed air. The solemn nun who was supervising the children had her hands tucked into her long sleeves. Marilyn noticed that the nun wore no makeup. She had never noticed this before.

"Has Father Finney given you penance?" asked the nun.

"Yes, Sister."

"You'll feel better after you do your penance," said the nun softly, nodding solemnly toward the altar rail at the front of the church. Marilyn Albion walked past the flickering flames of candles in tall red glass cups, past the passion of the twelve stations, past the thousands of pieces of stained glass. She knelt at the altar railing and said the prayers, carefully and precisely, and then she waited to feel better. Marilyn Albion did not feel better. She felt depressed and lonely. God hadn't shown up, and there would be no roses tumbling from heaven. Kate Albion would know how to handle this. Marilyn Albion genuflected before the altar and went outside to the dull, unmagic world.

Marilyn opened the door to her Commonwealth Avenue home and walked through the pristine reception area of inlaid black-and-white marble. Her mother would know what to do.

Marilyn was careful not to deliberately look at herself in the gilt-edged mirror as she passed. Vanity in a little lady, she had been taught, was a ticket to hell. It was all right to look at yourself in the mirror in order to make yourself attractive to someone else, but never for your own pleasure. Kate and Joe Albion had not taught this to Marilyn. She had learned it during religious instruction. Joe Albion had taught her table manners, and Kate Albion had taught her how to be popular. That was it.

Her footsteps silent on the thick pale rug, Marilyn walked up the staircase and paused outside the door to the master bedroom. Joe and Kate were inside, and they were making a lot of noise. Roaring. Howling. Purring. Oddly enough, clapping. Depressed, Marilyn sat on the chair outside their bedroom, her legs dangling heavy over the flat earth. Prayers tried to drone on in her mind, but she pushed them aside, preferring to recite the alphabet backward. At *H*, the bedroom door burst open, and Kate Albion, flushed and wrapped in a white sheet, her black hair magnificently tousled, entered the hallway, Joe Albion following closely behind. Kate had a long, thorny, lush red rose clamped between her teeth. Startled and uncomfortable at finding Marilyn sitting outside their door, Kate and Joe retreated into the bedroom. Through the closed door, Marilyn could hear hushed whispers and commotion.

Marilyn crossed her arms against her chest. She was angry. Did they know that God had not shown up? Had they known all along that he wouldn't?

Great Aunt Nellie Kelly, her cape draped on her shoulders, found Marilyn seated on the chair in the hallway.

"What is this now?" asked Great Aunt Nellie Kelly.

Kate and Joe emerged gracefully in their bathrobes.

Nellie Kelly looked at them and said, "In the daylight?"

Kate Albion smiled at Nellie Kelly and lit a cigarette.

"Mommy. Was Saint Theresa real?" asked Marilyn Albion.

Kate Albion thought about that.

"Of course Saint Theresa was real," said Nellie Kelly.

"Isn't she the one who got her breasts cut off?" Kate asked Nellie, taking a drag off her cigarette.

Marilyn Albion felt sick and crossed her arms against her chest.

"Kate. For God's sake," said Nellie.

"Apparently so," said Kate Albion.

Joe Albion swooped Marilyn Albion up into his arms. "Don't worry about that, darling."

Marilyn felt like the little girl she had seen tied to the prow of the wrecked *Hesperus* in Madame Toussaud's Wax Museum on Tremont Street.

"Mother," said Marilyn Albion.

"Yes, dear," said Kate.

"I don't like confession."

"Always remember that the priest goes to confession, too. Even Senator Kennedy goes to confession. And Frank Sinatra. Remember that." Kate took another drag from her cigarette and brushed Marilyn's cheek with her lips.

"But God never came," said Marilyn.

"When you're a woman," said Kate Albion, "God will come."

"I don't think that's in the Baltimore Catechism, dear," said Nellie Kelly to Kate Albion, who shrugged and flicked her cigarette ashes into the palm of her free hand.

Nellie Kelly said, "How about a little lunch, Marilyn? Where would you like to go?"

"Someplace where I'll become a woman," demanded Marilyn.

"Then it's Woolworth's, to see Mrs. Finnegan," said Nellie Kelly. "If that doesn't make a woman of you, nothing will."

Marilyn Albion was excited at the prospect of becoming a woman, which might be easier to handle than becoming a martyred saint. Joe Albion gently lowered Marilyn to the floor and watched Nellie lead his daughter out the door toward Woolworth's fabulous Woolworth's, where there are so many things to choose from, where all is good and there is no evil, where there are so many small plastic and rubber items to purchase, to enjoy, to lose, to buy again in the spirit of truly atomic-age merchandise. Woolworth's understood the doctrine of planned obsolescence; wherein its greatness.

Alone in the hallway, Joe Albion looked at his wife, who had made a little ashtray out of her free hand. He was worried. He had unexpectedly surrendered to Kate erotically. It made him uncomfortable. Now, had he planned on surrendering and then surrendered, he would still be in charge. He thought a moment about tactics for resuming command.

"I'm going to position myself for mayor of Boston," he announced. Hello hello! Kate and Joe Albion returned to the master bedroom.

En route to Woolworth's, Marilyn Albion and Great Aunt Nellie Kelly walked past a newspaper rack where the *Boston Herald* trembled in the spring wind, almost animating the front-page picture of Marilyn Monroe and Nikita Khrushchev.

Nellie Kelly purchased the newspaper and said to Marilyn Albion, "Now there's a girl who'd be better off behind a counter at Woolworth's. Mark my words."

Marilyn Albion marked Great Aunt Nellie's words and thoughtfully examined the photograph. Pressing her hands against her chest, she said to her great aunt, "That lady is very big. Do they hurt?"

Nellie Kelly laughed and said, "Don't worry, Marilyn. If they get too big, you can always sling them over your shoulder."

Marilyn Albion never was sure when someone was joking, because so many things that she would have thought impossible happened on such a regular basis that she dismissed nothing. She was horrified at the prospect of becoming a woman and having to sling her breasts over her shoulders, so by the time they stood at the portals of Woolworth's Five and Dime, in between the paperback book racks and the small tender plants, Marilyn Albion wanted to remain a little girl in an unmagic world with no experience of God and with manageable breasts, which would be a terrific consolation.

With a stately nod, Nellie Kelly made eye contact with Mrs. Finnegan, who privately referred to herself as Our Lady of the Lunch Counter. She was a close personal friend of Nellie Kelly.

Marilyn saw that Mrs. Finnegan, standing across the store behind the lunch counter, was surrounded by a white light. Marilyn preferred spiritual manifestations to occur in the dark, with her eyes closed. To have to meet Mrs. Finnegan in broad daylight terrified her. She longed for the safety of the dark, incensed air, the flickering candles in red cups, the thousands of pieces of shimmering stained glass.

Mrs. Finnegan's blue hair was curled just perfectly beneath her light brown hair net, which sat on the back of her head like a cocky halo. Mrs. Finnegan knew what she was doing. Mrs. Finnegan was in charge.

Marilyn's heart thumped a dark beat of fear as the seven ladies who worked the lunch counter stopped, silent as submarines, and turned toward her and Nellie Kelly in the entranceway. As if a silent signal had been given, each of the blue-haired ladies, and the young Irish and Italian mothers with their sweetly behaved children lunching at the Woolworth's counter, stopped chewing and spun toward the entranceway on their round, perfectly upholstered, red leather stools, the silver chrome side-plating shining like Flash Gordon's spaceship. Aunt Nellie smiled graciously and nodded like visiting royalty, but Marilyn tried to back out of the door. Aunt Nellie, however, was not going to allow a retreat, and Marilyn, forced to stand and face her fear, felt mildly enticed by the festive beauty of the lunch counter and the obvious camaraderie of those present.

The orangeade and lemonade bubbled in their transparent coolers, neither flavor having been sullied by real oranges or real lemons. The Woolworth's pies, especially the Boston cream and the lemon meringue, contained absolutely no essential vitamins and minerals, not even riboflavin. They were seductively presented on spinning platforms enclosed in clear plastic. Dangling from the ceiling on long strings and catching the sudden blasts of wind from the rotating fans were colored cardboard cutouts of a triple banana split, a hot fudge sundae with a cherry on top, and *la pièce de résistance,* a three-foot Woolworth's lunch-counter hot dog with mustard and relish on a grilled roll. That these very brightly colored cardboard jewels would one day bring about the death of Mrs.

Finnegan was a sad fact hidden in the beautiful spring day.

Mrs. Finnegan looked to the east. Mrs. Finnegan looked to the west. Mrs. Finnegan saw that all was well and emerged from behind the lunch counter, her pale blue uniform glistening under the bright lights. Imperious and as awesome as the queen of England, Mrs. Finnegan walked to the door to greet them. Marilyn was dizzy with fear, having never been in the presence of such a being.

Mrs. Finnegan reached Nellie Kelly and they brushed each other's cheeks. They were old friends. Mrs. Finnegan called Nellie Kelly "Mrs. Kelly," and Nellie Kelly called Flora Finnegan "Mrs. Finnegan," but neither had ever married, and neither had lost much sleep over it. Mrs. Finnegan always said, "The Irish love to tell lies that make the truth clearer. It's a form of prayer."

Nellie Kelly said, "Mrs. Finnegan. Our Marilyn has reached the age of reason and is now qualified to go to hell."

"Isn't that nice," replied Mrs. Finnegan, giving Marilyn a quick wink.

Marilyn felt a little magic in the air, but she was skeptical.

"So she is also qualified to select her own lunch and choice of restaurant," said Nellie Kelly.

Mrs. Finnegan looked at Marilyn Albion and said, "The world's full of secrets no priest ever dreamed of. Don't you forget it."

Marilyn would not forget it.

"There's nothing like a little girl-talk to soothe the soul," said Mrs. Finnegan to Mrs. Kelly.

"Two for lunch and a little girl-talk, please, then, Mrs. Finnegan," said Nellie Kelly, and they glided to the lunch counter, two high priestesses and one acolyte who still resisted the undeniable power of Woolworth's and Mrs. Finnegan. The blue-haired ladies, the well-behaved children, and the Irish and Italian mothers turned back to their cakes and hot dogs and chewed, chatted, and observed themselves in the mirror that ran the length of the lunch counter. Marilyn was jolted by the way they unabashedly played with their reflections, touching their hair, smoothing their eyebrows, pursing their lips. Marilyn had been taught that vanity was the sin of sins. Woolworth's seemed an evil and debauched place to Marilyn, a certain ticket to the infernal regions.

"I have two seats. Excellent seats in between the pies and the coolers, Mrs. Kelly," said Mrs. Finnegan. "And I might add that there's a clear shot at the mirror from these seats, so you can always see what's going on behind you, not to mention what you look like as you chew."

Marilyn Albion and Nellie Kelly sat on their spinning red stools. Marilyn kept her eyes averted from the mirror.

A shadow cast itself over Marilyn, and when she looked up to find the source, she saw that Mrs. Finnegan's heart-shaped face was inches from her own. Marilyn decided to be brave. Kate Albion would be proud of her.

"What would you like, dear?" asked Mrs. Finnegan. Marilyn looked at the dainty, powdered hairs in Mrs. Finnegan's nose.

"A hot dog with mustard and relish on a grilled roll, please," said Marilyn.

Mrs. Finnegan licked the tip of her pencil and with a flourish noted Marilyn's request on her order pad.

"And you, Mrs. Kelly?"

"Tea. Steeped fifteen minutes."

"And beautied up with a little dab of Borden's evaporated milk, I'd be willing to bet," said Mrs. Finnegan with a wink.

Mrs. Finnegan was certainly knowledgeable, thought Marilyn.

"You've got your hand in my mind," said Nellie Kelly.

Marilyn tried to imagine Mrs. Finnegan's hand in Great Aunt Nellie's mind and wondered if Father Finney would think it a sin.

Mrs. Finnegan snapped her fingers and relayed their orders, in hushed tones, to the second in command: the grill lady, Biddie O'Brien. In fifteen years, Biddie O'Brien would help Marilyn Albion to enter the White House and bring about the dramatic fall of Richard Nixon and insure the survival of both the free and Communist worlds, but neither Biddie nor Marilyn were aware of their destinies.

Although there were eight ladies behind the lunch counter, including Mrs. Finnegan, they never collided or became irritable because they operated as one perfect being.

Mrs. Finnegan held her head high and said, "Marilyn. What do you want to drink?"

"Orangeade, please."

Mrs. Finnegan filled an enormous, heavy glass to the brim. Marilyn liked drinking something the color of Howard Johnson's roof.

Refreshed, Marilyn asked, more to remind those present of the dangers of mirrors than for her own knowledge, "What is hell, Aunt Nellie?"

"So who's filling her up with that now?" asked Mrs. Finnegan.

"It wouldn't be me," said Nellie to Mrs. Finnegan; and to Marilyn, "Hell is an endless cover-all bingo game, dear, with one number missing. And that one number is on your card." Mrs. Finnegan smiled with great affection for Mrs. Kelly.

"Who's in hell, anyway?" persisted Marilyn.

"Fallen angels," said Nellie.

"Where do they come from?"

"They were the counter ladies at Woolworth's," said Nellie Kelly. Mrs. Finnegan and the seven counter ladies in their pale blue uniforms laughed as Biddie O'Brien tapped her metal spatula on the hot grill.

"Like Mrs. Finnegan?" asked Marilyn.

"Oh. Especially like Mrs. Finnegan."

"Isn't that the truth!" said Mrs. Finnegan.

Everyone went back to chewing, chatting, and playing with their reflections.

"What about the ladies at Dunkin' Donuts?" asked Marilyn.

"God, no!" said Nellie Kelly. "Just the ones at Woolworth's."

Mrs. Finnegan and Nellie Kelly laughed as loud as men.

Marilyn looked at herself in the mirror, then turned away.

Mrs. Finnegan leaned across the counter to Nellie Kelly. "Take a gander at Nora Shaw at the end of the counter," she said. Marilyn followed Nellie Kelly's eyes to a lady seated upright but without light flickering in her face. Nora Shaw stared straight into the mirror and had a great big smile, but the smile was vacuous and confused. She did not seem to know her own reflection. She could just as well have been looking at a potholder.

Mrs. Finnegan whispered to Nellie Kelly, "Do you see the two red splotches on her forehead?" Nellie Kelly nodded. "Mrs. Kelly. They hooked up this electric gadget on her forehead and tic toc, she got electroshock."

"Why did they do that?" asked Nellie Kelly.

Marilyn was horrified.

"She couldn't make friends with her reflection, so life couldn't make friends with her," said Mrs. Finnegan.

Marilyn studied Nora Shaw. Nora Shaw wasn't there. Marilyn looked at herself in the mirror. Vanity o' vanities. Sin o' sins. Marilyn did not want tic toc electroshock. Marilyn blew herself a great big kiss, and a wave of fear flooded up her spine into the top of her head, and then bright white light spun around in her crown. Peace. She rested on the dark side of the moon. She was beautiful. She was in love.

Marilyn looked more deeply at her reflection. Unashamed, she looked into her own eyes, in front of Great Aunt Nellie Kelly and Mrs. Finnegan, in front of all the blue-haired lunch-counter ladies, in front of the young Irish and Italian mothers and their sweetly behaved children, who were also intoxicated and at peace in the glow of their reflections.

Marilyn Albion spun herself on the round, red leather stool with the shiny chrome sides and dangled her legs just above the Woolworth's floor.

"Beyond good and evil," said Mrs. Finnegan, "there's a little dab of makeup." Mrs. Finnegan reached into the cleverly designed pocket of her uniform and presented Marilyn with her first little pancake-makeup-and-mirror compact.

Her hands planted on her generous hips, Mrs. Finnegan said, "Men use Brylcreem because they, too, love beauty. Remember that."

Marilyn would remember that.

Mrs. Finnegan, Great Aunt Nellie Kelly, the blue-haired lunch-counter ladies, and the young mothers with sweetly behaved children laughed as loud as men.

Mrs. Finnegan wore entirely too much makeup. Deliberately. Woolworth's had everything anyone could ever need for transformation, and Mrs. Finnegan used it all because she had a love of adventure. She looked like a Revlon explosion as she leaned across the counter, her lips almost brushing Marilyn's, and instructed, "Never go out without your war paint, Marilyn, and always remember that the only difference between you and a man is . . ."

At this, Mrs. Finnegan looked to the east, Mrs. Finnegan looked to the west, Mrs. Finnegan discreetly cupped her breasts in her hands and said, "He'll never have these. And he'll never get over it."

Mrs. Finnegan pursed her lips, closed her eyelids slowly, nodded her head once, and let go of her breasts, which settled for a moment on the lunch counter, then lifted and hovered beneath the colored cardboard treats.

Marilyn folded her hands on the Formica counter top and privately vowed to always tip heavily at Woolworth's lunch counter.

"This is what we call 'girl-talk,' Marilyn," said Nellie Kelly.

Marilyn loved girl-talk. It filled her with holy life.

Late that night, in her bedroom on Commonwealth Avenue, Marilyn slept. She dreamed that she was playing dead to keep alive. Marilyn held her breath as the mourners passed by her little white casket. A nun and a priest held a small compact mirror beneath her nose, to try to catch her breathing. They failed because two large-breasted women wearing emerald green cloche hats and riding spirited gray horses pushed them aside.

Isn't she beautiful?
Just like in real life.
She's happy now.
We're so sorry. So very sorry.

Kate and Joe were making a lot of noise in their bedroom. Again. Kate and Joe believed in America, where any boy could grow up to be president, no matter who he was or wasn't.

Roaring. Howling. Purring. Growling. The sounds drifted in and out of Marilyn Albion's dream, where the two gray horses stepped smartly, Brylcreem taming their manes.

She was such a good little girl.
Gave Boston cream pie to the poor.
Brylcreem to the needy men.

Marilyn Albion awoke, and she was happy to see the dawn, because she believed in Woolworth's, and she believed in Mrs. Finnegan, the true religion.

CHAPTER 4

Hail to the Chief

There hasn't been anyone like Nixon before because the rest of them at least had souls.

—*Marilyn Monroe*

1960

John Fitzgerald Kennedy battled Richard Nixon for the presidency, and Joe Albion found himself flying toward the mayorship of Boston on the glittering coattails of JFK, courtesy of Kate Albion. Kate Albion believed JFK to be the sensual messiah. Kate Albion believed that Richard Nixon, whom she referred to as "the beast" and "the devil," had "666" embroidered on his sheets. Kate also believed that Joe Albion would hold court at the Blue Lagoon while she ran Boston.

Marilyn Albion's crisp little white sailor dress with red piping billowed in the light September breeze as she stood transfixed before the large oak across the street from their Commonwealth Avenue home. Someone, perhaps an evil fairy, had stapled to the tree a picture of Richard Nixon. Marilyn ran her finger around the outline of his head. Marilyn Albion thought Richard Nixon had a long strange nose, like Pinocchio, the wooden puppet whose nose grew longer with every lie he told. Marilyn looked carefully around her, as if the world was especially alerted to eight-year-old girls in sailor dresses. She looked again at the poster. Mr. Nixon seemed to glow with high jinks and devil-may-care gaiety. She pulled at the poster until it dropped into her hands, little ragtag corner pieces still crucified to the tree. Folding the poster neatly, Marilyn tucked it down her neck, under the long sailor's bib, and turned to face her house. Yes. She would bring a picture of Richard Nixon inside Kate Albion's house.

Marilyn flushed with excitement as the noon sirens burst like air raid alerts to the accompaniment of sonic booms. Marilyn flung herself to the ground, the sirens and sonic booms seeming a response to the devil's image pressed against her chest. Marilyn stood up, looked both ways before crossing the street, and up into the sky. As she rocketed across the wide avenue, where blossoms fell from the dandified trees in the wind, she could feel the poster shifting position.

She entered the house and, following her daily ritual, went directly to the television set in the library. It was important that she not draw attention to herself by breaking with routine. A tall glass of milk was waiting for her on the tray table with the embossed presidential seal. At the stroke of noon each weekday, Big Brother Barry Boston, white haired, amiable, and a little bored, appeared on the television screen. Marilyn Albion lifted her glass of milk as Big Brother Barry Boston greeted his young viewers and lifted his glass of milk.

"Do you have your milk? Very good. And now we'll play 'Hail to the Chief' and drink our milk in honor of our president, President Dwight David Eisenhower. 'Hail to the Chief' is only played for our president," said Big Brother Barry Boston, rising to attention.

The camera panned to the official photograph of President Dwight David Eisenhower, benevolent, detached, and most noticeably bald. "Hail to the Chief" began to play, and Marilyn Albion drank her milk to the beat, synchronizing her gulps with the music.

> *Da da, da daa da,*
> *da da, da da,*
> *da daaa da.*
> *Da da, da daaa, da,*
> *da da, da da, da daaaa.*

Marilyn had it timed perfectly, and she swallowed her last gulp of milk at the final beat. As she tilted her head back for the last drop to the last "daaaa," the poster of Mr. Nixon gathered momentum and slipped beneath her waistband.

> Gravity catches up with us all.
>
> —*Marilyn Monroe*

Kate Albion burst into the room with Marilyn's peanut butter and jelly sandwich on pure white Wonderbread. Kate was one of those people whose hair entered the room before the rest of her. Kate was dynamic, and her daughter admired her, although she was very unlike the other mothers Marilyn had met. The other mothers did not, as Great Aunt Nellie explained it, "go on tour" very often, but when they did, they went away and came back with bright red splotches on their temples and great big smiles. Marilyn wondered what Kate would do if she knew there was a picture of Richard Nixon in her house. Marilyn hoped that Kate would not go away and get the bright red temple splotches and the great big smile.

Kate looked at the official picture of President Dwight David Eisenhower on Big Brother Barry Boston's television show.

"Not much longer for him," said Kate.

"What?" asked Marilyn. The poster of Nixon slipped just the slightest bit further. Marilyn puffed her belly out as far as possible in an attempt to arrest the slippage, quite taken by her mock pregnancy.

"He's on his way out. Your daddy's going to be mayor of Boston, and Jack Kennedy is going to be president."

"Mr. Kennedy on the posters?"

"That's right."

"But Mr. Kennedy is alive."

"Of course he's alive."

Richard Nixon's bad hair began to reveal itself at Marilyn's hemline.

"Is President Eisenhower alive?"

Kate Albion considered answering this question from a metaphysical viewpoint but decided against it. Marilyn, after all, was only eight, and as it was, she'd gotten enough misinformation from Nellie Kelly and Mrs. Finnegan. Last year, in Kate Albion's presence, Nellie and Mrs. Finnegan told Marilyn that Jimmy Durante was a Supreme Court justice, and "ink-a-dink-a-do" was a reference to drawing the lines for political districts.

"President Eisenhower plays golf," said Kate Albion.

"What is golf?" asked Marilyn.

"It's like being dead, but you still move around."

"Oh." Marilyn thought about that.

"Will Richard Nixon be president, too?" asked Marilyn.

Kate froze. "Richard Nixon is a scourge on this country. He will never be president. He's dangerous. He's vile. He's a liar." Kate Albion looked down at Marilyn's knees. The upside-down image of Richard Nixon's bad hair and cheap-shot eyes peeked out just below the hem of Marilyn's sailor dress.

Kate Albion let out a scream that was heard across Formica America.

Gosh. Maybe Mommy will have to go away for tic toc electroshock, thought Marilyn, who felt terrible about that.

Kate leaned down and pulled the poster out from under Marilyn's dress as if it were a king cobra. Kate backed away from her daughter, seeing superimposed flickering images of Lizzie Borden and the Bad Seed. Kate walked to the study, dropped the poster into the fireplace, and set it on fire. Little Marilyn stood in the doorway.

"Poor Mr. Nixon. No milk for him," said Marilyn.

Kate stirred the ashes and then looked at the beautiful little girl in the doorway, who smiled beatifically. Kate returned the smile and nodded, secretly considering exorcism. Marilyn took a slow bite from her peanut butter and jelly sandwich on white Wonderbread, and Kate felt tiny teeth. Everywhere.

Marilyn loved campaign headquarters. The phones, the red-white-and-blue ribbons and posters, and the endless members of the Finney clan plotting and loving and hating gave the place a warm family feeling. Kate was a genius at coattailing Joe's candidacy for the mayor of Boston with John Kennedy's candidacy for the presidency. She took a long hat pin and secured Marilyn's straw hat in place. A bright red ribbon encircled the crown and read ALL THE WAY WITH JFK AND JOE. Kate tied a wide banner ribbon across Marilyn's chest that read MY VOTE BELONGS TO DADDY. This had been Joe Albion's idea. He had seen Miss Monroe's latest movie, *Let's Make Love,* in which she sang the most comprehensive version of "My Heart Belongs to Daddy" that Joe Albion had ever heard. It was downright inspiring.

Satisfied with her work, Kate Albion took Marilyn along with her to buy a package of cigarettes at Star Market on the next block. Marilyn liked Star Market because it had the aroma of dead red meat, Lysol, and Hostess cupcakes. It was wonderful.

Kate Albion liked to be seen with the people, if she was sure there would be enough of them present. Nods, winks, and thumbs-up signs from everyone told her how they would be voting. No hoity-toity type of lady here, this Kate Kelly Albion, but smart and dangerous, said the people, which is the way they liked it.

Standing in the checkout line of Star Market, waiting to pay for the cigarettes, Kate and Marilyn heard a strange voice over the loudspeaker. The voice had that surprising "silent-movie queen talks" quality.

"Just keep on with your shopping while I tell you about my husband, John F. Kennedy. . . ."

Kate Albion did not hear another word as she walked slowly, Marilyn following, toward the source. All of the women in the store stopped shopping and walked toward the source. No one picked up the Quaker Oats. No one wanted a Swanson's TV dinner. Even the children became quiet. Marilyn Albion was reminded of the atmosphere during the sixty-second tests of the emergency broadcasting system.

"He cares deeply about the welfare of this country. Please vote for him."

Then the voice stopped. It was not a familiar voice. It was from another class, another world. The word *horse* popped into the minds of most of the women. They loved her. She had descended to their world. Kennedy *ex machina.*

Embarrassed, Kate's face flushed. She loved this woman but she wouldn't think twice about sleeping with her husband if the opportunity presented itself. She would, of course, be discreet, because Kate Albion had the greatest respect for the Family. Absolutely.

Mrs. Kennedy came down from the store manager's perch wearing a great big smile—graceful, all angles, and deadly unreal in her white gloves. Her eyes seemed to say, "I will shake your hands and I will touch you because I have a destiny, and you will have a destiny by touching me." Marilyn searched Mrs. Kennedy's temples for red splotches. There were none, but there was heavy makeup and the aroma of cigarettes.

Mrs. Kennedy extended her hand to Kate Albion, who took it very firmly, a little too firmly for a lady. Kate Albion was disturbed by the regality of Mrs. Kennedy. This is America, not Europe, thought Kate Albion, masking her thought with a bright, confident smile. Kate waited for Mrs. Kennedy to recognize her, but she did not. Kate Albion's feelings were hurt, a rare event. Kate Albion no longer loved Mrs. Kennedy. Jack Kennedy would have known me in a minute, she thought. Mrs. Kennedy withdrew her hand and looked at it for a moment, as if she were afraid she might draw back a nub. Hand intact, Mrs. Kennedy passed through Star Market, past the Swanson TV dinners, the dead red meat, the Lysol, and the Hostess cupcakes.

Kate Albion said, "You've been a part of history, Marilyn." Marilyn Albion was proud to be a part of history.

Kate Albion knew that at the end of the day, Mrs. Kennedy would throw away her white gloves.

The Great Debate between Senator John Kennedy and Vice President Richard Nixon had to be scheduled so that it would not conflict with "The Flintstones," a prime-time cartoon that had taken the country by storm. Marilyn Albion wasn't really all that impressed with "The Flintstones," but Kate and Joe watched the show religiously, calling Marilyn into the library to sit in front of the television set and, unbeknownst to them, to absorb low levels of radiation.

"Marilyn. Come in here. We're going to be like a family now," called Joe Albion.

Marilyn was grateful for the laugh track, which helped her to know when to laugh, so that Kate and Joe didn't have to keep asking her, "Isn't that funny, Marilyn? Isn't that funny?"

Marilyn hadn't seen anything that had struck her as funny, or even as interesting, since the time when Dale Arden, dancing to the music of the evil and beautiful space witch, almost stabbed Flash Gordon to death, right on television! Marilyn was, however, enjoying this "Flintstones" episode which featured "Marilyn Monrock." Joe became especially excited when he saw this.

"Turn it up! Turn it up! Marilyn! You were named for her, Marilyn," said Joe Albion, Democratic nominee for mayor of Boston.

Marilyn Albion was surprised to learn she was named for a cartoon.

"The Flintstones" over, the Great Debate was about to start. Kate Albion kept saying, "Focus it! Focus it!" Kate Albion spent the entire debate fine-tuning the focus on the television set.

"I can't hear a thing, Kate," said Joe Albion.

"It doesn't matter," Kate said. "Look at Nixon! He looks like a grave digger."

"But what's he saying?"

"He's saying he has a special on cemetery plots."

"Kate. I can't hear a thing," said Joe.

"Look at Kennedy's tan. Just look at him! This man is going to be a great leader."

After the Great Debate, the national consensus was that Nixon needed a new suit and a shave, and that Kennedy had fantastic teeth and charisma. Charisma. The secret ingredient. You can't learn it. You can't buy it. You have to be born with it. And if you're not born with it, you have to destroy anyone who is.

Kate and Marilyn Albion stood at the sidewalk's edge, in front of the pack of women precinct workers. They waited for the motorcade. *Motorcade.* The word triggered erotic sensations in Kate Albion. Motorcade. It was as good as *Sputnik.*

Kate could have ridden in the convertible with Joe, behind JFK's car, but she didn't want JFK to think she was just a wife. She wanted him to see her with the precinct workers, with the people, to know she worked for him and for her husband, that she was not just a woman, not just for show.

The motorcycle sirens approached and several women began to squeal.

"He's coming! He's coming!"

And a strange phenomenon occurred. Some of the women began to jump up and down. Some of them linked arms and jumped up and down. The sirens gained in power, and the jumpers gathered momentum.

"Here comes the motorcade! Oh my God!"

Up and down, back and forth, like a wave, like an orgasm, the women swayed and leaped, like the sea Jack Kennedy loved to navigate in a sailboat, like Dale Arden dancing to the music of the evil and beautiful space witch. The motorcade turned the corner.

Aides trotted alongside JFK's shining red convertible, keeping the women who were trying to climb onto the car from falling off and injuring themselves. As the convertible passed, Kate Albion was embarrassed at her excitement. She concealed it, however, and this gave her power.

JFK looked toward the women precinct workers. He knew exactly where they would be standing. He knew each of their first names. Divine and golden in his red convertible, he waved to them. He spotted Kate Albion, who was keeping her dignity. Everything in her wanted to jump, to sway, scream, pull his hair, French-kiss him, really French-kiss him. But she had poise.

JFK looked directly at her and shouted, "I like your hat, Kate!" She was wearing the ALL THE WAY WITH JFK AND JOE straw hat. She was his.

A wild woman, who Kate recognized as Cherries Deaner, was carrying a baby on one hip and missing a shoe on one foot. She stopped in front of Kate Albion and yelled to her sister Lynn, who was jogging happily alongside JFK's car, "Touch him for me! Touch him for me!" Lynn touched him for her and screamed in delight, looking at her hand for signs of contact with divinity.

Joe Albion's car approached in the motorcade. The women who couldn't get to JFK figured, What the hell, and grabbed Joe Albion, who smiled politely as his shirt buttons were ripped off, his hair caressed and pulled, his cheeks squeezed. Joe Albion would be a popular mayor.

Marilyn Albion was frightened as she saw her father being grabbed and seized like a sale item. Kate Albion knew Marilyn was afraid, and she leaned to her daughter and said, never taking her eyes off the taillights of JFK's convertible, "No one touches Richard Nixon. Remember that." Marilyn would remember that.

JFK was out of sight, having successfully negotiated the waves. Kate and Marilyn watched as Joe's convertible drove by. Joe Albion was in an almost postboudoir disarray. Kate Albion was then certain that Joe was about to become mayor of Boston. Perhaps Mrs. Kennedy would recognize her in the future, she thought defiantly. Marilyn Albion pressed against her mother's thigh, and Kate, delirious and gracious in power, put a hand on Marilyn's shoulder.

Joe Albion shook so many hands that his fingers were sprained. He kissed so many babies that he became immune to the smell of dirty diapers. He was going to be mayor of Boston. He wondered if he would have time for the Blue Lagoon. He would not have time to paint pictures of palm trees or talk to God. He would be mayor of Boston, but there was only one thing that truly interested him: Marilyn Monroe.

> *My heart belongs to Daddy,*
> *So I simply couldn't be bad.*
> *Yes, my heart belongs to Daddy.*
> *Da da, da da da, da da Dad!*

Joe Albion blew Marilyn Albion a great big kiss, but it landed on Kate, who cupped it in her palm and blew it back to him.

Walter Cronkite, all eyebrows and codified facial tic-tac-toes, announced the ascendancy of John Fitzgerald Kennedy to the presidency, and then, as an aside, Walter Cronkite himself announced the mayoral victory of Joe Albion. Kate Albion collapsed in pure triumph as she listened to Richard Nixon's concession speech. The applause meter had selected John Fitzgerald Kennedy and Joe Albion.

"Nixon is finished," said Kate Albion, and she felt a touch of cruelty in her, which caused her to burst into song:

> *I've got a loverly bunch of Cocoanuts,*
> *There they are a-standing in a row . . .*

Mrs. Finnegan, Nellie Kelly, and Joe Albion sang with gusto:

> *Big ones, small ones, some as big as your head.*
> *Give 'em a twist, a flick of the wrist,*
> *That's what the showman said!*

"And no one," declared Kate Albion, "no one will feel sorry for this president. And no one, no one will feel sorry for this mayor!"

Joe Albion saw something mean in Kate Albion's eyes and he smiled at her and howled inside. He was a gentleman but he loved her mean streak, and she knew it.

"Let's go to City Hall before your victory speech at headquarters," said Kate.

"At this hour? How will we get out? We're surrounded by reporters."

"The back way."

"How will we get into City Hall?"

"Through the front door."

"They'll let us in?" asked Joe.

"We are the mayor of Boston. We can get in anywhere," said Kate.

Marilyn looked at Kate in awe. There were no doors Kate could not open, no inner sanctums she could not violate.

Kate and Joe paused on the quiet gray sidewalk in front of City Hall. The bright green grass, freshly cut and watered, glistened in the lamplight. Kate looked at the statue of Benjamin Franklin and imagined a statue of Joe and Kate Albion, wind-blown bronze glowing in the dark across a century or two. Hand in hand, they walked up the steps to the entranceway, the mammoth arched windows like sleepy glass eyes in the night. The night watchman, Franklin Finney, Fatty Finney's cousin, was delighted to see Kate Albion. Franklin Finney was one of Kate's dozens of confederates, and he provided her with fascinating bits of information about the infidelities and Sunday afternoon perversions of her enemies and friends, information she never used but kept on file in case she was ever blackmailed. Franklin Finney opened the front door and admitted them to the silent rotunda. They climbed the wide marble steps to the upper floors.

Kate and Joe stood before the mayor's office as Franklin unlocked the door and let them inside. Franklin Finney disappeared into the night like the bellhop who brings the honeymooners to the bridal suite.

The plushness of the exterior offices was surprising: long comfortable couches, oak secretarial desks, lush plants, oriental rugs, and IBM typewriters. Inebriate of power were they as they crossed the threshold to the moonlit inner sanctum and closed the heavy door behind them.

Kate Albion swelled with pleasure as she ran her hand along the huge mahogany desk. Joe Albion rubbed the leather on the mayor's chair and let one hand brush the cold brass of the floor lamp. As they fondled the furnishings, their hands met near the antique ink pot. They looked deeply into each other's eyes and rested on the highly polished mahogany desk top. Hello hello. Kate Albion breathed heavily and said, "Just keep on with your shopping while I tell you about my husband, Joe Albion." Joe Albion's teeth glittered in the dark.

Marilyn Albion, one hand in Nellie Kelly's, one in Mrs. Finnegan's, strolled the long hallway and entered the kitchen.

"The Old Man's jigging inside Kate tonight," said Nellie Kelly, pouring a tall glass of milk for Marilyn.

"They'll be doing the cupcakewalk 'round Blarney Heaven in Southie," said Mrs. Finnegan, as she prepared the victory tea, putting on the kettle and breaking open a fresh can of Borden's evaporated milk.

Marilyn lifted her glass of milk and drank slowly, poor Richard Nixon dead-ended in her heart.

> *Da da, da daa da,*
> *My heart belongs to Daddy.*
> *Hail to the darling chief,*
> *My heart belongs to Dad!*

Studying the cow on the Borden's label, Marilyn put her empty glass on the table and said, "No milk for the devil. Poor devil."

CHAPTER 5

Happy Birthday to You

No one had the nerve to say it, but there was a party hat on the presidency.

—Anonymous

May 1962

In the history of New York City, there had been no hotter day in May. Ninety-nine degrees. Nevertheless, it was the Albion family's destination. Joe, Kate, and Marilyn Albion flew toward New York City on the Logan–LaGuardia shuttle flight from Boston. Mayor Joe Albion had three tickets for the President's Birthday Salute, a Democratic party fund-raiser to be held at Madison Square Garden, with tickets priced from $300 to $1,000, the original sliding scale.

Marilyn Albion had a long nap before the airplane ride so that she could stay up late and be a part of history, although she was tired of her uncomfortable black patent-leather shoes, even for history's sake. She preferred her Red Ball Jets.

The hum of the airplane was comforting in the first-class section of the jet and as close to a meditative experience as Kate Albion would ever come. Kate couldn't have been happier. It was a great time to be a Democrat. The president had unlimited access to the press. The president had charisma. The president had fabulous teeth. The causes of the Democratic party were just and noble: Medicare, the ownership of large red convertibles, physical fitness, and unlimited milk were on the lips of the nation. Millions of white milk moustaches hailed the chief every day.

"Let's face it," said Kate Albion. "Life wouldn't be the same without the Kennedys."

Joe Albion agreed. He noticed that would-be heroes were always showing up, young men longing for Japanese destroyers to cut their PT boats in half, that they might haul a crewmate to safety at great personal risk. Joe Albion suspected that most men create danger. The question "What if a madman pushes the button?" was repeated over and over, in Europe in Peoria in Baton Rouge in Venice Beach, in England in Budapest in Sweden in Havana.

Party-poopers, thought Mayor Albion.

For the West and its allies, Nikita Khrushchev was the perfect madman candidate. Sitting in the heart of the deepest, darkest Kremlin, banging his shoe on the table for show, will it be him?

"Clearly, his problems stem from his baldness," said Kate.

"But is that enough to make him a madman?" asked Joe. "He's never seen a palm tree. That's his problem."

"Wait'll he gets Cuba. He'll get Cuba and he'll still be the same. You'll see," said Kate Albion.

The jet hit an airpocket, and Joe held Marilyn close to him. "It's just a little hole in the sky," he said soothingly.

Marilyn loved Joe Albion, because she knew that, if necessary, he would save her life by tying her to the prow of the *Hesperus*.

Marilyn watched her mother take a long drag from her charcoal-filtered Tareyton. Marilyn couldn't wait to smoke.

"Men are as jealous of each other's looks as women are," said Kate. "But more frustrated. A woman can go to Filene's and get herself some lipstick, some blusher, some eyebrow tweezers. If a man did that, he could lose an election. Look what happened to Richard Nixon when Jackie Kennedy said she was proud that at least her husband had not worn any makeup during the Great Debate."

Kate Albion was still not reconciled in her heart to Jackie Kennedy. Kate Albion had decided that, should she meet Mrs. Kennedy again, she would pretend not to recognize her. Kate was pretty sure that would drive her crazy. Kate blew a smoke ring. Marilyn watched it rise and become invisible.

"Nikita Khrushchev accused President Kennedy of setting up an atomic-war challenge," said Joe Albion.

"Like a touch football game?" asked Marilyn, but she got no response.

"Khrushchev says it would be suicide to start such a war," said Joe.

Marilyn Albion wondered how many buttons, how many madmen there were. In theory, the supply of madmen could be endless. Marilyn was fairly certain it was not her father, because Joe Albion loved Marilyn Monroe and Marilyn Monroe was against the bomb. Miss Monroe once dated Mr. Khrushchev, remembered Marilyn Albion. Great Aunt Nellie Kelly had shown her their picture on the front page of the *Boston Herald.*

> My nightmare's the H-bomb.
> What's yours?
>
> —*Marilyn Monroe*

"There's a rumor," said Kate Albion to Mayor Joe Albion.

Marilyn listened carefully to rumors. Marilyn felt like a smoke ring, rising into invisibility.

"The man in the dark suit and sunglasses who is always near the president," said Kate. "You know the one. Well. Did you notice that he is always carrying a black metal box? Well. That black box has the button in it, the button that could destroy the world. If you push it, the bombs go off." Kate paused, then said in a muffled tone, "The button is green."

"Why is it green?" asked Marilyn Albion. No response.

"There's another rumor," said Kate to Joe. "Under the White House there's a special place where the most powerful men will go if the madman pushes the button. In this special place is everything that would be needed to survive an atomic attack, including Alka-Seltzer and servants' quarters."

Kate Albion had acquired an absolute obsession with atomic fallout shelters. Who had them, where they were, how long the oxygen would last, fanned her barely manageable fear of atomic holocaust.

"You know, Joe," said Kate. "Senators can probably get into that room. I want you to think about that."

Joe Albion thought about that as their plane landed in the hellish heat wave at LaGuardia.

The Albions passed the rotating beams of star-sized searchlights and entered Madison Square Garden. Inside the Garden, Marilyn felt the thrill of the circus; Joe the ring-flattened boxer's bloody nose; and Kate the hype of the political convention.

Kate noticed that she was not alone in her fashion selection. In spite of the heat, there were hundreds of pillbox hats, A-line dresses, and Jackie-flip hairdos. Kate, seeing the hundreds of Jackie replicas, took off her pillbox hat and discreetly dropped it into a trash can.

They were escorted to their seats; Kate was impressed. Fatty Finney had done exceptionally well. She had prepared herself to be seated high up and far away, high enough for a nosebleed, slightly embarrassed that she had dressed so fashionably and yet was seated with the nobodies. Kate wanted to be with the people, but only if she were in front. Her seats were on the 50th Street side of the Garden, facing the stage that had been constructed in the center of the arena. The president's box was also on the 50th Street side of the Garden, and she would be able to see him very clearly, without the binoculars discreetly tucked in her purse.

Marilyn Albion looked up to the ceiling and saw hundreds of red-white-and-blue balloons drooping in what appeared to be giant hair nets.

"Mrs. Finnegan would like this," said Marilyn.

On the left of the stage was a lectern bearing the presidential seal, and behind and to the right there was a fifteen-piece band dressed in elegant tuxedos. Marilyn recognized the presidential seal from the tray table she used to eat her TV dinners. Marilyn wondered if Sputnik was still going around. There were lots of American satellites going around now, too, and a Russian cosmonaut.

As they took their seats, from the corner of her eye Kate Albion watched the people in the nosebleed sections take note of her. She tried to move casually, with no trace of excitement, as if she knew all along that these were to be her seats. She felt a wave of hot anger. She was vulnerable to her desire for JFK's acknowledgment, but she was sick of her obsession, which was like patting a beloved cat that claws your furniture when you turn your back. With her terrific peripheral vision, Kate's eyes were riveted on the presidential box. She pretended they were not, appearing to look just off center, but she didn't miss a thing.

Joe Albion did not feign indifference, but his eyes were riveted on the stage, two small blue searchlights looking for Miss Monroe.

The woman Marilyn Albion was named for was in this Garden, and Marilyn wanted to get a good look at her. Marilyn got up from her seat, and to her surprise, her parents let her just walk away. Joe and Kate were drunk on history.

Marilyn made her way through the crowds of Jack and Jackie imitations, feeling out of place that she was not pretending to be somebody else, which seemed to be what everyone was doing.

Down on the floor of the Garden, Marilyn was able to walk anywhere without restriction. Looking at Marilyn, a Jack look-alike murmured to his Jackie-blowup wife, "Kennedy kid," and the guards let her pass backstage. No one wanted to admit they did not recognize a member of the clan, which was, as far as Marilyn could tell, as extensive as the Finneys, although not nearly so diverse.

Marilyn had always wanted her mother to look at her with the same interest she took in pictures of Caroline, the president's young daughter. The only true passionate interest Kate had exhibited toward Marilyn had been when she gave birth to Mr. Nixon's poster. Marilyn would remember that.

Searching backstage for Miss Monroe, Marilyn discovered that it was very useful to be a Kennedy, even an imaginary one. To be able to go anywhere in an adult world because you are a pretty little girl who is believed to belong to the powerful was almost as good as eating at Woolworth's and being greeted at the door by Mrs. Finnegan.

Marilyn Albion observed a young man in a pin-striped suit and black shiny shoes. It was Bobby Darin. And there was that man with the big nose, the Supreme Court justice, Jimmy Durante. Marilyn loved to see famous people up close because it made her feel as though she were dead and in heaven.

A heavy black lady whom everyone called "Ella" was standing nearby, singing soft gospel hallelujahs and bobbing her head like a buoy on the ocean.

Except for Shirley MacLaine, the white people around Ella seemed very awkward as they tried to be hip and bob their heads and clap their hands in rhythm. Unfortunately, while the sophisticated Ella looked inhabited by holy life, the white people looked like those heads on springs that jerk up and down in the back window of your car when you slam on the brakes. Clearly, Ella was as important as Mrs. Finnegan.

"Excuse me," said Marilyn. "Could you tell me where

Marilyn Monroe is? I'm a friend of hers." Marilyn had learned from Kate Albion that some lies are acceptable if they justify the means.

Ella leaned her wide dark face near Marilyn's and said, "You got some friends in mighty high places."

The white people laughed and laughed. One of the white men with a giant Jack-like lock of hair down to his nose decided this was a perfect picture.

"Ella Fitzgerald and the little blond girl."

Ella Fitzgerald was bored with the Jack-like man but tolerant. She turned her attention to Marilyn.

"Who are you, honey?"

"Marilyn Albion."

"That's a nice name," said Miss Fitzgerald.

"Albion . . . Albion . . ." said the white man, snapping his fingers not in time. Marilyn would not help him to identify her. Marilyn wondered if these were the people who would get to be in the atomic shelter under the White House.

The photographic flashes exploded in Ella's and Marilyn's eyes. They smiled as a delivery man brought Miss Fitzgerald an armful of spring flowers, freshly sprayed with water. Ella gave a white carnation to Marilyn.

"Where are the photographers?" yelled the white man.

All the white people said, "Awwwwww."

Marilyn looked carefully at their temples for signs of red splotches.

Miss Fitzgerald took Marilyn's hand and led her to a door with a small, bright green star. Miss Fitzgerald knew what's what. Miss Fitzgerald was in charge.

"It's green," said Marilyn Albion. "Like the button."

Miss Fitzgerald looked to the east. Miss Fitzgerald looked to the west. From behind the green star, there was a peal of laughter as the unmistakable Monroe voice mildly slurred, "Khrushchev looked at me the way a man looks at a woman."

Miss Fitzgerald opened the door and said, "Hello, Miss Monroe," and entered the dressing room with Marilyn Albion.

A delighted Miss Monroe said, "Hello, Miss Fitzgerald."

They're friends, thought Marilyn Albion, like Mrs. Finnegan and Great Aunt Nellie. She could just picture Ella Fitzgerald and Marilyn Monroe at the Woolworth's lunch counter together wearing their glistening dresses, their beautiful large breasts at rest on the counter, their voices rising up into the colored cardboard treats.

Miss Fitzgerald said, "I'd like you to meet Miss Albion, Miss Monroe. She's a personal friend of mine."

Marilyn Albion saw one tuxedoed boy-man and two drunken, highly coiffed women in the dressing room, champagne glasses perilously lolling in their hands.

"Well, thank you, ever so, Miss Fitzgerald," said Miss Monroe.

"You're welcome, ever so," said Miss Fitzgerald. Marilyn Albion thanked Miss Fitzgerald, who left the dressing room, glitter sprinkling her path.

Marilyn Albion saw that Miss Monroe's dress was unzipped up the back so that she could sit and bend. Marilyn Albion had never seen breasts like Miss Monroe's. They were the kind of breasts upon which children want to rest their heads. But Miss Monroe frightened Marilyn with the thickness of her stage makeup, and the taxidermical way in which she held her lips parted and stretched tight. Marilyn searched Miss Monroe's temples for the red splotches, but so cosmeticized was the goddess for whom she was named that Marilyn Albion had to close her eyes to try to feel if there was indeed someone named Marilyn Monroe in the dressing room.

Her head bent and eyes closed, Marilyn lifted the white carnation through the air toward Miss Monroe. Gentle and a little drunk—charming drunk, like Joe Albion liked to be—Marilyn Monroe put the flower to her lips and her hand on Marilyn's head.

"Are you afraid of me?"

Marilyn Albion nodded her head.

"So am I," said Miss Monroe.

Marilyn Albion opened her eyes and Miss Monroe's lips were relaxed.

"What's your name?" asked Miss Monroe.

"Marilyn."

"Marilyn? That's my name."

"I was named for you."

Marilyn Monroe looked closely at Marilyn Albion, and traced the perimeter of her face with the white carnation. Marilyn Albion dipped her longest finger into the white light around Miss Monroe's fame-ridden head, and they smiled across the feminine no man's land.

"Aren't you up kind of late?" asked Miss Monroe.

"I have to be a part of history," said Marilyn, with a sigh.

"So do I," said Miss Monroe. "But be careful of history. It's just some guy in a suit telling a story."

Miss Monroe took Marilyn Albion by the hand, and they walked to the backstage area, people stepping aside as they passed. No photo opportunity this because sex goddesses are not to be seen with little girls because someone might remember the sex goddess was once a little girl. Someone might feel strange about that.

"Not many miles before I sleep," whispered Marilyn Monroe, who looked like a mermaid trying to maneuver on land.

Marilyn Monroe squeezed Marilyn Albion's hand, and thunder rumbled across New York City.

The crowd was very anxious. They wanted to know why the president was late. Where was he? Had something happened to him?

"He's probably tied up with the riffraff outside," said Kate Albion. When Kate was in front of them, they were the people; if they blocked her path, they were riffraff rabble who only got to see his motorcade. Motorcade. Hello hello. She was inside. Finally. Inside. And in such a good seat. They arrived just before the thunderstorm. They didn't get wet because they were leading charmed lives. The heat and the night air collided, and thunder and lightning flashed. But the Albions did not get wet. That's what it was like to be a Kennedy. To be the president's wife. To ride in the bubble-top limousine. To have someone drop your Alka-Seltzer into the glass for you.

Joe Albion felt like an astronaut in a weightless condition. He would never be more perfectly happy as he waited patiently for the entrance of Marilyn Monroe. This was better than Camp Pendleton, better than the Trans-Lux Theater.

Marilyn Albion had made her way back to her seat, her absence unnoticed. Marilyn enjoyed having a secret. It made her feel powerful.

Everyone stood as the band struck up with "Hail to the Chief":

Da da, da da da,
Da da, da da,
Da daaaa da.

President John Fitzgerald Kennedy entered Madison Square Garden and took his seat in the presidential box.

He sat in the special upholstered chair to support his bad back. He was always in pain, which, in the aesthetic of Kate Albion, endowed him with great beauty.

Marilyn Albion was startled. She had not seen John Kennedy for two years, when she was eight years old, and he looked different. His face looked puffy and his head seemed bigger. Too big. It was disturbing to see him in person. It was as difficult for her emotionally as that time when she was in the car with Joe and Kate, driving along the Massachusetts Turnpike toward the Howard Johnson's with its glowing orange rooftop, and she saw the man-sized Mr. Peanut in his black top hat and white gloves, looking like President Kennedy at his inauguration. Mr. Peanut's monocle had caught the sun and his walking stick had pointed toward heaven.

"Look at Mr. Peanut, Marilyn! He's waving to you! Wave to Mr. Peanut!"

Marilyn Albion turned away from the president and collected herself.

The great liberal stars of Hollywood and New York began their performances. Joe Albion's eyes filled with tears. Just the thought of "There's No Business Like Show Business" being sung from a stage, no matter where, elated him, and if the performers formed a chorus line and kicked their legs in unison, it had the power of a spiritual experience. But he was a mayor, and mayors don't cry about chorus lines in public. Joe Albion dug his fingernails deep into the flesh of his hand. Pain brought him back to his duties.

Kate Albion stole a glimpse of JFK. JFK had his feet propped up on the railing. What dash! Kate Albion looked at the men and women in the presidential box, and she felt shame sweep through her body and a bright red flush beneath her skin. It became clear. She could never be a Kennedy. And she was furious. Jackie Kennedy was not in the booth with the president. That was some consolation. She turned away and took Joe Albion's hand in hers, for better or worse.

Joe Albion hadn't bothered to look toward the presidential box all evening. He had grown weary of JFK and JFK's incessant high expectations: perfect physical fitness, high milk consumption, and races to the moon. At least with Eisenhower, no one asked him on a daily basis what he'd done for his country lately, and he was not expected to carry any torches, which, as Joe Albion explained in the Blue Lagoon, could be used as easily to set the world on fire as to light the way.

Marilyn Albion pushed Mr. Peanut out of her mind, and looked back at JFK. He was smiling. He was in proportion. Marilyn relaxed and watched the stage, but Kate Albion's eyes were riveted on the tall thin man with crewcut, tan, and sunglasses, seated behind the president's box. The thin man was wearing sunglasses, at night, inside Madison Square Garden. It was quite possible that as a young child he had owned a Captain Marvel decoder ring, thought Kate Albion facetiously. The Captain Marvel devotee held a black metal box on his lap, and Kate Albion knew it was the box with the button in it, and that the button was lime green. This man, this tan, crewcut man with sunglasses, sitting perfectly still with the black box on his lap, this man's head turned slowly to the left, slowly to the right, then rested front and center; slowly to the left, slowly to the right, then rested front and center. He was on the lookout for the madman. Kate wondered, What if the madman sneaks up behind him?

The houselights dimmed and the stage became illuminated. A man's voice with a British accent, which gave the festivities a royal air, said, "Ladies and gentlemen, Marilyn Monroe."

The audience held its breath. There had been an uproar among the fundamentalist groups when they learned that Miss Monroe was to sing for the president in public.

There was an uncomfortable pause. The spotlight was on the left of center wing. But there was no movement. Joe Albion became agitated.

The British man's voice again said, "Ladies and gentlemen, Marilyn Monroe."

The spotlight swept to the wing entrance, but there was no movement. Joe Albion was concerned. "Where is she?" he said.

"She's probably trying to zip up her dress," said Kate.

The British man said, "Mr. President. In the history of show business, there has been no one female who meant so much, who has done more—"

A surprise attack! Marilyn Monroe burst onto the stage and ran like a foot-bound geisha halfway to the presidential podium. Then she stopped, and performed that slow, perfect walk through the fields of media hype. Miss Monroe had cut one quarter-inch from one spike heel to get that slight wobble effect, and oddly enough, President Kennedy wore a quarter-inch lift inside one shoe. It was speculated that Miss Monroe saved her little cut off pieces for him, as a gesture, the way eunuchs save their organs in a box that will be buried along with them.

With a great big smile, the British man said, "Ladies and gentlemen. Mr. President. The *late* Marilyn Monroe."

Miss Monroe arrived at the podium in full-bloom grace, wit, and Jell-O magnificence. An atomic cloud of white mink surrounded her in lush rings. Satisfied that she had been properly introduced, that no one was sure if she was sacred or profane, she dropped the mink to the floor.

The audience gasped and the blood rushed to Joe Albion's feet. Miss Monroe appeared to be naked. Miss Monroe appeared to be naked, and this was being televised. There was that nervous *snap crackle pop* laughter of collapsing adrenal glands. She was wearing a flesh-tone dress, with beads sewn into it. Skin and beads. She was toying with the audience. She was on the edge. She had the driver's wheel in her hand, and they all knew it, and she was pretending she wasn't watching the road. Or was she really not watching the road? Miss Monroe was at the wheel for the national thrill ride. Marilyn Monroe shielded her eyes from the stage lights and looked up into the nosebleed section, ignoring the sultanic president.

Kate Albion was disgusted. Marilyn Monroe epitomized the reason that women had not taken direct power. But her disgust collapsed when she saw the secret weapon of Monroe's magnetism: Kate Albion could not take her eyes off Marilyn Monroe any more than she could turn away from the aftermath of a bad accident. Marilyn Monroe was in control by the power of allurement, vulnerability, and impending disaster; and Marilyn Monroe knew exactly what she was doing. She looked to the east. She looked to the west. She looked directly at President John Fitzgerald Kennedy, and in the sweetest voice the land of cosmetic surgery and beach parties could imagine, she prepared to sing, tentative and tender as a small child in a big role in the Christmas pageant.

Would she remember the words? worried Joe Albion.

Could she remember the words? wondered Kate.

Would she break out of her dress? Would she fall? thought Joe Albion.

Was the president smiling? Oh yes, saw Kate Albion. The president. The president was smiling. And laughing. He snapped his big head back with laughter. But he was not laughing at her. He was afraid. The president was afraid! Kate Albion was impressed.

Marilyn Albion was frightened for Miss Monroe. "Her dress is too tight, Daddy. She can't breathe."

"Miss Monroe is an actress," said Joe Albion. "It's all an act, Marilyn. Don't worry. It's all an act."

"Or is it a toaster, Mr. Mayor?" said Kate Albion, a mean little smile playing on her lips. "A one-hundred-and-twenty-pound toaster, made of skin and beads, orbiting Madison Square Garden?"

It passed on the horizon like a gleam of light.

"It's a cake, Joe!" said Kate, delighted with the pageantry. "These Kennedys throw great parties."

Miss Monroe took a deep breath. Torrid and electric, she sang, like it's never been sung before or since:

> *Happy birthday to you,*
> *Happy birthday to you,*

Marilyn Albion did not understand why the people were laughing, and she was glad that Miss Monroe did not seem to know.

> *Happy birthday, Mr. President,*
> *Happy birthday to you.*

"God. What a cake," said Kate Albion.

The five-foot, five-tiered presidential birthday cake was wheeled around the Garden by two chefs in billowing white bakers' hats.

Thanks, Mr. President,
For all the things you've done,
The battles that you've won . . .

Forty-five large blue candles flickered on the perimeter of the world.

The way you deal with U.S. Steel . . .

Miss Monroe hovered a heavy breast in midair above her cupped hand.

Marilyn Albion relaxed and said, "Mrs. Finnegan would love this."

Miss Monroe clenched and raised her fist, the blond-bombshell albino panther.

And our problems by the ton
We thank you so much!

The roar of the crowd was alarming, out of control, as Miss Monroe cried out from the wilderness:

Everybody! Happy birthday!

And Miss Monroe was blacked out in a flash as the thousands of charmed Eves and Adams chanted as much to her as to President Kennedy.

Welcome to the Garden.
Welcome home.

In the blacked-out arena, Joe Albion put his head between his legs. He did not want to pass out from the heat.

"What happened to Miss Monroe?" demanded Marilyn Albion. Joe Albion lifted his head and quietly said, "She's gone home now. Miss Monroe has gone home to sleep."

Marilyn Albion sighed deeply as the lights came up to reveal President John Fitzgerald Kennedy mounting the empty stage. Kate Albion was transfixed. Now that the president was far enough away from her, she was again comfortable with him. There was no need for alarm.

The president stood at the podium with the presidential seal, where Miss Monroe had stood, and said, "I can now retire from politics after having had 'Happy Birthday' sung to me in such a sweet, wholesome way."

The crowd roared and Joe Albion, circulation intact, liked JFK for the first time.

President John Fitzgerald Kennedy continued:

> These Republican leaders have not been content with attacks on me, on my wife or my brothers; no, not content with that, they now include my little girl's pony, Macaroni.
>
> Well, I don't resent such attacks, but Macaroni does.

The applause meter quivered wildly against its upper limits, almost setting off a dangerous harmonic tremor in the Garden, but Marilyn Albion fell to sleep in her father's arms.

> Actually, there's another speech by a former vice-president of the United States in 1952 which is even more pertinent.
>
> It was just a little pony, and you know, the kids, like all kids, loved it. And I just want to say this right now: that regardless of what they say about it, we're going to keep it.

I feel about Macaroni like the vice president did about Checkers. . . .

Hot hot hot.
Flash flash flash.
Hot hot hot.

Kate Albion put her head between her legs. She did not want to swoon, but there was so much heat in the Garden that it was almost tropical. She took a deep breath and lifted her head. In the hallucination-inducing heat, she saw her head on a spring, bobbing in the back window of the black stretch mayoral limousine that transported her in Boston. She made a note to never travel in the tropics and wondered if President Kennedy's malaria ever caused him to see imaginary palm trees during press conferences.

Kate Albion looked at her husband and child, posed like a queer little pietà. Marilyn Albion was asleep in Mayor Joe Albion's lap, her head dangling over his arm. In her dream, she ran along the sandy beach with Mr. Peanut, his white gloves immaculate, his walking stick, top hat, and monocle bright and dazzling. They were chasing the Captain Marvel devotee who had the black box, the black box with the green button that, if pressed, would destroy the world. Marilyn could not keep up with Mr. Peanut, and in compassion, Mr. Peanut lifted her into his arms—as Joe Albion carried Marilyn out of the Garden, and Kate, walking beside him, stepped over discarded pillbox hats and empty candy wrappers.

"Well," said Kate Albion, "this certainly was history."

Part Two

CHAPTER 6

"How Fearfully and Wonderfully She Was Made by the Creator!"

—*Book of Psalms*

... But Hollywood and Americans who live everywhere else were and are also accountable before God for the elevation and eventual destruction of this woman.

—*Christian Century*

In a way we are all guilty. We built her up to the skies, we loved her, but left her lonely and afraid when she needed us most.   —*Hedda Hopper*

The poor girl ... Like a white dove ... One that hunters throw up in the air and shoot as a target.   —*Djuna Barnes*

... Sacrificial lamb destroyed on the altar of capitalism.

—*Pravda*

August 1962

It was late in the afternoon on Sunday, August 5, 1962, the sun was hot and declining, and the sky was a seamless blue in Boston. Mayor Joe Albion escorted Kate, Marilyn, Nellie Kelly, and Mrs. Finnegan toward the small green wooden dock to board the swan boats on the lagoon in Boston's Public Garden. The excursion had been planned before he learned that Marilyn Monroe had died the night before. Nellie Kelly and Flora Finnegan watched Joe carefully for any signs of going on tour.

Joe Albion's emotions ripped through him, but he had remained as silent as the hard earth in a hurricane. He stopped before the Victorian-style flower beds, and he thought of graves covered with bright flowers. Unable to conceal the tears that welled in his eyes, he put on his sunglasses, which horrified Kate Albion.

"Politicians do not put on sunglasses, unless they are military dictators in South American countries," she said quietly to her husband. Joe did not respond.

Nellie Kelly leaned toward Mrs. Finnegan and whispered, "Here we go. He's going to lose it."

Joe Albion would not lose it. Not this time. He was a dandy, but he was not weak. He hated weak men. When he was a child, he had lived for a short time in Whittier, California. He had beaten a whining boy in the schoolyard. The teachers turned their backs and pretended they didn't see, as the other boys cheered Joe Albion on. Puppies can whine, he believed. That's their job. But a whining boy is a disgrace to his country and must never be allowed to become president. Joe Albion had beaten the boy so badly that he frightened himself. No one had stopped him. They should have stopped him, but they had cheered, and Joe Albion had become excited. His fists had struck this boy like he was hitting a toy. He had been seduced by violence. Later that day, he was alone in his backyard, sitting on the green grass near the flower bed. He saw the boy's blood on his shirt and he vomited onto the flowers.

Joe Albion composed himself. He was the mayor of Boston. He had never again beaten anyone, but Miss

Monroe's death, her helplessness, her victimization, her vulnerability had made her too beautiful for him to bear. He believed that Miss Monroe could have lived happily with the snake in the garden, but that she'd left with Adam out of compassion. Pathological compassion. His hands and thighs ached from tension and remorse. He felt part of the collective responsibility for her death. Looking up from the flower bed, he saw his wife's eyes. He drew strength from Kate. Kate Albion would never have vomited on the flowers, but she did motion to Joe to remove his sunglasses, which he did. They continued on to the dock.

It was the last ride of the day, and Kate wanted to get this ride over with as quickly as possible. To her the swan boats were the type of ride you take in a bad dream where someone is chasing you but you cannot seem to run fast enough to get away from them or slow enough to be caught.

Ten-year-old Marilyn Albion looked at the swan boats. She had never seen anything quite so lovely, but her pleasure was tempered by the fact that Miss Monroe had killed herself. Marilyn Albion did not understand suicide.

The swan boats had six wide wooden seats, each long enough to sit six people. The bottom of the boat was a bright Kool-Aid green, and a red stripe ran along its wooden edge. The man-sized white swan at the rear of the boat, its feathers full and wide, its red beak and black Oriental eyes pointing down toward its breast, concealed in its back the seat for the young man who would steer and power the boat through the lagoon by peddling, his head riding just above the swan's.

Joe, Marilyn, Kate, Nellie Kelly, and Mrs. Finnegan

boarded the swan boat and sat along the first bench. As they took their seats at the front of the boat, Marilyn thought of the *Hesperus.*

"Mr. Mayor, it's a pleasure to have you aboard, sir," said the young man who would be powering the swan boat.

"It's a pleasure to be here," said the mayor. "What's your name, young man?"

"Freddie Finney, sir," replied the young man, as he went to his position on the swan's back.

"Well, Freddie Finney, let's board these people and sail," said the Mayor.

"Fatty Finney's youngest brother's oldest son," murmured Nellie Kelly to Mrs. Finnegan, who was discreetly adjusting her breasts to the absolute fascination of a little black-haired boy who was seated behind her.

"They're everywhere," said Kate Albion. "Like cockroaches. And every one of them votes. I love that family."

Excited citizenry boarded the boat behind the Albions. This was certainly history. No one could remember it happening in a nonelection year. Boarding behind them was a rollicking Italian family who took up two benches; a stern Irishwoman who had a fear of water, and her young son, who was the Mrs. Finnegan fascinatee; and two young women wearing bright summer peasant blouses and carrying newspapers and large pink cotton-candy swirls.

The last to board was Frances Bright, a strangely quiet bleached blonde in her late thirties. Her makeup was slightly heavy, and although it was a hot, windless afternoon, she protected her perfectly built beehive with a small, sheer blue kerchief. Joe Albion studied her for a moment and turned away, embarrassed at his interest in her, Miss Monroe's body barely cold in its crypt. But this woman seemed out of place to him, as if she usually traveled in dark places. She sat alone on the last bench at the back of the boat, her knees locked together, her purse gripped tightly in her hands on her lap. Her fingernails were long and highly polished a deep and dangerous jungle red, and her white summer dress was made of such a fine light material that it lifted up around her on the power of whisperings and her own breath. She stared dreamily into the water of the lagoon and absently fingered the gold letter *F* pinned to her white dress near her heart. She was strangely alone, not a woman you would expect to see without a man on a hot Sunday afternoon.

The long strands of the weeping willow trees surrounding the lagoon brushed the side of the swan boat as it began its slow hypnotic glide across the water, beneath the bridge, and around the small island, just as it had done for almost a hundred years, probably powered by one of the Finney family.

The Irishwoman's young son tried to stand up and press against Mrs. Finnegan, but his mother grabbed him and made him sit, the slightest rocking motion of the boat terrifying her.

> *This is the hanged man.*
> *Fear death by drowning.*

One of the young women in a peasant blouse opened the late edition of the newspaper she was carrying and read it to her friend, who was chomping slowly and deliberately on her pink cotton candy like a praying mantis eating the head of her partner after sex.

It was learned that medical authorities believed Miss Monroe had been in a depressed mood recently. She was

unkempt and in need of a manicure and pedicure, indicating listlessness and a lack of interest in maintaining her usually glamorous appearance, the authorities added.

"Well, I guess she was depressed," said Kate Albion, quietly and sarcastically. "Whoever wrote that better not be planning on the Pulitzer."

Marilyn will be dressed in a plain green dress, of a light shade, which she obtained in Florence, Italy. There will be no jewelry. The solid bronze casket will be lined with champagne-colored velvet.

"Champagne-colored velvet. Can you believe it?" said one young woman to the other.

The words "solid bronze casket" stabbed Joe Albion's consciousness and caused him great pain. Kate, Marilyn, Aunt Nellie, and Mrs. Finnegan stared straight ahead into the pleasant lagoon, knowing that the death of Miss Monroe was a tragedy for Joe Albion.

Looking as beautiful in death as she did in life . . .

The swan boat stopped dead in the water.

"It says that here. Isn't that the killer," said one of the young women. "She's dead! A beautiful dead body?"

Each member of the Italian family made the sign of the cross, like a row of holy dominoes, tears flooding their eyes.

Unclad body of star found on bed near empty capsule bottle.

The Italian family rattled their rosary beads for Marilyn Monroe's soul.

Marilyn Monroe committed suicide.

"She was killed," said Joe Albion. "She'd never kill herself. We all killed her." He crossed his arms against his chest.

Nellie Kelly and Mrs. Finnegan rolled their eyes and looked to Kate. "She better reel him in before it's too late," said Nellie Kelly to Mrs. Finnegan.

Marilyn Albion was sickened to learn they had all killed Marilyn Monroe.

The swan boat began to rotate in a circle. The Irishwoman with a fear of drowning was nearly in a faint, and her young son took the opportunity to reach from behind Mrs. Finnegan to cup that too tempting breast in his hand. Mrs. Finnegan took the little fellow's hand and would not let go, no matter how intensely he squirmed and pulled. He went into a panic, fearing he would draw back a nub as the rosary beads clicked and jostled for God's attention.

Kate Albion looked at Joe Albion, who stared straight ahead, marinelike, no tears, no movement. She tried to find the cause of the swan boat twirling in a slow-motion Edgar Allan Poe whirlpool. Freddie Finney had his face in his hands, and his shoulders heaved around his neck to shelter his sobs.

"Do you know what an autopsy is like?" said the young lady to her friend, who had gnawed the cotton candy down to the paper bone.

No. Joe Albion and Freddie Finney did not know what an autopsy was like, but they were about to learn. They were about to hear all about it, as the weeping willows tossed their long strands toward the water: how the medical examiner takes a saw and carves, as discreetly as possible . . .

"How discreet can you be with a saw?" said Kate Albion, looking up to the heavens. She turned toward the swan seat and commanded, "Freddie Finney. Pull yourself together!"

". . . through the skull, takes out the brain, weighs it."

"Freddie Finney. Your city needs you," said Kate Albion.

". . . takes out the liver, weighs it . . ."

"The ghouls, the photographers tried anything to get a 'good shot' of the corpse," said Mrs. Finnegan.

"Freddie!" said Kate Albion.

Freddie dropped his hands, and looking as much like the ancient mariner as a young man can, he dutifully peddled the swan boat through the lagoon. Mrs. Finnegan let loose the little boy's hand from her snare. He sat very obediently beside his mother, whose whole morbid life was flashing before her eyes. If she survived the swan boats, she promised St. Jude, her son would be a Benedictine monk.

"Miss Monroe was as popular in death as she was in life. And there are many who now say, Thank God she's dead. In six months, it will be as if she'd never lived," said the young lady licking away the last of the cotton candy.

The swan boat pulled into the dock, the last ride of the day.

"Marilyn Monroe will just be another dead sex symbol in hell," said the Irishwoman, whose son began to leap up and down in protest.

Everyone unboarded the rocking boat except Freddie Finney, the bleached beehive blonde with the floating white dress, and Mayor Joe Albion. The two young women took their newspapers with them. The articles about Miss Monroe's death would be good material for their scrapbooks.

Kate, Marilyn, Nellie Kelly, and Mrs. Finnegan looked at Joe Albion, who remained in his seat at the front of the boat. Without speaking a word, Freddie Finney steered the swan boat back out onto the lagoon, his two passengers silent at opposite ends of the boat. Frances Bright's white dress hovered slightly above her body.

As they circled the tiny island, Joe Albion whispered, "Marilyn Monroe, why did you go?"

Mrs. Finnegan, Nellie Kelly, and Kate Albion sat sipping sherry in the library. Marilyn Albion, now in her pajamas, sat near them, playing with her Barbie doll in evening dress, the tiny zipper open at the back down to Barbie's waist. Barbie hopped like a foot-bound geisha back and forth at Marilyn's crossed knees.

The windows were open and not a breeze moved the draperies.

"Well, Mrs. Finnegan, have you heard about the copy cat deaths?" asked Nellie Kelly.

"What are you harping on?" said Mrs. Finnegan, sipping her sherry.

"Beautiful women are swallowing bottles of Nembutal. They are being found dead with telephones in their hands. Nude. They leave notes that claim they follow in the steps of Marilyn Monroe," said Nellie Kelly.

Barbie was now naked and undergoing autopsy at the hands of the make-believe coroner, Marilyn Albion.

"Her soul's not going to go without taking a lot of them with her. It's the nature of the beast," said Mrs. Finnegan.

Marilyn Albion weighed Barbie's imaginary body organs.

"What would you be saying?" demanded Nellie Kelly.

"Marilyn Monroe was not just some poor little naked girl with a telephone in her hand. Marilyn Monroe had power. And you can bet that her power's going to look for somewhere else to settle in," said Mrs. Finnegan.

"I see what you're saying. Like the Banshee, in a sense," said Nellie Kelly.

Barbie's head was now separated from her body, and Marilyn put her finger into its surprisingly hollow cavity.

"Everybody! Happy birthday!" said Marilyn Albion as the sherry glasses were refilled.

Barbie's hollow head was as disappointing to Marilyn as the chocolate Easter rabbit she had bitten into last spring, only to discover it was an empty shell.

"What I'm saying," said Mrs. Finnegan, "is that a suicide makes the soul heavy, like any kind of violent death, and it stays on the earth for a longer period of time until it can work out its problem and move on."

"Little pitchers have big ears," said Aunt Nellie Kelly, noting at last the horrific Barbie doll scenario on the library rug. Kate watched Marilyn in silence. Nothing about Marilyn surprised her. This was, after all, the child who smuggled a picture of Richard Nixon into her house.

Lightning flashed. "Count the seconds until the thunder, and you know how far away the storm is," said Marilyn Albion.

"Aren't you clever!" said Nellie Kelly.

"Now back to where Monroe's soul goes," said Mrs. Finnegan.

"She wasn't just another brain-damaged blonde, you know," said Nellie Kelly.

"Did you see that one at the back of the swan boat?" said Kate Albion. "The one my husband's still floating around with?"

Marilyn Albion could not get Barbie's head off her finger, which had swollen inside the cavity.

The thunder rolled more deeply toward Boston.

Mrs. Finnegan looked up and held her left index finger by the side of her head. "The thunder talks."

"What's it say?" asked Marilyn Albion, wondering if the thunder could be saying something specifically about her.

"It says, 'Time for bed, Marilyn Albion, so I can tell you my secrets,'" said Nellie Kelly.

Kate Kelly Albion said, "Does he see her face when he sleeps with me?" And for the first time, Kate felt jealousy, because now that Monroe was dead, she was perfect and ageless, and it was impossible for Kate to compete. Kate had been counting on Monroe becoming old, fat, and alcoholic.

This was too personal for Mrs. Finnegan, who adjusted her breasts while Mrs. Kelly escorted Marilyn up the pale staircase to her bedroom.

Alone and safe in her room, Marilyn Albion listened to the thunder and counted the seconds between rolls. Marilyn Albion believed that Marilyn Monroe was in between the thunder and lightning, trying to find a safe place for her soul, so it would not have to race through the world looking for a home. Marilyn tugged at Barbie's head, but the more she tugged, the tighter it held. A huge lightning bolt cracked through the sky and Marilyn's bedroom was as bright as a stage set. The bolt was followed by a thunderburst of such proportions that the vibrations poured into every house below, rattling the windows, knives, and toasters. Marilyn Albion looked at Barbie's head and decided it would be a nice safe place to keep Marilyn Monroe's soul. Small hot tears spilled from her eyes onto the decapitated toy.

In silence the swan boat plied its way through the lagoon until the night sky was slashed with lightning.

As a damp gust circled the swan boat, Joe Albion demanded, "What have we given?"

The blonde then stood at the edge of the boat, heavenly and awful, as Freddie Finney peddled and Joe Albion sang a sad and soft sort of "Taps" for the dead goddess:

> *Goodnight, ladies,*
> *Farewell, gentlemen,*
> *So long, everyone,*
> *It's time for me to go.*

The swan boat tipped in one violent rock as Frances Bright jumped into the water . . . she did not surface. Freddie Finney backpeddled and shouted, "Mr. Mayor!"

Joe Albion turned to see the woman facedown in the dark green water, her beehive still intact. He jumped into the water and lifted her in his arms from death. As he stood up, he saw that the water was only a few feet deep. All she would have had to do was stand up. Lucky for Joe, she didn't know.

"Are you all right?" asked Joe Albion.

"If you save me, really save me," said the bleached beehive blonde.

Joe Albion lifted Frances Bright into the swan boat, and Freddie Finney helped to get her seated. "It's time to go ashore, Freddie," said Joe Albion, the life force surging through him, a hero at long last. It wasn't the PT-109, but it would do.

Freddie Finney returned to his perch on the swan's back and peddled into the gusting wind and rain to the dock.

"Who are you?" asked Joe Albion, and the blonde replied, "Frances Bright."

"Miss Monroe once said something that truly moved me," said Joe Albion to Frances Bright. Freddie Finney listened.

"What was that?" asked Miss Bright.

" 'You're always running into people's unconscious.' "

"Is that bad?" asked Miss Bright.

Joe Albion placed his arm around her shoulders and smiled. He would be patient. He would explain the world to her. She would be safe, and he would be redeemed.

The swan boat docked. Freddie Finney tied the boat up and followed Joe Albion and Frances Bright across the Public Garden toward the Blue Lagoon.

The abandoned swan boats bobbed on the dark green water, gentling nestling each other as birds do in a storm.

So long, Miss Monroe.
Fame has had you.

CHAPTER 7

Save Little Ricky!

October 1962

On Monday, October 22, at 7:00 P.M., a somber Kate Albion turned on the black-and-white portable television in the mayor's office to watch the special address to the nation of President John Kennedy.

After a close-up of the presidential seal, an eagle bearing an olive leaf and arrows in its claws, the camera panned to the intense expression of the president, who said:

> There are nuclear missiles in Cuba capable of striking the United States. Any nuclear missile launched from

Cuba would mean a full retaliatory response upon the Soviet Union. We have created a military blockade. No Soviet ship will be allowed to cross this line, or we are at war.

"If you cross this line," said Kate Albion to the mayor. This morning, Joe Albion, upon being questioned about his constant attention to the Blue Lagoon and lack of attendance at the mayor's office, had risen to his feet in uncharacteristic fury.

"You're running it yourself! You and your imaginary Kennedy," Joe Albion had said.

Kate Albion had backed away from him, narrowing her eyes, the hair on her head lifting slightly. Kate Albion had never seen this behavior in Joe before, and she had thought, It's about time.

She had looked at Joe Albion's hands and said, "Cut your nails, Joe. You look like a Mandarin prince, not a mayor. Remember who you are." Then Kate Albion had slowly turned her back on him and left the room. You couldn't see a trace of fear in her, but she was on alert, and any movement on the periphery of her vision would have signaled her to spring back. But Joe had not moved. He was a gentleman.

President Kennedy was walking by Nikita Khrushchev in this same way, but Mr. Khrushchev was not a gentleman, and because of this, the world was on the verge of nuclear confrontation. The madman was about to reveal himself.

"If you cross this line," Kate Albion said to Joe Albion, plucking a strand of Frances Bright's bleached hair from his deep gray suit. She snapped the hair easily.

"Damaged ends, Joe," said Kate, standing very close to Joe. She reached up and patted his chest.

"Maybe I like things damaged," said Joe, taking Kate's hand from his chest and squeezing it a little too intensely. The madman was about to reveal himself.

Kate Albion said to Joe Albion, "I didn't kill Marilyn Monroe, and Frances Bright didn't bring her back to life."

Joe Albion's guts knotted and he dropped Kate's hand.

> There is no need for alarm.
> Citizens have been expressing their concerns.
> Citizens have been buying up
> all of the canned foods
> for their atomic fallout shelters.

Later that morning, standing at the window in the mayor's office that overlooked Boston, Kate Albion could think of only one thing. Where are the best atomic fallout shelters? She was, after all, the wife of the mayor of Boston. She knew things that the average citizen did not. She would be, in her opinion, an invaluable person to have around after an atomic blast. She knew, for instance, how to keep her balance while wearing spike heels during an explosion. Kate Albion practiced the position. She posed herself in an open-legged stance with her knees locked, and threw her pelvis back and her chest forward, her arms poised at her sides. Kate Albion then experienced a moment of recognition: this was precisely the stance of Marilyn Monroe.

In anticipation of the end of the world, David Marat, Jackie Bright, and Marilyn Albion played atomic war on the lawn in front of city hall. David Marat was the blond and toothy son of a Boston brahmin, a diplomat. David wore tweeds and polished cotton, and lived on Pinkney Street on Beacon Hill. Jackie Bright, tomboy deluxe in honky-tonk bright red jacket and dungarees, had thick black braids as long as whips, and lived near Scollay Square, a more colorful neighborhood of exotic dancers and tattoo parlors. She lived with her mother, Frances Bright.

The children watched Joe Albion and Frances Bright behave as if they had never met, because they were standing on the lawn, in public, in front of city hall. The three ten-year-olds knew that Frances Bright had tried to kill herself in what amounted to little more than a puddle during a thunderstorm the day of Marilyn Monroe's death, and that Mayor Joe Albion had saved her.

Mayor Joe Albion turned to the children. "Children. I have something important to tell you. There are nuclear warheads aimed toward the United States from Cuba. Cuba is an island where people used to go for vacations. Try not to worry about it too much. We might have to go to the atomic fallout shelters, but we will be safe there. Remember. If you hear a loud siren, run to the nearest armory or shelter."

Marilyn Albion was getting absolutely sick of potentially fatal things threatening to fall out of the sky. It started with Sputnik, then there were Saint Theresa's roses, and now there were these missiles in Cuba.

Mayor Joe Albion asked Frances Bright, "What do you think of the missiles in Cuba?"

Frances Bright paused. "It will ruin the beaches."

"Yes. Havana has beautiful beaches."

"No," said Frances Bright. "The beaches here. Cape Cod."

Joe Albion stepped back from Frances Bright. Not another one, he thought. Not his Frances, too. Cape Cod's Hyannisport. Hail to the Kennedy. He'd almost like to see Nixon come to power. What a thought. He'd have to say that to Kate. He'd say that to Kate just as she was going to sleep. He would pretend he was talking in his sleep, so he could always deny it. It could be like that movie, *Gaslight*. He would drive Kate crazy. He would take absolute control. Better still. He would tell her he was going to become a Republican. She would prefer he announced an interest in Satan worship, in the ritualistic killing of children.

"War is the ritualistic killing of children," said Joe Albion. "Only whores and idiots survive."

Frances Bright thought about that.

Jackie Bright, David Marat, and Marilyn Albion hadn't thought of that. "We'd better prepare some entertainment for the adults, so we don't get killed," said Marilyn Albion. Marilyn Albion was showing signs of cynicism.

"I'm sorry," said Frances Bright to Joe Albion. "But I have no opinion. I only try to make the rent."

Joe Albion felt the protective gentleman rise within him once again. Hello hello. Frances Bright wanted to make love with Joe Albion. The tension he created was unbearable, his formality amazing. It was as if the marine at attention in the dress-white uniform had sunken down to his soul. Frances Bright remembered seeing pictures of the guards at Buckingham Palace standing perfectly still while short, squat Welsh corgis with enormous teeth, loud barks, and little white chests tormented them. No matter what she did, he would not consummate their love. Joe Albion wanted Frances Bright to remain pure, distant, untouched, and holy.

Joe Albion did not care that Frances Bright was a professional prostitute.

He thinks he's the only one, thought Jackie Bright.

"Well, Mayor Albion, if the world might be about to come to an end, shall we go to the Blue Lagoon?" asked Frances.

Joe Albion smiled; ecstatic, his body trembled. The world might be about to come to an end. There was no reason for pretense. "Will you children be all right without us?" asked Joe Albion.

"They'll be just fine," said Frances Bright as she took Joe Albion's arm.

Certain that Frances and Joe had gone on ahead and that Kate was busy governing, Marilyn Albion, Jackie Bright, and David Marat went to the forbidden Rapid Transit, the old and rickety underground Metropolitan Transit subway system. They ran below ground down the echoing stairs and boarded a train. Sparks flew from the screaming wheels as the old green cars careened around the curves of the subway's underground tunnels and the lights flashed on and off as the electrical system shorted out and started again. The children let themselves tumble to the floor and played at being inside the belly of an insane rocking horse. At the Park Street station, they disembarked and stood on the deserted platform. There was a sign: DANGER—THIRD RAIL. Mothers' voices echoed in the walls of the Boston subways.

> Stay away from the edge.
> Stay away from the third rail. It's live.
> Just touch it, you'll die.

The three children played dead in a little heap near the edge of the platform. Passersby were not amused. The nuclear missiles in Cuba had ruined their day.

Marilyn Albion came back to life and said, "When electricity goes through your body, it makes your hair all broken. It's like electric shock."

Jackie Bright climbed down onto the subway tracks and placed a penny on the rail. Not the third rail. Jackie Bright did not want to die, or to get electric shock; she just wanted to make an impression. She climbed back up to the platform. The train screamed toward the station, and its metal wheels ground to a stop. The passengers disembarked, most of them looking worried and fearful. The madman was about to reveal himself. The train pulled out of the station and Jackie Bright again climbed down onto the subway tracks. She retrieved the penny and presented it to Marilyn Albion.

"Thanks, ever so," said Marilyn.

Mr. Lincoln was all flattened. David Marat was jealous that he was not brave enough to do that for Marilyn Albion's love.

If you cross this line, you might get a kiss.

At the mayor's office, Kate Albion tried to decide which atomic air-raid shelter she preferred. There will be an awful lot of riffraff at the armory, she thought. But the accommodations will be better. Surely there must be special considerations for Boston's mayor and his family. Why wasn't there a shelter under city hall, the way there was a shelter under the White House? Oh, yes. Kate Albion never forgot about that. A special shelter for all of those who would be the ones to press the green button in the black box. They, of course, had the best shelter. She also knew about the doomsday test, when the army helicopters flew the big shots to Honolulu, which was too beautiful to be affected by fallout. Kate Albion had a tremendous secret: she toyed with socialism when she felt cheated.

Kate Albion decided to take a tour of the city's atomic fallout shelters, select a good location, and make reservations. Kate felt a wave of pride as she realized that, since the age of four, her Marilyn had known what to do in case of an atomic blast.

"Duck and cover," said Kate Albion, a smile playing across her lips as the nostalgia hit, and the streetlights grew brighter in the deepening darkness. In a flash of humanitarianism, Kate decided to take Mrs. Finnegan and Nellie Kelly with her. She would inform them immediately.

Kate stepped out of the taxi in front of their Commonwealth Avenue home and entered the house to give Mrs. Finnegan and Nellie Kelly the good news: they would have reservations with her at the very best atomic fallout shelter available. However, Mrs. Finnegan and Nellie Kelly were drinking twenty-minute tea with Borden's evaporated milk, one and a half teaspoons of sugar per cup. Mrs. Finnegan and Nellie Kelly were unaware of the dangers, and they humored Kate Albion as they talked simultaneously to each other in parallel conversation genetic to the Irish.

"Cockroaches survived atomic testing . . ." said Mrs. Finnegan to Mrs. Finnegan.

"The world's gone on tour. . . ." said Mrs. Kelly to Mrs. Kelly.

". . . because they have no function. . . ."

"Electroshock therapy, let's wire up the boytime brawlers. . . ."

"If you adapt," said Mrs. Finnegan to Mrs. Finnegan, "you can catnap through history."

"Get them to sit down," said Mrs. Kelly to Mrs. Kelly, "to a good cup of tea."

Kate Albion concluded that Mrs. Finnegan and Nellie Kelly were becoming senile and would be better off dead. Kate Albion believed in Darwin. Mrs. Finnegan and Nellie Kelly were not interested in how to keep their balance during an explosion. Kate felt insulted.

If you cross this line. Or fall over it.

The superpowers rumbled through the consciousness of the world, yet Mrs. Finnegan and Mrs. Kelly just kept drinking tea, bursting into occasional song.

I'm the king of the mountain,
The big bad king of the mountain.

—

At the Blue Lagoon, Joe Albion sat beside Frances Bright in a secluded, dim booth at the back of the cocktail bar. He had never touched her, except to help her up an invisible step or across an imaginary threshold, and she had become unnerved by him. She wondered if he was some sort of psychopathic killer. She'd met a psychopathic killer before, the white-collar kind. They were polite and charming, and there was no dirt under their fingernails. No. Joe Albion was probably not a psychopathic killer, she decided. He was, after all, the mayor of Boston. Then she remembered that Khrushchev was some sort of king, yet he was willing to risk murdering everyone.

ed vest soft and
these missiles?"
short drag off his
cally calm-lagoon

l me they've got it

o, I'm not about to

meet at Finnegan's

d South Boston," said

goon, which was filled
for a Monday evening
The threat of annihila-
tion brings p_ _   ns bonds, makes them
ignore the cockroaches scatte_ _ _g in the alarm of daylight.
"Let's have a party."
"Let's wear hats."
"Let's hire a good fiddler."
"Let's put green dye in the beer."
"Let's get Saint Patrick to charm the snakes."
"Saint Pat could charm the missiles out of Cuba!"
Joe Albion leaned toward Frances Bright, and with all
his love flowing as only imminent death can release, he
pressed his lips against hers and hello! he put one foot
across the line.

David Marat, Jackie Bright, and Marilyn Albion were in
the sunflower garden at the back of the Commonwealth
Avenue house. The garden was lit by low-wattage electric
bulbs covered by Japanese lanterns. They could hear the

constant scream of the teapot, and the *tinkle rattle* and *roll* of silver spoons against china teacups and saucers.

"Where is Cuba?" asked David Marat.

"You don't know much, do you?" said Jackie Bright, twirling a long black braid.

"It is in Hollywood," said Marilyn Albion.

"Yes," said Jackie Bright, exasperated with David Marat. "Where Lucy and Ricky Ricardo live."

"Little Ricky is there, too," said Marilyn Albion.

"Babaloo. What does *babaloo* mean?" asked David Marat, straightening his tweed play suit. He knew they could not possibly know that. No one knew that. It was like in religion class, learning about the secrets behind the terrible face of God. No one knew until they died, unless they were the pope.

"He doesn't know what *babaloo* means, Marilyn. Why do we let him play with us?" said Jackie.

Marilyn sighed and said, "What will happen to Little Ricky if the missiles go off?"

They were silent.

David Marat said, "Lucy's hair is already red."

"Ricky will be at the club," said Jackie Bright.

"The Blue Lagoon," said Marilyn Albion.

"With Ethel but not with Lucy," said Jackie.

Marilyn was very quiet, but then she erupted, "Someone will have to save Little Ricky!"

"You don't know what *babaloo* means. I don't believe it," said Jackie Bright to David Marat.

David's neck was stiffening with fury, but he smiled and played cocky because he was the son of a diplomat, and he loved and coveted Marilyn Albion.

"You know," said Marilyn. "I know a secret. There's a man with a black box. He goes around with President

Kennedy, and in the box is a button, and the button's green. My mother said it's the doomsday box, and if you push the button, it would be the end of the world."

"No more school!" said Jackie Bright.

Marilyn Albion thought about Mr. Peanut and the size of President Kennedy's head.

"Watch this," said Marilyn. Marilyn stood up and walked straight up to a sunflower her height, confronted it as though she were Kate Albion, and turned her back on it. Jackie and David howled, rattled, and rolled.

If you cross this line, be ready to be on the other side.

CHAPTER 8

Everyone Loves Berlin
in the Springtime

June 1963

Freedom has many flaws
and democracy is imperfect.
But we have never had to put a wall up
to keep our people in!

The Telstar satellite transmitted the image of President John Kennedy to the black-and-white television screen in the library on Commonwealth Avenue, where Kate Albion stood at attention, Nellie Kelly and Mrs. Finnegan engaged in competitive clairvoyance, and Marilyn Albion ate Hostess cupcakes. The crowd of two million swaying, chanting Germans was pressed together in such intimacy that their bodies seemed to blend into one head with millions of eyes. The four-million-eyed, emotion-flared Argus concentrated on President Kennedy, who stood on a platform in front of Schöneberg Rathaus, West Berlin's City Hall.

> *There are people in the world*
> *who really don't understand,*
> *or say they don't,*
> *what is the great issue*
> *between the free world and the Communist world.*
> *Let them come to Berlin!*

John Kennedy's eyes shot laserlike at the wall that Khrushchev had built across Germany to prevent more East Germans from crossing to the West. It was Khrushchev's turn to say, "If you cross this line."

> *And there are even a few who say*
> *that it is true that Communism*
> *is an evil system,*
> *but it permits us to make economic progress.*
> *Lass' sie nach Berlin kommen!*
> *Let them come to Berlin!*

From the forbidden zone in East Germany, beyond the wall, a small group of East Berliners cheered. John Kennedy's image in black and white flickered over satellite, rattling windows, toasters, and knives across the world as he stared at the concrete and barbed-wire wall.

All free men, wherever they may live,
are citizens of Berlin,
and therefore, as a free man,
I take pride in the words:
Ich bin ein Berliner!

The crowd in the square, Rudolph Wilde Platz, spun into an elegant frenzy. They wheeled higher and higher into a spectacular single voice chanting his name, honing his name into a fine strong blade with which they pierced the sky, expecting roses to fall from the heavens. No roses fell, but one small bouquet was tossed over the wall from East Berlin.

So charged was the crowd, at his command they would have marched to the wall and torn it down. This was not the same John Kennedy. The crowd had recast him into another type of being, a being who would challenge the archetypal beast for them and call forth its mate, beauty, whose self-righteous anger could be more violent than anything the beast could have dreamed. They had recast the American president into a symbol that would allow them to believe they were on crusade, a religious form of being on tour with a lot of crowd activity.

Mr. Kennedy looked surprised. Very surprised. Or was it fear? Kate Albion had seen that expression before, when Marilyn Monroe had sung for the president at Madison Square Garden. Marilyn Albion was eating her third cupcake.

Mrs. Finnegan and Nellie Kelly paused to watch the televised canonization by the Berliners of "Kennedy, Kennedy." Mrs. Finnegan jerked upright and omen-heavy in her chair.

"Who is that beside him?" she said, then she nodded in

recognition, adjusted her breasts and reached for her teacup. "You can't bring up that pitch of passion without it coming, I suppose."

Nellie Kelly said, "That's just the man with the black box who's with him." The guardian of the black box lingered in the sunlight behind the president.

"Not him," said Flora Finnegan. "The creature, neither man nor woman, with the brown hood."

"What the hell are you talking about?" said Kate Albion, peering closely at the television set. Kate Albion never picked up on omens and it irked her.

Marilyn Albion, however, believed she saw the hooded figure quite clearly, but it transfigured into a sly, seductive Mr. Peanut. Marilyn took a big bite out of her cupcake. Marilyn Albion was certainly imaginative.

"The Banshee looks like that," said Mrs. Finnegan. "I saw that hooded figure when Pope John XXIII was ready to make his exit."

"Oh, here she goes again," said Nellie Kelly, "Clara Voyant herself. Prediction happy you are, Mrs. Finnegan."

"Deep in the heart of the Vatican," persisted Mrs. Finnegan, "he lay on his bed. One of those bishops all in red skirts like a woman took a little silver hammer and struck him lightwise but firm on the forehead."

"You make so many predictions that of course you hit it square on the head now and then—but mind you keep the bats in your belfry jigging like a team, because just one loses step and it's off to tic toc electroshock for you. Remember Nora Shaw."

Undaunted, Mrs. Finnegan continued, "And as he struck him, he said, 'Are you dead, Angelo?' "

"Who the hell was Angelo?" said Kate Albion.

Mrs. Finnegan replied, "Angelo was the pope's Christian name. Three times they took the little silver hammer and said 'Are you dead, Angelo? Are you dead, Angelo?' Seeing as he did not answer—"

"They probably killed him knocking him on the head like that," said Kate Albion.

"Seeing as he did not answer," continued Mrs. Finnegan, her brogue rising to the challenge, "they removed the papal ring from his hand and smashed it with the little silver hammer. He got too powerful. Drew the world into his spell. They would have bought Saint Peter's Basilica from him. They won't let anyone get that much passion stirred up around them again. Not in Europe, and certainly not in Germany."

"Who's 'they'?" demanded Kate Albion.

With studied pity, Mrs. Finnegan stared at Kate.

"What are you looking at?" said Kate.

"A cat can look at a queen," said Mrs. Finnegan, "so I can look at you."

Marilyn Albion had devil's food all over her face.

"They," said Mrs. Finnegan, patient and condescending, "are the charmed ones stuck between times."

"Suffering Christ," swore Kate Albion, taking a long drag from her charcoal-filtered Tareyton, "can I get a straight answer around here?"

"She means the dead, Mommy," said Marilyn. "The dead who weren't good enough for heaven or bad enough for hell."

Kate Albion blew a smoke ring and, *sotto voce,* asked Mrs. Finnegan, "Is she right?"

Marilyn licked the frosting from her fingers, and Mrs. Finnegan nodded in assent.

In Berlin, two million Germans chanted John

Kennedy's name, and in Boston—"they" or no "they"—Kate Albion elevated JFK to the pantheon of divine-right Irish politicians. Kate drew her coat upon her shoulders with a flourish usually reserved for silk-lined, ermine-trimmed imperial capes.

Before her grand exit, she opened the library closet and from its stand she pulled a large black umbrella with a carved handle of a snake's head that sported a pair of silver fangs. Nellie Kelly and Flora Finnegan were plagued by the superstitious Irish fear of opening an umbrella indoors, which to them amounted to inviting death, disease, and apocalypse to dinner.

Kate stood in the center of the library, raised the umbrella slowly overhead, and flipped it open. Nellie Kelly and Flora Finnegan, momentarily paralyzed, began to wail. Kate smiled and closed the umbrella, for there was a trace of compassion in her, and she returned it to its stand in the closet. Kate Albion left the library, no longer feeling too badly about not being able to see the hooded creature, neither man nor woman.

Marilyn smiled nervously amid the hyperventilation. She did not know if it was true that passion and power awaken jealousy on the part of the unseen world, as Great Aunt Nellie Kelly and Mrs. Finnegan would have her believe. But she was comforted because she knew her mommy did not believe in the gossipings of the ghosty dead.

Kate Albion descended the outside stairs of the Commonwealth Avenue house. She walked along the broad white sidewalk toward City Hall, the black limousine piloted by Freddie Finney trailing slowly just behind her through the rarefied June world. Imperious and blinded with command, Kate sensed that she could overrule by sheer willpower any and all pretenders, losers, dilettantes, Madison Avenue advertising executives, and visiting extraterrestrials who might be of non-Irish descent and Republican sympathies. Kate Albion verged on an amoral state of enlightenment.

> *My wild Irish tsarina*
> *The power behind*
> *Boston's mayor*
> *The air is quite thin*
> *But she can get in*
> *My wild Irish tsarina*

—

"Marilyn, dear," said Joe Albion, benevolent as Eisenhower seated at his desk in the mayor's office. He carefully dropped the note from the teacher just above the desk. It floated down, fascinating Marilyn. "Did you actually do this?"

"Yes, I did it," said Marilyn Albion, not terribly contrite.

"Mrs. Murphy says that you hypnotized the entire class and gave them a posthypnotic suggestion."

"What?"

"Mrs. Murphy says that every time she said the word 'class,' the students sang, 'Plop plop, fizz fizz, oh what a relief it is.' Is that true?"

"Yes, Daddy. Let's go on the swan boats."

"Well, Marilyn, I had no idea you were so talented."

Marilyn brightened. "Do you think so, Daddy?"

"Oh, yes," said Mayor Joe Albion.

"Hypnotizing is wonderful," said Marilyn. "I can take you on a journey and stay with your body while you go, and you will do whatever I say. I am the master."

"Marilyn. You can never hypnotize someone into doing something that they really don't want to do."

"Do you want me to hypnotize you?" asked Marilyn Albion.

Joe Albion looked at his eleven-year-old daughter and thought that there was something incredibly peculiar about that proposal.

"How did you learn to do this?"

"I got a pamphlet called *How to Hypnotize Your Friends.*"

"Where did you get this pamphlet?"

"Woolworth's."

"Ah. Woolworth's. Hypnosis is a very tricky business, Marilyn. People with too much power get crazy."

"Are you crazy, Daddy?"

There were no red splotches on Joe Albion's temples, but he did have a great big smile, like a god at poolside.

"Crazy enough to let you hypnotize me."

A delighted Marilyn stood before her father. She took three deep breaths, closed her eyes, ran her hand through her curls, and said:

Relax, Daddy, relax.
Listen to the sound of my voice.
 There are beached mermaids glistening in the sun, said Joe
 Albion.
You will notice a pleasant sensation of heaviness coming over
your entire body and head.
 I am the beautiful blue-and-green Pacific.
Listen to the sound of my voice.
Listen to the sound of my voice.
 The green palm trees breathe in the heat.
Breathe slowly and deeply into every muscle and nerve in your
body.
 The divine savage female lays naked in the saltwater.
Your arms are becoming very heavy.

Your legs are becoming very heavy.
I have eaten her but all her parts grow back.
Your head and eyes feel very pleasantly tired.
Continue to listen to the sound of my voice.
The jungle birds are sleeping.
Your eyes are becoming very heavy and sleepy.
Your eyes are beginning to water.
The island has an unlimited supply of green Jell-O.
Your eyes are beginning to water.
Like oysters.
You would like to close your eyes and fall fast asleep.
Allow your mind to become very passive.
God cannot fail to see me in the jungle.
Allow your mind to become very passive.
Let your eyes close now.
Let your eyes close.
In the beautiful green-and-blue Pacific.
You are entering a deep hypnotic sleep and will not awaken until
I tell you to do so.
Continue to listen to the sound of my voice.

Marilyn prepared for the ultimate test. From deep in her beautiful blue pocket, she took a tiny ammonia capsule that she had purchased from Woolworth's. She broke it open.

"I want you to smell this beautiful rose, Daddy. This beautiful rose." She waved the ammonia capsule under Joe Albion's nose, and he smiled. Joe Albion was still a master of self-control.

"Now you can open your eyes and do whatever you want," said Marilyn Albion, the queen of Wonderbread, creator of miracles.

Joe Albion slowly rose from his chair and walked to the glass French doors that led to the small balcony across the front of the mayor's office and overlooked the bright green lawn. He opened the doors. The cut glass sparkled in the sunlight as he stepped onto the balcony. Feigning trance, he looked up into the sky. So refined was his vision that he believed, for an instant, that he saw Telstar, "Or is it Sputnik?" he said.

"What, Daddy?" said Marilyn, terribly pleased, in fact as pleased as Mary Shelley must have been when she created Frankenstein's monster.

"Broadway. The Great White Way," said Joe Albion, filled with enthusiasm.

"What, Daddy?"

"I should have been on Broadway, Marilyn. No damned torches to pass from generation to generation. Just tap-dancing lessons for everybody!"

Joe Albion, mayor of Boston, in choreographed steps, reentered the office and leaped on top of his desk in a move as breathtaking as Gene Kelly's in the rain. Joe Albion stood on top of his grand mahogany desk, which was riddled with history. And why shouldn't he? It was, after all, his desk. He moved his hands and arms like Al Jolson, and then he burst into song with a lovely tenor voice that curled and spilled through the room, making even the rug feel happy to be alive.

> *When you're smiling,*
> *When you're smiling,*
> *The whole world smiles with you.*

Joe Albion lifted Marilyn Albion onto the desktop.

> *When you're laughing,*
> *Yes, when you're laughing,*
> *The sun keeps shining through.*

Joe and Marilyn tap-danced in the fashion of Shirley Temple and Bojangles. Marilyn was a natural.

> *But when you're crying,*
> *You bring on the rain,*
> *So stop your crying,*
> *Be happy again—*

Kate Albion stood in the doorway, as unreadable as the sphinx. Marilyn pretended that Kate was a flickering image coming in over satellite, an image she could see but could not be seen by. Joe Albion didn't give a damn.

> *'Cause when you're smiling,*
> *When you're smiling,*
> *The whole world smiles with you.*

There was the sound of one hand clapping. Kate's.

Marilyn, scrambling from the mahogany desk top in full alert, said to Joe Albion, "You will return to your chair, and you will not remember anything."

Oyster-eyed, Joe Albion pounced from the desk top and sat on his chair.

Marilyn Albion said, "Close your eyes, Daddy. You will now come out of trance. Five, four, three, two, one. Open your eyes."

Quiet as a cat who can't decide if she wants the mouse or the cheese, Kate studied Marilyn and Joe.

"I wonder," said Kate, turning to Joe, "if that would get many votes?"

Only Joe Albion knew that he could not be hypnotized because he was already spellbound. What Marilyn and Kate did not know wouldn't hurt them, he decided. No. Joe Albion was not Mary Shelley's Frankenstein monster. He was Kate Albion's, and he was wide awake.

Kate Albion turned and walked past the open French doors onto the balcony, certain she would take even greater power, that her image would one day spill across the world via Telstar, if only her husband would not dance upon his desk.

Marilyn Albion wondered if her hypnotic power could be trained to conjure an unlimited supply of Hostess cupcakes with the squiggle on top.

Mayor Joe Albion paused prestigiously behind his desk, then rose up, walked beyond the French doors onto the balcony, stood grandly beside the first lady of Boston, and announced: *"Ich bin ein* Bostonian.*"*

CHAPTER 9

The Great Filene's Basement Sale

November 22, 1963

Marilyn Albion closed the front drawing room window, which she had opened to test the air and determine what clothing she should wear. The Friday air was brisk and saturated with the smell of frying fish that floated to the rooftops. Small jagged pieces of icy snow lay randomly throughout the streets, melting and collecting dirt. How could something so beautiful as snow get so ugly? wondered Marilyn. She looked up. The sky was the same slate blue from which Bostonians love to make suits. She closed the window and went to find her mother.

Kate Albion was seated on the pink vanity chair before the mirror in her dressing room beside the master bedroom. Marilyn Albion arrived at the doorway of the dressing room and, with great admiration, watched her mother make up. Kate was completing the finishing touches on her disguise: large dark sunglasses, a thick paisley kerchief tied under the chin, and red lipstick. She leaned toward the mirror as she outlined her lips, slightly exaggerating her lip line in a Bette Davis smear. She would be unrecognizable. Problem was, everyone going incognito these days wore this outfit.

Kate looked at Marilyn and said, with a smile, "Very interesting."

Marilyn was pleased with Kate's reaction. Marilyn had tucked her hair beneath a Red Sox baseball cap, the visor pulled down close to her eyes, and pink plastic sunglasses were perched on her nose. Slung over her shoulder was the pink clip-on strap to her small white plastic transistor radio, which hung just above her waist. The tiny white earphone was tucked into one ear, transmitting in monophonic echo-tin through its delicate cord. Marilyn Albion couldn't believe how cool she felt, listening to the Kingsmen perform "Louie Louie." She had on her Red Ball Jets and green knee socks, and she rolled her plaid skirt up at the waist. Her blue pea coat hung open.

"Great," said Kate Albion. "No one will know us, and no one will want to. We look like trouble."

To "look like trouble" was the highest compliment Kate Albion could pay to anyone. "Here comes trouble" was the most often heard comment upon her approach.

Kate and Marilyn left the house and descended into the subway. Kate looked at the third rail, and it excited her. Marilyn looked at the third rail, and she thought of poor Mr. Lincoln's flattened face. They took the screeching train to the Park Street station and ascended to Park and Tremont in the Boston Common, also known as Brimstone Corner. Wild-haired citizens were continually propping themselves on top of soapboxes and shouting their version of the truth, the whole truth, and something like the truth.

Kate and Marilyn walked slowly past today's orator, an old man whose wisps of white hair floated about his bald head as if he had just ascended from the netherworld. His long black coat hung askew on his thin shoulders.

He pointed at Kate and Marilyn and shouted, "Repent. The time is at hand when the elegiac darkness shall descend, the world shall be ripped open, all the monsters of the Broken Mind joining forces with the Beast, and the Beast . . . the Beast shall rise again."

"What is he saying?" asked Marilyn.

Kate Albion studied him carefully. "He's saying Richard Nixon will probably run for office again." Kate Albion burst into a laugh as loud as a man's.

Peering from beneath her Red Sox cap visor and through her pink sunglasses, Marilyn Albion took a good look at Kate Albion. She admired her mother, but to live up to her was a formidable task. Sometimes Marilyn wished she had a mommy with red splotches on her temples and a great big "Queen for a Day" smile.

Kate and Marilyn walked past the Old Granary Burial Ground, where there was a gravestone marked MOTHER GOOSE—who, according to Kate Albion, was actually a man—and onward Christian soldiers they went to Bromfield Street, Washington Street, and finally, Filene's Department Store came into view.

As they marched onward toward Filene's, they were commented upon.

"Isn't that sad?"

"Don't stare. They can't help it."

Kate and Marilyn stood silent at the entrance to Filene's. Filene's was to Kate Albion what Woolworth's was to Marilyn. It was minutes before ten o'clock in the morning, the hour when the doors would open. The horde of women pressed near the door, girl children in tow, a boy here and there, certainly potential Mother Gooses whose fathers were not exerting enough influence. The horde stared at the guard inside the Filene's glassfront, who stared back at them with an expression of power laced with fear. Today was the Great Basement Sale, when the finer things from the upper floors were dumped on large wooden tables and crushed together on hanging racks, prices slashed by as much as 80 percent.

The huge silver Christmas bells hung like milk-heavy tits above the gathering competitors—which explained the presence of Kate Albion, who could well afford to buy these spoils on the upper floors, salesladies crooning to her, the mayor's wife. But Kate Albion enjoyed shopping as a sport because it kept her instincts sharp.

Kate looked down at Marilyn, took her hand, and instructed: "Don't lose sight of me. It can get pretty tight in there. And don't lose your nerve. And keep your elbows out from your sides about half a foot, so you'll always have breathing room. And don't mind the fainters. Just keep on going."

Filene's ornate timepiece was perched high above the women. The hour hand was solidly on ten, and the minute hand, large and hyperreal, moved seductively toward the twelve like an exaggerated Hitchcockian device, moving constantly yet in such slow increments that time seemed to be standing still. Kate Albion's spike heels moved with anticipation on the wide sidewalk. Then she zeroed in on the guard, the living starter gun who was slowly approaching the front door from the inside of Filene's.

"Oh, look," she said to Marilyn Albion. "It's Ronny Finney, Fatty Finney's brother's son's second boy." Ronny Finney approached the door and began to work on the lock. The women pressed closer to the door, silent and calculating. Just pushing to the front would not be feminine, so the push toward the door was polite, concentrated, and done in feigned unconsciousness, similar to "Did I spill that red wine on your white dress? Silly me."

Marilyn felt very short. She pressed the earphone deeper into her ear and turned up the volume on her transistor radio. The news crackled on.

President and Mrs. Kennedy will be arriving in Dallas . . .

Marilyn's earphone fell out and dangled at her side as the press of women became more intense, the crowd fusing into one shopping body. Kate half-expected a chant of "Filene's, Filene's" to explode from the compressed female energy.

Kate Albion studied Ronny Finney's face. He did not know her in disguise. He was having trouble opening the lock. His eyes, slit narrow, peered in his limited peripheral vision out to the women, a sadistic smile playing along his clamped lips.

"He'd better watch out how he milks power. If he irritates the cow, she'll kick him in the head," said Kate Albion. The women closest to Kate Albion laughed as loud as men.

By his movements,
the way his eyes flashed,
the way his lips tightened to conceal laughter,
Ronny Finney revealed himself as Charon,
ferrying the dead souls
across hell's river
for a gift certificate.

Kate Albion saw an unexpected crack in the world, and her consciousness jolted to an uncomfortable self-awareness. She had stumbled into being on tour, and she lost her balance for a moment, but the crack sealed itself and she made a note to drink less coffee. This loss of balance, however temporary, alarmed Marilyn. Kate had never faltered.

The lock clicked and Ronny Finney opened the glass doors. The massive body of women and girls swelled and pushed through the open glass mouth into Filene's, pouring like a flash flood past the makeup and lingerie counters to the steep narrow stairway that angled downward to the basement. A black banister ran down the center of the narrow red-and-yellow passageway, and to avoid being impaled upon it, it was very important not to resist the flow of women. Kate Albion felt unpleasant. Her mind was thinking of things besides the sale, an unusual occurrence for an absolutely focused Zen shopper with a taste for the hunt.

They were the Furies,
and their sisters
were daughters of the rivers of hell:
Acheron, the river of passage;
Cocytus, the river of wailing;

> *Lethe, the river of forgetfulness;*
> *Phlegethon, the river of fire;*
> *Styx, the river by which*
> *the gods seal their oaths*
> *and ordain game show hosts.*

At the foot of the stairs, salesladies stood poised, eyeglasses hanging from silver clamps on black cords around their necks. Down came the Furies and their sisters, heels clacking on the staircase, stepping on down along the black borders of the red-and-yellow steps.

Kate Albion made a direct hit on a French designer dress as Marilyn Albion plugged the earphone back into her ear.

> *I will follow him*
> *Follow him wherever he may go . . .*

Two women broke into a tugging match, and they ripped the blouse in two. Others began to try on clothing in the aisles. Kate Albion leaned close to Marilyn.

"If you see something you want, don't let on. Look at it with one hand. Or else—Well, look over there."

Marilyn and Kate observed an unseasoned shopper lift a skirt and say, "I love it!" In split seconds she was surrounded by human female shopping locusts.

The heat level rose and winter coats were dragging on the floor. The hours passed until Marilyn Albion was in a daze. The sound of hangers screeching metal against metal as the women raced through the hanging racks sounded like the scream of exotic birds deep in a humid jungle. Kate Albion watched the service elevator carefully. She knew that there would be a restocking in the early afternoon. Endurance tests like this were good for her, good for Marilyn. The cash registers rang and voices hovered and slammed onto the sale tables.

As Kate had predicted, the restocking began. The green elevator doors opened, and young men pushed the pendulous gray cloth bins toward the sales arena.

"Oh," said Kate, looking at the stock boy, "if it isn't Danny Finney, Fatty Finney's nephew's son."

> *Oh, Danny Boy,*
> *The pipes*
> *The pipes are blowing . . .*

The excitement mounted and the women became nearly wild. Marilyn began to feel short again. She raised the volume on her transistor. It was twenty minutes before two in the afternoon.

BULLETIN

In Dallas, Texas, three shots were fired at President Kennedy's motorcade.

Marilyn Albion stared at her mother, then at the gray cloth bins wheeling toward the women, heavy and swaying with costumes and pretty blouses and green and blue sweaters. Marilyn felt she was suffocating in a cartoon hyperstate. She did not want this secret.

"Mother."

"Are you hungry? You have to learn to endure. Endure. Don't you want to survive the next war? Of course you do."

> *From glen to glen*
> *And down the mountainside. . . .*

Yes. Marilyn Albion wanted to survive the next war in the atomic fallout shelter of her choice, but she did not want to tell Kate about the gunshots in Dallas.

> *The summer's gone*
> *And all the roses dying . . .*

"Mother. The president was shot."

Kate Albion was silent in the narrow, fashion-strewn aisle. A young woman, her blouse untidily hanging from her skirtband, turned to Kate and said, "What's the matter with that kid? What'd she say? That's a sick kid you got there."

Kate gently took the radio from Marilyn and unplugged the earphone. She tuned the radio and raised the volume as if she were cracking a safe that contained explosives, but the sound of the women's voices drowned it out.

> **Kennedy . . . scheduled to speak . . . political luncheon . . . blood all over her pink suit. . . .**

"Silence!" ordered Kate Albion. The women's voices stopped. Kate's voice was unmistakable. One last ring of the cash register was recorded, and the little plastic radio vibrated in monophonic echo-tin as Kate Albion adjusted the tuner.

> **From Dallas . . .**
> **A flash . . .**
> **The president died at two o'clock**
> **Eastern Standard Time.**
> **The president**
> **is dead.**

146

The silence poised above the women in a fantastic blanket of shock. They began to wind through the aisles like a serpent just hit on the head with a silver hammer, their shuffling shoes dragging across the floor of Filene's basement.

Kate Albion pulled off her disguise and the women were relieved to see her commanding presence. She ran her hands through her hair, caressing herself, and the women and girls followed her lead. A small old woman, dressed in black, cracked into a smile, the smile of the helpless looking at God's bad joke. The women's hands touched their faces and necks.

> *It's you, it's you*
> *Must go*
> *And I must bide.*

Each woman looked into the eyes of each woman, and each little girl looked into the eyes of each little girl, as they wandered across the basement. Then it began, as stranger touched stranger, placing a hand upon a shoulder, upon a cheek. It began. The waters churned the first sob of mourning. Cocytus, the river of wailing, flooded the world, but Kate Albion did not cry. She was too shocked to cry. She was on tour. She studied her hand, and then she ran her fingers through her hair in an attempt to feel the presence of the president. He was not there.

Leaving the sobbing women, she moved with dignity and flashes of madness up the red-and-yellow staircase with the black border. Forgotten, Marilyn trailed behind, her white radio hanging by its long strap from Kate Albion's hand, cracking against each step of the long staircase. The plastic split and broke into jagged random fragments that scattered and flew as Kate lifted the radio high above her head at the top of the steps and smashed it onto the golden floor.

"Bad radio," said Marilyn Albion, who took her mother's hand and patted it.

Joe Albion was overwhelmed by desire for Kate, but he could only wait in the distance and watch the spectacle. He wished to protect her, to protect his daughter. Now that the president was dead, he loved him deeply. But Kate Albion was untouchable, inconsolable, her sense of well-being and control nothing more than shattered pieces of imperial jade.

It was now Sunday, and the same pictures had flickered relentlessly over the television since the assassination: the president and Mrs. Kennedy's arrival at the Dallas airport that Friday; shots of the Texas School Book Depository and the sixth-floor window where the rifle was later found; the casket being loaded into Air Force One for the flight back to Washington; the swearing in of Lyndon Johnson, Mrs. Kennedy at his side in her pink blood-and-brains-splattered suit.

"The identity of the assassin was the final insult," said Kate Albion. "The assassin wasn't even the Beast. He was just an errand boy. A whining, weak bastard who wanted to star on 'Assassin for a Day.'"

Kate spoke whether or not there was anyone listening, for "they," the disembodied, were as much an audience. "I admire Mrs. Kennedy for keeping on that bloody suit. Let them see what they did." Now that the president was dead, Kate Albion loved Mrs. Kennedy deeply.

Just keep on with your shopping while I tell you about my husband, John F. Kennedy . . .

From the kitchen came the relentless sound of Mrs. Finnegan and Nellie Kelly rattling teacups on saucers, the tinkling of silver spoons churning milk and sugar into the tea leaves and boiling water. Marilyn cupped her chin in her hand, rested her elbow upon the kitchen table, and studied the cow on the Borden's evaporated milk can. She felt depressed.

Mrs. Finnegan looked down the hallway for any sign of Kate. The coast clear, she whispered to Nellie Kelly, "I told you. In Berlin. You can't wake that pitch of passion without it taking its due. He was taken by it. Charisma kills. They can't stand it. If it can't be theirs, they have to kill. Lay low. Lay low." Nellie Kelly nodded, her eyes bulging and flashing under the influence of seven cups of tea and fourteen spoons of sugar.

In West Berlin, the citizens marched in a silent candlelight ceremony and renamed their square for John Kennedy, but Marilyn was not seduced by history. She vowed not to hypnotize the world because she wanted to live.

Kate Albion walked into the kitchen. Mrs. Finnegan, Nellie Kelly, and Marilyn were silent and attentive. They looked at Kate as they would look at the aftermath of a bad accident.

"The assassin has just been shot. Live. On television. Jack Kennedy said a man could kill him if he was ready to trade lives. He's not dead yet but he will be."

Kate Albion poured herself a cup of tea and walked serenely from the room. She had just witnessed a possible murder, and she was glad. So be it.

It was true. Lee Harvey Oswald had just been shot by a nightclub owner, Jack Ruby. On the air.

It was true. Millions witnessed the murder, but not many shed tears.

Kate Albion sat quietly in the library and watched the televised pandemonium as if it were a "Gunsmoke" rerun. She approved of Jack Ruby's verdict. Joe Albion watched her from the doorway. He wanted her back, but he was distracted by Jack Ruby, who had now given club owners a bad name. Or had he?

Relentlessly, the television replayed the footage of the shot until the images were seared into the brains of the world.

Marilyn walked to the garden in the back of the house and bent back the wide green stem of a sunflower. Its withered winter petals stretched toward her like the arms of an old madman. She peered cautiously at the dangerous sky.

Kate Albion remained in the library, drinking tea, smoking Tareytons, watching the procession of images. The president's body left the East Room of the White House for its journey to the Capitol rotunda. The caisson bearing the casket rolled from the front of the White House. Muffled drums. The hooves of seven white horses and their four riders beat the pavement and pulled the caisson. The dark and formidable Blackjack, the eighth horse, was riderless, but bright black cavalry boots hung reversed in Blackjack's stirrups and a sword was strapped to his saddle. The skittish and powerful horse toyed with the private trying to control him. No one would toy with Blackjack.

FLASH

Lee Harvey Oswald is dead.

"Blackjack will calm down now," said Kate Albion. And he did, as "Hail to the Chief" played in dirge time, for the last time, for Jack Kennedy. Being on tour, Kate Albion read the signs of beast and fowl and wind and fire, and the weeping Mrs. Finnegan and Nellie Kelly, standing in the doorway to the library, thought the fairies might have made a mistake, opening the door of prediction to Kate Albion.

Joe Albion waited in the shadows to catch Kate, should she fall. Oh, please fall, Kate, he thought, and I'll save you.

Seated in the dead sunflower garden, Marilyn Albion heard the sad music and the muffled weeping of Mrs. Finnegan and Great Aunt Nellie Kelly in the library. She entered the abandoned kitchen, opened the refrigerator, and poured herself a tall glass of milk. She returned to the cold garden, and stared at her milk. The milk was hyper-real, bright white liquid that had dripped from the heavy silver tit of a Filene's Christmas bell. She brushed the hot tears from her cheeks, and she drank her milk slowly in honor of the chief.

CHAPTER 10

Mrs. Finnegan's Wake

> Wasn't it the truth I told you?
> Lots of fun at Finnegan's wake.
> —*Old Irish Ballad*

August 24, 1964

Nellie Kelly said to Freddie Finney, "Hurry up, Freddie. Mrs. Finnegan'll be coming looking for me right here in this limousine if I don't show up soon. She'll be complaining that I didn't get to her before the little wild violets started sprouting from her chest." Freddie Finney hit the gas pedal. Freddie Finney was deeply superstitious.

The black stretch limousine of the mayor of Boston pulled up smooth as a cat before the porch to Mrs. Finnegan's house. The children playing kickball paused to watch Freddie Finney open the streetside door to the limousine. Nellie Kelly emerged, followed by Marilyn Albion, who had never been to Mrs. Finnegan's house. On the sidewalk side, Freddie Finney broke loose the dignified Kate Albion and Mayor Joe Albion, as the neighbors on the narrow street peeked from behind their curtains. Nellie Kelly and the Albions wore black, and they were dignified as hell.

Close beside Nellie Kelly, Marilyn Albion walked up the steps into Mrs. Finnegan's wood-frame house, following Joe and Kate. Fat black cats luxuriated on the porch near their small china saucers filled with milk. A black wreath hung on the front door, a large green ribbon fastened to it by a plastic shamrock with "Mrs. Finnegan Go Bragh" emblazoned across it in gold lettering. Poor Mrs. Finnegan had cracked her skull falling from the ladder while dusting the cardboard hot fudge sundae with a cherry on top. Marilyn burst into tears, and Kate turned sharply, bent over to Marilyn and said, "Mrs. Kennedy didn't cry. She had dignity. Grandeur."

Nellie Kelly stiffened and took a surprised Kate's jaw firmly in her hands. "Mrs. Kennedy," said Nellie Kelly, "is French, not Irish." Nellie let go of Kate's jaw.

"Marilyn's part English. What about that?"

"She can't help it."

Deeply impressed by the presence of the mayor and his Kelly wife, the tipsy mourners opened Mrs. Finnegan's door to greet them, moving aside and allowing them to pass, nodding sorrowfully, sighing splendid in their wake black. They were shown to the parlor.

There was a long table that ran the length of the room, piled high with massive quantities of potato salad, rare roast beef, turkey, breads, condiments, angel food cakes, pies, devil's food cupcakes, glass bowls overflowing with apples and pears, a rum-soaked plum pudding that was periodically set ablaze, plates of mixed nuts, and celery sticks carefully stuffed with cream cheese and green olives, with wide-awake red pimento eyes staring helplessly at the looming cannibals. A thirty-gallon coffee pot perked at the table's end near the napkins, forks, knives, and plates. Against the rear wall of the room ran a table half as long but twice as deep, packed tight with glasses and bottles of scotch, gin, vermouth, brandy, rum, and whiskey. Joe Albion went straight to the liquor table and prepared a tumbler of sherry for Nellie Kelly and a scotch on the rocks for Kate Albion. He gave Marilyn Albion a small crystal glass with a short thin stem, filled with sherry. Joe drank a bourbon, straight.

Marilyn sipped her sherry and admired the wallpaper, which was a rose, pastel blue, and unripened green floral design. The slipcovers on the couch and the matching overstuffed chair were a light- red-and-yellow print of a seaside scene with a two-inch green fringe along the bottom. Mrs. Finnegan was partial to fringe. White lace doilies were pinned into the arms of everything that could not move. A bald gentleman mourner had one on his head. Mildly drunk, the gentleman had been telling a joke and pretending he was a little girl at her first confession. He forgot he was wearing the doily and he sat in one of the two overstuffed chairs in the dim hot corner, sipping his whiskey and watching the end of the Red Sox game on the black-and-white television.

Marilyn looked down at the rug, which was pink, green, and gold, with a splash of red, depicting the decapitation of Mary Queen of Scots, whose head was barely visible under the banquet table. Marilyn took a little swig of her sherry and discreetly poured herself another one. Twelve years old is old enough to be discreet.

The draperies, drawn shut in reverence for the dead, were a carefully woven scene of horses pulling sleighs through snow, and men in black top hats and dress suits helping ladies in billowing skirts to keep their balance.

Kate Albion, finishing her second drink, recited:

> *The woods are lovely dark and deep*
> *But I have promises to keep . . .*

She couldn't remember the next line. Kate Albion sat near the bald man in the stuffed chair near the television, and on an empty stomach drank a third scotch on the rocks.

"Bobby Burns, that's Bobby Burns," shouted the bald man by the television set.

"Edna St. Vincent Millay," shouted Red Byrne from the back of the crowd.

"Bullshit. It's Jack Frost," said Mary O'O.

"Robert Frost, you ninnie," said her brother, Madden O'O.

"Edna St. Vincent Millay," said Red Byrne, getting nasty.

"I'll Millay you," said Mary O'O.

Joe Albion handed a fourth drink to Kate. Taking her drink from Mayor Joe, in a voice loud enough for everyone to hear without strain, Kate Albion said, "It's hard to think with your eyes open in here, which is probably the point of it. The thinking Irish mind can be suddenly struck insane. Like a flu. On tour with no baggage, no change of underwear. And no gradual deterioration. Just a surprise event. A sort of seeing in between the cracks. So we fill up the cracks."

Great applause and chatter jostled in the room, and everyone gobbled another fine hard drink.

Joe Albion was concerned that Mrs. Finnegan's untimely death added to Kate Albion's trauma. He feared that Kate would go on tour permanently. Kate Albion had not revealed any deep emotion since President Kennedy's death, and when Joe questioned her on her behavior, she said she was "having dignity." Joe had been relieved that she seemed to have forgotten that the Democratic presidential convention was to begin at any moment at Convention Hall in Atlantic City, where waves licked the dark sand. But now, just as she was loosening up, the convention was about to be telecast. He tried to get to the set, to turn it off, but it was too late. Kate was transfixed by the image on the black-and-white television of Bobby Kennedy, his head bowed, then raised, gesturing with one hand, smiling with love. Kate leaned toward the television and turned up the volume. Rintrah roared from the heart of the crowd at the Democratic convention, and Mrs. Finnegan's mourners pressed around the television set.

Marilyn watched her mother, riddled with emotion in the silent room. Dignity. Poise under pressure. Marilyn was afraid that Kate would explode from self-control. Joe Albion also wanted the old Kate back, the Kate with a mean streak, the Kate with the demanding voice in the wilderness.

The convention crowd was silent but on their feet, and Bobby Kennedy, beneath the picture of his slain brother, like a lover lost at sea, recited:

> . . . *When he shall die,*
> *Take him and cut him out in little stars,*

And he will make the face of heaven so fine
That all the world will be in love with night
And pay no worship to the garish sun.

At that a terrific wail burst out from Mrs. Finnegan's bedroom, and Kate Albion had another drink, tears rolling from her eyes.

Marilyn worried that Mrs. Finnegan lay unattended, dead in her bed in the next room. Marilyn Albion did not want to see Mrs. Finnegan's body, but it would have been disrespectful not to. She followed the sherry-fortified Nellie Kelly down the short hall to view the corpse. Marilyn considered a fake faint but remembered Kate's disdain of the fainters at Filene's basement.

An intimidating wail sounded from the bedroom at their approach, but Marilyn Albion forced herself to pass through the doorway, eyes closed, hand clamped onto Great Aunt Nellie's black sleeve. Marilyn opened her eyes. Mrs. Finnegan lay splendid and dead in her four-poster bed. Marilyn was amazed. Mrs. Finnegan was wearing her Woolworth's uniform, with hair net. Seated in chairs that circled her bed were the blue-haired Woolworth's counter ladies, their makeup heavier than usual. In fact, it was as heavy as the makeup on Mrs. Finnegan's corpse.

Marilyn Albion was startled, the way she had been when she had seen President Kennedy at the Garden, and his head had seemed too big. As she looked at Mrs. Finnegan, in her peripheral vision she saw cardboard cutouts of a hot fudge sundae and a hot dog on a grilled roll rotating slowly above Mrs. Finnegan's bed. Marilyn Albion turned away to collect herself, knowing there were, of course, no cardboard cutouts hovering in the air. Anxiety, a little sherry, and an opulent imagination produced mild hallucinations in Marilyn Albion.

Mrs. Finnegan's bedroom was overflowing with massive funeral arrangements, including a crowd-pleasing horseshoe of green-dyed carnations that said GOOD LUCK FROM KATE KELLY ALBION.

"They got all these flowers to cover up the smell of the corpse," said Jetsam Finney to Flotsam Finney, commenting on the floral masterpieces.

"That's a damned lie," said Nellie Kelly, surprising Jetsam and Flotsam Finney from behind. "And in my presence. Mrs. Finnegan has her favorite perfume, Nights of Araby, sprinkled all over her thick as holy water, I'm sure."

The veil fluttered, and Marilyn saw the brown-hooded apparition, neither man nor woman, at Mrs. Finnegan's bedside. The price of power was very high. Another wail pierced the bedroom causing Jetsam and Flotsam to cling together in momentary fear, then to push each other away in a horror of imagined homosexual advance.

"You'd terrify the Banshee herself," said Nellie to the ladies. "Finney would have loved it."

"Finney" was Nellie Kelly's private pet name for Mrs. Finnegan. Marilyn followed Nellie Kelly to Mrs. Finnegan's corpse. As Nellie Kelly was leaning close to Mrs. Finnegan, inspecting the makeup job, Marilyn found herself nose to nose with Biddie O'Brien, the heiress to Mrs. Finnegan's Woolworth's throne. Biddie O'Brien let out a sudden wail that kicked off the cacophony of the other ladies and terrified Marilyn.

Nellie Kelly, bent over and now patting Mrs. Finnegan's rouged cheek, dabbed a glistening tear from each eye. Nellie Kelly then sat in the chair beside the bed and held Mrs. Finnegan's powdered hand. She sobbed and talked, talked and sobbed without inhibition, the ladies punctuating with sighs and arias of wails:

"Well, Mrs. Finnegan. We didn't let them wrap that rosary around your fingers. But we could never have laid you out with the counter menu in your hands. Don't you be worrying, though. I'll slip it into the casket at the last moment. The ladies will create a diversion."

Nose to nose with Biddie O'Brien, Marilyn whispered into Biddie's nostrils: "Who is the Banshee?"

Biddie O'Brien, her large, deeply powdered nose aimed at Marilyn, twitched and sniffed, to make sure Marilyn was a worthy receiver of this information. Biddie O'Brien never took her eyes off Mrs. Finnegan's corpse as she said to Marilyn, "The Banshee is death. She has a long comb. If she can run the comb from your crown to the ends of your hair, you're hers. That's why you've got to keep the doors and windows locked tight when there's sickness in the house. If the Banshee gets in, there's no stopping her. She lets out a long shriek when she wins."

The inebriated Kate Albion sliced through the parlor, the short squat hallway, and stood at the foot of Mrs. Finnegan's bed. There was silence. Kate Albion looked to the east. Kate Albion looked to the west. Kate Albion moved closer to Mrs. Finnegan's corpse and, bending over it, kissed Mrs. Finnegan lightly on the lips.

Kate trembled and cried, her long black hair falling, thick with drama, and she raised her fist toward heaven like a barbarian. The ladies followed suit, surrounding the body. Released of broken-hearted rage and led by Kate Albion, they began to anoint and primp the corpse, as if

Mrs. Finnegan were a huge doll. Kate Albion was returning from tour.

Joe Albion took Marilyn's hand. These women. What were these women doing? The Irish were colorful and poetic but hopelessly barbaric. He did not yet understand that Kate was returning to him.

Marilyn Albion laughed as loud as a boy. Marilyn Albion suspected that she was on tour as she triggered a laughing spell among the women. Joe Albion's heart pounded.

"There are only so many things you can do in good taste with a corpse," he said. His remark only served to up the volume on the laughter.

Marilyn pried her hand from her father's and slipped beneath the bed to board a little boat that rocked in the beautiful dark Atlantic. Marilyn became sleepy with sherry, as she toyed with the crystal glass in the shadows, and observed from beneath the bed that Kate Albion was surrounded by a bright white light.

The room was now jammed with mourners, the drunken men and women having made their way into the bedroom. Kate's hair was crackling with static electricity.

Kate Albion launched herself. "Another death. Another vote lost." Kate paused.

"Here we go," said Mary O'O.

"The Beast is coming," said Kate Albion. "And those of us who remain alive must be ever vigilant and willing to fight, or this society will be ripped apart."

Nellie Kelly adjusted her breasts and said quietly, "Mrs. Finnegan would have loved this."

Kate Albion moved through the room, and at each statement confronted eye-to-eye a different individual whose mouth was invariably filled with rare roast beef or rum plum pudding.

"Leave a hat on the bed, radiation will get you," she said to Mary O'O.

"Open an umbrella inside your house, you'll get locked inside your atomic fallout shelter," she said to Flotsam Finney.

"And most importantly," said Kate Albion to Joe Albion, "prostitutes will determine who shall control the world. As they always have."

"So good to have you back, darling," said Joe Albion. Kate smiled at him. We'll have sex later, she thought.

Kate realized how far away she had been, how far the tour had gone, and that an Irishwoman cannot afford to stuff her anger into her purse.

"Sometimes," said Kate Albion to Mrs. Finnegan's corpse, "it's important to go as close to the edge as possible, as close to out of control as Miss Monroe." Kate Albion locked her knees in a open-legged stance, threw her pelvis back, and dug her spike heels into the rug. "And sometimes it's important to get angry."

Marilyn awoke to the sound of the squeaking springs of Mrs. Finnegan's bed. Early morning light glimmered in the room. A dark green coffin on rolling wheels was pressed up against Mrs. Finnegan's bed. Marilyn watched as Nellie Kelly discreetly tucked the Woolworth's menu below the casket's satin lining, and the ladies lifted the body into the green box. Marilyn was surprised at how tiny Mrs. Finnegan had been.

The ladies arranged Mrs. Finnegan carefully, and Nellie Kelly bent to her ear and whispered, "May the wind be at your back, Mrs. Finnegan." Nellie Kelly gave Mrs. Finnegan one last kiss and closed the lid, fastening the bright brass locks on the casket.

The Woolworth's ladies, led by Biddie O'Brien, rolled the casket from the bedroom, down the short hallway, past the parlor, and onto the front porch. Nellie Kelly followed immediately behind. The ladies hoisted the casket easily upon their shoulders and stepped smartly to the waiting hearse, past the fascinated black cats and their china bowls of milk. As they carried her out, the drunken mourners gathered on the porch and, led by the now radiant Kate Albion, sang:

> *"She'll ride forever*
> *'Neath the streets of Boston.*
> *She's the woman who'll never return."*

And then silence.

Marilyn Albion crawled from beneath Mrs. Finnegan's bed and walked along the short squat hall and into the parlor. The banquet table was picked locust clean, the liquor bottles dry. Marilyn liked wakes but thought it was too bad that someone had to die in order to have one. Marilyn joined the fascinated black cats on the porch and watched Kate Albion being Kate Albion again, at last. Kate was directing the loading of the casket into the hearse. Marilyn closed the door to Mrs. Finnegan's woodframe house in South Boston and walked down the steps to the sidewalk and the waiting cars.

Bright yellow signs bearing the black-lettered word FU-NERAL were placed in the windows of the long line of cars, their drunken occupants singing the praises of Mrs. Finnegan: her beauty, her passion, her sense of fashion.

The funeral cortege pulled stately grand into the street, the Albions and Nellie Kelly in the long black limousine behind the hearse, behind the overflowing flower car, the bright spectacle of a happy good-bye. Marilyn Albion no longer felt afraid of death, as long as it wasn't her own.

> *Whack folthe dah, dance to your partner,*
> *Welt the flure, yer trotters shake,*
> *Wasn't it the truth I told you,*
> *Lots of fun at Finnegan's wake!*

Part Three

CHAPTER 11

The Tupperware Party

In 1860 ivory was hard to get, because the wild elephant herds were nearly slaughtered for the greater cause, so a manufacturing firm—Phelan and Collander—had a contest with a $10,000 prize: a contest to find an alternative material with which to produce billiard and pool balls. So John Wesley Hyatt created Celluloid. John Wesley Hyatt lost the contest, but Celluloid begat Bakelite, Bakelite begat Tenite II, Tenite II begat Lucite, Lucite begat Plexiglas, Plexiglas begat Polystyrene, Polystyrene begat Nylon, Nylon begat Orlon, Orlon begat Dacron, Dacron begat Polyethylene, Polyethylene begat Teflon, and Teflon begat Silicone. And the tribes multiplied, and Rintrah, the MGM lion, the celluloid father of them all, wed Sheba Sheik, the mother of political taste tests, and they were pleased when their progeny begat Tupperware.

1965

It was with such biblical passion that thirteen-year-old Marilyn Albion prepared for her first Tupperware party, which was to be hosted by Jackie Bright's mother, Frances, in Scollay Square, the significance of which did not escape Kate Albion. Joe did not know the exact location of the Tupperware party, and Kate Albion anticipated his surprise with enthusiasm.

Joe Albion smoked a cigarette as he watched Kate sit before the mirror in her dressing room, combing her hair, and Marilyn eavesdropped in the hallway.

Kate said, "The ladies of Scollay Square have silicone tits."

"I want her to see what women do," said Joe Albion.

"I am a woman. I do," said Kate.

"You're not . . . typical."

"What makes you think she is?"

"She has had nothing but strange examples of the world of ladies since she was born, the last of which, the most impressive fiasco, being Mrs. Finnegan and her theory of breast envy. Marilyn must be prepared to take her place as a woman in history."

Kate Albion smiled, adjusted her breasts, and said, "To carry the torch for the next generation of men?" Joe Albion leaned over and nipped Kate's closest breast, which earned him a long friendly scratch on the back of his neck.

Marilyn Albion walked to her bedroom, wondering if her breasts would grow big enough for history, as big as Marilyn Monroe's, and if that would be painful.

"Couldn't he come as a sort of game show host?" asked Marilyn Albion.

Although his voice had not yet changed and only minor facial hair growth had begun, David Marat was not allowed to attend the Tupperware party because he had a penis.

"We wouldn't feel free," answered Jackie Bright. "It's for women only. It's always been for women only. We have our reasons."

Marilyn was quite impressed with Jackie's deep knowledge of the secret rites of womankind. "How many Tupperware parties have you been to?"

Jackie crossed her arms across her slightly developing chest. "This will be my first."

"So how do you know what it's like?"

"I listen to things in the dark."

"What time will it be?"

"Tupperware parties are always held at night."

Nellie Kelly had a bad cold; nevertheless, she went to the Tupperware party, especially since it was in Scollay Square and life had become quite boring without Mrs. Finnegan. In fact, Great Aunt Nellie seemed to have more or less gone on tour permanently since the loss of Mrs. Finnegan, touching down now and then but only for special occasions.

Joe Albion escorted Marilyn and Nellie Kelly, driving Nellie's vintage Buick and taking directions from Marilyn. They cruised past the bars and the tattoo parlors, the pawn shops, and the open windows where muscular, dangerous men in tight white undershirts and women in bright, low-cut blouses hung their heads out for fresh air, smoked long, foreign cigarettes, and drank domestic beer from bottles. Marilyn Albion was at the stage when danger, pawn shops, and people who disappear without a trace in the middle of the night are romantic and glamorous; for that matter, so was Joe. For Marilyn and Joe, the potted red geraniums behind the barred tenement window were tragic, and thus beautiful.

"Pull over, Daddy. This is it," said Marilyn. Nellie Kelly peered at the large blue house with the extraordinary number of windows.

Joe Albion was stunned. Marilyn Albion had directed him to pull over in front of Frances Bright's house. Did Nellie know? Did Marilyn? Just keep smiling. Why do women know these things? Hello. Hello out there.

The blue house was a large cheerful house, full of large

cheerful women in the windows on the staircase in all of the rooms. Even in the tiny turret a woman brushed her long red hair in the orange twilight.

> *In the room the women come and go*
> *Talking of Tupperware and Jell-O.*

Marilyn and Nellie Kelly entered the blue house with a level of fascination that would rival a tour of the Queen's Chamber in the Great Pyramid. There was a large entranceway with red tiles, red wall hangings, and a red phone. They climbed the wide grand staircase immediately before them, escorted by Joe Albion. The stairs creaked and spoke in a sort of tongues, tattling on all the foot traffic that had passed that way.

Jackie Bright, dazzling in nylons and pumps, was at the top of the staircase to greet Marilyn and Nellie Kelly, but not to greet Joe Albion. Marilyn and Nellie Kelly followed Jackie into the large living room, where a long table had been set up and the demonstrator, Pixie Finney, was arranging her wares. Pixie was old but flashy. Near the front bay windows was a refreshment table with an assortment of crackers, Kraft cheese spread, potato chips, and spiked punch.

Joe waited politely on the threshold with a great big smile. It was bad-dream time for Joe Albion, but he'd fake it, romanticize it, Peck's Bad Boy it.

> *When you're smiling,*
> *When you're smiling,*
> *The whole world smiles with you. . . .*

Joe Albion remained in the doorway, but Frances Bright was not smiling.

A great commotion broke out in the hallway behind Joe

Albion as the gang of Woolworth's counter ladies, led by Biddie O'Brien, entered the premises in a tight, spinning knot, whirling past Joe Albion like a toy top. They were all magnifying eyes and examining fingers, having clearly never been on the premises of a blue house. Marilyn and Jackie had invited them. The ladies' crisp uniforms glistened, and their large powdered noses sniffed for scandal and good scotch. They spotted Nellie Kelly who had taken a seat near the bay window overlooking the busy boulevard. Nellie Kelly waved to the friendly passers-by on the street below, and the Woolworth's ladies moved toward her as one body. Nellie felt them coming before she saw them, and she was overjoyed. She felt tugged back into the world.

"I read you in the cards this morning, ladies," she said.

"The girls invited us as a surprise," said Biddie O'Brien, winking at Marilyn and Jackie, who had taken their seats near the refreshment table, where they waited patiently for Revelations. Marilyn was curious as to why her father remained in the doorway.

"Marilyn. You'll be wearing a bikini soon enough," said Biddie O'Brien, who had worked her way across the room for the express purpose of commenting on Marilyn's plump little breasts, which had only recently made their appearance. In the absence of Mrs. Finnegan, Biddie O'Brien took up the slack.

Jackie Bright cast a cold eye on Mrs. O'Brien, who had never married. "You know where they got that name *bikini?*" demanded Jackie.

Biddie's nose sniffed.

Jackie said, "Far away, deep in the beautiful green-and-blue Pacific, there are some islands where the men tested the atomic bomb. And everything on the tiny islands was

wrecked. Bang! Boom! There go the Bikini Islands!" Jackie
Bright was tremendously satisfied with herself. "Only the
cockroaches survived, because they could adapt. Think
about that."

Biddie O'Brien thought about that.

Marilyn could hardly breathe in her girdle. She wore
the girdle because she had heard that any sign of movement of her flesh could invite rape. But most of these
women did not wear girdles. In fact, she had never seen
so many women with round flowing bodies and holiday
war paint. Marilyn felt helpless in her body, as if it were
going on ahead without her. Her breasts were sore and
seemed to grow larger every hour. She worried that in six
months they'd be hanging down around her knees and
she'd have to sling them over her shoulders for any peace.
As if that were not enough, pubic hairs were appearing,
thickening like a virgin forest, and no matter how much
Dippity-Do she used, her long bangs flew up in synthetic
electrical salutations to the four directions. Her garter
belt held up the nylons that bagged in the back because
her legs had not yet developed. The black patent-leather
high heels were uncomfortable on Marilyn's feet, the nylons bagging ever so slightly, ever so uncomfortably into
the hard, polished heel; her legs were cold in the draft
that roared up the grand staircase, into the demonstration
room, and up her short dress.

Joe Albion was mesmerized by Marilyn Albion, and he
felt wondrous strange as the image of Marilyn Monroe
straddling the grate at the Trans-Lux Theater superimposed itself upon his daughter. Did she know her destiny?
he wondered. He felt like John the Baptist, like Norman
Mailer crying out in the jungle of Scollay Square.

"Looking beautiful hurts," confided Marilyn to Jackie with resignation, waiting for Revelations to give the pain meaning.

Jackie Bright, similarly attired, pulled the twisted metal garter out of her thigh flesh and said to Marilyn, "At least we're not men."

Joe Albion remained in the doorway, looking at his daughter, then Frances Bright, his daughter, then Frances Bright.

"You look beautiful," he said.

Frances and Marilyn turned to him at the same time, and Frances Bright went to the doorway and touched Joe Albion's arm. "Joe. Please go."

Perhaps it was the way she touched his arm, or the way she said his name. "Joe." Marilyn knew what she had seen, and Jackie saw what she already knew.

"It kind of makes us blood sisters, or something," said Jackie.

Marilyn was not interested in being a blood sister. She was interested in being enraged at her father. Marilyn stood up, went to the refreshment table, and picked up the dull short knife, which still had some bright orange Kraft cheese spread stuck to it. Hypnotized by Frances Bright, the evil and beautiful space witch, Marilyn Albion walked toward her father, who flashed and smiled in her direction.

"There are two things I need to tell you, Daddy," said Marilyn.

"Yes, darling?"

"Sputnik is not a toaster, and Marilyn Monroe is dead."

As Marilyn neared her father, she looked down and saw blood trickling down her leg. Attacking daddy lost its urgency as the Woolworth's ladies and Great Aunt Nellie surrounded her and immediately demanded that Joe Albion leave.

Nellie Kelly lifted the cheese knife from Marilyn's hand, commenting, "If you're going to have a weapon, dear, be sure it's sharp." Aunt Nellie wasn't touring as extensively as everyone thought.

"You women. What are you women doing?" demanded Joe Albion. They had surrounded Marilyn Albion, and she was almost hidden by them. They were primping her like a big blond doll, like they had done to Mrs. Finnegan's dead body.

"Let me in here," demanded Joe Albion.

"You've got no business here," said Biddie O'Brien.

"She's my daughter," said Joe Albion.

"You're a man," said Biddie O'Brien, definitively.

"Well, of course I am," said Joe Albion, rent with frustration.

"Enough said," said Biddie, crossing her arms against her chest, forbidding Joe Albion to cross the invisible line she drew with the toe of her white work shoe.

Marilyn had gotten her first period. The redness of her blood frightened her. It was actual real blood. Jackie Bright watched it trickle down Marilyn's leg, and she felt sad.

Marilyn's fury at Joe Albion was unabated by real blood. He had handed her over to the ladies of Scollay Square. He had not told her about Frances Bright. She looked at him with disdain. How dare he make a fool out of her mother? And he had named her after Marilyn Monroe, the tramp whore laughingstock madwoman of Madison Square Garden. How dare he look her in the eye? Jackie

Bright and Nellie Kelly led Marilyn to the privacy of the bathroom.

Joe Albion was backed into the hallway by the wave of women. He knew violence would be ineffective and that he would lose. This pack of women could mangle him. He would go to the Blue Lagoon, deep in the beautiful green-and-blue Pacific, to the Bikini Islands that exist no more.

Kate Albion stood behind Joe Albion in the doorway to the Tupperware demonstration room.

Not seeing Kate, Joe said in a last effort at diplomatic manipulation, "She's my daughter. She's my Marilyn. I understand her. You don't. I can help."

The Woolworth's ladies laughed as loud as men as his wife, the mayor's wife, stood behind him and said, "They understand perfectly, Mr. Mayor. Now go home."

Joe Albion stepped aside. Kate Albion looked into the Tupperware party the way Charlton Heston must have looked into the Red Sea, because the wave of women separated for her to pass through easily. As Joe Albion tried to follow, the wave of Woolworth's uniforms rolled unstoppable into the floodgate and the door slammed in his face.

"So keep your blood and plastic, then," he shouted, but it was all bravado. Who would love him? What would happen to Flash Gordon? He left the blue house and walked to the Blue Lagoon, his driver, Freddie Finney, following closely in the limousine. Yes, it was bad-dream time for Joe Albion. Frances Bright was inside the blue house with Marilyn and Kate Albion; and Nellie Kelly and the fallen angels, the Woolworth's counter ladies, were as impenetrable as the caesarean guard.

In the room the women come and go
Talking of Tupperware, blood, and Jell-O.

—

Kate Albion moved through the silent women. With deep interest, she studied Frances Bright, who turned away. Kate noted Miss Bright's peroxide hair and firm buttocks. How do you do? She also noted the inner doors of this blue house had no locks.

"Where is my daughter?"

Marilyn Albion came out of the bathroom, led by Nellie Kelly and followed by Jackie Bright. She looked at her mother.

"Do you want a Jell-O mold, Mother? Or how about a lettuce crisper. Have you met Frances Bright?"

"We've never been formerly introduced. You're the lady from the swan boat, aren't you? Tried to drown in a puddle."

"Isn't she something else?" whispered Biddie O'Brien.

Frances Bright said nothing.

To everyone's surprise, Kate Albion sat in the most comfortable chair at the center of the room. She motioned for Marilyn to sit beside her, and Jackie Bright beside Marilyn. They obeyed. Everyone was grateful that Kate knew what was what and had opted to remain civilized and in control in the face of her husband's mistress and her furious, menstruating daughter. Only Nellie Kelly, who had bounced Kate Kelly on her knee and had lost to her at Old Maid, knew the concealed wrath Kate Albion was calmly stirring in the cauldron of her heart.

Kate Albion lit a charcoal-filtered Tareyton and took a deep drag. She said, "Men are weak. That's why there was 'Queen for a Day,' to make them feel stronger. But some women have forgotten that was a game. Emotional instability is the perfect feminine weapon, because there will always be men who will dedicate themselves to a beautiful and sick woman."

Kate Albion took another long drag from her Tareyton and blew a smoke ring at Frances Bright.

"Would you like some punch, Mrs. Albion?" asked Frances.

"I'd prefer a lowball. Wouldn't you?"

Frances Bright backed away into a corner as Biddie O'Brien sniffed twice and located the liquor cabinet. The Woolworth's ladies gathered glasses and ice cubes and served drinks all around.

Settled in their seats, the anesthetization begun, Kate Albion raised one hand and signaled for the demonstration to begin.

Pixie Finney, the demonstrator, oblivious to anything but her pastel Tupperware, stood bright and flashy before her table. A cigarette dangled from her mouth, hanging on by the stickiness of her lipstick. Each time Pixie described an *objet de* Tupperware, the ladies repeated after her in call-and-response fashion, as with a Gregorian chant. It reminded Marilyn of hypnosis. It reminded Marilyn that everyone loves Berlin in the springtime.

Pixie Finney said:

> *This is the lettuce crisper.*
> *See the lettuce crisper.*
> *This is the ice cube tray.*
> *See the ice cube tray.*
> *This is the two-gallon Kool-Aid container.*
> *The Kool-Aid container.*
> *This is a set of graduated plastic bowls*
> *with airtight covers.*

The airtight covers.
See how to burp them.
Again.
See how to burp them.
This is the age of leftovers.
   The age of leftovers.
Here are the Jell-O molds,
Suitable for green Jell-O red Jell-O orange Jell-O . . .

Marilyn leaned into her mother's ear.

"Mother. Frances Bright and Daddy . . ."

Kate looked at her daughter. "I know." Kate leaned into Marilyn's ear. "Do you know what kind of a house this is?"

Marilyn was silent. Kate was not.

"The women who live in this house are all prostitutes. And one of them, the woman who is the demonstrator, Fatty Finney's tramp cousin Pixie, has gotten too old for it, and doesn't have enough money to be a madam or open a cigarette shop, so she's gone into Tupperware."

   . . . scarlet Jell-O ruby Jell-O . . .

"Are the Avon ladies ex-prostitutes?"

"Marilyn. All women are prostitutes."

Marilyn did not want to become a woman. She wanted always to be a little girl, her feet dangling high above the floor of Woolworth's Five and Dime, forever and ever. She put her arm around Jackie Bright's shoulders because they were the only two virgins left in the blue house.

Rintrah roared as Sheba Sheik licked her paws.

   . . . and cherry Jell-O.
Again.
See the Jell-O molds.

CHAPTER 12

Blackout

1968

Marilyn Albion was sixteen years old, and she was afflicted with the subterranean Tupperware blues. Her place in society, as a young woman, had been a cruel shock to her, and she had given up any pretense of caring about anything except her comfort. Her friendships with Jackie Bright and David Marat had become more distant as the two of them became more fashionably political. The last time she had heard from them, all they could discuss was the counterinaugural, should Richard Nixon be elected.

Marilyn could not imagine going to an inaugural, counter or otherwise, if she herself were not to be crowned queen. But the price of crownings was high this year, and she was not willing to pay it in any case. She wasn't stupid. After all, she did watch television, her window on the world. She watched the assassinations of Martin Luther King and Bobby Kennedy. She watched the police riot at the Chicago Democratic convention. She watched the body bags arrive from Vietnam on the evening news on a daily basis. She had become emotionally two-dimensional, like the television. If nothing else, she was going to survive.

She considered following the Maharishi Mahesh Yogi, like Mia Farrow, but she didn't like Indian food, so in Marie Antoinette style, she luxuriated on her bed, eating chocolate-covered cherry after chocolate-covered cherry from a deluxe gold-papered Schrafft's candy box. Outside her window, in the streets of Boston, she saw two-dimensional antiwar protests and racial violence spoil Sunday afternoon glides on the swan boats in the Public Garden. Marilyn Albion, as the daughter of the most popular mayor in the history of Boston, felt rock-a-bye safe in a city that secretly lusted after royalty, even if that royalty was homemade, as it was with the Kennedys and the Albions. Whatever dangers there were in the world, her Yankee Doodle daddy protected her, and she enjoyed her chocolates.

No one seriously challenged her father. He was the walking cabaret of political bandwagons. But although he sang and danced and his popularity could not have been greater, it was her mother who was powerful. Marilyn searched inside herself for her mother's power, but found only her father's circle of security.

Marilyn heard the front door close, and walked to her window. She watched Joe Albion wrap his white silk scarf around his neck and slowly take each step to the sidewalk as if he were being filmed. He looked at the tree branches, black line drawings in twilight against the pure November night air. His driver, Freddie Finney, who had paddled the swan boats in August five years ago, opened the door to the limousine. Joe settled on the plush seat, and Freddie Finney closed the door. Marilyn was fascinated by her father.

The back passenger window of the limousine rolled down, and Marilyn could see that her father was using his silver nail clipper, which glistened cold and hard. Joe Albion was glamorous and well manicured. He knew who he was, and he could create a new you if you let him. It was his gift.

The limousine rolled away to the Blue Lagoon, where Joe Albion was having an election-night party. The black car absorbed every shock like a muffled drum.

Marilyn lay back down on her bed, cherubic, Lolita-esque yet virginal, curved and pouty, a masterpiece of decadence. She'd shown them what it meant to be daddy's little girl. Studying a chocolate-covered cherry, Marilyn rested her head against a large, exotic Marrakesh pillow, her long legs and delicate feet kneading the blue satin sheets.

The door to Marilyn's room burst open.

"In the French revolution," said Kate Albion, "you would have been decapitated."

Marilyn Albion was undisturbed by Kate's presence. When you've moved into the second dimension, it's hard to get worked up.

"Mother," said Marilyn, "is there really a Love Potion Number Nine, and if I drank it, would I hear a symphony?"

"Don't be fresh. When Johnson quit, when he couldn't

take being president, do you know what that meant?" asked Kate, looking at the poster of Cher in Las Vegas high drag, captioned with the name of her greatest hit: "Bang Bang My Baby Shot Me Down."

"He wouldn't get assassinated." Marilyn had turned into an observant brat.

"That bastard . . ." Marilyn knew her mother was about to discuss Mr. Nixon. ". . . will probably be elected tonight. This could never have happened if Bobby Kennedy hadn't been killed."

"Twinkle twinkle, Bobby Kennedy," said Marilyn, licking the chocolate from her fingers.

Propelled across the room by her anger, Kate's open hand raised up swift and true and slapped Marilyn across the face.

"Don't you ever speak with disrespect again," said Kate Albion.

"What do you want from me?" asked Marilyn, enraged and rising from the blue satin sheets, the faint welt of Kate's wedding band swelling on her cheek.

"To remember who you are," ordered Kate.

Marilyn straightened her minidress, pulled her Sgt. Pepper jacket onto her shoulders, and prepared to enter the cold night. This was the first time that Kate Albion had ever sunk to physical violence, which she considered too primitive because it required constant repetition.

"I want you to take your place in this world," said Kate Albion, shocked by her actions but desperate to conceal it.

"Do you want me to make a big scrapbook of all the dead heroes? I'm tired of dead heroes. Aren't you? I'd prefer to be alive!"

Kate Albion looked at her daughter. "Never."

Marilyn turned her back on her mother and left the bedroom. "I'll take my place in the world the way I want to," she said. Furious and full of blind energy, she found herself opening the front door and standing in the cold on the front steps. She decided to walk to the Blue Lagoon, by way of Beacon Hill. The riot-ridden city would be suitably dangerous. If she was killed or raped, her mother would never be able to forgive herself, and Joe Albion would never forgive Kate. Good, thought Marilyn.

The darkness deepened and the street lamps glowed brilliantly. Marilyn was enjoying herself. Her senses were acute. This was the most adrenaline that had moved through her body since the Tupperware party three years ago, when she had considered stabbing her daddy with the cheese knife.

She walked purposely along Pinckney Street, the most eccentric street on the south slope of Beacon Hill. In the distance, there were the explosive sounds of Molotov cocktails, police sticks tapping the ground and cracking bones, and the occasional whir of helicopter blades.

Quick and easy, she walked past the houses made of red brick and painted clapboard, past the tunnels and narrow walkways that led to courts in the center of the blocks. The sound of an explosion in the distance propelled her into one of the dark and damp tunnels. She stopped, and heard footsteps, a man's footsteps—a dangerous man's footsteps, she was certain—coming toward her. She ran back through the tunnel, her heart tightening in a knot, as a dog ran past her, chasing a cat.

She crossed to the north slope of the hill and rested at the entrance to Holmes Alley, which had been a stop along the Underground Railroad for fugitive slaves. She knelt and felt the petals of a small red flower that grew at the alley's entrance. Marilyn was never too angry or frightened to notice beauty, and anger only heightened her appreciation. But Marilyn felt spooked. So this was the way her mother lived. Her mother was in her, but where was the power?

Marilyn plucked the red flower and, kneeling on the ground, raised it to her nose. Its scent was powerful, unusual. It smelled like blood.

Marilyn remembered Bobby Kennedy, who had sounded like Bugs Bunny but offered hope. She dropped the flower, and the light of the black iron, Revolution-era street lamp extinguished itself. Marilyn stood up and watched as, one by one in a dreaded domino effect, the streetlights, the house lights, the traffic lights, the searchlights, the riot lights, the romantic lights of Harvard Square cafés, the beacons of Beacon Hill, and she assumed, the neon light of the Blue Lagoon in Scollay Square flickered, choked, and faded into the night. Boston was as dark as the belly of a starving rat.

The absence of electricity revealed the stars. Thousands of stars that had been invisible glimmered over Boston. Thousands of Bobby Kennedys. Marilyn was enchanted and raised up her hand to trace the Big Dipper. Marilyn Albion studied the distant moving lights that gleamed on the horizon, but in the beauty of this sudden darkness, Marilyn swiftly lost her courage. The lights on the horizon became 184-pound toasters twenty-three inches in diameter taking 96.2 minutes to orbit the earth, and Kate Albion's voice echoed from the far Sputnik past: "They could have bombs on those things."

Marilyn Albion knew what to do in case of an atomic blast, so she made her way to a subway entrance. As she descended, the familiar subway transformed into a black hole in the ground. The smell of urine and sweat, which before had not been noticeable, became dominant without sight to dilute it. To find their way out, those who were lucky enough not to be trapped on the trains lit matches that illuminated their faces like jack-o'-lanterns. Marilyn had forgotten that the trains ran on electricity, that the third rail would be cold. Angry phobic voices jostled deep in the tunnels, trapped in the stalled green cars.

"Are we being attacked?"

"I can't breathe."

"Is it the Russians?"

"It's probably Nixon!"

Nixon, thought Marilyn. Has he won? And she felt a freakish sensation: compassion for Kate Albion.

Marilyn ascended again to the darkened city and made her way home, trying to appear dangerous and armed, but Kate was no longer there, and Great Aunt Nellie Kelly was in South Boston for her weekly bingo. Marilyn felt abandoned, even though she had been the one who left. She found some money in the desk in the library and hailed a cab, her imagination rattling the knives and windows in her mind.

"The Blue Lagoon, please," she said to the driver, who did not need to ask directions. The cabdriver did not look like the enemy, although Marilyn would not have recognized him if he was.

Marilyn watched and listened as the cab passed the roaring, struggling men who looted and rampaged the city. Marilyn Albion wondered if it was the beginning of the revolution. She closed her eyes and saw her blond head rolling down Holmes Alley. Seized with panic, she opened her eyes. She did not know from what dark recess of her memory the next thought sprang, but it was clear:

Royalty is allowed the privilege of hanging to death by a silk cord. Marilyn Albion did not want that privilege.

She struggled to breathe as the cab pulled up to the Blue Lagoon. Her cab door was opened by the doorman, innocent in his bright red costume. The blackout had not stopped him from doing his duty. This startled and then comforted her.

"Good evening, Marilyn," he said.

"Good evening."

The doorman pulled open the highly polished brass door to the club, and Marilyn Albion pressed a Kennedy half-dollar into the palm of his white glove. He tipped his hat and closed the door behind her.

She had expected to step into darkness and the stumble of panic, a few flashlights and matches burning and jiggling in nervous hands in the darkness. She was greeted instead by the lights of hundreds of white candles reflecting on the exotic shimmering fish that swam in the recessed aquariums along the walls. Cigarettes and highballs flashed in the darkness, a tequila sunrise sloshing in a hand here and there. Laughter and expensive perfume mingled and were yanked into death nooses that floated unnoticed above the party.

Indignation at the crowd's blindness to the chaos of the outside world wrestled in Marilyn's head with her desire for peace and chocolates. She made her way through the beautiful crowd to her father, to presumed safety. With Frances Bright hanging on his arm, he appeared to be strong. Joe Albion was smiling, singing, dancing in the face of danger. Marilyn could not feel his presence, but his image was magnificent. Joe was the king of Carpe Diem, not a hair out of place, and his smile defeated the Beast. But where was he? His presence was like a mirage. Marilyn slowly realized there might be no Flash Gordon to rescue her, and that Dale Arden was nowhere in sight.

"Where's my mother?" Marilyn demanded.

"Under City Hall, my darling, hiding from the Beast," said the mildly inebriated Joe Albion, unaffected and pure. "Richard Nixon certainly can make an entrance. We've got to give him that, even in his badly cut suits!" said Joe Albion. Laughter erupted throughout the room and fluttered about his shoulders like ticker tape at a hero's parade.

"Don't you just love blackouts?" asked Frances Bright. Frances was drunk, and Marilyn ignored her. If she were not Jackie's mother, Marilyn would have engaged in active hate.

"I need to find Mother, Daddy," pleaded Marilyn.

Joe Albion kissed Marilyn on the cheek. "Stay here with me. It's safe. I'm keeping up everyone's morale." He patted Frances Bright's hand.

There is no need for alarm. Citizens have been buying up all the canned foods . . .

Shaken, Marilyn backed out of the Blue Lagoon and away from Joe Albion, who glistened in the candlelight. It was clear that the party was not to be disturbed. Daddy appeared so elegant, so in charge, but when she got close to him, he was like everyone else: lost in the swamp of history, but wearing a top hat.

Marilyn paid the taxi driver and stepped out of the cab in front of City Hall. She passed Benjamin Franklin and walked across the hard, frosty grass, up the white granite steps, and through the wide doorway. She stood in the silent rotunda, feeling very alive beneath the tremendous height of the ceilings and on the black-and-white marble of the floors. The seat of power appeared abandoned.

Marilyn climbed the grand staircase and entered the unlocked mayor's office, but Kate Albion was not there.

"Under City Hall, my darling," Joe Albion had said.

Steeling her nerves against the spiders' webs and the bats that hung upside down in her head, Marilyn descended to the tunnel beneath City Hall. The sounds of exploding tear-gas canisters and sirens became more distant as she worked her way deeper into the tunnel. The tunnel was lit by construction lamps, small heavy steel balls with slits across the top from which one thick tongue of flame shot. The imaginary bat wings beat hard in the real tunnel, and the spiders worked overtime as she made her way by using the distinct but distant sound of a metal-on-metal SOS to guide her.

> *Dot dot dot.*
> *Dash dash dash.*
> *Dot dot dot.*

Marilyn followed the sound to a heavy metallic door that was being pounded from the inside. She grasped the black steel handle in both hands and pushed down upon it. With a heavy hydraulic thrust, the door opened.

Kate Albion stood inside, holding a crowbar. Kate Albion had locked herself inside her private atomic fallout shelter. There was electricity, a cot, some books, and enough powdered food to sustain, from the looks of it, one person: Kate Albion. In the corner, beside the cot, there was an elaborate ham radio powered by an independent electrical generator. Marilyn wondered why she had thought she would feel safer with her mother.

Angry and hurt, Marilyn asked, "When did you build this?"

"This is Richard Nixon's fault," said Kate Albion.

Hot hot hot.
Flash flash flash.
Hot hot hot.

"When did you build this?" demanded Marilyn.

"Too early. Forty-four's too early for menopause," said Kate as she flushed with red blood. Kate Albion, no stranger to sensations of power, had never felt such a tremendous focus of her being. Thoughts of possible possession by the violently dead, such as Mrs. Finnegan, had passed through Kate's mind when she had believed that she might well be buried alive. Now, she was embarrassed that Marilyn had had to save her from her private shelter. It wasn't terribly maternal.

Marilyn said, "It's not so hard to go from power to paranoia."

Kate Albion assumed the take-off position in the chair she had brought from her father's study. She wrapped her hands around the carved claws of the chair, held her knees slightly parted, and pressed her spiked heels onto the hard underground floor. Kate Albion knew the Beast was about to take power. The ham radio crackled, the amber tubes flashed, and the dial and tuner trembled like the applause meter on "Queen for a Day." Walter Cronkite announced the fall of each state to Richard Nixon. As each state fell, Kate Albion said, "They're turning in their graves. It's Nixon's fault. And Jackie's."

"Jackie who?" asked Marilyn.

"When Jackie Kennedy married that Greek and abandoned Jack Kennedy's memory, anything was possible."

"She was a young woman, Mother," said Marilyn.

"The final blow was Jackie O," said Kate, slamming a fist on the chair.

Marilyn remembered Jackie Kennedy's blood-stained pink suit and felt a tremendous sadness.

"Then they could forget everything. They forgot the great debate. They forgot Nixon looked like a grave digger," said Kate Albion. "All Nixon could say was, 'Him and that damned hairdo.' They forgot the slush fund. They forgot he used his wife to make them feel sorry for him. They closed their eyes to his hair."

Marilyn believed Kate Albion to be on tour. She had never felt so alone.

"You're wondering if I'm on tour, aren't you?"

Marilyn hated it when Kate could guess her thoughts.

"Well, I'm not. But I am sorry I hit you, Marilyn," said Kate. " 'Twinkle twinkle, Bobby Kennedy' wouldn't have been so bad on any other day."

"I thought it sounded kind of nice," said Marilyn. "Like when he said about his brother, that he'd cut him out in little stars, and all that. You know. That's all I meant."

Emotion welled up in Kate's eyes.

"You get your sentimentality from your father, not me," said Kate.

"And what do I get from you?" asked Marilyn, the anger rising in her again.

"A mission. A purpose. Something beyond chocolates."

Marilyn was impressed, and as Walter Cronkite announced the fall of California, Kate Albion began to scratch the finish off the mahogany claws.

"When your life hung by a thread, Aunt Nellie predicted that you would come to great things and have a special purpose if you survived. You survived, and now you owe something to the world. I want you to know that you have my permission to do anything at all that will help to bring about the fall of Richard Nixon."

Marilyn was impressed. She had not known that she had a debt to pay, or that she could possibly do anything that would even remotely influence Richard Nixon.

"I could never be an assassin, mother."

Kate stopped clawing and stared at her daughter, recalling her daughter's suspected perverse partiality to Richard Nixon. "Marilyn. I am not suggesting that you literally murder him." Kate Albion involuntarily brought her hand to her beating heart.

"But that's how it's done. You know, Mom."

Kate Albion rested her hand on the carved claw. "I have to remember that you have lived in the age of assassins. I meant through honest political manipulation."

Marilyn understood. "I could go to the counterinaugural with David and Jackie. If the lights ever come on again."

Kate Albion's eyes twinkled like a pack of nasty fairies. "Counterinaugural?" she said slowly.

"Yes. They're going to protest his election."

"No passing the torch to another generation? No asking what you could do for your country? No promises of unlimited green stamps for all?" said Kate. She paused. She looked her daughter cold in the eye and said, "Never forget, Marilyn. You're part animal. It will ruin you or make you."

"What?" said Marilyn Albion, but Kate Albion was fine-tuning the ham radio. "Was that the birds and bees lecture I've been waiting to hear?" asked Marilyn.

Kate was busy. Too busy to bother with Marilyn's sarcasm.

Sheba Sheik was hungry for Richard Nixon.

Marilyn sat upon the cot and said, "You were only going to save yourself, weren't you?" But Kate was very, very busy, much too busy to answer, perhaps too busy to hear.

Marilyn walked out of the tunnel alone. Kate's paranoia was so deep that she preferred to stay below ground. Marilyn ascended into the city and made her way quickly and cautiously to the Blue Lagoon. At least Joe Albion had invited her to the party.

Marilyn entered the Blue Lagoon and saw that the festivities hadn't skipped a beat. They had actually become more elaborate. Joe Albion stood at the center of the club and announced, "Everyone, of every race, creed, sect, and country of national origin, is invited to go with me on vacation to the beautiful blue-and-green Pacific." No one protested. In fact, there was great applause. What a Democrat!

Marilyn watched her father glisten in the candlelight. When Joe Albion saw her, he became silent and lifted his arms, like Moses leading the children of Israel to the promised land. As the Woolworth's ladies had parted for Kate Albion at the Tupperware party, the people before him, including Frances Bright, cleared a path between him and his daughter.

"Ladies and gentlemen," said Joe Albion. "The new Marilyn." Ahhhh, said the guests.

The candlelight glistened, but Marilyn Albion did not move. Miss Monroe in her atomic cloud of white mink, barely breathing in her skin and beads, stepped through Marilyn's mind as if she were crossing a mine field, then floated up to the surface as Marilyn Albion walked toward her father. Marilyn Albion felt intoxicated by the sexuality swirling through her body. Marilyn Albion felt sweet power. The men, the women, even Frances Bright were captivated by her. Marilyn Albion breathed deeply, her mind a blank white sheet in the wind. But then she stopped. Joe Albion was the poison apple, and she would not take a bite. He would not draw the perfect animal from her. But then, his hair gleamed and his eyes were perfectly clear, and he wanted her, so she moved beside him as he whispered, "You could save every man. Even Richard Nixon."

Marilyn believed him.

Joe Albion, mayor of Boston, drew Marilyn's arm through his and worked the room: smiling, laughing at terrible jokes, shaking the hands of even those with bad haircuts, proudly leading Marilyn through the light.

Marilyn Albion,

> *Looking as beautiful*
> *in death as she did in*
> *life,*

suddenly remembered that Marilyn Monroe had committed suicide. She pulled herself slowly away from her father and toward the door as if in a strange and deadly dream.

> *Wake up, little Marilyn!*

As she retreated, Marilyn pushed her sexuality down into hiding, as deeply as she could, but it could get no further than her feet where it camped, hot with life and forever undeniable.

The lights came on as Marilyn slipped from the Blue Lagoon. Everyone cheered as if Joe Albion were personally responsible for the return of illumination, but Marilyn Albion had abandoned them all, like a gold crown during the French revolution.

CHAPTER 13

The Counterinaugural

January 1969

Within two months of the election of Richard Nixon, Marilyn Albion had become a radical-left celebrity. But she was deeply depressed. A dedicated life on the left meant brown rice, not chocolates. Marilyn forced herself to eat the politically correct cuisine because colorless food would have to be tolerated if she wanted to be in on the party.

Marilyn Albion rode through the streets of Washington, D.C., toward the counterinaugural via a Volkswagen bus decorated with peace signs. Jackie Bright and David Marat were seated behind her on the bus, which was packed with politically correct young men tossing and fingering their long hair. They were fascinated with themselves, Marilyn observed. It was a shame they'd been denied their own beauty so long that they were now blinded by it.

Sphinx Whalen was the organizer. He was a bushy-haired, jumpy fellow who wore jeans, boots, and a leather jacket, the Billy Steinway uniform of the left.

Sphinx Whalen shouted into the bus, "Billy Steinway might make an appearance." The thought of seeing Billy Steinway in person made the radical fellows fluff up their hair into as unruly and windblown a look as possible.

Jackie Bright leaned toward Marilyn and said, "They look like they're getting ready for a date."

Marilyn and Jackie laughed as loud as men.

Marilyn Albion felt a desire to undercut the effect on these men of the impending arrival of Billy Steinway. A mere man could never compete with me, thought Marilyn. But she flushed, and stuffed her sexuality deep into her pockets. She wanted real power. She did not want to be a political aphrodisiac.

Sphinx Whalen spoke constantly on a walkie-talkie as he turned the wheel of the bus sharply at the Washington, D.C., street corners.

"We're approaching the stage area. Clear the route for us, please."

The VW bus turned near Pennsylvania Avenue as the official inauguration of Richard Nixon boomed from the sound system across Washington, D.C. Marilyn saw a cheering throng and the frantic waving of hundreds of little American flags. She had never seen anyone cheer for

Richard Nixon. It horrified her. The sight would have tormented Kate Albion, who was probably spending the day in her private fallout shelter. Marilyn turned away from this perversion and collected her self, which had scattered across the mined political terrain.

Marilyn said to Jackie and David, "Those are Republicans." The three activists stared at the Republicans with suspicion and revulsion.

Marilyn Albion had never actually seen a Republican display of power in the flesh. She had seen them on television, holding signs and parading, but over the black-and-white telewaves they had seemed no more real than Flash Gordon. She conjured a mental image of Queen Elizabeth, who excelled at handling odd situations: white gloved, flower print dress blowing in the breeze, a purse hanging from her wrist, chatting up the king of the cannibals. Inviting him to tea. Politely refusing a human toe appetizer but diplomatically taking one along for later. Putting the toe in her purse, unwrapped. Snapping the purse shut. Click! Hanging it nonchalantly from her wrist. Marilyn understood that God must have had a very good reason for creating cannibals and Republicans.

By their behavior in a crowd, Marilyn concluded that Republicans turn their essence over to a leader, whereas Democrats steal the essence of their leader, hide it in their purses, and open it late at night in their bedrooms, long after the Secret Service has tucked what's left of the little fellow into bed for the night.

> *Now I lay me down to sleep,*
> *The Secret Service my soul to keep.*

The VW van passed the last Republican and approached a far more disconnected, rambling group: the counterinaugural. Marilyn's spirit lifted, the slightest tingle of Kate Albion moving through her feet. The rally resembled a gypsy camp with bright banners flapping in the cold wind and tambourines gleaming hard, cold, and beautiful. The crowd parted Red Sea–style for the VW van, Sphinx Whalen rapping like a dexedrine casualty over the walkie-talkie.

"We're on the approach. On the approach. Just went by the moron tribe Republican jelly flag-mad freaks."

Marilyn thought Sphinx Whalen a bit extreme.

The van screeched to a halt behind the oblong wooden stage, and Marilyn Albion stepped out. She thought it odd that only two months before she had been luxuriating in her satin sheets, eating chocolate-covered cherries one by one from a Schrafft's candy box.

The air was frigid as she concentrated on Sphinx's instructions to her.

"Be sure to mention the war, and the women's movement is important—but let's face it, we have to deal with the war first," said Sphinx Whalen.

Marilyn felt a piece of emotional shrapnel fly by her forehead.

A reporter from *Rolling Stone* magazine approached her. He had a scraggly black beard, and his cold fingers clenched a stubby pencil. He asked Marilyn, "As the daughter of the mayor of Boston, how do you feel about the election of Richard Nixon to the presidency?"

Marilyn looked at the reporter carefully. He was not making eye contact with her. He was looking directly at her breasts. Mrs. Finnegan had known what was what. Marilyn Albion looked to the east. Marilyn Albion looked to the west. Marilyn Albion looked at the reporter from *Rolling Stone* magazine and said, "No one will sing

'Happy birthday, Mr. President' to Richard Nixon. No one will lift a glass of milk to hail this chief."

"What kind of answer is that?" demanded the reporter in a patronizing tone, still staring at her breasts.

"My kind," said Marilyn.

"Yeah, you tell him!" said a darting bundle of multicolored scarves and hats, representative of the unionized worldwide cloth industry, that arrived at Marilyn's side. "My name's Starshine O'Schwartz and I'm from the radical free press of the Lower East Side chapter of Burnt Toast Offerings. What do you think, *Ms.* Albion, of those who believe Richard Nixon should be killed before he destroys the world?"

Marilyn thought carefully and said, "Richard Nixon has bad hair, but does he deserve to die for it?"

Starshine O'Schwartz laughed at a pitch of about dog-whistle level—barely audible to human ears, yet definitely interfering with telecommunications satellite dishes and electronic surveillance devices already being installed by Mr. Nixon's CIA. Starshine O'Schwartz gave Marilyn Albion a little electrostatic hug, then retreated in her wools and mixed cottons.

Sphinx Whalen announced: "That's enough questions. We have to go to the stage." Sphinx Whalen, Marilyn thought, likes to imagine he's in control.

Sphinx spoke into his walkie-talkie: "We're coming up the steps now." The steps were directly behind him and not a soul was on them. Marilyn laughed at his pretensions, as a photographer focused on her for a candid shot. Sphinx put his hand up in front of the camera lens.

"This is a free country, man. We got a free press here," said the photographer.

"The revolution will not be photographed, man," said Sphinx.

On stage, Marilyn was seated beside a very young black woman, thin and electric, deep black complexioned, a magnificent Afro framing her head like a halo in a photographic negative.

Sphinx made the introductions. "Marilyn Albion, Belle Washington. Belle, Marilyn." Marilyn put her hand out to Belle, who examined it carefully. Marilyn felt self-consciously blue-eyed and blond under Belle's microscopic glare. The darkness of Belle's skin startled Marilyn, who had never been this close to such a perfect example of everything she knew nothing about. She was very familiar, however, with the look in Belle Washington's eyes: it was the same as Kate Albion's.

As Marilyn's hand touched Belle's, Sphinx Whalen yelled "Photo opportunity!" and the radical flashbulbs popped and sizzled in the freezing temperatures.

Loud thundersnaps of applause for Richard Nixon lingered in the distance and dissipated over the Potomac. Marilyn's stomach twisted and braided into itself, and she wanted to escape the sound of Sphinx Whalen's voice, the applause for Richard Nixon, and especially the stare of Belle Washington.

Beneath Belle's eyelids crackled a thousand unspoken words and colors. Then Belle spoke. "Rapunzel, Rapunzel, let down your golden hair."

Sphinx commanded, "Could you girls do that again. Some of the guys didn't quite get it."

Marilyn and Belle looked solemnly at each other and wrapped their fingers together. Marilyn looked at the intertwined black and white fingers and was delighted by their beauty. She relaxed as she thought that a touch of dark green would look lovely. Belle spoke under her breath so that only Marilyn could hear what she was saying.

"Slave hunters chasing runaways a hundred years ago, that's who these boys are descended from." Her voice was ceremoniously low, like the first woman sounded before the Great Oppression. Belle gripped Marilyn's hand more tightly.

"Could you both please look over this way, girls?"

Marilyn snapped at Sphinx Whalen, "I am not a girl. You're beginning to sound like a game show host." Belle loosened her grip slightly in respect for Marilyn's flash of anger.

Sphinx smiled. "You're cute." Marilyn did not respond, and Belle again tightened her grip.

"Yes, Miss Albion, daughter of the mayor of Boston," said Belle quietly. "I am the maid's daughter. I am a descendent of George Washington, Father of Your Country, slave owner with wooden teeth, which left their mark."

Belle Washington is as odd as the Republicans, thought Marilyn, who had in her life spoken to only one other black person.

"Could you raise your hands up together, girls?"

"What do you represent?" asked Marilyn as their hands bonded above their heads.

"The destruction of your race."

"I'm surprised you're a Republican! The Democrats have much more to offer your people," said a startled Marilyn. What would Queen Elizabeth do? thought Marilyn. Pull the human toe out of her handbag and start nibbling?

"We may spare a couple of you, as token figureheads."

"What city are you from?" demanded Marilyn, who had never met anyone from outside the northeastern United States.

"I come from where the mumbo jumbo voodoo sisters mix up potions to make you people crazy. It's not 'Green Acres,' and even the black cat on 'I Spy,' that Cosby brother, he does not know where I've been, nor can he find me."

It sounded to Marilyn like Belle was from Mississippi. They disengaged their hands.

Belle glared over her shoulder at David Marat, and Marilyn followed her eyes. Marilyn was disappointed in David. He was tripping again, staring at his hands with dilated eyes.

"Do you know Ella Fitzgerald?" Marilyn asked Belle, to prove she did indeed know another black person.

Belle's eyebrows raised up and she smiled as wide as a Kennedy. "Oh, sure! Me and Ella go way back."

Why is Belle lying? thought Marilyn.

"Is your mother really a maid?" she asked.

Belle's teeth flashed and Marilyn felt small psychic bites in her arms. Belle said, "My mother is a maid in the White House."

Marilyn was silent, and certain that Belle was telling the truth.

"My mother's name is Martha."

Marilyn smiled and said with great appreciation, "Martha Washington."

"That's right, baby. Martha Washington."

"And she's a maid in the White House?"

Belle nodded and Marilyn was absolutely delighted. Belle thawed ever so subtly, and Marilyn detected in her a trace of pride in her lineage.

"BITCH!" shouted a woman's voice. Belle and Marilyn turned defensively toward a wild woman with a beautiful round face. She was dressed in black and carrying a sign that read

B.I.T.C.H.

Sphinx Whalen was trying to force her down from a pole that overlooked the stage. She had exotic long brown hair decorated with little brightly colored fake birds strategically fastened to clumps of her hair by their flexible claws. Marilyn had seen these birds in Woolworth's. The wild woman's facility at climbing was aided by a scuffed and beaten pair of beige desert boots.

"I wanna talk!" she shouted.

"Don't you know how to cook?" said Sphinx.

"Yeah. I cook ball soup."

Belle leaned toward Marilyn. "That's Betty Bloom. She's a BITCH. Only white girl I've seen got her ass on right."

"If she's a bitch, why is she your favorite white girl?"

Belle shook her head. "You don't know anything. BITCH is the Bitch's International Terrorist Conspiracy from Hell."

"I know that!" said Marilyn. Marilyn lied with poise. Thinking David might offer her some support, Marilyn glanced back. David was absolutely fascinated with his hands. No. David was not going to be much help. Jackie? Jackie Bright was missing.

Marilyn turned back to the Betty Bloom commotion and saw that Jackie Bright was assisting Betty Bloom with her BITCH sign as she climbed down the pole.

Betty shouted at Sphinx Whalen, "Women have as much a right to talk as any man."

Sphinx smiled patiently and said, "When you chicks have to get drafted to Vietnam and bleed, you'll be equal."

"Women bleed every month. Great big clots," said Betty Bloom.

"That's not real bleeding," shouted Sphinx.

"Let's get some and show it to him. Anyone got any?" shouted Betty Bloom.

"What are you going to say to the crowd, Belle?" asked Marilyn, trying to strike up conversation. Belle laughed and shook her head.

"What makes you think these boys are planning on letting us talk? You're cheesecake, baby, and I'm devil's food." Marilyn and Belle laughed as loud as men. Belle caught herself short and manufactured an icy stare. It was not a photo opportunity.

Free of Betty Bloom, who was unsuccessfully attempting to collect blood clots from the women in the crowd, Sphinx Whalen cradled the microphone, keeping his walkie-talkie pressed to his right ear at all times. Marilyn Albion thought, Sphinx Whalen would enjoy guarding the black box with the green button.

"Men and women of the revolution. We are honored to have here today the poet laureate of our movement, Billy Steinway."

Billy Steinway took the stage, pausing briefly before Marilyn Albion. Close enough to touch. Close enough to bite. Marilyn Albion smiled and lowered her lids to half-mast.

Billy Steinway's walk was predatory, his expression saintly. His neck was bent forward in deference to his harmonica and rack, his folk cross. He strummed his guitar as he approached the microphone, minstrel of the people, channel of the do-right do-wah-diddy gods. He looked back at Marilyn Albion with large baby-blue eyes, eyes that wanted to be saved but had long since reconciled themselves to a life of lonely beauty. The lost boy-man turned away from Marilyn Albion in philosophical suffering and flicked the microphone with his index finger. The sound shock produced a friendly roar from the revolution. He smiled. He's coy, thought Marilyn Albion. A coy man. That's interesting.

Belle said, "This dude is terminally correct."

But Marilyn did not hear her because she was falling in love with Billy Steinway's black radical curls, his poet's oyster eyes, and his cigarette-thin body that twitched and spasmed beneath the boots, faded jeans, and battered leather jacket, the body that sacrificed itself to channel the message of the revolution.

Hello hello oh yes a thousand times hello.

This was it for Marilyn Albion. It was perfect. Singing and politics wrapped into one package. Rintrah and Sheba Sheik were delighted. Billy Steinway. He didn't dance, but Marilyn couldn't ask for everything.

> *When you're smiling,*
> *When you're smiling,*
> *The whole world smiles with you.*

Billy Steinway had a voice like a bagpipe. It was fabulous.

> *No! Mr. Richard Nixon,*
> *I won't be your whore.*

"Whores have rights too!" shouted Betty Bloom. Marilyn felt embarrassed. These women had no respect for this young god.

Jackie Bright raised a defiant fist beside Betty Bloom.

Betty had let Jackie carry her sign. A pack of women from
NOW, the National Organization of Women, moved toward Betty and Jackie in a tight body and put little pieces
of cake into their mouths.

I won't fight in your sick war.

Betty and Jackie were shouting with their mouths full,
cake spewing in the four directions. Not good representa-
tion, not with television cameras present. Machismo set in
when the men of SDS, the Students for a Democratic
Society, and SNCC, the Student Non-Violent Coordinat-
ing Committee, started shouting down Betty and Jackie:
"Why don't you chicks find a dark alley where you're
wanted?"
Marilyn was horrified. She had never heard such words
from a man. But she was again distracted by Billy Steinway. Every woman for herself, she thought, as the heat in
her feet raised up into her legs but got caught just below
her heart.

You wanna be King for a Day
In an Armageddon photo-play.

A handsome black man, a radical-chic maumau master,
shouted at Betty Bloom, "The only position for a woman
in the movement is prone." The white men surrounding
him cheered. Thank God all men aren't like that, thought
Marilyn. Jackie and Betty are asking for it, too.

You'll go down like a lead shoe
For just one last babaloo.

"Babaloo!" said Marilyn Albion. This could be her long-
awaited paramour, to whom she could be joined at the

subconscious, safe and sound above ground as she'd always dreamed.

"Babaloo?" said Belle.

Billy Steinway was above it all and at the heart of it.

Belle stared at Billy Steinway, but all she could see was a skinny white boy.

"Hey, cheesecake," said Belle, disappointed that Marilyn's attention had been so completely diverted.

"Hey, devil's food," said Marilyn, feeling stronger and more alive as her attraction to Billy Steinway accelerated.

Belle said, "You really know Ella Fitzgerald?"

"Yes! She introduced me to Marilyn Monroe." Marilyn never took her eyes off Billy.

Belle pondered the complex weave of random events that would have been necessary for that introduction to happen, as Marilyn watched Billy Steinway, folkmaster deluxe.

Marilyn then turned to Belle and said, "If all men could be like him." Marilyn's eyes again riveted on Billy as she wove fantasies like long daisy chains on a summer's afternoon by the river to hang about his harmonica rack.

Belle flashed like the Cheshire Cat. "I don't want to trash your daydream, baby, but remember this: You may be blonde, but you're still a piece of meat."

Marilyn thought Belle a bit extreme. Perhaps the men Belle knew were like that, but certainly she had not met anyone the caliber of Billy Steinway.

Betty Bloom and Jackie Bright had now swallowed all of their cake, and they chanted:

> *What the hell are we fightin' for?*
> *Janis Joplin's chain and ball?*
> *Death in a cheap motel?*

Billy Steinway strummed and his bagpipe voice overruled them.

Hot hot hot.
Flash flash flash.
Hot hot hot.

Marilyn Albion wanted Billy Steinway. Marilyn wanted sex, a virgin voyage. She brimmed with the spirit of every girl group she had ever loved: the Ronettes, the Supremes, the Shangri-Las, the Dixie Cups.

A few blocks away, the Republicans hailed the new chief, Richard Milhous Nixon, as music of the military bands broke over the Potomac and scattered like the heads of assassinated heroes.

I love him I love him I love him
And where he goes
I'll follow

As Billy Steinway blew heavy and sensual on his harmonica, Marilyn was surprised at how deeply she loved America, politics, brown rice, and heroes. She hadn't known that political activism was such a good way to make new and interesting friends like Belle Washington, and to meet men: mature men, perhaps great men, like Billy Steinway.

Billy Steinway closed his performance, and as he left the stage, he brushed close by Marilyn Albion and whispered: "Never has one woman given so much, or looked so good."

Marilyn's lips parted, but no sound came out. She was too full of beauty, desire, and the cold air of January.

I will follow him.

CHAPTER 14

I Went Walking
on the Moon One Day

July 1969

BLAST OFF

Walter Cronkite had never been so animated. His excitement with the impending moonwalk had transfigured his face into a startling resemblance to the Man in the Moon.

Here we are, live at Cape Kennedy, where the Saturn Five booster rocket will thrust the Apollo Eleven into space. Its mission: to enter into the moon's orbit and separate the command module from the lunar module. The lunar module, manned by two astronauts, Armstrong and Aldrin, will then land upon the moon. They will take a stroll in their bubble-top spacesuits.

Along the banks of the Mystic River, Marilyn Albion, Billy Steinway, and Billy's harmonica and rack drifted in the summertime heat. Marilyn was transformed by his presence into a state of carnal desire. Her eyes met his, and they were cold but freaky with desire. He breathed lightly onto his harmonica and spoke.

And the spaceman of your dreams
Could not your hot soul redeem
With green stamps

Marilyn Albion was determined to seduce—and save—this prince from his lonely eagle's perch. She would appeal to his intellect.

"The moon is two thousand one hundred and sixty miles in diameter," said Marilyn Albion. "Its daytime temperature is four hundred degrees Kelvin. Its night temperature is one hundred degrees Kelvin."

Marilyn took a drag from her charcoal-filtered Tareyton, and Billy Steinway took a drag from his Marlboro. They got into Billy Steinway's Mercedes and drove to Boston, past the Sea of Tranquillity.

THE LANDING

On the thirteenth revolution, Mission Control held its heart as the lunar module separated from the command module, and radio communication was out during the undocking. Then Armstrong's voice: "The *Eagle* has wings."

As they cruised across the Mystic River Bridge, Marilyn saw what appeared to be a halo around Billy Steinway's dark radical curls, but rather than the nimbus of the saints, it had the consistency of a large, white-powdered donut with a hole in the middle. Mrs. Finnegan's ghost took a large bite out of it, a shower of white powder falling around Billy's head. Marilyn smiled at the large dandruff flakes on Billy's shoulders.

The next twenty-two seconds will determine the success of the moon landing. Can the lunar module safely land?

The beige door to Billy Steinway's apartment was simple enough. The simplicity that cloaks the rare and protects it—thought Marilyn Albion—from the intrusion of the riffraff. A loon, radically off course from Thoreau's Walden Pond in Concord, raced overhead screaming to itself and in deep need of Thorazine, the new wonder drug. The loon narrowly missed the belfry of the Church of the Holy Bean Blowers across the street, with its carved angel heads blowing with all their might on thin trumpets to get man's attention.

Neil Armstrong has had to take manual control of the flight, as the computer cannot distinguish between boulders and flat landing space.

Billy opened the beige door and entered. Marilyn held her breath slightly, as this honor was tremendous, to be allowed behind the beige door into the home of the greatest living poet, the leader of young men, the radical-chic prince. Marilyn shut the door behind her and adjusted her eyes to the dim lights.

Every object in the room was beige, and in the atomic style. The floor lamps were formed in scooping lines like mushroom clouds suspended in space forever. How odd. It must be to avoid interference with his vivid imagination, thought Marilyn Albion. The lamps were radar dishes that picked up the frequencies of dead alcoholic poets. The only splash of color was created by the cupcake crumbs, which were everywhere, trailing through the house as if someone was not sure if he could find his way back to the door without a trail. The little pleated paper cups that had held the cupcakes were stained red and green from baking dyes and were exactly where they must have landed upon being discarded. They created a surreal landscape in Billy Steinway's beige and desolate living room. Marilyn Albion discreetly pulled aside the heavy drape and looked out the window to make sure the rest of the world was still there. It was. She let the drape fall back across the window.

Billy Steinway turned on his black-and-white television set. Marilyn had not expected Billy Steinway to have a television set, but of course he too would have to keep up with current events.

> We don't think the astronauts will be able to see it, but there is a lot of lunar junk up there. Sort of like a big spacecraft wrecking yard. There are also a lot of cupcake liners. What's great about it, though, is that since there is no gravity, and no oxygen to cause rust, and no water to cause erosion, the junk is preserved for all time.

Billy Steinway turned and presented Marilyn with his all-knowing smile. She alone would hear his observation on the event that riveted the world. With the formality of

Napoleon tucking his hand inside his breast pocket, he rested his fingers on the harmonica rack around his neck.

He spoke: "If Marilyn Monroe's body had been put on the moon, we would all have been able to see what she looked like. The sleeping beauty. She once said gravity catches up with us all."

Billy Steinway sighed into his harmonica.

Marilyn Albion was surprised to hear these words from Billy Steinway. He was so ofthepeoplebythepeople and here he was talking about the blue-eyed-blonde suicided sex goddess.

The right of genius, thought Marilyn.

> Tranquillity Base here. The *Eagle* has landed. Welcome to *terra nullius,* or no-man's-land, as this moon of earth was declared by Washington and Moscow in 1966.

MOONWALK

The shadows played across the screen as the first man stepped outside. It was 10:56 P.M. Eastern Daylight Time, July 20, Sunday. At first there appeared to be Hollywood klieg lights on the moon, but in fact it was the harsh lunar morning playing across the ashen surface.

Marilyn touched Billy Steinway's white, pock-marked face. She hadn't noticed its imperfections before, but these scars only intensified Billy's charm, as President Kennedy's pain had heightened his beauty for her mother.

Neil Armstrong placed one of his hoofed boots onto *terra nullius.*

"Nine and a half," said Billy Steinway.

Marilyn remained silent for the explanation. None came.

"What?" she prodded, bravely preferring not to feign understanding.

"His foot. It's a size nine and a half."

Armstrong had just said something, but they both missed it, and now the astronauts were bouncing around in the one-sixth gravity like Tweedledum and Tweedledee.

> *Will you, won't you, will you,*
> *won't you, will you,*
> *join the dance?*

Marilyn Albion and Billy Steinway moved through space, exploring the new world, removing their earth suits. Billy Steinway ran his fingers over the exotic virgin landscape, where no man had gone before. Marilyn reached down as they rolled space-brained and body-drunk. She picked up a strange exotic artifact, a book entitled *The Apollo Rhyming Dictionary.*

Marilyn said, "This is like finding a paint-by-number kit in Michelangelo's rumpus room."

The astronauts planted a three-foot by five-foot American flag that appeared to be flying in the dead air by means of thin wires that held it erect forever.

> *Oh, say can you see*
> *By the moon's lunar light*

The astronauts stood at attention near the rigid flag as President Richard Nixon placed a phone call from the White House to the moon. Hell of a toll charge. Twenty-four billion dollars.

Marilyn and Billy, naked except for Billy's harmonica and rack, stood at attention and saluted the president.

The president said, "This certainly has to be the most historic phone call ever made. . . ."

Marilyn ran her hands over her breasts, and Mrs. Finnegan's ghost preened.

The astronauts spoke:

> **ALDRIN:** Beautiful view!
> **ARMSTRONG:** Isn't that something? Magnificent sight out
>   here.
> **ALDRIN:** Magnificent desolation.

Billy Steinway, all parts at attention, breathed on the
harmonica and his voice, in fine bagpipe form, sang:

> *Women do seem to have more control*
> *But its only because*
> *you can't see their hello*
> *harmonica*
> *o harmonica*
> *o motorcade of harmonicas*
> *My blue-eyed, blond goddess*
> *Oh say I'm the lotus*
> *You'd sit upon*
> *Get your kicks from*

Marilyn Albion felt like an alien. Billy Steinway, liberal
ringmaster, believed in the blue-eyed, blond goddess.
Marilyn thought, if he thinks I'm the goddess, maybe I am.

> *Here she comes,*
> *Miss Radical America*

LIFT OFF
The astronauts lifted off, leaving behind a tiny silicon disk
with words, 200 times reduced, of presidents Eisenhower,
Kennedy, Johnson, and Nixon, and the leaders of seventy-
two different countries. A cosmic fortune cookie.

You will travel to strange lands.
You will meet distant relations.

They lifted to couple with the command module, a move that required surgical precision. If handled clumsily, they would be unable to dock with the *Columbia* or would smash themselves to their death onto the moon.

Billy Steinway explored and plowed and fantasized a life-size, blow-up party doll with a wide-open Marilyn Monroe mouth.

As they orbited over the desolate landscape below, one of the astronauts reported, focusing on a triangular-shaped peak,

"Just going over Mount Marilyn."

> *But square cut or pear shaped,*
> *These rocks don't lose their shape*
> *In one-sixth gravity*
> *No rust*
> *No erosion*

The spaceship passed over Sidewinder and Diamondback, twin winding rills in the lunar face.

Astronaut Collins commented, "It looks like a couple of snakes down there in the lake bed."

Billy Steinway lifted himself from Marilyn Albion, having given the great hello to her landscape. But Billy Steinway, folkmaster deluxe, did not give her time to wave back. Wave to Mr. . . .

Billy spoke: "And the serpent charmed the woman into eating from the Tree of Life, and she gained the knowledge of Good and Evil, and she in turn charmed Adam and got them both thrown out of Eden. Armageddon photo-play."

Billy Steinway turned his bare back on Marilyn and watched the television.

SPLASHDOWN

> If the controls fail, the spacecraft could reenter the earth's atmosphere at too steep an angle. The craft could burn to a cinder. Or it could reenter at so flat an angle that it would bounce off the outer rim of the atmosphere and ricochet deep into space, where its oxygen would eventually be exhausted.

Marilyn's fingertips felt numb as she touched the crumbs that were scattered over the beige floor. The air was too thin here. She dressed as the moonsteps were re-replayed on Billy Steinway's black-and-white television. Riveted to the repetitive pictures, Billy sat on the floor. Smoking his Marlboro, harmonica spent, shades drawn, his dog-eared *Apollo Rhyming Dictionary* at his side, he glanced up at Marilyn and said, "The cow jumped over the moon." He smiled softly, suffering beauty/beast revolutionary, as Marilyn backed out of the Crater of Desolation and opened the front door, closing it softly behind her. She was certain that she would be useful raw material for lyrics on Billy's next hit album.

Marilyn Albion stood on the steps of the town house, the bright Boston sun overhead. Her feet were hot, but her hands were cold. Atop the belfry of the Church of the Holy Bean Blowers across the street, where cherubs blew spitballs at the passersby, the loon screamed with betrayed desire. Marilyn Albion knew exactly how the loon felt.

Marilyn walked along the sidewalk that sparkled like a broken mirror, and as she passed the newsstand, she saw that the typesetters had broken out their Second Coming typeface to report the lunar cupcakewalk of Misters Tweedledum and Tweedledee.

Marilyn Albion descended into the belly of the subway and sat inside the lunatic green subway car en route to the boardwalk at Revere Beach. Marilyn wanted to see the sideshow freaks. Marilyn wanted to ride the rickety roller coaster. Marilyn wanted to shoot the sitting ducks with a high-powered rifle. The subway car screeched and sparks flew from the electric third rail.

Would not, could not, would not,
could not, would not
join the dance.

CHAPTER 15

The Crowning

Atlantic City, September 1969

Betty Bloom's Thunderbird convertible tore along the final stretch of the coast road to Atlantic City. The September winds whipped through the open car, but Betty Bloom, Jackie Bright, and Marilyn Albion liked their hair to have that windblown look. They were, after all, radicals.

"I don't want to do it," said Marilyn Albion. "Why don't you do it, Betty?" Billy Steinway had joked about women's liberation, and Marilyn Albion did not want to be a joke, especially not on a national basis.

"I wouldn't be as convincing," said Betty Bloom. "You've got all that blond hair. Use it for the women's movement!"

Marilyn Albion never ceased to be amazed at the political power of hair.

Jackie Bright put her hand on Marilyn's shoulder. "Your father's the mayor of Boston. If you do it, it will attract attention."

"I attract attention anyway," said Marilyn. "If there was a real revolution, I'd probably be the first one to get my head chopped off. There it'd go, rolling down Beacon Hill."

"Marilyn," said Jackie Bright. "Sometimes sacrifices have to be made."

"But why should I do it?"

"Because you could actually win. You could actually be Miss America. And when you pop out of the coffin, the nation will be watching." Jackie paused for the coup de grace: "Walter Cronkite will say your name."

Marilyn Albion was seduced by the idea of Walter Cronkite saying her name. Walter Cronkite had never, as yet, said Kate Albion's name. Kate Albion would be impressed, perhaps even a little jealous. Kate would think twice about dismissing Marilyn.

"I'll do it," said Marilyn.

Marilyn Albion had never been to Atlantic City, had never seen the waves pounding against the dark sand beside the boardwalk. A tight little knot formed in her chest as she wondered if Billy Steinway had ever wandered past the tourist shops, the family stores, the overflowing bins of saltwater taffy, the Taylor's porkroll displays, the porcelain knickknacks. It was lunchtime as they drove along the sea. They passed a Woolworth's, and Marilyn snapped to attention.

"Let's go to Woolworth's for lunch!" she said.

Betty Bloom and Jackie Bright looked at Marilyn Albion with pity. "That is not cool," said Betty Bloom. Marilyn Albion was silent, but angry. She felt as if her religion had been insulted.

Leaning back in the convertible, Marilyn watched the large white powder-puff clouds transmute against the gray sky to form a great, tiered birthday cake that orbited Atlantic City in slow motion. Out from the birthday cake cloud popped a naked blonde, who was blown away in one big wind.

Marilyn seized the dashboard in her hands. She reconsidered the attractiveness of the role of debutante and eater of chocolate-covered cherries, as opposed to radical feminism. Marilyn Albion had a terrific imagination.

Betty Bloom pulled the Thunderbird to a stop alongside the long wooden boardwalk. Jackie Bright and Betty Bloom could barely contain themselves in their rush to join their sisters on the boardwalk in protest of the Miss America Pageant. Marilyn, however, would not get out of the Thunderbird.

Jackie Bright said quietly to Marilyn, "So do you want to go back to Revere Beach and shoot the fake ducks in the shooting gallery?"

"No."

"Or swallow a bottle of Nembutal on a Saturday night like Marilyn Monroe?"

"No."

"Or get paraded around the ballroom of the Ritz-Carlton by your father?"

"Well, maybe just a little I'd like to go dancing. But I'm afraid your mother already filled up his dance card," said Marilyn.

Jackie paused. "You could always join your mother in her atomic fallout shelter."

"Did you tell anyone about that?" asked Marilyn, feeling betrayed.

"No. Did you tell anyone about my mother?"

"No! How could you even ask me?"

"Then just get out of the car. Please. I put pennies on the MTA tracks for you. You could at least get out of the car for me."

Marilyn Albion felt it was a lot to ask for a flattened President Lincoln penny, but she also did not want to be left out. It was lonely in her bedroom with the Schrafft's chocolate boxes and her mother demanding to know what she planned to do for her country.

"Apologize," said Marilyn.

"For what?" asked Jackie.

"Both of you," said Marilyn.

"What's the matter, Marilyn? This is Atlantic City. Over there is the protest. Let's go!" said Betty Bloom.

"Apologize for making fun of Woolworth's," said Marilyn. "I think it's very classist of you both."

That hurt. That dug in beneath Betty and Jackie's political fingernails. It was too true.

"I'm terribly sorry, Marilyn. I had no idea how you felt," said Betty.

"It's Mrs. Finnegan's memory you insulted," said Marilyn, delighted to at last be the one in the group who was politically correct.

"I said I'm sorry," said Betty. "Jackie. Apologize to Marilyn."

"I'm sorry, Marilyn," said Jackie, with questionable sincerity. "Will you now grace us with your presence?"

Marilyn Albion graced them with her presence. They

boldly linked arms and walked toward the protest at the boardwalk. They wore boots, jeans, and leather jackets. Marilyn, however, had discreet lace around her neck and wrists. She couldn't resist a little frill. No one wore a harmonica rack. No one stood out too much. But every woman was proud of her breasts. The more they hovered and rolled, the more powerful the woman felt. Mrs. Finnegan had believed that breasts were a woman's secret weapon, the envy of man. Mrs. Finnegan knew what's what.

It was a sparkling blue day, and as they neared the boardwalk, the two hundred assembled women hooted and cheered their approach. They recognized each other immediately because they were wearing the same uniform. Young drunk men along the way offered such interesting commentary as, "What are ya? A pack of lezzies?" and "All you need's a good fuck." But Marilyn saw that there were also young couples, holding their children, standing and staring at them in true confusion. Marilyn stared back at them, just as confused. They smiled. She smiled. It was better than suffocating in the thin air on the moon in Billy Steinway's apartment.

After a short powwow, a coven's worth of feminists formed a line, with Marilyn discreetly placed at one end. Marilyn leaned into Jackie Bright's ear and said, "David would have liked this."

"He's busy trying to levitate the Pentagon," said Jackie.

Marilyn thought about that as, following the lead of the other women, she rolled up her jeans and displayed her legs. She lifted a Lady Schick razor high above her head. The cameras closed in, finding Marilyn's legs especially interesting.

Guerrilla theater was in the making, and the sacrifice would be the blond Noxema girl's shaving cream ad, where she talked like a stripper, mugged the camera, and said, "Take it off. Take it all off."

The feminist can-can line slid the razors along their legs and sang to the accompaniment of an all-woman jug band.

Da da daaaaa

        bump

Da da da dah

        bump

Da da daaaaa

        bump

Da da da dah

        grind

The young drunk men cheered, believing all to be right again in the world, and the surprised camera crews zeroed in for the unexpected feminist cheesecake. A covert signal was given, and the women, including Marilyn Albion, Jackie Bright, and Betty Bloom, dug the razors deeply into their skin. Blood rolled down their legs.

The women proceeded as if nothing unusual was happening, as if they were happy mannequins with great big electroshock smiles, but the horrified young men and the camera crews turned their heads in disgust. Congratulatory war whoops from the other women protesters greeted the conclusion of their little theater piece.

Marilyn examined the drained ampule of chicken blood that she had concealed in her palm. Marilyn Albion was enjoying herself as the late afternoon sun hung low on the horizon. Revolution could be fun.

It was early evening when Marilyn entered Convention Hall. The hall was concrete, stark and cold, not something you could lay your weary head upon, and the audience did its best to make itself comfortable on the hard metal folding chairs. Marilyn was shocked by the hall. Over the years, as she had watched the pageant on television, it had appeared so sumptuous. But in truth, Convention Hall in Atlantic City had the kind of decor one could expect at a rodeo or a livestock show. There was, however, one little slice of beauty: where the cameras were aimed.

Dressed in polite dresses and polite shoes, holding little purses, Jackie and Marilyn joined the twenty fake ladies, feminist infiltrators in high drag, and took their seats in the balcony of Convention Hall. Marilyn Albion was wearing a pair of wrist-length white gloves. She was disappointed at the ugliness of the palace of beauty pageantry, where the women wore big stuck smiles like cocktail waitresses working for tips, and smeared a sheen of Vaseline on their teeth. Oh, well, thought Marilyn Albion, not everyone can be a Kennedy.

Marilyn took a seat at the end of the infiltrators, and focused her attention on the slice of beauty in front of the cameras. Abruptly, a young man in his early twenties sat in the vacant seat beside her. His hair was tied tightly at the nape of his neck by a piece of rawhide. He was thin but muscular, and wore jeans, brown boots, and a brown leather jacket. His face was unusually handsome, his eyes a striking green. A light brown pencil-thin moustache, groomed in the Fu Manchu style, delighted Marilyn. The man was alone, and he looked deeply into Marilyn's eyes and nodded, as if she were expecting him. Marilyn felt like the little girl tied to the bow of the *Hesperus,* and she leaned away from the man and toward Jackie Bright, who was seated beside her.

Bert Parks walked onto the stage, the ultimate game show host. Marilyn missed David Marat for a moment and then dismissed him. The last time she'd seen David, he was at the Blue Lagoon, discussing a trip to Canada to keep his body parts intact. Bert Parks did a full turn in his tuxedo, the cameras rolled, and the show began its international telecast.

"Good evening, ladies and gentlemen," said Bert Parks. "Welcome to the Miss America Pageant."

This was the signal. The feminists looked to the east. The feminists looked to the west. The feminists erupted from undercover into loud unladylike yells. Over the metal railing they threw girdles, bras, wigs, false eyelashes, and instructions for operating the Hoover Princess Deluxe vacuum cleaner. A banner fell open declaring women's liberation, and one wild-eyed woman—Marilyn could hardly believe her eyes but yes! it was Betty Bloom! how did she get down there?—ran past the judges spraying Toni hair spray in toxic clouds above their heads. Marilyn spontaneously stood and shouted "Duck and cover!" and in her enthusiasm came perilously close to falling over the balcony rail. The young man beside her slipped his arm around her waist and gently stabilized her. Marilyn was furious at the idea of this strange man touching her, even if his touch was as pleasant as a mild drug.

"Don't touch me again," said Marilyn Albion. The young man was not watching Marilyn. He ran his finger along his thin moustache as he looked in all directions around her, patient and vigilant as the man who held the black box in his lap and sat behind President Kennedy. The man beside Marilyn then sat in his seat as Marilyn sat down and neatly arranged her dress.

Politically incorrect objects stopped dropping from the balcony as security guards escorted the slogan-shouting feminists from Convention Hall. The nation and the world saw an unusually long series of commercials on their television screens.

Marilyn Albion sat very politely in her seat, staring at the strange man beside her. Then on the floor at her feet, she saw a compact mirror that had been tossed up into the air, fallen, and cracked on the cold cement. She felt sad and a little lost, and she wanted to go to Woolworth's.

The security guards did not remove Marilyn Albion and her wrist-length white gloves from Convention Hall because the gentleman seated beside Marilyn had raised his arm along the back of her chair. Marilyn let him, and she watched as Jackie Bright struggled with a security man who was leading her away by the arm with unnecessary roughness. Jackie turned and locked eyes with Marilyn, and Marilyn turned away from her, straightening her little white gloves and trying to piece together the broken compact.

"Collaborator!" shouted Jackie Bright.

Marilyn remained uncomfortably in her metal chair, watching the stage. The chairs on one side of Marilyn were now abandoned, and the pageant continued as the contestants began their swimsuit promenade. It brought tears to Marilyn's eyes. It was so lovely to see people do things together. But this lovely choreography was not enough to keep Marilyn Albion in her seat. She stood up to leave, and the young man said, "My name's Jones."

"Good-bye, Mr. Jones," said Marilyn Albion.

Marilyn took off her white gloves and tossed them gently toward the cold metal railing, but Mr. Jones plucked them from the air.

WOOLWORTH'S BY NIGHT
In the cool of the September evening, Marilyn walked along the sidewalk, the light sea breeze blowing the folds

of her dress between her legs. She felt as if she were being followed, but when she looked back, she could see only a brown-clothed figure, neither man nor woman, with very long and wavy hair. "The Banshee could get her comb through that hair easily enough," thought Marilyn.

The figure looked like John the Baptist one moment and a drug pusher the next, and then sometimes it resembled Joan of Arc. Marilyn wondered if this creature were insane or just another admirer. She did not feel safe, but she was too embarrassed at not being thrown out of Convention Hall to return to the boardwalk. She slowed down to look at the sea, and the figure slowed down. It watched her. She could sense its breathing, which it had timed with hers. She walked away quickly, her heels clicking on the silvered sidewalk, but the figure hovered at her back like a loose kite that could slam down on her at any sudden loss of wind.

She stopped and looked dead-on at the figure, and it took this as an invitation to approach her.

"You're so beautiful, I'm overcome. I believe I saw you earlier today in my meditation." Marilyn now saw that it was Mr. Jones. He had untied his hair, and it was as long as a woman's.

Marilyn studied Mr. Jones. She had never seen anyone quite like him. He was not like David Marat, sincere and recreationally drugged. He was certainly not like Billy Steinway, who, although the winner of the cupcakewalk, was nevertheless marooned forever 'neath the streets of Americana.

"What's your name?" said Mr. Jones.

"Marilyn."

"Marilyn," he repeated. "Mine's Yogi. Yogi Jones."

Yogi Jones smiled. There was something about this man that made Marilyn think he was a liar. She was afraid of him, even if he was handsome, even if he did have beautiful hair.

"Like Yogi Bear?" How strange, thought Marilyn. Someone named after a cartoon.

"Not like Yogi Bear. Yogi as in India. As in enlightenment." His voice was like a narcotic, and Marilyn could see and feel that this man was obsessed with her.

There was a long sterile pause.

"You were born with a purpose," said Mr. Jones. "I can see it. You have the Goddess within you. The kundalini waits to crawl up your spine." Mr. Jones ran his hand through his hair to push it back from his face. This was a movement Marilyn had seen President Kennedy perform.

Invisible fingers of fear and unwanted possession ran along Marilyn's back. She continued to walk toward Woolworth's, the twilight ready to crash into night.

"I know who you are," said Mr. Jones, following like a good dog or a bad dog, Marilyn could not decide.

"So do I," said Marilyn.

"No. I'm the voice crying in the wilderness to announce you."

Marilyn smiled. Never let a crazy person know that you know he's crazy. Kate Albion had said that at one time in reference to a particular member of the local Democratic committee.

"You mean a voice crying in Woolworth's?" she said.

"The humor of the divinity," said Yogi Jones. "Your beauty betrays your mission."

"My mission?" said Marilyn. Everyone thinks I have a mission, thought Marilyn.

"You are here as the ecstatic incarnation of woman, and I am here to honor it."

Marilyn wondered if Yogi Jones had any chocolate-covered cherries in his pockets. His flattery was cracking her clarity, but not enough to let him join her. She found him disturbingly feminine, yet highly sensual in a very male style.

"I have to go now," she said, but he persisted in following her.

There it was. Woolworth's. And it was open.

Marilyn entered slowly and was relieved that Yogi Jones did not follow. In a state of hello, he pulled his own hair tightly back from his forehead and leaned against the outer wall of Woolworth's to await Marilyn Albion's return.

Marilyn entered slowly, half expecting to be greeted by Mrs. Finnegan, but Mrs. Finnegan was not there. There were, however, fallen angels very much like the ones in Boston, glistening in their uniforms. Above them were the cardboard cutouts of a triple banana split and a hot fudge sundae with a cherry on top, dangling from the ceiling on long strings, catching the blasts of wind from the rotating fans. Before them were the Boston cream and lemon meringue pies in their go-go-girl spinning booths, hermetically sealed to retain freshness. Marilyn wanted to stay in Woolworth's forever. There was enough food and entertainment for quite a while. Dangerous men were not allowed to pass by the book racks and the small tender plants.

Marilyn Albion took a seat on the red leather stool. The silver chrome side-plating still shone like Flash Gordon's spaceship. She was rounder now. She was a young woman. Marilyn smiled.

"My feet touch the ground now," she said to the Fallen Angel behind the counter. The angel's bright blue eyelids fluttered, and her ruby lips puckered as she licked the tip of her pencil and poised it for Marilyn Albion's order. Marilyn picked up the distinct aroma of the perfume, Nights of Araby, Mrs. Finnegan's and Nellie Kelly's favorite. A deep sadness invaded Marilyn. Great Aunt Nellie Kelly had been on tour ever since Mrs. Finnegan's death. Nothing short of a visitation from beyond the grave would bring Nellie Kelly back. Marilyn reached deep into herself. It was important to carry on.

"Hot dog on a grilled roll, please. And orangeade," said Marilyn.

A flourish of paper and pencil, a knowing nod.

The broken compact had broken Marilyn's heart. How foolish. How sentimental. She felt like a traitor to the protest, but she did not want to turn her back on Mrs. Finnegan's memory. How could she crush underfoot the little mirror? After all, she had learned at Mrs. Finnegan's knee that a girl has to make friends with her reflection, "or it's off to tic toc electroshock," as Great Aunt Nellie had described it.

Marilyn leaned on the counter and said to the blue-haired counter lady, "Beyond good and evil, there's a little dab of makeup." The counter lady winked and pursed her lips, seeming to recognize the Finneganism.

Marilyn ate her hot dog on a grilled roll and drank her orangeade, the counter service being, as usual, prompt and impeccable. She rested her breasts upon the counter top and appreciated how large they had grown. This comforted her.

"Never go out without your warpaint, Marilyn, and always remember that the only difference between you and a man is . . ." At this, Mrs. Finnegan discreetly cupped her breasts in her hands. "He'll never have these. And he'll never get over it."

Marilyn studied her breasts, and thought of Yogi Jones outside of Woolworth's. She was afraid of him, but she was curious. She knew she could rule him, like her mother ruled Joe Albion, but she wasn't sure she was strong enough for that. One mistake, the tables would turn, and she would be the possession of an obsessed man.

"It's getting time to close, honey," said the counter lady, pulling off her brown hair net and shaking her hair loose. It was almost ten o'clock. The grand finale of the protest was due to start in thirty minutes.

Betty Bloom and Jackie Bright passed through the portals of Woolworth's Five and Dime and took seats on either side of Marilyn Albion at the lunch counter.

"I knew you'd be here," said Jackie Bright.

"You got scared, right?" said Betty Bloom.

Marilyn was so happy to see them because she would now be able to escape Yogi Jones.

"All you have to do is jump out of the coffin and say, 'I am the Anti-Marilyn,' " said Betty.

"The Anti-Marilyn," said Marilyn Albion. "And Walter Cronkite will say my name."

"Yes," said Jackie Bright.

Marilyn had absently cupped one heavy breast discreetly in one hand and looked at herself in the Woolworth's lunch-counter mirror. She saw that she was surrounded by a bright white light. Walter Cronkite would say her name over national television if she jumped out of the coffin, a sort of women's movement version of a girl in a cake. Marilyn felt a wave of guilt because she was being asked to desecrate the memory of Miss Monroe, but she also felt a surge of arousal for the first time since Billy Steinway. "Marilyn Albion" from the lips of Mr. Walter Cronkite would make it all worthwhile, and it would certainly compel her mother's attention and respect. For at least a minute.

Marilyn said, "Woolworth's is lovely, dark, and deep, but I have promises to keep."

Marilyn tipped heavily and walked outside, flanked by the exuberant Jackie and Betty. Only Marilyn took note of Yogi Jones, who was still leaning against the outside of Woolworth's eating penny candies on the dark side of the moon. Marilyn's heart went out to him because he seemed so alone, because she was compassionate, because empty candy wrappers had fallen around his ankles. He ran his finger along his thin moustache and smiled.

The newswoman in her gray suit and pink shirt, with matching gray pumps, spoke in that trained flatland commentary voice, even though she was from New Jersey:

> Inside Convention Hall, they are down to the last five contestants. Outside Convention Hall, a coven of BITCH members, representing "Bitch's International Terrorist Conspiracy from Hell," led by Betty Bloom, is attempting to levitate Convention Hall in preparation for a Second Coming, which they promise will occur. And ladies and gentlemen. Believe me. It's going to be a "She."

Betty Bloom, surrounded by two hundred spirited women, lifted her black-cloaked arms and spaketh unto the denizens of the female netherworld.

"Lift up and throw to the ground like a broken toy this monument to the shame and degradation of womankind! O Emily Dickinson! Aren't you pissed?"

"Yes!" shouted the women, raising their fists toward heaven like divine barbarians.

The newswoman's hand quivered expectantly as she looked down the boardwalk . . .

"O Sojourner Truth!"

past the shops . . .

"Elizabeth Blackwell!"

the family stores . . .

"Louisa May Alcott!"

the saltwater taffy . . .

"Susan B. Anthony!"

the Taylor's porkroll . . .

"Mary Wollstonecraft!"

and the porcelain knickknacks. . . .

"Tina Turner!"

"Tina Turner?" said Starshine O'Schwartz.

At the other end of the boardwalk, Marilyn Albion climbed into the pine coffin and lay down. Her sisters encircled her, and Marilyn Albion remembered Mrs. Finnegan, and how the Woolworth's counter ladies and her mother had anointed and primped her corpse.

Marilyn heard a man's voice say, "What are these women doing?" She recognized it as the voice of Yogi Jones. Marilyn laughed as loud as a boy and wondered if this was "being on tour." Her laughter triggered a laughing spell among the sisters. They closed the lid carefully, and Jackie leaned into one of the air holes.

"Are you all right, Marilyn?" she asked.

"Sometimes," whispered Marilyn Albion, "it's important to go as close to the edge as possible, as close to out of control as Marilyn Monroe."

Jackie Bright stepped back in alarm from Marilyn Albion's unfamiliar voice as the sisters hoisted Marilyn in her pine coffin high upon their shoulders. They were as strong as men, as strong as the Woolworth's counter ladies had been. They sang Marilyn's praises as they walked along: her beauty, her passion, her sense of fashion. The coffin swayed like a little boat rocking in the beautiful dark Atlantic.

The funeral procession proceeded along the boardwalk, the coffin balanced on the shoulders of six feminists and encircled by seven solemn women bearing candles and flowers.

> **"What appears to be a coffin is being carried toward the steps of Convention Hall," said the newswoman.**

As Betty Bloom saw the approach of the coffin, she heightened in enthusiasm.

"O Gertrude Stein! O Julia Child!"

Marilyn Albion breathed heavily and fought the mild nausea induced by the uneven rocking and the muffled pounding of the waves outside the pine box. She had given her body to the women's movement, but the air was unexpectedly thin. She remembered the overflowing flower car following Mrs. Finnegan's hearse, the bright spectacle of a happy good-bye.

"Cast out the demons of Toni and Tonette," commanded Betty Bloom.

> **The protesters have explained that the purpose of this funeral is to expose the fact," said the newswoman, "that women in this society must play dead to keep alive.**

Marilyn heard that. Good point. Mrs. Finnegan would have agreed.

"O souls of the copy-cat deaths of Marilyn Monroe, who swallow sleeping pills on Saturday nights . . ."

Marilyn heard that, too.

The women began to beat on drums, crash finger cymbals, wave lights. Marilyn wished she could see it. It was probably as pretty as Sputnik and Telstar on a clear night.

The knotty-pine coffin was placed in the center of the BITCH circle, amidst great photo-play. There was absolute silence as the drum beat out a voodoo cadence. At its crescendo, the lid burst open for the Second Coming, and Marilyn Albion rose up happy with divine oxygen, radiant as a new-made animal. She locked her knees in an openlegged stance, threw her pelvis back and her chest forward. Heavy with energy, thick blond hair streaming in the sea breeze, Marilyn Albion smiled into the sizzling light bulbs. She was aware of the location of every camera as she adjusted her breasts in a manner strangely reminiscent of Mrs. Finnegan.

Yogi Jones came into Marilyn's sight line, and although her curiosity remained, she no longer feared him. After all, she had just risen up from the dead, and Walter Cronkite would soon say her name. Marilyn knew she would dominate Yogi, sooner or later, with his permission.

Betty Bloom placed the victory wreath of Athena upon Marilyn Albion's head.

"Who are you?" cried Betty Bloom to Marilyn. Her rehearsed "Anti-Marilyn" response would be sure to make a great headline.

Marilyn Albion looked to the east. Marilyn Albion looked to the west. Marilyn Albion said with sexy grace, as she cupped her heavy breasts in her hands, "He'll never have these, and he'll never get over it!"

The feminists cheered and Marilyn Albion said, "Listen to me, Walter Cronkite! Let me tell you all about it!"

Late that evening, on national television, Kate Albion and Joe Albion watched Walter Cronkite raise his right eyebrow, which pulled up the right corner of his mouth ever so slightly. His eyes twinkling, unnervingly riveted into the camera's heart, he smiled like a secret lover and said, "Tonight, Marilyn Albion, the daughter of the mayor of Boston, told me all about it, and I'll never get over it. Thank you, Marilyn."

Kate Albion was mesmerized but turbulent with mixed emotion. "What the hell is she doing," said Kate, "hanging out with a bunch of lesbians? Does she have to insult Miss America? What will this do to our future? To the governorship? Look at her hair! It looks like she hung out at the third rail a little too long!"

"She's having fun, darling," said Joe. "And I didn't see more than one, maybe two lesbians in the group."

Kate shot up from her seat, fists clenched, hair on edge, dangerously close to short-circuiting. Joe Albion was absolutely delighted that Marilyn had not only Walter Cronkite's complete attention, but Kate's as well.

"Relax, darling. It's just a young girl spreading her wings," said Joe.

"I'll spread your wings, you son of a bitch," said Kate. Kate had been so damned superior to him lately, just because he had a mistress, that Joe Albion had absolutely no sympathy for her devil.

Against the news credits, the newsroom again ran Marilyn's coffin extravaganza scene in Atlantic City. Angry and jealous, Kate stormed into the kitchen for her Alka-Seltzer. She was unable to predict the political ramifications of Marilyn's behavior, but most importantly, she was shocked that her daughter was so out of her control.

Mayor Joe Albion, however, had one of the heartiest laughs he'd had in a long time. And he believed there would be no political ramifications. He knew that the antics of a girl could never affect the true course of history.

Wave to the cameras, Marilyn.
Wave to the cameras.

Part Four

CHAPTER 16

Alpha/Omega House

September 1970

The black stretch limousine slipped through the September evening, the air a crystal bell reflecting sound as distinctly as each instrument in the perfect symphonic orchestra: car doors closing, heels hitting pavement, dogs barking in the distance, keys jangling on dangling rings, BITCH covens incanting against the evils of game-show-host worship.

I'll take ritual sacrifice for one hundred, Bill.

Freddie Finney parked the limousine in front of the large, brown-shingled house with the sprawling green lawn, incandescent under the stately glow of the Revolution-era, black iron street lamps. The vacant lot next door to the house was grassless, rocky, and desolate, an urban moonscape. A wide porch ran the length of the front of the house, and the paint was peeling from its face and sides. At the correct angle and by the light of the full moon, it was said that you could see in the pattern of the peeling paint the distinct outline of a naturally created feminist Mount Rushmore, consisting of the wise profiles of Susan B. Anthony, Elizabeth Stanton, Mary Wollstonecraft, and Sojourner Truth.

The twenty-foot letters A and Ω, like show-and-tell from a giant's alphabet book, were side by side at the crown of the roof. They were lit up like an A&P supermarket sign.

Two identical women stopped gliding on the porch swing and sprung to their feet, revealing long black dresses, with bright-red long underwear tastefully exposed at the neck, elbows, and ankles—devotees of the devil-may-care school of fashion. Their thick waves of long red hair made them unmistakable: they were the famous hyperactive radical twins, Molly and Dolly Gunn, in person.

The screen door swung open and a tall woman emerged. She lifted her long brown hair from her face and revealed shocking green eyes. Her eyes had the permanent expression of an Egyptian cat about to be disemboweled and buried along with its recently dead queen: flattered yet horrified. This striking creature positioned herself at the top of the steps. She was Christina Smythe-Corduroy Stuckey, founder of the feminist counter-sorority, Alpha/Omega House. Alpha/Omega House promised its members that womankind would have the last word.

Christina had declared: "No man has ever set cloven hoof within these doors, and no man ever shall. Not even a plumber."

Freddie Finney, chauffeur's cap jauntily in place, opened the rear door of the limousine. Marilyn Albion and Jackie Bright stepped out onto the sidewalk to survey their new home, leather jackets glistening, boots vibrating with anticipation, jeans snug but not trashy. So fabulous had been the response to the Atlantic City Action, also known as the Miss America Pageant Protest, that under Betty Bloom's sponsorship, Marilyn and Jackie had been offered tenure in Alpha/Omega House for the duration of their stay at Boston University.

Freddie Finney closed the car door for the two eighteen-year-old radical feminists, opened the trunk, and pulled their luggage onto the sidewalk. Marilyn and Jackie headed up the pathway to the front door, Christina Smythe-Corduroy Stuckey's broad smile looming larger and larger, like one of those Macy's Thanksgiving Day Parade helium balloons. Freddie followed behind, dragging makeup kits and steamer trunks.

Christina Smythe-Corduroy Stuckey was the kind of woman who, five years earlier, would either have formed a civic organization such as Debutantes for World Peace or thrown herself into electrocution upon the third rail of the MTA. Since it was 1970, she was instead the founding mother of BITCH.

Molly and Dolly Gunn, who stood beside her on the porch, were the self-avowed lunatic fringe of the women's movement. They had never, and would never be, invited to a National Organization for Women strategy session.

Christina spoke to Marilyn and Jackie as if she were

rolling a hot potato around in her mouth. "We're honored to have you both here. But 'that' is not to set a foot on these steps."

Freddie Finney had been called a lot of things, but never "that." "That" was low, especially from a woman. Marilyn smiled uncomfortably.

Jackie Bright, however, wanted to fling herself into Christina's arms and sob with relief that in this vast world someone finally had some common sense.

Freddie Finney scowled at Christina, his eyes hard and cold like little discarded rocks he'd love to place in a slingshot and aim at Miss Stuckey.

"I'll take these by way of the servant's entrance, Miss Albion," said Freddie.

"No!" said Molly and Dolly Gunn, leaping to the ground on either side of Freddie, four blue eyes pinballing at world-class speed. He was shook up.

"Just leave the trunks there," said Dolly Gunn.

"We're not helpless, and we will not be made helpless by your male-chauvinist-pig attitudes," said Molly Gunn.

They hopped around Freddie, shadowboxing with each other.

"I'm not a chauvinist," replied Freddie Finney icily. "I'm a chauffeur." The mayor wasn't going to like this. Not one bit, Freddie was sure.

Freddie, cool as a Popsicle, turned and walked down the pathway to the sidewalk, hoping nothing would hit his back but playing it a bit cocky, because, after all, these were girls, except for that big tall thing on the steps. If he was a "that," she was certainly a "thing."

Victoriously unscathed, he broke open the front door of the limousine and slammed it closed behind him. He turned the key in the ignition, and only then did he look back at Alpha/Omega House, expecting to see those nasty twins struggling with the luggage or staring after him, worried about his feelings and his possible violent retribution in the dead of night. The porch, however, was deserted, the luggage gone, the door to the house closed—the slight movement of the porch swing the only indication that lady life in all her glorious mutations had recently glided past.

Those sorority girls better shape up, thought Freddie Finney, or no man will buy them a Speed Queen washer and dryer in avocado green to make life easier. Freddie imagined them beating their clothes clean on the rocks in a suburban backyard, which made him feel good. He pulled away from the curb and cruised to the Blue Lagoon, where he was loved and appreciated.

Christina Smythe-Corduroy Stuckey took Marilyn and Jackie on a tour of Alpha/Omega House. Dolly and Molly led the way like inbred flower girls at a wedding.

There was an entrance hall, with a staircase to the bedrooms on the upper two floors. The lower floor was used as community space and a communications center. Long tables were set up in the living room, similar to the Tupperware demonstration tables. Kitchen chairs were scattered throughout the room, the legs sharply tangled in the hooked throw rugs that decorated the politically correct, gouged wood floors. A bright afghan was tucked over the long, overstuffed couch. A crystal chandelier in good condition hung incongruously from the ceiling, lighting the highly detailed map of Massachusetts that hung on the wall. Bright green tacks were stuck in the map.

"What are those tacks for?" asked Marilyn.

Christina smiled. "Those are our targets."

Marilyn noted there was a bright green target tack on City Hall. What if the madman pushes the button? thought Marilyn.

Three black rotary-dial desk telephones with long cords were on the tabletop, and Starshine O'Schwartz, looking ravishing in her new fall bundle of mixed wools and African dashikis, was working paste-up for the *BITCH Times*. Marilyn could not read the inverted letters.

MAYOR'S DAUGHTER JOINS BITCH

In the back of the first-floor area was a large dining room with more tables and unmatched chairs, and through a set of swinging double doors was a large kitchen with pots and pans hanging from hooks twisted into the ceiling. With so many women present, Marilyn had expected the great house to be filled with the aroma of baking cakes, but instead the house was permeated with the smell of mimeograph ink. The sound of the rotating drum and the round-the-clock *flup flup flup* of newly printed BITCH manifestos rolling hot off the mimeograph would, over the next four years, become so steady a background sound in Marilyn's consciousness that its absence would trigger paranoia.

"This is our forecaster," said Christina, introducing them to a tiny, wiry blond woman with Shirley Temple curls, who was madly spinning the barrel of the mimeo.

"I'm Marilyn Albion, and this is Jackie Bright."

The tiny curly-top shouted over the sound of the mimeo drum roll, "You're the Anti-Marilyn. Your coming was foretold. I got something in a Cornflakes box that looked intriguing, even for Kellogg's. I'm Felicity Cuntwise. Pleased to meet you."

Jackie was ecstatic. "Felicity Cuntwise," she said luxuriously and with great approval.

Marilyn thought "Cuntwise" a bit extreme.

"That's not my given name. It's 'Finney.' 'Cuntwise' is my taken name," confided Felicity. "Welcome to the revolution."

Betty Bloom, cool and radical, came down the stairs to greet Marilyn and Jackie. "Your rooms are next to mine, on either side," she said. Dolly and Molly Gunn had a special love of Betty Bloom, who still secretly believed in animal magnetism.

"I'll leave you women, now. But the house rules are: No hexing after ten," said Christina Smythe-Corduroy Stuckey, laughing at her own joke.

They watched Christina climb the staircase like the Tsarina Josephine, her Marlboro leaving a trail of smoke behind her. Jackie Bright was in love.

Marilyn Albion was surrounded by the Gunn twins, who touched her hair and patted her cheeks and took her by the hands up the staircase to her bedroom, her first room away from home. She wondered what Kate Albion would think of this. She had told her she was going to live at a sorority, having artfully omitted the word *counter*. Poor Joe Albion, mayor of Boston, would not be allowed to come into Alpha/Omega House.

> *In the room the women come and go*
> *Talking of Steinem, Friedan, and Sappho.*

Marilyn, in private at last, put away her clothes, slipped off her boots, and opened the window. The rarefied September air was sweet and intoxicating, but the serenity was disturbed by an animated figure jumping up and down on the edge of the green grass, waving to her and blowing kisses. Marilyn's heart pounded. Was it the hooded creature, neither man nor woman? Under the light of the iron street lamp, the creature revealed itself to be Yogi Jones, long brown hair flowing in the breeze.

"I love you! I love you! I'll die for you!" shouted Yogi.

This was not going to make a good impression for the first night, to have the enemy so infatuated.

Marilyn leaned out the window. "Go away, Mr. Jones."

"I shall treasure these words and interpret them the best I can for eternity."

"Just go away. There are electrical shock wires surrounding this house."

Yogi Jones spaketh to his Juliet:

> *O, speak again, bright angel, for thou art*
> *As glorious to this night, being o'er my head—*

"Yogi, you must understand the dialectical problem this is posing."

> *"As is a wingèd messenger of heaven*
> *Unto the white-upturnèd wond'ring eyes—*

"You're an embarrassment to your sex!"

> *"Of mortals that fall back to gaze on him*
> *When he bestrides the lazy puffing clouds*
> *And sails upon the bosom of the air."*

"Yogi, forget my bosom."

> *Shall I hear more, or shall I speak at this?*

At that Molly and Dolly Gunn leaped from the trees and surrounded Yogi Jones.

Using guerrilla Shakespeare, they spoke to each other as if Yogi were invisible, a tactic designed to fry the nerves of their prey.

"Where hast thou been, Sister?" inquired Dolly.

"Killing swine. Guess I missed one," replied Molly. "Sister, where thou?"

"Here I have a chauvinist's thumb, chopped off as homeward he did come."

Marilyn closed her window and drew the curtains to dissociate herself from Yogi Jones, who ran into the shadows as his instinct for self-preservation kicked in. Dolly and Molly Gunn pranced back into Alpha/Omega House.

Marilyn ran her hand through her hair. Hello hello, Yogi Jones, you naughty boy.

Candymad, Yogi Jones stood beneath the tree in the shadows, determined to protect the Anti-Marilyn.

Out of the dark side of the trees, he dragged a colorful tent onto the desolate empty lot beside Alpha/Omega. Having been a boy scout, he erected the tent in moments, a rainbow of color in an abandoned landscape. He fixed stakes into the ground and hung bright silver pots and pans from ropes. He strung small sterno lanterns on parallel cords, and fastened wind chimes to the tent's entrance. Inside his tent, he laid plush Moroccan pillows and blue satin sheets. A gold paper box of Schrafft's chocolates was just visible through the open tent flap. As the fresh coffee brewed, he set a small dish of birdseed upon a pedestal near the entrance to his tent. Yogi Jones was a seductive homemaker.

Christina Smythe-Corduroy Stuckey watched Yogi set up camp, then let the drape fall back across the window of her third-floor sitting room. She sat for tea with Dolly and Molly, who were hotly debating Kant's *Prolegomena to Any Future Metaphysics*.

Dolly Gunn said, "As far as it represents judgments as *a priori*, it constitutes transcendental concepts of pure reason."

Molly Gunn threw up her hands in frustration. " 'Pure' and 'reason' necessarily negate each other."

Christina's green eyes were looking at the Gunn twins, but she was seeing beyond the veil of the informal press blackout that had plagued her organization. Christina Smythe-Corduroy Stuckey knew she finally had a newsworthy resident from Boston's seat of power, a refugee from the dark side of the moon.

Marilyn Albion wanted to smoke a Virginia Slims cigarette as she turned off the lights and put her head on her pillow, but Virginia Slims were being boycotted. Marilyn Albion hoped that someone would create a feminist cigarette, perhaps pretzel shaped. Otherwise, she would settle for Tareytons.

Marilyn became drowsy, hypnotized by the chants of Betty Bloom next door. Muffled yet unmistakable words drifted through the wall: "imperialist . . . chocolates and blood . . . I may say no no no but do it again. . . ."

Marilyn Albion was startled into wakefulness, a sheen of mild fever on her skin. She was not sure if she had been asleep or awake, but even dreaming of Betty Bloom singing a Marilyn Monroe song qualified as a nightmare.

Marilyn Albion put on her yellow terry-cloth bathrobe and walked downstairs. She passed Felicity Cuntwise, who was spinning the mimeo drum by candlelight, an anachronistically medieval sight. Felicity smiled in the flickering flames. Marilyn masked her fear with a great big Kennedy smile and walked into the kitchen. She dropped two Alka-Seltzer tablets into a tall glass of water and watched them blow up.

> *Plop plop*
> *Fizz fizz*

Oh . . .
Do it again.

—

Photographic light bulbs flashed for a year around Marilyn Albion, and the local press—leftist, rightist, upist, downist—never tired of her.

MAYOR'S DAUGHTER IN FEMINIST SIT-IN

MARILYN NAUGHTY AGAIN

MARILYN NOMINATED B.I.T.C.H. OF THE YEAR

DOESN'T HER HEART BELONG TO DADDY ANYMORE?

SOME LIKE IT COLD

WHATEVER HAPPENED TO BABY MARILYN?

MARILYN HEXES FRANK SINATRA

GENTLEMEN DON'T PREFER FEMINISTS

THE SEVEN MONTH B.I.T.C.H. STRIKES AGAIN

THE BALL SOUP PAPERS AND THE DAUGHTER OF ALBION

In the vacant lot next door to Alpha/Omega, which Marilyn had designated as "the Moon," the ever-faithful Yogi Jones waited through the blizzards of winter, the minimonsoon of springtime, and now the passion of summer. For some reason, it was impossible to get the Boston police to evict him.

It was early in the evening on Friday, August 1, 1971. That morning, Christina Smythe-Corduroy Stuckey, Jackie Bright, Felicity Cuntwise, Starshine O'Schwartz, and the Gunn twins had gone for a day-long action at

Revere Beach. Marilyn Albion and Betty Bloom had remained behind. They had spent the day depressed, feverish, side by side on the overstuffed couch—the word *lipstick* having come up from the murky lagoon of repressed desire, only to sink back down into the heat of summer.

The mimeo drum was silent, and the two young women sat quiet and causeless in Alpha/Omega. At eight o'clock, Betty leaped to her feet and, with the speed and dexterity of the Gunn twins, negotiated the staircase to her room.

Marilyn was alone with the tic toc of the clock and no chocolates. She had rarely seen Joe and Kate, although they were only minutes away. Joe Albion thought Marilyn's behavior was cute, which made her angry, and Kate Albion refused to speak to Marilyn because of her irresponsible actions, which endangered her father's career and, according to Kate, the course of history. Marilyn Albion hoped ever so that she would alter the course of history, and there was a part of her that enjoyed taking on her mother with the same tactic her mother used: apparent dedication to a cause greater than herself.

The clock ticked, and Marilyn's thoughts shifted to Jackie Bright, who had become as submissive to Christina Smythe-Corduroy Stuckey as Frances Bright was to Joe Albion. David Marat was safe in Canada with his body parts intact, and Billy Steinway was semiretired in his beige, crumb-strewn world. Nellie Kelly was fairly senile, on a worldwide tour, still carrying on conversations with Mrs. Finnegan. Mrs. Finnegan must have turned in her grave when they allowed a man behind the counter of Woolworth's, even if they did call him a "soda jerk." Nostalgic, sleepy, with a taste for cherries, Marilyn Albion climbed the staircase to her room.

As she lay in her bed in the dark, she heard a strange sound through the wall from Betty Bloom's room. It sounded like a television, but it was certainly not tuned in to Public Broadcasting. There was the nasal sound of a man's voice, a woman's deep, rolling voice, and audience laughter. Marilyn Albion pressed herself against the wall.

Marilyn was stunned. Betty Bloom, who would ever have suspected Betty Bloom of tuning in to "The Sonny and Cher Comedy Hour"? There was the sound of Betty's muffled laughter and a lot of moving around. Marilyn couldn't hear the television. More movement. A phonograph record began to play Cher's "Gypsys, Tramps and Thieves" in monophonic echo-tin on Betty Bloom's cheap record player.

Marilyn Albion could not decide if she was delighted or betrayed, or if Betty Bloom had simply lost her mind. She left her room and stood in the hallway outside of Betty's door. Ignoring the Bill of Rights, Marilyn opened Betty's door without knocking.

Betty Bloom was stunning in a costume appropriate for a Las Vegas showgirl: feathers, beads, sequins, and heavy makeup suitable for the stage or a casket.

Betty Bloom spun around and saw Marilyn. Betty Bloom took the offensive and said, "I like to dress up, I love Cher, and I'm just as much of a feminist as any other woman."

Marilyn Albion moved her hips and raised her arms above her head. Her pent-up sexuality crawled up from her feet like a thirsty woman to an oasis and poured like Niagara as the 45 played the sacred Cher mantra over and over.

Marilyn said, amid gyrations, "My favorite Cher is still 'Bang Bang My Baby Shot Me Down.'"

"I've got that album!" said Betty Bloom.

In girl time they partied—erotic, dark-side-of-the-moon style—selling kisses for the milk fund but drinking the milk themselves. They were, after all, feminists.

Ms. Albion said to Ms. Bloom, "Let's go visit Yogi Jones."

"Both of us? At once?"

"Some people ask, 'Why?' I say, 'Why not?' "

Downstairs, the front door opened, and Christina Smythe-Corduroy Stuckey, followed by Jackie Bright, Felicity Cuntwise, Starshine O'Schwartz, and the Gunn twins, entered Alpha/Omega House.

But Marilyn and Betty did not hear them. They were busy dancing to "The Beat Goes On."

Christina, flanked by the sorority, arrived in the doorway of Betty Bloom's room as the Cher mantras played.

Marilyn and Betty dropped dead silent in Christina Smythe-Corduroy Stuckey's presence, and their flesh burned as red as the scarlet letter. They had been seduced by a slave of Las Vegas. They had almost gone to the tent of the infidel.

Bless me, Christina, for I have sinned.

In the heat of the August morning, Betty Bloom and Marilyn Albion wore black turtlenecks and sat for penance on the front porch, reading Betty Friedan's *The Feminine Mystique*. The Gunn twins sat on the porch swing, sullen and depressed, for they loved Betty and Marilyn and their animal magnetism. Yogi Jones sat in his tent, strategically placing the Schrafft's chocolate box so that it would reflect in the sun and draw Marilyn's eye to his tent.

Christina Smythe-Corduroy Stuckey sat on the front lawn with her back to Yogi Jones. She called into the house for Jackie Bright, who emerged immediately. As Jackie trotted down the steps, Marilyn, from the deluxe-perversion corner of her heart, barked. It was the first harsh sound that had ever passed between them. Jackie turned, her back on fire, in blinding, fury-crowned hostility. Marilyn was delighted: Jackie Bright was still alive.

Betty Bloom whispered to Marilyn Albion, "I'm sick of ball soup," but returned to the Book of Friedan. They had gone too far to go back, but as yet could not fathom where to go.

Marilyn Albion ran her hands over her breasts as she watched Jackie Bright take instructions from Christina Smythe-Corduroy Stuckey, and Yogi Jones jiggled his candy box.

Will you, won't you, will you,
won't you, will you
join the dance?

CHAPTER 17

The Bridal Fair

February 1972

Madison Square Garden was cold and ugly, and cluttered with wedding and bridesmaid gowns. Long tables bore little plastic pastel swans whose backs were filled with almonds, matching pastel netting securing their loads. Marilyn Albion closed her eyes and drifted on the swan boat through the lagoon in Boston's Public Gardens.

Marilyn Albion was a confederate for BITCH. They had not had an action in quite a while, and the bridal fair at Madison Square Garden seemed to be an opportune moment. Outside the Garden, her compatriots were carrying signs.

ASK NOT FOR WHOM

THE WEDDING BELL TOLLS

was Marilyn's favorite.

Marilyn Albion opened her eyes and walked to the seats on the 50th Street side of the Garden, where she had sat with Kate and Joe Albion for President Kennedy's birthday party. Marilyn Monroe had spoken to her then.

> **Be careful of history. It's just some guy in a suit telling a story.**

Marilyn Albion knew that it could just as well be some woman in an A-line dress, spikes, and white gloves telling a story.

Marilyn walked to where President Kennedy had been enthroned and sat in the seat behind his, the seat that had been occupied by the tall man with the crewcut, tan, and sunglasses. The Captain Marvel devotee had held the black box on his lap, the box with the green button that could signal the destruction of the world. Marilyn looked into her lap and tried to imagine possession of the black box and how it would make her feel. She remembered her mother's constant refrain: What if a madman pushes the button? Marilyn knew that women's liberation now expanded the roster of button pushers to madwomen.

Marilyn folded her hands on her lap and looked to the floor of the Garden. The president would have easily seen Miss Monroe's breasts from his seat. Wondering if he had spent much time as a boy looking up girl's dresses, Marilyn Albion smiled. President Kennedy's indiscretions had been charming because he had wit, and his vulnerability to women endeared him to them even if they were discarded like broken toys the day after Christmas.

Marilyn Albion watched the brides and their mothers swarm slowly past the bridal industry displays. The intimacy between mother and daughter was painful for her to observe. They seemed so welded to each other, so American dream–ish, so terribly clear on who they were, so much an extension of each other, reaching into the future, a chain of girls and women giving birth and exchanging recipes. Marilyn resented them. In spite of everything, she would like nothing better than for Kate Albion to help her select wedding favors. She would be proud and fulfilled to walk with her powerful mother, welded in mother-daughter bliss, past the cakes and gowns.

The Garden darkened and a hush as profound as when they play the mystery notes on "Name That Tune" fell across the crowd. The sounds of "The Wedding March" piped through the Garden as a painted, wooden, five-tier wedding cake revolved in a spotlight. A plastic bride and groom were cranked up in holy matrimony out of the top of the cake, and the audience burst into applause as the first model took to the runway, dripping with lace and chiffon, even if it was February and a light snow had begun to fall.

At that, Marilyn Albion looked to the east. Marilyn Albion looked to the west. Marilyn Albion saw that all was ready, and delayed.

"Where is love?" she said, but no one heard her. She remembered holding hands with little girls in the schoolyard and circling, orbiting to rhymes that would solve that riddle.

> *Turn to the east, Sally.*
> *Turn to the west, Sally.*
> *Turn to the very one*
> *That you like best.*

"Where is love?" she demanded of herself, but she had no answer, so Marilyn blew the whistle that signaled the release, from all four directions, of 500 white mice across the floor of the Garden.

The brides and their mothers ran for higher ground, and the models lifted their wedding gowns and veils and ran in hysterical circles, flashing like 120-pound toasters circling the globe, like wedding cakes on a crash course with history. The spotlights careened through the air, as at a Hollywood opening, trying to locate the source of the mice.

Marilyn sat in her seat like a lady and remembered Yogi Jones' chivalry at the Miss America Pageant. She wanted to master Yogi Jones, to practice being man and woman, but she was still not sure she could keep control of his obsession. If she lost control, she would become his party doll, like she had with Billy Steinway. If she kept the reins, she would be on an equal footing with her mother. Marilyn Albion longed for romance and her mother's respect.

From the secure distance of the doomsday seat, Marilyn watched BITCH conclude their hex and retreat with the brides and their mothers into the street. The Gunn twins, Jackie Bright, and Felicity Cuntwise discovered they did not have any greater affinity for 500 white mice than did the brides and their mothers, whom, in some instances, they beat in the footrace to the snowy outside.

Marilyn Albion felt no remorse.

She walked down to the deserted Garden and stood over a little pastel swan that had fallen and spilled its almonds onto the hard, cold floor. Marilyn was not afraid of the swarming white mice, but she was distorted with sexual desire and there seemed to be no way to satisfy herself without collaborating with the enemy.

There were 500 white mice scuttling along the floor in the darkness of Madison Square Garden, white mice about to turn into coachmen, coachmen with little checkered jackets, guiding six white horses, each one of them named Macaroni.

P_{AWS}

in the Name of Love

Early Summer 1972

In the warm twilight, beneath the trail of a brilliant summer sunset, Marilyn Albion stood in the gray dust outside of Yogi Jones' tent on the rocky, empty lot she had christened "the Moon." The wind chimes tinkled lazily and the sterno lanterns glowed, but the seductive beauty and peace was broken by the overhead screech of a loon that narrowly missed colliding with the twenty-foot letters *A* and *Ω* side by side at the crown of Alpha/Omega House.

Marilyn slowly drew the tent flap aside, her every

movement erotic to the surprised occupant. Yogi Jones did not move. He relaxed every muscle in his body. Marilyn saw that he did not want to frighten her away, and she smiled because she knew he was not in control. Yogi was sprawled upon thick Persian cushions like a refugee from the hippie movement. Kool-Aid green fabric lined the tent walls. The tent was much larger on the inside than it appeared from her window in Alpha/Omega House. Books on Eastern thought and treatises on enlightenment were stacked alongside the sleeping area. There was an entire section devoted to tantra and sex.

Marilyn lifted one of the books and fingered the pages. There were a number of positions illustrated in the book.

"What is tantra?" asked Marilyn, not looking at Yogi Jones but still examining the positions shown in the book.

"The object of tantra is to delay orgasm," said Yogi, "so as to reach a peak experience of enlightenment during the sexual act."

Marilyn was very interested in becoming enlightened during the sexual act. It was much more appealing than the traditional monastic vows of celibacy, poverty, and a large consumption of raw vegetables, which disturbed her digestion. Marilyn dropped the book on the futon bed. She noted the blue satin covers, the Moroccan pillows, the Schrafft's candy box. She believed the candy box to be a good omen and took it as a sign to claim Yogi Jones as her paramour. For the summer.

Marilyn was not shy. She looked at Yogi carefully, from head to toe. "Can you do it on your back, with your eyes closed?" asked Marilyn.

Yogi extinguished the lantern so that only the twilight, tinged green from the hanging fabric, colored the tent. She watched him slowly remove his clothes, and when he looked up, she was upon him, her blouse unbuttoned. She placed one hand firmly across his eyes.

Marilyn Albion was in charge. Marilyn Albion knew what was what. She was not thinking of marriage or enlightenment but of mastery and pleasure. She straddled Yogi Jones the way Marilyn Monroe had straddled the grate outside the Trans-Lux Theater. True to his word, Yogi Jones had the control of a Michelangelo. As Marilyn rocked without thought of time, she grabbed Yogi's John the Baptist hair with her free hand and said, "You're a saint."

Marilyn pulled hard on Yogi's hair, and it seemed to inspire him. Marilyn Albion forgot she was on the Moon, that Yogi Jones was beneath her. She was crossing the exotic landscape of sensation, exploring the life-size, blow-up party doll with the wild lock of John Kennedy hair. She pulled one last time and Yogi flashed poetic.

She released his hair from her fist but continued to toy with it, keeping her free hand over his eyes as she bent down and kissed his mouth.

"There's nothing wrong with saying thank you," she said.

Marilyn Albion lifted herself from Yogi Jones, having given the great hello to his landscape. She dressed, and the rustling of her clothes intensified in the warm silence. Yogi Jones smiled peacefully and said, "What a good boy am I."

Each day, Marilyn took a crack at enlightenment, and the loon sat silent, at last, on the crown of Alpha/Omega. Cha cha cha.

It was the dead of a hot midsummer night. Having again returned from Yogi's tent, Marilyn Albion sat in the large, warm kitchen of Alpha/Omega House. She smoked a charcoal-filtered Tareyton and drank a glass of milk. There was something disgusting about the combination of cigarettes and milk, and Marilyn loved it. Men, women, and small children would turn their heads away when she did this in public, but Marilyn was no stranger to controversy.

She looked out the wide-open window beside her. The night was stark still, hot and silent, the kind of night that seems more like an echoing stage set than the arena of real life. Yogi Jones' colorful tent was snug on the Moon, surrounded by yellow No-Pest strips covered with dead insects. Even Yogi Jones made this one exception to his position of nonviolence.

Marilyn Albion wanted to become more like a woman, but she knew this had somehow become synonymous with becoming more like a man. She was shocked at how easily she had relegated Yogi Jones to the "party boy" category. She was certain that her explorations gave him great pleasure, that her mere presence in his tent captivated him, but was his vulnerability to her an invitation for sex without love? She was not sure if he understood that she did not love him. She considered paying him to make it clear, but no, that would get too expensive. Marilyn took another drag from her cigarette. That would seem cheap, too. She could never be cheap, but she did want to have a good conscience. She didn't mind being dominant, but she did want to be thoughtful.

She wondered if these thoughts crossed her father's mind.

She consoled herself with the fact that men apparently enjoy being treated as sex objects.

She was barefoot, her long hair uncombed loose and

thick as a horse's tail. The belt to her white summer robe was tied carelessly at the waist, and the small flashes of skin that became visible as she moved were more afterthought than seduction. There was, in fact, no one left to seduce except herself. She wondered how to accomplish that. Her arm hung limply along the window sash and one bare foot rested on a nearby chair rung. She blew an artful, charcoal-filtered smoke ring that disintegrated above her head like a broken halo.

I wonder what my mother is doing tonight? thought Marilyn.

Betty Bloom walked softly on the grass past the window, carrying her phonograph. Dead-of-the-night curious, Marilyn got up and tied the sash on her robe. She pushed through the swinging kitchen doors and climbed the wide staircase to Betty's room. Except for the Cher poster on the wall, a box of records, and a pair of open scissors lying in the corner, it had been cleaned out. Christina Smythe-Corduroy Stuckey was standing in the room, her hands behind her back like a horsemaster hiding the crop. Betty returned for her records.

"What's going on?" Marilyn asked Betty.

Betty said, "I'm Audrey Hepburn breaking her vows and leaving the convent in *The Nun Story.*"

Betty Bloom laughed wildly as only redheaded women can.

Christina Smythe-Corduroy Stuckey was not amused.

Betty put her hands on Marilyn's shoulders. "I'm going into business, Marilyn. Wish me luck. It's a sort of social service work."

Jackie Bright stood in the doorway, bitter and beautiful. Christina ignored Jackie. That was how it went after Christina got you under control. No more attention.

"I've formed an organization called PAWS in the Name of Love," said Betty Bloom.

"Tell her what PAWS stands for, Betty," said Christina sarcastically.

Marilyn did not like Christina's tone of voice. It wasn't very "all for one and one for all."

Betty planted her hands on her hips and said, "Prostitutes Are Workers Society, Marilyn. I feel that women should be well paid for their contribution to helping the survival of humanity by allowing the male an outlet besides murder and rape for his unmanageable hormones."

Marilyn Albion hoped she would not have to begin to pay Yogi Jones. Marilyn looked at Jackie Bright, who averted her eyes.

"I've liberated the blue house in Scollay Square," said Betty, "and I'm moving in."

Jackie Bright played with her long black hair, and Marilyn wondered if Frances Bright was involved in PAWS.

"The place is crawling with history," said Betty.

"I hear they give a hell of a Tupperware party," said Marilyn, but Jackie Bright did not smile.

Betty continued. "It's near what used to be Scollay Square, where Sally Keith, Queen of the Tassels, lived. And Tempest Storm used to dance nearby at the Old Howard. And then there was Gypsy Rose Lee, exotic dancer supreme—and mystery writer! Those were the stars. But there were plenty of ordinary sex workers."

Jackie Bright looked at Betty Bloom and said, "People romanticize desperation."

"Sex workers?" said Marilyn to Betty Bloom.

Jackie Bright picked up the cold scissors from the floor in the corner of Betty Bloom's room. They glistened. They were dangerous, attractive.

"Yes. And I'm going to fight for disability, unemployment, workers' compensation—"

"Vacations in the beautiful blue-and-green Pacific," said Marilyn Albion.

"You name it," said Betty Bloom. "We intend to announce on television that we'll go on strike if we don't get our demands met."

"She's selling her body, Marilyn," said Christina.

"I'm not selling my body," said Betty Bloom. "I rent on occasion. And I like my work."

Betty Bloom marched out.

"Filthy slave! Closet heiress!" said Christina.

That was low. "Heiress?" asked Marilyn.

"It's not as if Miss Bloom needs the money. Do you know who she is?"

"No."

"Elizabeth Crocker Duncan Swanson Campbell Bloom. What a fake," said Christina Smythe-Corduroy Stuckey, who turned to march out of the room.

Jackie Bright shouted, "What about your stud farm in Virginia, Christina?"

Christina Smythe-Corduroy-Stuckey turned with ill-advised vengeance. "It's rather similar to your mother's profession, isn't it, Jackie?"

Jackie Bright slapped Christina.

"You bitch!" shouted Christina. "Violence will not be tolerated at Alpha/Omega."

"Violence doesn't have to be physical," said Marilyn, putting her arm on Jackie's shoulders.

Christina left the room, trailing righteous anger behind her.

Marilyn was very pleased with Jackie Bright, who sat beside her on the bed, opening and closing the scissors.

"Jackie. Are you and Christina lovers?"

"For Christ's sake, no!"

"Too bad. At least then I could understand it," said Marilyn.

"Understand what?"

"All that passion," said Marilyn.

Jackie Bright was surprised. Now she would surprise Marilyn. Jackie took the scissors and in three sharp movements cut off her hair and handed it to Marilyn. Jackie Bright stood and walked to the door with the cool defiance of Jackie Kennedy walking down the aisle with Aristotle Onassis.

"Where are you going?" demanded Marilyn, horrified. She had loved to look at Jackie Bright's hair, but when it was on her head, not chopped off in her hand.

"Underground, where I'll be loved and appreciated."

"Jackie Bright! You're loved and appreciated right here."

"Jackie X. Got it? Jackie X."

Jackie X left Alpha/Omega House.

Marilyn sat on Betty Bloom's stripped bed, holding Jackie Bright's hair. Marilyn had never before felt true sadness. Molly and Dolly Gunn stood marooned in the doorway, then sat on either side of Marilyn, each putting a hand on her shoulders.

Marilyn felt a deep longing. Her best friend had become someone's naughty pet and had run away, which in a sense was good news. And now Betty Bloom was leaving.

Betty Bloom returned for her Cher poster on the wall.

"What is passion?" asked Marilyn Albion.

The Gunn twins were perplexed by this question, and they put their heads together like a team on a quiz show.

Molly spoke for them: "There are two kinds of orgasms. Vaginal and clitoral. The clitoris is the only organ in the human body whose sole function is pleasure. Vaginal orgasms are a sort of consolation prize."

"Sex doesn't necessarily have anything to do with passion," confided Marilyn. Oh, the sad revelations of liberation.

Betty Bloom, red hair flashing, heart face twinkling, planted her feet in the center of the room and said, "Now you know the secret men have been keeping from us. Love doesn't necessarily have anything to do with sex."

Betty Bloom looked like Harve Presnell about to perform in *The Music Man*.

"What's the relationship between passion, sex, and love? First you've got to know who put the *o* in *orgasm*. And the answer to that is women's liberation!"

The Gunn twins erupted in applause: "Who put the *o* in *orgasm?* Women's liberation!"

Marilyn Albion said, "But what about love? What about passion?"

Betty looked at Jackie's hair in Marilyn's hand. "That's passion," said Betty.

Marilyn lifted Jackie's hair. "I feel like some sort of cannibal."

"Do you want to spend the night with me at the blue house?"

"This is passion?" demanded Marilyn, shaking the tail of hair.

"Yes!" said Betty Bloom.

"But is it love?" asked Marilyn.

Betty Bloom looked at Marilyn and shook her head in pity. "It's anger, Marilyn. Can't you tell the difference?"

"Apparently not," said Marilyn.

* * *

Inside the Blue Lagoon, Frances Bright stood up and leaned into Joe Albion's face.

"I'm tired of being your party girl, Joe."

"I love you, Frances."

"Then marry me."

"I'm married. You know that."

"I want to die," said Frances Bright, and she left the club.

Frances Bright had torn the heart out of the master of the Blue Lagoon, but it was a calculated risk. Frances Bright decided that manipulating Joe Albion into marrying her was preferable to killing herself. She knew he couldn't live without her, because she was the depository of his broken fantasy of Marilyn Monroe. He would have to follow her home, to be sure she would not kill herself. He had a fear of open, empty bottles of Nembutal floating downstream like broken coffins come above ground in a flood.

Carrying a crammed Filene's shopping bag, Marilyn Albion, accompanying Betty Bloom, arrived at the large, cheerful house, which was full of large, cheerful women in the windows, on the staircase, in all of the rooms. In the turret, there was a woman brushing her long blond hair in the moonlight. These were not victim prostitutes or drug addicts. They were simply practitioners of the oldest profession. And there were no pimps. That was the power of the blue house, and if Betty Bloom had her way, the power of the union and a potential strike. The Chamber of Commerce would never admit it, but the convention business would be badly hurt if the hookers struck. The blue house did a brisk and lucrative business. Betty Bloom hurried to an organizational meeting in the rear of the house and left Marilyn to herself.

Marilyn climbed the grand staircase and entered the living room, where the Tupperware party had been held. Frances Bright was looking out the window to the street below. Frances Bright had lost her pathos, that "If you don't save me, I'm going to drown myself" look.

Frances and Marilyn were alone, and Frances turned and faced her. Her eyes were cold. They were not the eyes of someone who was considering suicide.

"Are you going to the meeting?" asked Marilyn.

"I don't have to go to any meeting," said Frances with hostility.

"I don't care if you go or not," said Marilyn.

The two women were silent as they stalked each other.

"Your mother thinks I'm a joke," said Frances Bright.

Marilyn said nothing.

"Kate Albion is the only woman I've ever known whose husband's mistress is a source of amusement," said Frances.

Marilyn was not interested in Frances Bright's feelings about her mother. She lifted Jackie Bright's hair from her Filene's bag and handed it to Frances.

"She cut it off. Then she went away."

Frances Bright took the hair in her hands.

"Jackie?"

Marilyn nodded.

"I did the best I could. I wasn't bad," said Frances. She left the room and dimmed the lights behind her as if Marilyn were not there.

> *Yes, my heart belongs to Daddy,*
> *So I simply couldn't be bad.*

Marilyn sat by the window in the moonlight and lit a cigarette.

"Where is love?" she said.

> Yes, my heart belongs to Daddy,
> Da da, da da da, da da Dad!

—

Joe Albion stood before the blue house and looked at the PAWS IN THE NAME OF LOVE banner that hung as still as the American flag on the moon. He entered the house, which was strangely deserted, and walked up the grand staircase to the living room in search of Frances Bright, whom he hoped was still alive. Framed in moonlight and smoke and studying the sky was his daughter, his Marilyn. In the blue house—and not for a Tupperware party. Why? He could not approach her, and he remained in the shadows, the daddy who named her for Monroe. Guilty daddy, bad daddy, hanging the golden *M* around his little girl's neck.

He slammed to the bottom of his soul, and when he closed his eyes, the dust devils swirled around Marine First Lieutenant Joe Albion, stationed at Camp Pendleton, and the gold buttons on his dress-white uniform burned as hot as branding irons. The heat waves rose up from the ground in the distance like a snake charmer's pets.

> DRIVE CAREFULLY—
> THE LIFE YOU SAVE
> MAY BE MARILYN MONROE'S

Imaginary men, bubbling with hormones, heads filled with red-light districts, came ranting toward his daughter.

Joe Albion's mind screeched and sparked like the underground subway.

I'll chop off their penises before they get to her, he thought.

He ran his free hand through his hair. For a flash, they were Miss Monroe's hands, Marilyn Albion's hands.

Joe Albion wanted to cry for mercy, but it would not be manly. There were mice, vicious mice, chattering on the dark side of the moon. He felt little teeth make their marks all over his beautiful body.

Kate will stab Flash to death for this.

But he was a good man. He was a kind man. He was the most popular mayor in the history of Boston.

Good-bye. Good-bye.

Crack-up in the moonlight.

Joe Albion left the blue house. He didn't care if Frances Bright killed herself. She had killed him by making him come here. He would never save her again. He'd rather go crazy.

Marilyn Albion blew a smoke ring and watched it dissolve in the moonlight.

> *Da da da,*
> *da da da,*
> *da da Dad.*

In the sultry summer night, Freddie Finney mounted the swan's back and peddled through the lagoon. Mayor Joe Albion was seated at the helm, and the large white swan, its feathers full and wide, its red beak and black oriental eyes enlightened and silent, plied the waters.

Well, what are we gonna tell your Mama?
What are we gonna tell your Pa?
What are we gonna tell our friends
When they say—
The blonde jumped into the lagoon.

Joe Albion clenched and opened his hands, then ran them through his thick blonde hair. All his beauty and all his pain couldn't put Joe Albion together again.

"Freddie," said Joe Albion.

"Yes, Mr. Mayor."

"Do you remember what Miss Monroe said?"

"What was that, sir?"

"'I'm always running into people's unconscious.'"

"Yes, sir."

"Well, Freddie. I ran into my own."

Joe Albion did not care any longer. He saw Kate Albion standing at the dock as Freddie Finney brought in the swan boat. The gleaming black stretch limousine was on the street behind her, and at her side was a bald man in a suit, smoking a pipe. Freddie Finney recognized him. He was Dr. Mason Squibb, the Doctor of Electronics, the shock therapist.

"Joe," said Kate as the swan boat docked. "It's not the end of the world. For God's sake. There are so many other things to worry about."

Joe said nothing.

"You've been riding around here for days. It's time to stop. You're needed."

"To sing and dance?"

"You're the mayor."

"I no longer cut my nails, Mrs. Albion," said Joe Albion, displaying his nails, which he had honed to neat sharp points. "I must be the dangerous prince."

"Joe. I've rented a lovely house on Walden Pond. This is Dr. Mason Squibb. He's very famous. State of the art. He'll be attending to you."

"How do you do, Mayor Albion?"

Joe Albion pitied Dr. Squibb. He'd never seen such a sight in his life.

Joe Albion said to Dr. Squibb, "I'll chop off your tail with a butcher's knife."

"Paranoid delusional," mumbled Dr. Squibb to Kate Albion.

Kate Albion was frightened—a thoroughly unfamiliar experience—and angry. Men were always breaking down like this. They had to control their emotions as intensely as they did, they had to punch each other in the arms to say hello, because the slightest brush with deep emotion made them break like sticks that can't bend in a strong wind. She knew that this is why men need to have women feel for them.

She took Freddie's arm. "Freddie. You're to go with the mayor, and please keep this quiet. Keep me informed of everything. And if you need anything, tell me."

"Yes, Mrs. Albion," said Freddie Finney, tipping his chauffeur's cap.

"Freddie."

"Yes, Mrs. Albion."

"Do you suppose it would help if I got him Frances Bright back?"

Freddie Finney was too shocked at her question to even venture a reply. He thought, Mrs. Albion has brass balls.

Kate Kelly Albion looked at Freddie and said, "I guess not."

Dr. Squibb, Kate, and Joe entered the limousine, and Freddie Finney put the car into gear and drove slowly from the dock, as if he were carrying a hundred unboxed eggs.

"If there's a nuclear war," said Joe Albion, looking out the window at the lagoon, "the paint will peel off the swan boats. Khrushchev is an animal." Joe was enjoying himself. The insane don't age and I like that, he thought.

Kate wondered if Joe was faking it. She couldn't be sure. "Khrushchev is dead," she said. "Remember? Dead."

No. No, Joe did not remember.

He can never campaign in this condition, thought Kate Albion. She hoped Dr. Squibb could help Joe. She herself knew nothing about psychotherapy. Kate Albion felt that an examined life was a wasted life.

And as it is with all those who play games and forget they are playing games, Joe Albion went far, far away, deep in the beautiful green-and-blue Pacific to the Bikini Islands, before they dropped the atomic bombs. The day before.

So long, Joe Albion. Love has had you.

CHAPTER 19

Looney Tunes

August 1972

Early that August, the passionate summer heat surrounded Walden Pond and its passive, dead-weight water. The grass was green in patches, but mostly browning, the dirt parched. The occasional fitful breeze did no more than rock the heat in waves and irritate it into slapping philosophers with mosquitos.

Marilyn Albion walked along the narrow path toward the back entrance of the private house where Joe Albion was staying, or being kept, as she thought of it. Marilyn wore a long, loose, white cotton summer dress and sandals that laced up her legs. She knew that Joe Albion liked to see ladies in white.

Marilyn was angry at her father. She could not hate him, but she did resent that his beast was weak. Where was the hormone-blinded male animal, capable of destroying all in its path that it may survive, throwing deadly hatchets across the treetops?

A loon raced madly along the surface of Walden Pond, its laughlike cry screeching to a halt as it abruptly stopped in the air and dropped headfirst into the water, resurfacing with a bloody little fish in its mouth. Marilyn Albion understood loons.

She saw the white clapboard house, innocent and have-a-cookie-ish, and she saw Dr. Squibb sunning himself on the porch. Marilyn had a visceral hatred of smug, fat white men sunning themselves. She approached him. She had a special hatred for smug, fat white men sunning themselves in flowered trunks, and so she cast a cold eye on Dr. Squibb's boxer-style shorts and their gaudy sunflower pattern.

"Marilyn Albion?" asked the doctor.

"How are you treating my father? What is his diagnosis?"

"We're giving him special treatment, and we have him on Thorazine, which seems to be working quite well."

"I thought Thorazine was for schizophrenics," said Marilyn.

"Let the doctor handle this. A little zip here. A little zap there. Good as new tomorrow."

Marilyn turned her back on the paragon of psychiatric medicine and approached the house. As she neared the rear entrance, she heard the sounds of early morning cartoons. She entered through the back screen door and turned to see that the doctor had once again made himself comfortable on the porch. Moving toward the front of the house, she looked out the window to the circular driveway and saw Freddie Finney. He was smoking a cigarette, leaning against the limousine, looking around, following the loon with his eyes, holding his chauffeur's cap in one hand. He was looking inside his cap for the answer to the riddle of being, but the answer to the riddle of being was not in Freddie Finney's cap. In frustration he jammed the cap back on his head and mumbled, loud enough for Marilyn to hear, "I love my mother." Marilyn felt a surge of brotherly love for Freddie Finney.

Marilyn walked down a short white corridor and stood in the doorway to Joe Albion's room. Joe Albion was watching "Looney Tunes Cartoons" full blast, and Porky Pig and Elmer Fudd were having an argument about the riddle of being. Joe Albion watched without expression. He didn't laugh at the jokes. He didn't cry at the pain.

On an easel in the corner, Marilyn saw an absolutely horrible painting of a palm tree. Some things are better left in fantasy, thought Marilyn, relieved her father had not given up his life to his painting. Something resembling a big dead fish with a human head lay beached beneath the horrible palm tree.

> *The divine savage female*
> *lays naked in the saltwater.*

Marilyn moved between Joe Albion and the cartoons. "Are you dead, Joe Albion?"
Joe Albion studied the glow around Marilyn.
"The jungle birds are sleeping," he said.
"Are you dead, Joe Albion?"

"You're like the moon in full eclipse of the sun," he said.

"The Flintstones were better than that, don't you think, Daddy?"

Joe Albion looked at Marilyn Monrock and smiled.

When you're smiling,
When you're smiling,
The whole world smiles with you.

Marilyn Albion turned off the television. The silence permeated the world, and only the occasional laughing cry of the loon broke it.

"Father."

Joe Albion looked at Marilyn and closed his eyes. He said, "A woman like that looks into the eyes of a man and sees the hairy ape. Looks into the heart of a man and sees the killer."

"What woman?"

"I beat this boy up when I was small because he whined. I had to make sure he didn't grow up to become president. Then I vomited on the flowers. He did anyway."

"Did what?"

"Grow up to be president."

"Who?"

"Richard Nixon."

Marilyn had never heard her father's secrets.

"I never once missed the urinal, you know."

"Yes, Dad. You were always quite polite."

"But there's too much wrong with me."

"There's nothing wrong with you."

Marilyn brushed her father's hair from his forehead with her hand. Red temple splotches, but no great big smile.

Marilyn completed her eclipse and returned Joe Albion

to "Looney Tunes Cartoons." She walked out of the room, down the short white corridor, and outside to the circular driveway where Freddie Finney had resumed his search in his cap for the answer to the riddle of being.

"How long has he been like this?" asked Marilyn.

"A few weeks. For Christ's sake. I don't like this, Miss Albion."

"What's this doctor like?"

"All transmitter, no receiver, if you know what I mean."

"We're getting my father out of here. Tonight."

"We can't, Miss Albion. This doctor's like a jailer."

"I'm not a member of Alpha/Omega for nothing, Freddie."

The evening was bright with moonlight, perfect for a kidnapping. Dr. Mason Squibb was taking his constitutional along the path, fantasizing restructuring entire personalities in his own image. He was unaware that the Gunn twins, for whom the American Psychiatric Association did not even have a category, were perched in the tree branches as emergency backup for the abduction of Joe Albion. Felicity Cuntwise had supervised the operation. She gave the cry of a loon, which was the signal for Betty Bloom.

Betty Bloom appeared on the pathway, wearing a splendiferous feather-and-sequins gown and gold platform shoes. *Très* showgirl. Marilyn watched from a window back at the house as Betty's "Gypsys, Tramps and Thieves" outfit reflected the moonlight. It was one short, fat moment before Dr. Squibb's sunflower boxer shorts glimmered.

"His psychology is so simple, it's sad," said Marilyn Albion quietly.

Marilyn knocked on Joe Albion's door. He was still drugged on the Thorazine, it was difficult to assess the damage of the tic toc electroshock, and he was obsessed with his painting—so Marilyn had brought him a special outfit to wear, something that would seduce him into coming with her, something that would appeal to a Yankee Doodle dandy.

Freddie Finney waited anxiously, chain-smoking outside by the limousine. He had not informed Kate Albion of Marilyn's visit, and she'd be royally pissed when she found out they'd suckered Squibb, but he trusted Marilyn Albion with affairs of the soul, and Mrs. Albion with affairs of the voting booth.

Joe Albion did not open the door. "Come on, Daddy," said Marilyn, trying not to betray any anxiousness on her part. "It's time to go."

The door at the end of the short white corridor opened, and Mayor Joe Albion emerged, a great smile on his face. The black silk top hat was cocked perfectly on his head and the silver monocle glittered before his eye.

"You look wonderful, Father," said Marilyn.

Joe Albion put his arm through Marilyn's, adjusted his white gloves, and lifted his walking stick toward heaven.

They emerged from the house on Walden Pond, entered the limousine, and drove off to Logan Airport to catch the next flight to Hollywood. Freddie Finney smiled nervously.

Christ, thought Freddie. The mayor looks like a fucking Mr. Peanut.

Cruising down the Massachusetts turnpike, they passed the orange rooftop of Howard Johnson's. Joe Albion moved to the edge of his seat. Spellbound and delighted, he announced, *"Ich bin ein* Looney Tunes."

Pandora's Box

August 1972

It was dawn when the plane landed at Los Angeles International Airport. Joe Albion was alert and attentive, like a prince awaiting the fireworks display in his honor. It was pleasant that no one in Hollywood would recognize the mayor of Boston and his daughter, although the top hat and monocle did attract some attention.

They disembarked and walked in the warm predawn to the curb outside the airport. A red Dodge Dart convertible in impeccable condition, its white top down, spun into the space before them. A young man, hair black as Freddie Finney's, unusually tan for an Irishman, hopped from the convertible. His yellow rayon shirt was bright with flamingos posing for tourists.

"Flash Finney here. Freddie called me from Boston. At your service!" Flash Finney opened the bright red door for Marilyn Albion and the mayor. Joe Albion removed the top hat and placed the monocle and the white gloves inside it as he and Marilyn sat on the backseat of the car. Joe Albion was elated to have finally solved the mystery of "What happened to Flash Gordon?"

"Where to?" asked Flash, smiling as wide as a Kennedy.

Marilyn leaned near Flash Finney's ear and said, "Westwood Memorial Park." Flash smiled and gave the thumbs-up sign, and they pulled away, leaving rubber behind them.

At Jetson speed, they drove from freeway to freeway. A delighted Joe Albion pointed his walking stick toward a palm tree at the foot of the Hollywood Hills and fell into a state of grace. Marilyn, alarmed by Flash's exotic driving, held tightly to her father's arm.

"Don't be afraid, Marilyn," said Joe. "It's just a toaster."

Dawn lifted its warm, milky breast as Flash pulled up to a tiny cemetery behind a movie theater. The cemetery sign was of the same design as a motel's. How peculiar, thought Marilyn, but then again, this was Hollywood. Rintrah was silent, and Sheba Sheik was curious.

Marilyn got out of the convertible, and Flash Finney hopped from the driver's seat and lit a cigarette. Joe Albion did not get out of the car. Joe Albion did not want to haunt a cemetery in the morning, especially before medication.

"Marilyn. What are you doing?" he asked, still waiting for his fireworks display.

Marilyn Albion did not answer him. She walked the short deserted path, beneath the two trees, past the graves. Joe Albion would not move from the red convertible. Marilyn Albion turned the corner around what appeared to be some sort of cement wall, and Joe Albion's darling disappeared into the death yard. Joe Albion leaped from the car, his heart beating too hard, and he chased after his daughter, the walking stick clenched in his hand as a weapon to defend her. He turned the corner, and his gleaming black shoes stopped.

Joe Albion saw before him a wall of crypts, neatly stacked one on top of the other, like drawers in a strange filing cabinet. Marilyn Albion stood before one of the crypts, her light white dress lifting and hovering in the gentle breeze. A small bronze flower vase was hooked into the cement facing stone, and in it two red roses stood fresh as any rose Saint Theresa could have conjured. Marilyn touched the flowers and bent to kiss the facing stone. The stone was chipped by souvenir hunters and covered with the lipstick marks of women's kisses.

Joe Albion moved up behind Marilyn Albion and saw the small bronze plaque.

MARILYN MONROE
1926-1962

Joe Albion touched the bronze plaque like a blind man trying to fit the key into a strange door. In a flash he felt his body slip from him as if his soul were a hanger. Joe Albion wept, a deep sobbing cry that would have silenced even the loon of Walden Pond. Marilyn Monroe was dead. She was dead, and her body, or what was left of it, lay inside this crypt whose facing stone had been mutilated by souvenir hunters, whose occupant had been worn away by the fantasies and failings of men and women.

Marilyn pressed her hand against the crypt and felt a deep sadness. She looked at Joe Albion, who was transported.

Before him was the crypt, but within him Miss Monroe maneuvered her splendid body through his world. Joe Albion ran his fingers through his hair.

Joe Albion looked at his daughter and searched her eyes for the infant in the christening gown. His breathing became profoundly steady, and the crypt the ground the sky, his daughter, exuded flowers chocolates compassion. Within Joe Albion's mind stretched the existence of gods and men, and scoured of fear, his body hung back upon its hanger. Joe Albion knew he hadn't killed Marilyn Monroe. Marilyn Monroe had killed herself.

Joe forgave her, and said to his daughter, "Miss Monroe was the ecstatic incarnation of woman. She was fearless beauty in an evil and dangerous world."

"That ate her up," added Marilyn Albion, but Joe Albion was not interested in that, because Marilyn Monroe was dead, safely dead and perfect. Upon her memory, he would forever be able to explain and excuse the sacred and profane in himself, because Marilyn Monroe was pathologically compassionate, like most saints, and he believed it was her fault that he had been banished from Eden.

"There's nothing wrong with me," said Joe. Hello Hello. He looked at the sky. He looked at his hands.

"You love me," he said to Marilyn Albion.

My heart belongs to daddy,
Da da, da da da, da da Dad!

"Yes. I love you." Marilyn began to tremble and leaned against the wall of crypts for support. She was very quiet. She was very ladylike. She was a little crazy, but she did it for her daddy.

Joe Albion, empowered, mayor of Boston, was satisfied with his innocence and his sanity. He wanted to return immediately to his wife, his politics, his club. His walking stick poked at the graves as he wandered back through the cemetery and got into the red convertible.

Flash Finney said to Joe Albion, "You know, the fingernails and the toenails keep growing on the corpses. Did you know that? Long and kind of curvy."

"Like a Mandarin prince," said Joe Albion.

She was unkempt and in need of a manicure and pedicure, indicating listlessness and a lack of interest in maintaining her usually glamorous appearance, the authorities added.

Marilyn Albion remained at the Corridor of Memories and placed one hand on Miss Monroe's facing stone as she ran the fingers of her free hand through her hair.

"Ich bin ein Marilyn," she said.

Marilyn Albion's body quivered like the applause meter on "Queen for a Day." How do you do?

There was also the sinister fact that a well-made woman had always thrilled me to look at. **—Marilyn Monroe**

She could never seduce herself, thought Marilyn Albion, and that's why she died. Marilyn Albion backed away quickly from the crypt, turned, and walked, a little heavier, from Westwood Memorial Park. Her eyes were targeted on Joe Albion.

"If I were pure Kelly," said Marilyn to the dead, "I'd have chipped off a piece of the facing stone for a souvenir. But I'm part Albion, so I kissed it."

The toasters, knives, and windows rattled in the Hollywood Hills under the power of the sonic booms from LAX as Marilyn Albion got into the red convertible beside her father. She saw Joe Albion's clipped nails strewn across the leather seat. Marilyn scooped them into her palm and dropped them into the shallow pocket of her white dress.

"So the nails are gone," she said. How do you do?

"You're absolutely radiant, darling," said Joe Albion.

Flash Finney raced his red Dodge Dart convertible from freeway to freeway to Los Angeles International Airport, where at curbside he hopped from the driver's seat and opened the back door for Marilyn and Joe. Flash Finney's yellow rayon shirt with the pink flamingos posing for tourists was vibrant under the hot sun.

As the plane lifted from the ground like an unnatural act and headed for Boston, Joe Albion was again the master of his soul, his mind all nice and jigsawed together, but Marilyn Albion felt like someone had slipped her a Monroe.

Part Five

CHAPTER 21

Filene's Revisited

August 1972

The heat was almost solid in its oppressiveness, but Kate Albion was on alert. She had planted herself spikes-first in front of Freddie Finney at the VIP gate at Logan Airport. She concentrated on the landing airplane with the same attention she had given to the orbiting Sputnik.

"Jesus," said Kate when she saw the debonair Joe Albion approaching with his top hat, monocle, white gloves, and walking stick.

"Freddie," she said, her mouth open but not moving,

ventriloquist style. "Why is the mayor dressed like Mr. Peanut?"

"It's just one of Miss Albion's games, Mrs. Albion." Freddie Finney hoped he was telling the truth. He was sick of the swan boats. He was sick of Walden Pond, loons, and Dr. Mason Squibb in his sunflower shorts. He wanted to get back to City Hall and the Blue Lagoon. He wanted to have dinner with his mother on Sunday afternoons.

Marilyn Albion was in front of her father, and she reached Kate Albion first. Kate Albion kissed Marilyn on the cheek, but the kiss was only for show. Marilyn did not understand why Kate was so cold.

Mr. Peanut took Mrs. Peanut in his arms and kissed her. Kate Albion deepened the kiss until there was nothing in their heads but each other's tongues. They were nicely welded. Marilyn Albion did not exist for them.

Kate broke the kiss and said to Joe, "Do you want to go back to Walden Pond?"

Joe Albion said, "No. Marilyn Monroe is dead. Let's go home."

Joe and Kate, arm in arm, walked out of the airport, followed by Marilyn Albion and Freddie Finney. Joe Albion smiled like a Kennedy and adjusted his top hat. Kate Albion could taste the governorship as she discreetly placed the white gloves and monocle in her purse and snapped it shut.

Marilyn Albion laughed as if she were a little drunk. "You remind me of the queen of England, Mother, putting the cannibal's toe hors d'oeuvre in her handbag."

"Marilyn. Are you all right? You don't look well, Marilyn. Would you like to stay at Walden Pond?" asked Kate Albion solicitously.

"No," said Marilyn. No tic toc electroshock, thank you very much.

"It might do you good. A little rest," said Kate Albion.

"Yes," said Joe Albion. "There's such peace there. You could paint."

"I can watch cartoons anywhere," said Marilyn.

"Don't be disrespectful to your father," said Kate.

"Twinkle twinkle, Marilyn Albion?" said her daughter.

"Marilyn's tired, Kate. She doesn't know what she's saying," said Joe.

"Do you think it's because she's blond?" asked Kate, as if Marilyn were not there.

"What? What because I'm blond?" asked Marilyn.

"Tendencies . . ." said Kate.

"Sensitivities, darling," said Joe.

The divine savage female
lays bloody in the loon's mouth.

Freddie Finney opened the back doors of the air-conditioned black stretch limousine, and Kate, Marilyn, and Joe sat on the cushioned leather seats. Kate Albion powered up the smoked glass window, and the car rolled quickly in its muffled beauty toward Boston City Hall.

Joe Albion's power surged through him. "I'll always take care of you, Marilyn," he said. Marilyn smiled, feeling safer if she appeared to be weak.

"Thank you, Daddy."

Kate Albion clenched her hidden fist, as Joe Albion powered down his window to watch the approach of his city. The limousine entered the Callahan Tunnel.

In a quiet voice, Kate said, "Marilyn."

Marilyn leaned close to Kate. "Yes, Mother?"

This was the moment Marilyn had been waiting for, the moment that Kate Albion would thank her. Marilyn told herself not to be smug, but to be gracious.

"Marilyn." Kate's voice was somber, yet a faint sad

smile played across the light and dark shadows of her face. Marilyn knew it was very difficult for her mother to acknowledge her daughter's power.

Kate Albion said, "Yogi Jones works for me."

Callahan Tunnel was narrow and yellow like the eyes of a dangerous dog.

Marilyn Albion concealed all feeling as she fell through open space. She was certain that her mother was telling the truth.

"I pay him to protect you. To report to me. Try not to—what was that cute way he said you refer to it?—'walk on the Moon' so often, dear. It will ruin your reputation."

Marilyn Albion was so angry, and so sustained was her pain, that she thought she might well become enlightened from it, because the adrenaline pumped white light up into the crown of her head. Marilyn Albion glimpsed the secret of the masochists: if the pain becomes deep enough, it splits apart, and the soul lifts ecstatic into bodiless bliss. But she was a Kelly and the fruits of masochism could not seduce her forever. Her mind slammed into the limousine as it shot out of the mouth of the tunnel. This was not the reward Marilyn had expected for sacrificing herself, for corpse-hopping, for taking on Monroe.

As they entered the city, along the sidewalk Marilyn saw an entrance to the subway.

"Pull over, Freddie," ordered Marilyn.

"Where are you going?" asked Joe.

"Shopping," said Marilyn.

"Will you be all right by yourself?" asked Joe.

"I always have," said Marilyn, beginning to remember her power, though it seemed to fade with the offer of being taken care of. She pulled herself from the air-conditioned limousine, feeling heavy as the dead in the blast of hot August air.

Kate Albion blew Marilyn a kiss from the tips of her fingers and closed the car door.

Marilyn descended into the subway, which seemed to be deeper underground than she remembered. She dropped a token in the slot, pushed through the rotating gate, and boarded the green train, which rambled, flared, and screeched like the inside of a schizophrenic mind.

At Park Street station, Marilyn disembarked and ascended to Park and Tremont Streets at the corner of the Boston Common. It was too damned hot. Brimstone Corner was occupied by an old man standing upon a small wooden box, wisps of white hair floating about his bald head as if he had just ascended from the netherworld. His long black coat hung askew on his thin shoulders, revealing bermuda shorts decorated with meditative pink flamingos. He pointed at Marilyn.

"Repent. The time is at hand when the elegiac darkness shall descend, the world shall be ripped open, all the monsters of the Broken Mind joining forces with the Beast, and the Beast shall rise again."

Marilyn Albion said, "Don't worry about the beast. I can take care of him."

She sauntered along the sidewalk, surprised at the words that had come from her mouth. Men and women smiled at her as she wandered up Tremont Street to School Street, pausing in front of City Hall. Anger again welled up inside her, the rising water lifting memories of the deep past up into her consciousness to float like coffins come above ground in a summertime flood past the seat of power. Marilyn looked at the mayoral balcony and remembered standing on the edge of the Commonwealth Avenue rooftop, waiting for Sputnik. She remembered her mother plucking her from the edge, guarding her from the satellite's imaginary bombs.

Marilyn turned right onto Washington Street, passed the Boston Five Cent Bank, and stopped in front of the Orpheum Theater to follow the overhead scream of a loon radically off course from Walden Pond. The loon narrowly missed colliding with the Hitchcockian timepiece of Filene's, high above the street. Marilyn wanted a high-powered rifle.

> *O Marilyn,*
> *The pipes*
> *The pipes are blowing*

Marilyn crossed the street and entered Filene's. Who she was, how she felt, hung from a long and ponderous pendulum that was out of her control. She did not want to surrender herself, but she felt compelled to grab hold of any hand that would extend itself to her. She wanted to be held.

Inside Filene's, she walked to the steep and narrow downward stairway that led to the basement. Drugged by the heat, the salesladies stood dulled near the foot of the staircase. Their eyeglasses hung from silver clamps on black cords around their necks. Marilyn stepped on down the black-bordered, twisting red-and-yellow stairs.

Below ground in the basement of Filene's, there was a heat of bodies and boilers, a shuffling and hovering, a music of cash registers and elevator signals, but it was all in near slow motion, the faces of the women slightly depressed, not believing there would be anything down here that they could buy that would change their lives. There wasn't a sale today.

> *It's you, it's you*
> *Must go*
> *And I must bide.*

Marilyn scanned the racks and the tables, as curious salesladies perked up and trailed her like little cats toying with a mouse. Marilyn did not want to surrender, but she did not want to be alone. There was nothing here for her. There wasn't a sale today. She walked toward the staircase to ascend, but a saleslady blocked her path and said, "My dear, we just received a dress from the designer section that I think would do you justice."

The saleslady's name tag read FANNY FINNEY. Marilyn smiled. Fanny Finney held up a short, tight black dress with a plunging neckline.

"Do you really think it's me?" said Marilyn Albion. Marilyn was surprised at her voice. It played the girl game so well. The saleslady could not tell it was a game. Marilyn wanted to please her. She wanted the saleslady to love her. She knew that this is why women shop.

"If it's not you, dear, it's not anybody," replied Fanny Finney.

This game would be so easy to win, thought Marilyn, feeling oddly at ease in the role of man-trap and conspirator.

Marilyn wanted Fanny Finney to care about her. Marilyn wanted to feel safe and loved. Fanny Finney wrapped up the dress, and a pair of nylons. Their hands brushed as she took the package.

Marilyn Albion once again turned to ascend, but she was stopped by another saleslady, Fanny's sister, Nora. Nora Finney held a pair of three-inch black spikes.

"You can't get a better deal anywhere. Size six, right?"

"How did you know?"

"I know feet, honey."

The word "honey" went to Marilyn's heart, and she felt the loss of Mrs. Finnegan shoot through her with deep pain. She remembered the secret of the masochists and let the pain reach so far into her that, once again, it split into light. Nora Finney reached out and touched Marilyn's arm. Marilyn felt a flash of ecstatic peace.

> *But come ye back*
> *When summer's*
> *In the meadow.*

Marilyn took the shoes from Nora Finney's hands. Near the register was a small sharp knife with which the salesladies cut off unwanted tags.

> *I will be there*
> *In sunshine*
> *Or in shadow.*

Marilyn picked up the knife and swayed slightly to the jingling, ringing sounds of the basement. Slowly, deftly, as if she had done it a hundred times before, she cut one-quarter inch from the heel of one spike. She put the scrap of heel in her pocket. She saved it for the president.

Holding the spikes by the heels, Marilyn Albion entered the dressing room, with its sagging, pale green curtains and the toasty aroma of ladies' feet. She drew the curtain behind her and slid the nylons up her legs. A sensual shiver spun in her belly. She slid the black dress slowly over her body and arranged her errant breasts, braless and magnificent. Yogi works for my mother, she thought. The pain glowed and broke like lightning filling a dark bedroom at night.

Marilyn slipped on the spike heels with the same assurance that Cinderella must have had when Prince Charming put the glass slipper on her foot. She leaned against the dressing room wall, and her eyes got glassy for President Kennedy.

Bless me, Chief,
This is my first confession.
I love girl-talk.
It fills me with holy life.
But I'll be true to you.

Marilyn placed her traveling clothes in the Filene's shopping bag and emerged from the dressing room. The Finney sisters awaited her entrance. When they saw her, they were each so moved that they took out the neatly folded Kleenex wads they always concealed just under the wrist of their sweaters, and dabbed carefully at their eyes, so as not to smudge the mascara from all the emotion.

O Marilyn,
O Marilyn,
We loved you so.

"We haven't seen anything like this for so long," said Fanny Finney. "Ten years, at least, since Miss Monroe died."

"It does a soul good," said Nora Finney.

Marilyn Albion blew Fanny and Nora Finney a great big kiss, turned, and ascended from the heavy world of the basement to the thinner air of the main floor.

It's you, it's you
Must go
and I must bide.

Marilyn Albion moved slowly toward the makeup area, feeling intoxicated with the movement of her body. There were no customers in the area, only salesladies who seemed to be awaiting Marilyn's coming. The elevator bells began to chime, and the aroma of a very specific

perfume wafted through the air like an irresistible narcotic. Marilyn Albion headed toward the aroma of Nights
of Araby, the scent of choice for Mrs. Finnegan, Great
Aunt Nellie Kelly, and the Woolworth's counter ladies.

The cosmetic ladies smiled seductively at Marilyn Albion, and Marilyn moved to them as a child to a mother's
welcoming breast. The cosmetic ladies surrounded Marilyn as she selected a tall, silver chrome and pink-cush-
ioned stool to perch upon. They touched her hair, her
eyebrows, and her cheekbones. Bottles popped open,
compacts stood at attention, mascara brushes slid up and
down in their tubes, anxious to touch her lashes. Hands
fluttered about her, and veils of color and light swelled
and hovered as the voices crooned and lectured.

> *Men will do it to this one.*
> *Pity. What a pity.*
> *A little more rouge.*
> *A girl's got to play dead to stay alive.*

Marilyn thought of her mother. Okay, Mommy. You
think I'm ashamed of the moon? I own the moon!

> *Saint Marilyn of Hollywood.*
> *Saint Marilyn of Boston.*

As Marilyn Albion melted into perfect vulnerability and
disappeared into sacrifice and danger, she felt loved by
womankind. She felt power. She felt Marilyn. But she
could not sense her own presence as, when a child, she
had met Miss Monroe and could not feel another human
being in the room.

Marilyn rose up from the chair to the applause of the
cosmetic ladies. Slowly, her shopping bag dangling from

her hand, she walked from the dark side of Filene's out onto the street to take her place in a long line of lonely, self-destructive but beloved blond bombshells.

Marilyn walked into the street, careless of the oncoming cars. It was part of her new charm. She raised her hand for a taxi, and three cabs screeched to a halt. She spoke to the chosen one: "Thanks. Ever so."

The driver's eyelids struggled to remain alert, for Marilyn's voice had the effect of a narcotic.

"Take me home. Please."

The taxi driver fought his urge to possess and fornicate and transcended to his higher protective self. Reaching the destination, but with no memory of how he had gotten there, the driver pulled to the curb. He was transfixed and forgiven of all sin as he watched Marilyn move up the walkway into Alpha/Omega House. It was as long and ripe a walk as Miss Monroe had made in *Niagara*, the longest walking scene ever shot. Yogi Jones' bright tent was muted in the heat waves and Yogi stood at the edge of the rocky lot, eagerly waiting to be acknowledged by Marilyn. He's on my mother's payroll, she thought. It was now clear why the Boston police never evicted him from the lot. Marilyn knew that Kate would not bother to tell Yogi that he had been revealed. It would be more fun for her to wait and let him find out for himself.

Marilyn did not look to the east. Marilyn did not look to the west. Marilyn didn't bother to cover her back but instead looked at Alpha/Omega House.

Seeing he was to be ignored, Yogi shouted, "This is the most blatant misuse of kundalini in history!"

Marilyn swiveled toward him. "Are you getting this all down for my mother?"

Yogi's face flushed and tears stung his eyes.

Marilyn moved her hips with even greater concentration as if the air were liquid with sweat.

A frightened yet delighted Molly and Dolly Gunn greeted Marilyn on the porch and shadowboxed with each other with a good-natured vigor that had been missing between them for years. Christina Smythe-Corduroy Stuckey watched Marilyn's approach and saw in her a predatory little monster that would have to be tamed in order to be used properly. Marilyn mounted the front porch and stood, knees locked and pelvis thrust forward, toe-to-toe and eye-to-eye with Christina Smythe-Corduroy Stuckey, who would not move.

Marilyn heaved her breasts and pursed her lips, and in a motion so hypnotic that even the threat of death could not move Christina from its path, Marilyn kissed her softly, fully on the lips. Christina moved out of the way. Quickly. Startled. In fact, hellfire devil action fury face of the wrathful deities of the deep, but Marilyn was not concerned with Christina's response, because Marilyn Albion was not afraid of her sexuality.

The Gunn sisters had never seen this much power and they were ripe for idol worship. They did not understand that the power came from being willing to ride on the edge, to tour so close to the line, that Marilyn was willing to crack up in order to feel loved.

Marilyn moved her hands through her hair and walked through the front door of Alpha/Omega House as if she were passing through for the first time. Marilyn was surrounded by the white light of pain split wide open. Yogi Jones would have to wait. Yogi Jones might even have to watch as a madman took possession of her. That would be her greatest triumph, she thought.

Felicity Cuntwise, Starshine O'Schwartz, and the Gunn twins were all that was left of BITCH, but they belonged to Marilyn. They swayed in their protectiveness as Marilyn moved toward the mimeo machine to touch it, to examine it, as if she had never before seen it. Hello hello! None of the women looked into the other women's eyes, but they did smile, oh yes, they did smile and touch their own hair, their own breasts.

Christina Smythe-Corduroy Stuckey detested perversion, which was why she had driven Jackie Bright from the house. What could be expected of Jackie Bright, with a whore for a mother? Christina had said. But it would not be so simple to drive out Marilyn, because Marilyn had never loved her. The more powerful Marilyn became, the closer to the edge she walked in her spikes, the more fierce would be her bevy of protectors.

Marilyn walked up the stairs toward her room, paused midway, and turned to the women in the room below. She spoke:

> My mom may scold me,
> 'Cause she told me
> It is naughty, but then
> Oh! Do it again.
> Please.
> Do it again.

Giggles and deep laughter, feigned horror lifted and hovered in the air, slamming down around Christina Smythe-Corduroy Stuckey's ankles and morals. Christina Smythe-Corduroy Stuckey was busy making Alpha/Omega more acceptable to the masses, having been overtaken by the desire to obtain legitimate political office. The loony daughter of the mayor of Boston was now in her way. Christina and her political ambitions stormed through the swinging doors into the kitchen, where she filled a tall glass with water, dropped in two Alka-Seltzer tablets, and watched them blow up.

Plop plop
Fizz fizz
I'll get you bitch.

CHAPTER 22

On Tour

The god Vishnu disguised himself as the beautiful woman, Mohini, in order to vanquish by charm the violent beasts of the world. But so beautiful was Mohini, that the god lost himself in her reflection, which was his own, and it became the task of the world to remind the god who he was.

September 1973

Marilyn reached the top of the staircase at Alpha/Omega House. Propped against the door of her bedroom was a plain brown package and a bouquet of white carnations. Marilyn lifted the package and the flowers and entered her room. Placing her goodies on her unmade bed, she locked the door behind her.

She read the card in the flowers—"Happy birthday. Love, Yogi"—and, seized with a desire for vengeful enlightenment, she looked out the window to the Moon, but Yogi Jones had deserted.

Marilyn stood before the mirror and toppled down into her reflection. It was her birthday, and she was twenty-one years old. She knew it was Richard Nixon's fault. She had come into the world off schedule, not at her own time. She had been forced too early into life by the Checkers speech. It was Marilyn Monroe's fault. She had been named for the impossible woman by a father drunk on femininity. But Marilyn liked the power that her new position had given her.

She laid back against the pillows propped on her bed, fingering the wool blankets and her hair. Her dress was very tight for luxuriating, so she lifted it high above her knees so that she could maneuver comfortably. There were raspberries in a dish nearby, with a note: "We love you. Please don't die. Love always, Molly and Dolly."

"How sweet," said Marilyn.

She closely examined one of the raspberries. It was so like an erect nipple. She ate the raspberry slowly, curling the little seeds up in her tongue and snapping them in two with her teeth. She unwrapped the flowers and placed the loose bouquet of white carnations on her lap, taking the head of one in her left hand. She pressed the carnation into her face and bit a petal as if it were a human ear. She picked up the brown paper package, which seemed to take forever to open, as complex a task as building an atomic bomb. Finally, out tumbled a photographic book of Marilyn Monroe. In the frontispiece, Joe Albion had written, "Happy birthday, Marilyn. Love always, Mother and Dad."

Marilyn looked at the pictures, which radiated not deadly but forever lightly, and as she looked at the pictures, the left hand that held the carnation by the head wandered up and under the loose bouquet to her clitoris.

The thick white sturdy petals pressed and rubbed, calling forth the coy genie of sex and politics. She slipped into that twilit place, and she fell into a monologue witnessed by the hooded figure, neither man nor woman, that lingered in the corner of her imagination.

"Yes. Love the beast. He's been denied the scent of Nights of Araby. O yes. I'm on the dark side of the moon and my fingers are sticky with penny candy. Give me your hungry your tired your poor your huddled beasts yearning to destroy. I'm the yogini of love. I'm the apple. The snake. The kundalini. The cupcake. O yes, I am. O yes, I am that I am."

The carnation tumbled from her hand and Marilyn fell to earth, asleep, the Book of Monroe open on her chest. She knew that Monroe was Monroe not just for the love of men, whose demands and tantrums could be excused on the grounds of hormonal helplessness. Monroe was Monroe for the love of women, too, who knew exactly what they were doing.

Further and deeper into the hyperfeminine state of Monroeism sank Marilyn, but she did not find love. She found passion. And although there were days when she felt seduced by herself, it led her only deeper into fantasy, where she flopped helpless on the sands of the beautiful blue-and-green Pacific, her fingers stretched toward the saltwater, wondering if her mother could love her enough to throw her back into the sea.

CHAPTER 23

Death
of a Party Hat

CURSUM PERFICIO.
—The Latin, pronounced like Pinocchio, for "I am completing my journey," a phrase that was carved into the front
walkway of Marilyn Monroe's final residence

October 1973

Marilyn paused by the tree across the street from the
Commonwealth Avenue house. The noon sirens blasted
the birds into the sky. She scanned the horizon for any
suspicious movement. Marilyn had terrific peripheral vision. Saint Theresa of the Roses, the one who got her
breasts cut off, had destiny but no power. Marilyn wanted
both, but Marilyn wanted to keep her breasts.

The sirens gave one last deep blast, and Marilyn went
slowly into the atomic crouch, for old time's sake, then

stood up and entered the family house. She passed through the living room where Great Aunt Nellie was propped on a number of lavish pillows, sipping her tea, a can of Borden's evaporated milk and a bowl of sugar on the silver tray beside her, a second tea cup placed near her own.

"And there you are!" said Nellie Kelly. "You must have had your hand in my mind, as I was thinking about seeing you."

Marilyn kissed Aunt Nellie on the cheek. She was certain she did not have her hand in Nellie's mind, as she would probably have drawn back a nub if she did. The great whirling mechanism that was Nellie Kelly's mental city of the angels chewed and masticated indiscriminately, the Venus's-flytrap of Commonwealth Avenue.

"Aunt Nellie," said Marilyn. "Does my mother love me?"

"You were always beautifully dressed, sparkling clean, and you knew exactly what to do in case of an atomic blast. Thanks to your mother."

Great Aunt Nellie took a sip of her Lipton tea.

"But does she love me?"

"She saved you from falling off the roof when Sputnik went overhead. And she covered you with her own body when she thought we were being bombed. She was willing to die for you! That's love."

"Those were sonic booms."

"It's the thought that counts, isn't that the truth, Mrs. Finnegan?"

Great Aunt Nellie Kelly spun a silver spoon in the second china teacup, presumably for Mrs. Finnegan, and looked toward heaven.

"I wish you loved me enough to stay in this world," said

Marilyn, moving her body out of the line of Nellie Kelly's mind.

The silver spoon clanged noisily to the bottom of the teacup and was silent.

Marilyn walked the long hallway and found her mother seated in the study, the fire ablaze, the air conditioner humming. The television was tuned in to the Watergate hearings. Marilyn sat beside her mother in one of the formal black leather chairs with carved armrests and legs that ended in claws. She had not seen her mother for a year, since the ride in the limousine from the airport.

Marilyn wrapped her hands around the armrest talons.

"You know what John Dean just said?"

"No, Mother."

Marilyn realized they were to go on as if nothing had happened.

"He says he told Nixon, 'There's a cancer growing on the presidency.'"

Marilyn looked at her mother. "There are women in this country who are furious that their soap operas are being interrupted by the Watergate hearings."

Marilyn could play this game as well as Kate. She was, after all, Kate's daughter.

"You know, Marilyn, I'm forty-nine years old, and I still don't understand the perversity of my sex."

"I do," said Marilyn.

"I believe you do," said Kate, never taking her eyes from the Watergate hearings. "I should never have taken you to Filene's."

" 'Queen for a Day.' Do you remember that, Mother? The woman who was the most long-suffering, the most pathetic, was the winner, based on the applause of the women in the audience."

"I'm not interested in nostalgia," said Kate Albion.

Then why was that John Kennedy scrapbook still out of its box, still within finger's reach? The hearings off for the day, Kate slapped shut the television's cathode-ray tube, and Marilyn walked with her mother to City Hall.

The beauty of New England's October did not touch Kate Albion.

"You know who I most admire in this Watergate mess?" asked Kate Albion, bright dead leaves racing from her path.

"Martha Mitchell."

"How did you know?" asked Kate Albion, pleased at Marilyn's astuteness but disturbed at her accuracy. Kate thought of herself as inscrutable.

"I read an article that said the mere sight of Richard Nixon was enough to throw her into a frenzy. They're also trying to commit her to a mental hospital for saying that Richard Nixon thought the whole thing up. They're calling her the Cassandra of Watergate."

"Nixon's going mad, you know," said Kate Albion as they walked past Benjamin Franklin and the green lawn in front of City Hall. They passed through the rotunda and up the grand staircase, their heels clicking across the marble, and crossed to the private staircase and the back entrance to the mayor's office.

"He shoved his press secretary toward a pack of reporters, and he slapped a bystander because, in the glare of the lights, he had mistaken the man for a woman," said Kate Albion.

"Mrs. Finnegan's hooded creature, neither man nor woman," said Marilyn.

"Marilyn, you concern me sometimes. Which brings me to a point."

tic toc
tic toc

Marilyn and her mother went into the mayor's office through the rear entrance.

"Where's Daddy?"

"Where do you think?"

The Blue Lagoon.

Marilyn settled down on the couch as Kate stood behind the mayor's desk.

"I would like you to keep in mind that I'm positioning your father for governor."

Marilyn smiled. "Is he comfortable?"

"The mayor's daughter can get away with popping out of coffins and dressing her medicated daddy up like Mr. Peanut for a spontaneous trip to a Hollywood sex queen's grave. But a governor's daughter might exercise a bit more discretion. Quite simply, Marilyn, try not to go to the Moon quite so often, will you?"·

"Just being patriotic, Mommy." Kate had not won. Yogi was Marilyn's boytoy yet.

"The Republicans are dead in the water for the season. For a Democrat to lose anything this year, he'd have to sell his grandmother."

The telephone rang, and Kate Albion picked up the receiver.

"Yes." Kate Albion's hand trembled slightly as she placed the phone back in its cradle.

When the bough breaks,
The cradle will fall . . .

"Has something happened to Mr. Peanut?" said Marilyn.

"He's going to take the world with him," said Kate.

"Mr. Peanut?" Marilyn was alarmed.

"Stop playing. You're not on tour, and you never have been, Marilyn. You know perfectly well that I'm talking about Nixon."

Kate Albion bolted to the door. "He's launched a worldwide military alert," she said. In a fractional moment of maternal afterthought, Kate said, "You can come with me if you wish."

"Yes, I wish," said Marilyn, not really wanting to be locked underground with Mama, but certain that it was preferable to being blown to bits across the bright green grass.

Kate and Marilyn descended the private staircase to the tunnels beneath City Hall. The walls of the tunnels were slick, dark, and slightly damp, like a birth canal. Marilyn followed Kate through the complex web of altered space, steeling her nerves against the spiders' webs and bats that hung upside down in her head.

Kate said, "The order was, 'Assume Def Con Three,' which means 'Defense Condition Three.' And the order was for all U.S. military worldwide. It can only be issued by the president, the madman with his finger on the button. Seventy B-52s have taken up position in case of nuclear war." Kate's face was as taut as a gargoyle.

"Why?" asked Marilyn.

"Because Richard Nixon is going to take the world out with him."

> *Rockabye Nixon,*
> *Civilization and all.*

The bat wings beat past Marilyn's cheeks and the spiders worked overtime as they entered Kate's private

atomic fallout shelter. Kate sat on the cot, and Marilyn
stood near the door. Marilyn did not want to go into this
room, however attractively it was decorated. She remembered releasing Kate Albion from this shelter when she
had locked herself in, believing that the East Coast blackout was the beginning of a Russian attack.

Kate's mouth was dry as she said, "The last time we
assumed Def Con Three was when President Kennedy
was killed."

Marilyn closed her eyes and felt suffocated by the memory of the ladies crushed together in Filene's basement.

Kate Albion paced through the shelter, past the small
cot with its green army blanket, past the electrical generator in the corner. She sat in the straight-backed chair at
the ham radio and tuned in to the outside world.

Marilyn entered the fallout shelter. She was alone with
her mother for the first time in years. The requirement
for this blessed event was the threat of atomic annihila-
tion. Marilyn laughed quietly, on the verge of hysteria.
She closed the door behind them, making sure that the
release latch operated easily from the inside. Being
locked in a fallout shelter with her mother unto death
conjured visions of cannibalism.

Kate Albion moved the knobs and traveled up and
down the airwaves until she hooked into a military base.
The radio spluttered.

> This is a recall announcement for the 909th Air Refueling
> Squadron, 376th Field Maintenance Squadron, 376th Stra-
> tegic Air Wing, and the 82nd Strategic Reconnaissance
> Squadron. I repeat, this is a recall announcement. . . ."

"The hell with that. Anybody can get that," said Kate
Albion, slapping the side of the radio with her open palm,

as if inanimate objects responded to pain. "What I want to know is," she said impatiently, "are they sending the helicopters to the White House?"

Kate manipulated the dials, and the sounds of police commands and military alerts and taxicab pickup requests formed a radio Babylon that relaxed Kate and ushered her into a Zen condition. Marilyn sat and watched the intensity of her mother and the command she took of the dial.

Marilyn said, "I love you," in the quiet voice she saved for revealing secrets.

"Listen!" said Kate Albion.

"Did you hear me?"

"Listen to this!" repeated Kate. "Nixon's done this. We've got Eisenhower to thank for him. Listen."

Marilyn strained to make out what one shortwave radio was saying to another.

I can see the base from here.... They're setting up inoculation tents. . . ."

Kate was turning the dials with the precision and concentration of a safecracker, but suddenly she was rattled, her fear having rammed her nearer to the dream world, hyperaware of her daughter's declaration of love but afraid of drowning in the deep and beautiful Atlantic.

Dot dot dot.
Dash dash dash.
Dot dot dot.

"He'll crack up all right," said Kate with certainty.

"Who?" demanded Marilyn.

"Nixon, damn it! Nixon! Flirting with danger at the Saints and Sinners party. Sheba Sheik knew what's what. Are you angry? Are you dead? Have some tea! Huh!"

Kate Albion's voice lashed out toward heaven:

I've got a loverly bunch of cocoanuts.
There they are a-standing in a row.

"You even hate Nixon with more passion than you've ever shown toward me."

"That's what your grandfather used to sing when his enemies were going down in flames," said Kate Albion, ignoring Marilyn's statement. "That son of a bitch Nixon wears comfortable shoes you can bet. That hair. That cheap perfume of haughty poverty. A pathetic man, a whining man, is a man without sex appeal, Marilyn. A man without guts. And a man like that doesn't deserve to run this great country. Your father should have killed him as a child. But no. Failure of nerve. No one would have said anything, believe me. Children aren't supposed to kill other children."

"Mothers aren't supposed to eat their young," said Marilyn with anger.

Kate lost the thread of her thoughts and laughed with pleasure at Marilyn's statement, but the respite was short-lived. She stood, manipulating the radio dials, and shouted like a tent evangelist: "Damned Monroe and the Sputnik traveling overhead spilling down into the houses, rattling the knives and television sets. Why did it excite me like that? You know, Marilyn, Sputnik aroused me. You're not the only one who's orgasm happy. Does that surprise you?"

"Not at all," said Marilyn, moving behind the radio.

"I felt like a Communist traitor," whispered Kate, "but then there was always Walter Cronkite to reel me back in."

The static bubbles burst and Kate shouted, "Thank God

for Walter Cronkite! He's the closest thing we've got to a secular saint. I bet he's awful in bed even if he is great on television. He said your name. So what!"

"You're jealous, Mommy," taunted Marilyn.

"There you were. My little girl going on and on about some saint who had her breasts lopped off! I could barely look at you, Marilyn. I was sick with fear because I loved you too much, so much I couldn't look at you sometimes. The world's no place for a little girl who doesn't have claws." Kate Albion let go of the dials and walked behind the radio to Marilyn.

"We're the same height!" said a startled Kate.

Marilyn was pleased to look her mother in the eye.

Kate regained her momentum. "I watched the picture of Nixon peek out from under your dress. What was it I could have done to produce such perversions in my child?"

Marilyn smiled defiantly.

"Mothers are blamed for everything," said Kate. "Just you wait. You'll see. Everything."

Kate turned from Marilyn and walked to the poster of JFK on the back of the fallout shelter door. "The motorcade went by and he waved and waved. And my own husband dazzled beautifully in the sunlight. My president. How I hated that I couldn't be with him. His constant pain made Jack Kennedy too beautiful, the most powerful of the Yankee Doodle dandies. But the true dandy was your father, my Joe Albion, crazy on the swan boats twirling into the night."

Kate Albion turned from the poster and was surprised to find Marilyn standing close behind her. Kate's voice softened as if to ask for compassion. "My God," she said. "A woman with a crazy husband has her hands full. What difference does it make when your husband has a fantasy, or a mistress, if he fails the doomsday test? The big shots get lifted up off the White House lawn in the big, pregnant-looking army helicopters, and where does Joe Albion go? The Blue Lagoon. *Ich bin ein* Bostonian! Standing on top of the desk, hypnotized by my beautiful little girl. It was too painful for me to love you."

Kate's voice became even softer, and Marilyn had to bend closer to hear her words.

"If you had been just a little ugly it would have been easier. Beautiful little girls in the world of the Beast are changed by power into pets, and my heart would not break like that. Slam all the silver hammers on all the popes' heads for all I care. My heart wouldn't break like that. Joe Albion I loved precisely because he lived for the beauty of the Blue Lagoon, and there has to be a slice of beauty in the world, especially for girls."

> *Dot dot dot.*
> *Dash dash dash.*
> *Dot dot dot.*

Kate's voice raised up sudden and sharp like a fascist salute. "Yes, my Marilyn. Speedy Alka-Seltzer took my little girl to the whore castle. Stupid fool. Pixie Finney and 'This is the lettuce crisper.' So what does the queen of Wonderbread do? She bursts from a pine coffin in Atlantic City. I shouldn't have worried so much. My only way to say hello was to put Yogi Jones on the payroll, with orders to kill any killer who came near my baby. He's got a black belt in karate. You didn't know that, did you?"

Marilyn did not back away from her mother.

"That's why he can afford to be so passive. He can kill at will. This is a mother's love."

Marilyn thought, This is Richard Nixon's fault.

"But love can't stop the madman's finger if it diddles with the green button," said Kate. "I'm not as young as I was, but I can plainly see there's no party hat sitting on this presidency: there's a cancer growing in its belly. His own lawyers tell him so."

"Who?"

"Nixon. Nixon! Always Nixon! Aren't you listening?"

Kate took a deep breath, turned her back, and softened as she said, "And not the beauty of the Blue Lagoon, not the beauty of my daughter's hair, can stop it. The one thing I'm grateful for is that your father doesn't have time to paint. God, he's a shitty painter."

> *Dot dot dot.*
> *Dash dash dash.*
> *Dot dot dot.*

Kate Albion sat in the chair before the radio, tuned to the public air channel, and listened to the measured commentary.

> **This military alert has exposed the dramatic state of collapse of this presidency. There are many who now believe Mr. Nixon to be capable of exploiting the international crisis of the Arab-Israeli war, and perhaps leading the superpowers into a nuclear showdown, as a distraction from his illegal activities concerning the Watergate coverup.**

Marilyn looked at her mother, whose thick dark hair tossed around her pale skin like electrical snakes darting through water lilies, beautiful snakes filled with desire and lacking courtesy. A deep love stirred within her for this woman, a love that can stir only when it expects nothing.

With great courage, Marilyn crossed the short distance of the shelter, bent down, and kissed her mother's cheek. She felt the memory of Monroe's crypt against her lips.

Marilyn watched her mother's eyes flicker in the amber light of the communication tubes.

"Do you have to believe we're about to die before you mention loving me?" asked Marilyn.

"This is Richard Nixon's fault," said Kate.

Marilyn straightened up. "Yes. This is Richard Nixon's fault."

Marilyn pressed upon the hydraulic door handle, and the door opened with a hiss. "I love you, Mother. See you above ground."

Kate sat motionless at the radio, then ran her hands through her hair.

Marilyn left the underground chamber, infuriated at Richard Nixon, whom she held responsible for her mother's madness. Bat free, she traveled through the cool tunnel to the sunlight, to the green grass, to Def Con Three.

CHAPTER 24

Watergate
Fabulous Watergate

No milk for the devil.
Poor devil.
—*Marilyn Albion*

Summer 1974

The articles of impeachment were about to be voted upon by the House Judiciary Committee, and Kate and Joe Albion watched the televised political coup from the comfort of the mayor's office. Kate stood beside the television, and Joe sat casually on the leather couch against the wall, sipping a drink.

The television commentator's voice cut through the room.

> Outside of the White House, citizens are expressing their concerns. Citizens are wearing black-and-white striped prison costumes and masks of President Richard Nixon. Citizens are holding up signs with crude black hand-lettering that read "Honk for Impeachment." As the cars, trucks, vans, and motorcycles drive by the White House, the honking of horns creates a harmonic tremor that rattles the windows of the Oval Office and shakes the hell out of the roses in the presidential garden.

Kate Albion laughed wildly and patted the television as if it were a good pet.

The television switched live to the Judiciary Room, where the newsman's voice was as hushed as a commentator at a funeral.

> The vote for the first article of impeachment, for obstruction of justice in an attempted coverup of the Watergate burglaries, is about to begin. Chairman of the House Judiciary Committee, Peter Rodino, will call the role.
> "Representative Holtzman," said Chairman Rodino.
> "Aye," said Representative Holtzman.
> "Representative Drinan," said Chairman Rodino.
> "Aye," said Representative Drinan.

"Drinan better say 'Aye,' " said Kate Albion, pacing and chain-smoking charcoal-filtered Tareytons. In public she attempted to behave as if the demise of the presidency of Richard Nixon were a tragic event. Joe Albion smiled as Kate erupted into the Kelly gospel:

> *I've got a loverly bunch of cocoanuts.*
> *Every ball you throw will make me rich. . . .*

Joe Albion wanted to have sex, but it was impossible for him to compete with the televised drama of the vote.

"Representative Jordan," said Chairman Rodino.
"Aye," said Representative Jordan.

Joe Albion might have been mistaken, but he could have sworn he detected a wave of orgasm charging Kate Albion's body.

"Vote by the House to impeach or not, Richard Nixon has no intention of giving up the presidency," said Kate Albion. "He thinks it's just a case of public image, a case of bad hair. But there's more to the presidency than hair!"

Joe Albion took a sip of his drink and said, "Is there?"

"Representative Froehlich," said the televised chairman.

Kate Albion did not breathe. Froehlich was a Republican.

"Aye," said Representative Froehlich.

Kate Albion paced faster. "Republicans are crossing party lines to impeach! This is real! Richard Nixon and his gang thought, 'What's a little good-natured play to destroy the Democratic contenders by breaking the law and lying? What's a little obstruction of justice to cover up the burglary of the Democratic headquarters?'"

"Representative Railsback," said Chairman Rodino.

"Another Republican," said Kate.

"Aye," said Representative Railsback.

"Nixon and his gang thought, 'What's wrong with the suspension of the constitutional rights of citizens who don't agree with you?' " said Kate Albion. "He thinks because he's the president, he's above the law. He thinks he has a right to defy subpoenas, to wiretap, to burgle, to maintain secret funds, to launder money, and then to whine about it when he gets caught. Jack Kennedy didn't have to do that."

"Representative Kastenmeier," said Chairman Rodino.
"Aye," said Representative Kastenmeier.

"Every good politician has an enemies list, uses dirty tricks and character assassination. But they play fair," said Kate.
Joe Albion said, "You fascinate me, darling."

"Representative Wiggins," said Chairman Rodino.
"NO!" declared Representative Wiggins.

"God damn it!" said Kate Albion, stubbing her cigarette out on the television screen.
Joe Albion was delighted to see that Kate had snapped out of her depression.

"Representative Sarbanes," said Chairman Rodino.
"Aye," said Representative Sarbanes.

"That's more like it," said Kate, brushing the ashes from the screen. She looked at Joe, smiled, and said, "I get excited."

"I like that," said Joe. "It reminds me of our first night together in this office."

"Representative McClory," said Chairman Rodino.
"No," said Representative McClory.

"He'll swing to yes on article two, you watch," said Kate. Joe Albion was in a state of hello, but Kate was counting votes.

"To keep his place in history as thirty-seventh president of the United States of America, Richard Nixon took the only route open to him," said Kate Albion.

"What was that?" asked Joe, twirling his ice cubes in his scotch.

"He began to blow-dry his hair," said Kate.

"Representative Flowers," said Chairman Rodino.
"Aye," said Representative Flowers.

The commentator's voice rolled deep and dark as the Atlantic.

The first article of impeachment is adopted, twenty-seven ayes, eleven nays. The second article of impeachment charges Richard Nixon with abuse of power. Chairman of the House Judiciary Committee, Peter Rodino, will call the role.

"Representative Hungate," said Chairman Rodino.

"Aye," said Representative Hungate.

"Representative McClory," said Chairman Rodino.

There was silence in the office of the mayor of Boston, the silence before the guillotine falls sharp and neat, when the last thing the condemned man sees is the red carnation in the headsman's buttonhole.

"Aye," said Representative McClory.

Kate Albion's hand chopped through the air, trailing cigarette ashes like the tail of a comet. The deed was done.

McCLORY JOINS TO IMPEACH

—

The klieg lights, microphones, and all members of the media were magnetized to the mayor's daughter, the composite BITCH Fury and vulnerable bombshell, denied by both factions as a political liability trained at the Martha Mitchell Finishing School.

Marilyn was a walking happening, an endless event. She created street theater wherever she went, protected more or less by PAWS, of which she was an honorary member, and the constant surveillance of Molly and Dolly Gunn, who had become an endless source of interest to the American Psychiatric Association.

While the kingmakers wept in Bohemian Grove, and Diane Sawyer wept with the president's press secretary, Marilyn explained the fall of Richard Nixon to the press. Lowering her eyelids and pushing her thick blond hair from her round pure-fire face, the words came through her from beyond the grave—or at least from another city, a sort of cosmic Edgar Bergen and Charlie McCarthy.

Marilyn took a deep breath, her beautiful breasts hovering and landing safely beneath a tasteful long strand of pearls.

"I note that the president has taken to blow-drying his hair, but I must state that this is a case of too little too late," declared Marilyn. "When I close my eyes"—which she did,—"and I run my fingers through his mane"— which she did in the air before her and in the eye of the television camera—"there is no electricity. There is only the telltale stickiness of years and years of Brylcreem."

> She gave Boston cream pie to the poor,
> Brylcreem to the needy men.

Marilyn breathed. Marilyn continued. "The people of the United States are performing the ritual of Saturnalia, the ritual assassination of the mock king, who is given all the powers of the king for one long day and then must be destroyed."

"Could you elaborate?" asked Davey Finney, a reporter for the *Boston Globe*.

The media people roared with laughter as Marilyn smiled seductively, for elaborating was definitely her great power.

Marilyn spoke: "The election of Richard Nixon was an invocation of chaos so that everything could be wiped out and started over again."

Molly and Dolly Gunn couldn't agree more, based on their analysis of ancient fertility rites.

"What does this mean for the country?" asked Davey Finney.

"Well, Richard Nixon needs to resign. Richard Nixon needs to come into contact with his sensual self. Richard Nixon needs to keep his finger away from the green button in the black box, which does not contain a pearl necklace but the fate of the world." And my mother's sanity, thought Marilyn.

Marilyn grabbed the long strand of pearls that hung from her neck and bit it. The media loved her. Marilyn opened her big blue eyes and blew a great big kiss to the nation.

The reporters roared with Rintrah, while Christina Smythe-Corduroy Stuckey grimaced on the sidelines, and Fatty Finney, the local Democratic party boss, watched Marilyn become a political liability that might cost her father and the Democrats the governorship.

Christina Smythe-Corduroy Stuckey believed that Marilyn could trigger a wave of rape with her careless statements. Worse than that, Christina believed that Marilyn made women look silly. Christina Smythe-Corduroy Stuckey had just about determined that it was more important to sacrifice the individual for the sake of the many, the individual being Marilyn.

Kate and Joe Albion watched Fatty Finney's cigar snap to attention in his mouth and in the process drop its long, thick ashes on top of the great big mahogany mayoral desk. Fatty Finney was preparing to leave. In the relative coolness of the mayor's office, the passion of summer pulsated in a wave of heat out on the grass. He was angry.

"So this is how it is," said Fatty. "If you can't get her under control, how the hell are you gonna control the machine?" Trailing ashes behind him, Fatty Finney left the mayor's office, slamming the door behind him.

"Mentioning in public the possibility that Nixon might

blow up the world was very Martha Mitchell–ish of Marilyn," said Kate.

"Whatever happened to the poor woman?" said Joe.

"She's resting," said Kate. "She's happy now."

The televised voting process and media hunt around the White House for signs of movement was relentless. The arrival of a Mayflower moving van made prime-time coverage. The commentators' voices were cracking with anticipation, rent with preorgasmic frustration.

In Paris, the foreign minister, Jean-Pierre Fourcade, is frightened that the activities in the United States could unleash disaster in the world money market, and in London there were reports of a wave of fear in response to unidentified repercussions. Planets are said to be lining up in deadly syzygy, a large radioactive meteor is said to be on a collision course with the earth, and in the midwestern United States, a farmer and his wife claim to have witnessed the dead rising from their graves, demanding that a Kennedy sit again in the Oval Office.

That last comment got Kate's attention.

"There will always be a Kennedy," said Kate. "They can shoot them down, but like the sons of Banquo, they'll just keep coming at you."

You would have made a great monarchist, thought Joe Albion, who said, "Yes, my love."

"Poor Marilyn," said Kate. "Can we help her in time?"

tic toc
tic toc

The commentator's voice was tight with controlled frenzy.

The vote on article three to impeach, charging defiance of subpoenas, will now proceed.

Joe and Kate turned to the television.

"Representative Brooks," said Chairman Rodino.
"Aye," said Representative Brooks.
"Representative Hogan," said Chairman Rodino.
"Aye," said Representative Hogan.

Kate Albion was not ashamed as the slightly sadistic angle in her personality was titillated with excitement.

"He's going to have to resign or go to jail," she said, imagining Richard Nixon holding out his tin plate to a nasty jailer, who filled it with cold beans.

"Representative Sandman," said Chairman Rodino.
Mister Sandman, bring me a dream.
"Aye," said Representative Sandman.

"I can hear his tin cup on the cell bars," said Joe Albion, in an attempt to seduce his wife.

Kate Albion felt romantic.

Make him the cutest
that I've ever seen.

She ran one hand through Joe's hair, and tuned in on her police band radio with the other.

Please turn on your magic beam
Mister Sandman, bring me a dream.

In between the kisses and the static radio waves, Kate heard a very strange alert from the police station:

A kamikaze pilot just left National Airport in D.C. He's headed for the committee room. Says he's gonna plunge

**right into it. Kill everyone. Maybe we should shoot him
down?**

Breaking a kiss, Kate Albion looked out the window and
said, "Republicans are such fanatics."

Joe Albion laughed until he almost got sick.

"Don't overdo, Joe. You always overdo."

There was a buzz over the intercom, and the secretary,
Mabel Finney, said, "There's a Christina Smythe-Corduroy Stuckey here to see you." Kate Albion was very interested. "Send her in, Mabel."

Joe Albion posed on the leather couch, and Kate Albion
stood, hands clasped royally behind her back. There was
a knock at the door, but Kate said nothing. Was this be-
trayal? she asked herself. There was a knock at the door,
and Kate said, "Come in."

Christina Smythe-Corduroy Stuckey was surprisingly at
ease in the city's seat of power.

"We have a problem," she said, addressing Kate Albion.

"Yes, we do. Do you have any suggestions?" asked Kate.

Christina Smythe-Corduroy Stuckey sighed and said, "I
don't know what to do to help our poor Marilyn."

tic toc
tic toc

What a bitch, thought Kate of Christina Smythe-Corduroy Stuckey.

"Marilyn needs help," Christina continued. "Professional help. We can't let her be exposed to the media like
this any longer. If they push her any further, any closer
to that line, I'm afraid we might lose her."

If you cross that line, be ready to recognize the enemy.

"Lose her?" said Joe Albion. Christina Smythe-Corduroy Stuckey fascinated him. She's probably as bad as Nikita Khrushchev in bed, he thought.

Kate Albion said slowly, "There's a doctor who could possibly help her. Dr. Mason Squibb. I've already spoken to him about her."

You'd do that to your own daughter for power, you bitch, thought Christina Smythe-Corduroy Stuckey of Kate Kelly Albion.

"Old Sunflower Shorts?" said Joe Albion. "Yes. I don't know if he could help her, but I enjoyed myself. I painted."

Joe absently rubbed his temples, then gave the ladies a great big smile.

It was plain to Christina that Joe Albion's greatest asset was a lack of conscience.

"I agree with you that she must not be exposed to the dangers of this media coverage, what with the fragile condition of her mind," said Kate Albion.

"Yes. It's a difficult thing to do, but we need to save her," said Joe Albion. "I wish there was another way." Joe Albion really wanted to sit under the big gold dome up on top of the hill in the governor's office in the State House overlooking the Boston Common and Brimstone Corner.

"Maybe a vacation would do the trick," he said. "A trip to Hollywood. A look at a palm tree."

"It's too late for vacations. Marilyn's staying at that—that bordello, with PAWS, the fanatic whores," said Kate Albion. "Do you know what kind of press she's getting us?"

"Frances Bright might help," said Joe Albion. "For old time's sake."

Kate Albion and Christina Smythe-Corduroy Stuckey smirked at Joe Albion, then looked at each other. As their eyes met, they both knew the other was thinking the same thing: Men will use anyone to achieve their goal.

"I'll call her," said Joe Albion. Joe Albion lifted the receiver and dialed the number.

Kate noted that he still knew the phone number.

"Frances," he said. Christina and Kate studied each other silently, using a stare-down game at which they both excelled. Neither of them lost, because they both turned on Joe Albion as he spoke.

"Frances. Joe. . . . I need your help, Frances. Please understand I'm calling you only because I need your help. . . . I need to set up a place and time when I can discreetly pick up Marilyn. Any further media attention would be very dangerous for her. We're very concerned. We have a doctor, Mason Squibb, who will be able to treat her. . . . Yes, Old Sunflower Shorts. . . ."

> Red temple splotches
> And a great big smile to go,
> Please!

"We'll need two days to get the papers drawn up in case she refuses to cooperate. So let's say on Friday. Can you get her to . . . the swan boats? Frances? Are you there? Good. I'll be at the lagoon with Christina Smythe-Corduroy Stuckey, Kate, the doctor . . . Dr. Squibb. . . . Thank you, Frances. You're very kind."

Joe Albion placed the phone back into its cradle. He closed his eyes and sat beneath the big gold dome; Kate Albion adjusted her crown—strike that—tiara; and Christina Smythe-Corduroy Stuckey visited Marilyn in a locked ward.

* * *

It was a beautiful summer-fun Friday evening at the Boston Public Garden, even if the country did weep with pain, real and theatrical, at the loss of trust in the presidency. The solemn voting process ground on, and the Democrats were behaving oh so honorably, so impartially, seducing the Republican votes in the name of honor and decency and the Constitution. Two more articles of impeachment had been voted upon, and the tension in the country accelerated to an unbearable level as rumors spread like poison oak that the president was out of touch with reality.

The swan boats bobbed in the water at the dock, as the Gunn twins and Betty Bloom strolled toward the lagoon, Marilyn surrounded by them. Betty Bloom looked over her shoulder from time to time, like Illya Kuryakin, the man from U.N.C.L.E.

Marilyn was wearing a flowing white dress that hovered and slammed against her hot body. Large black sunglasses covered her eyes, Jackie O style. Marilyn had designed her hair differently this evening. She wore a perfectly built beehive that was protected by a small, sheer blue kerchief. She seemed out of place, as if she usually traveled in dark places. Her fingernails were long and highly polished, a deep and dangerous-looking red. She walked dreamily toward the swan boats, absently fingering the gold letter pin, the *M* pinned to her white dress near her heart. Her steps were unsteady as she maneuvered through the world and across the short, green, manicured grass.

The mayor's black stretch limousine pulled to the curb a discreet distance from Marilyn. Freddie Finney was at the wheel, tears in his eyes, but at the wheel: the good soldier following commands, with a broken heart, but following commands. Out of the limousine, like an endless string of clowns from a tiny circus car, came Joe Albion, Kate Albion, Christina Smythe-Corduroy Stuckey, Dr. Mason Squibb, a county law-enforcement agent, Findlay Finney, who bore the court-approved papers for Marilyn's commitment, and Yogi Jones, who had the obscure hope that if a lobotomy were performed on Marilyn, she might then agree to marry him.

Joe Albion was disappointed that Frances Bright had gone through with this setup of Marilyn. Kate Albion was disappointed that Marilyn was so ignorant as to fall into the trap. Christina Smythe-Corduroy Stuckey was disappointed that the Gunn twins were present and would witness her collaboration.

Dr. Squibb, Doctor of Electronics, was absolutely titillated by the prospect of curing Marilyn, having been Betty-Bloomed at Walden Pond by her design. Yogi Jones followed at a respectful distance, practicing his marriage proposal speech. Freddie Finney waited by the limousine, and smoked, and wondered if his mother would forgive him for not saving Marilyn.

Joe and Kate, Christina and Yogi, Dr. Squibb and Findlay Finney closed in on Marilyn, who turned and saw their approach.

Marilyn ran slowly and awkwardly, her heels digging into the grass, and jumped aboard one of the swan boats, the Gunn twins and Betty Bloom chasing after her—and yes! all aboard! Molly Gunn leaped onto the swan's back and began to peddle the swan boat out onto the lagoon like hell ripped loose, which amounted to a fraction of a knot per hour. Not to be outfoxed, Joe, Kate, Dr. Squibb, and Yogi Jones climbed aboard another swan boat, and Christina Smythe-Corduroy Stuckey settled into the paddle seat. Findlay Finney stayed on shore because he feared death by drowning.

The lumbering dream-time swan boats gave hypnotic chase to one another upon the lagoon, enlightened bright white swan feathers ruffling, black Oriental eyes in harmony with the gods, Kool-Aid green stripes gleaming on the water. Arms waved, and shouts broke out from swan boat to swan boat like sonic booms demanding that roses fall; but the swan boats were the swan boats, and pleasure will not be rushed. The weeping willows rustled in the light wind.

At the limousine, a spacy young man with a cap pulled over his eyes sidled up to the car and slid beneath it. Freddie Finney felt that someone was tampering with his insides—so tied to the car was his whole being—as a *snap crackle pop* jangled in his gut and chest. He thought he'd had a heart attack, but he looked down and saw a precious piece of engine rolling away into the sewer. He reached down and dragged the intruder out by the ankles. He was about to beat him to a pulp and throw him for dead into the nearest flower bed, but Freddie Finney had a rule about never beating anyone if you're not sure who it is. He was a gentleman. Instead, Freddie Finney tore the man's cap from his head.

"Mr. Marat, sir, what the hell are you doing?" asked Freddie Finney, letting go of the Boston Brahmin limousine mutilator.

David Marat smiled and between eye dilations explained, "Being patriotic. Getting our Marilyn to the White House, where she's needed."

Freddie Finney and David Marat laughed as loud as the Woolworth's counter ladies at the two swan boats jousting with each other in one of the clumsiest chase scenes ever witnessed.

"Marilyn! It's for your own good!" shouted Kate as the forces of evilesque won out, and Joe, Kate, Yogi, Squibb, and Christina boarded Marilyn's boat.

Marilyn turned toward them and smiled, but it was not Marilyn whom they had trapped upon the swan boat. It was Frances Bright. Frances Bright really liked coming out on top, and she and Yogi Jones locked libidos. They would meet later in one-sixth gravity, no rust, no fuss.

The Gunn twins and Betty Bloom were ecstatic, and Frances Bright blew Kate and Joe Albion, Christina Smythe-Corduroy Stuckey, Yogi Jones, and Dr. Mason Squibb a great big kiss.

At the limousine, Jackie X pulled up on her Harley Davidson motorcycle, custom built and displaying three dozen American flags. Jackie X had liberated herself.

Wearing her short black dress with the plunging neckline, her strand of pearls nestled in her cleavage, Marilyn was securely seated on the back of the Harley, a Filene's bag carefully tied onto the carrier rack behind her.

Freddie Finney took off his cap to Marilyn.

"Do you forgive me, Marilyn?" asked Freddie.

"Of course, ever so," she said.

Marilyn looked at David Marat, grabbed him around the neck, and gave him the deepest of kisses. Jackie X kissed David Marat on the cheek. David Marat kissed Jackie X on the hand.

Jackie X revved her engine, and Marilyn positioned her spike heels onto the footrests and waved to the swan boats, which drifted limp and spent upon the lagoon. Kate and Joe Albion smiled proudly, to the confusion of Dr.

Squibb, Christina Smythe-Corduroy Stuckey, and Findlay Finney. Yogi Jones and Frances Bright understood in a hot flash, and Betty Bloom and the Gunn twins waved and blew kisses to Jackie X and Marilyn, who disappeared in an Aladdin's-lamp cloud of blue motorcycle smoke, bound for Washington, D.C.

Kate Albion now knew that Marilyn was ready to play with the devil, and she commanded the swan boats to return to the dock. It was an unusual time to get maternal, but Kate, and anyone who wished to follow her, was going to Washington, where, hungry for meat, Sheba Sheik growled and stalked the Oval Office in the White House.

CHAPTER 25

Talk to Me, Richard Nixon, Tell Me All About It

> The World was all before them, where to choose
> Their place of rest, and Providence their guide:
> They hand in hand with wandering steps and slow,
> Through Eden took their solitary way.
>
> —*Paradise Lost*

August 1974

The morning of Thursday, August 8, 1974, Marilyn entered Washington D.C., on the back of Jackie X's Harley-Davidson, miniature American flags fluttering across the handlebars. The sultry air and light rain were peculiar for Washington, and the clouds had the power to lift the soul by the scruff of the neck up into the atmosphere, only to leave it dangling godless and without taxi fare, exiled from both political parties. Rumor had it that Billy Graham was nearby because it was feared that the president might commit suicide. Marilyn knew what everyone knew, but no one else would say: the president could take the world out with him.

As Jackie X circled the White House, Marilyn saw that the national drama had not affected the tourist line, which stretched around the block from the east gate.

Marilyn shouted into Jackie's ear over the roar of the Harley, "Americans don't let anything stand between them and their vacations."

Marilyn had not slept very much, but as they circled the seat of power, she could not dismiss as the product of sleep deprivation the image her eyes sent to her brain. Hovering near the entrance to the Executive Office Building were Nellie Kelly, Biddie O'Brien, and the gang of Woolworth's counter ladies.

Jackie X steered the Harley to the rear of the Presidential Ellipse, a tree-bordered circle due south of the White House. Marilyn dismounted, straightened her black stretch dress, and arranged her breasts within its tight top, plucking the long pearl necklace from her cleavage. Jackie X unfastened the Filene's bag from the back of the motorcycle.

Marilyn embraced Jackie, who climbed onto her motorcycle and revved the engine. The sight of a woman roaring, Rintrah-style, on a Harley down Pennsylvania Avenue horrified both Democrats and Republicans alike.

Marilyn looked to the east. Marilyn looked to the west. Marilyn made her way to her rendezvous at the northern corner of the Presidential Ellipse and the square stone stub that was to serve as a meeting point: the Zero Milestone, the belly button of Washington, D.C., the place from which all distances are supposed to be measured. She stood beside the Zero Milestone; and across the green grass, raven black and even more beautiful than Marilyn remembered from the counterinaugural, pranced Belle

Washington, daughter of Martha Washington, the White House maid. Belle was dazzling in a crisp white uniform, something Belle would wear only for a covert operation. Everyone Marilyn had seen since she arrived in Washington had adopted a somber attitude in response to the magnitude of the situation, but Belle Washington was in a party spirit.

"Hey, Cheesecake!" said Belle, her voice still ceremoniously low like the first female must have sounded. "Welcome to the end of your civilization. Sky's gonna open up and rain down all sorts of righteous crap. All seven seals gonna rip open like the surprise doors on 'Let's Make a Deal,' and all the angels and all the devils are gonna do the monster mash."

Belle Washington made some impressive mash moves upon the Presidential Ellipse. Belle Washington had soul, even if it had been sullied by the Father of Our Country.

"Miss Devil's Food. So nice to see you back at your ancestral lodgings," replied Marilyn, Queen Elizabeth style, dropping an imaginary human toe hors d'oeuvre into her Filene's shopping bag to save for later, with tea.

Belle Washington studied Marilyn and said, "Operation Babaloo requires something with a little less flash. That black dress with your tits dangling to the ground is not the ideal choice for the discriminating infiltrator's wardrobe this season." Marilyn was sexy, for a white girl, thought Belle, but dumb. Belle now knew that the dumb-blonde thing had some truth to it.

Marilyn held up her Filene's shopping bag and smiled. "Can you guard me while I duck behind that tree?"

"Duck and cover!" said Belle.

"Duck and cover!" said Marilyn, throwing her arms around Belle's neck and giving her a great big kiss on the cheek. As Marilyn slipped behind the trees, Belle made a note to limit her use of Love Potion #9, as it tampered with her dangerousness.

The rustle of the Filene's bag was heard round the world as Belle Washington studied the White House.

"You know why they call it the White House?" called Belle to Marilyn in the midst of her metamorphosis. "On plantations, the master's house was called the White House because that's where the white folks lived. Now there wasn't a black house. No no no. There were the slave quarters, right here on this pretty little Presidential Ellipse."

Tourists passed by Belle Washington at some distance, fearing she might be some sort of Black Pantherette, her glistening white maid's uniform suicidally wired with explosives. Marilyn emerged from behind the tree, holding her Filene's bag, which now contained her black dress. Marilyn was wearing a Woolworth's counter lady uniform, although she had not removed her spikes.

"You'll get arrested for impersonating a Woolworth's lady," said Belle Washington, approaching Marilyn and marveling at the authenticity of her outfit. "Where the hell'd you get that?"

Marilyn reached into the marvelously designed hip pocket, pulled out a name pin, and showed it to Belle.

" 'Flora,' " read Belle. "Is that some kind of vegetation?"

"Flora is Mrs. Finnegan's first name, and we had about the same body mass. It was just distributed differently," said Marilyn, adjusting her breasts.

"Who in hell was Mrs. Finnegan?"

"She said he'd never have these," said Marilyn, cupping her breasts, "and he'd never get over it."

"I think it's time for a tour of the White House," said Belle, fascinated by the white mind. "Now you watch for

me when you pass from the East Room to the Green
Room."

"Is this dangerous?"

There is need for alarm.

"Most of the staff is drunk," said Belle. "The Secret
Service is busy keeping Vice President Ford, who we call
'Cinderella,' from falling into the Potomac. And the joke
backstairs is 'Does President Nixon know the little black
box ain't the bell for the butler?' " Belle Washington
laughed with radical pleasure.

"While we're laughing, we could all be blown up," said
Marilyn.

"Not so big a loss, if you ask me," said Belle.

Marilyn pinned Mrs. Finnegan's name tag on her left
lapel and tightly clutched her Filene's bag. Marilyn could
not fathom the black mind.

"I'll be inside," said Belle.

"How will you get in?"

"I'm gonna go see my poor old slave Mama with
wooden teeth marks in her arms," said Belle. "You see
that skinny little slice of electric blackness over there by
the service entrance, kind of smiling and waving at me?"

"Yes," said Marilyn.

"That's Jackson Finney, and he's my main man. He's
also security," said Belle.

"Jackson Finney," said Marilyn, "of the Washington
Finneys," as Belle sauntered on over to the servants' gate
like an egg on a hot griddle. Belle gave Jackson a great big
kiss and walked right on in to the White House. Marilyn
was surprised that President Nixon had never been assassinated or even had an attempt made on his life; but she
knew that he was such an ideal depository for both ration-

al and irrational hate that he was of great cathartic use to the nation as long as he was alive.

Marilyn walked slowly toward the east gate, mixing with the tourists. It was late afternoon, and the crowds had swelled in front of the White House and across the Presidential Ellipse. As Marilyn moved across the ellipse, she saw Billy Steinway leading a small group in song. He looked exactly the same.

> *In one-sixth gravity*
> *No rust*
> *No erosion*

Billy's eyes were fixed on a blow-up doll of President Nixon in a chain-gang uniform propped against the black iron gate of the White House. He sang in his bagpipe voice:

> *Yes, Mr. Richard Nixon*
> *You thought you stole the crown*

Marilyn studied Billy Steinway and felt a flush of anger crackle in her head.

> *But square cut or pear shaped*
> *These rocks don't lose their shape*

And she remembered that she had learned to dance without him. Cha cha cha.

As she headed east, she saw tight knots of citizenry expressing their concerns as they awaited history, their dreadful faces thronged at the gate.

Near the doorway of the byzantine Executive Office Building across from the White House, Marilyn saw Nellie Kelly at the head of a pack of Woolworth's counter ladies.

They were pretending to be absorbed by the bronze tablet to the left of the entrance, which commemorated the "services and sufferings of 243,135 horses and mules used in World War I." Their eyes were on the bronze tablet, but their large, heavily powdered noses sniffed at the White House. Marilyn felt a small and friendly inhabitation by Mrs. Finnegan.

Nellie Kelly and the Woolworth's ladies spied Marilyn, and in her peripheral vision, Marilyn saw Nellie Kelly point her long and terrible finger at her. The pack of Woolworth's ladies began to close in. They had seen the uniform. Marilyn did not step up her pace toward the White House. She did not wish to appear suspicious. She joined the line for the White House tour, Nellie Kelly and the Woolworth's ladies hot on her heels. They entered the line as the security guard placed a rope behind them, announcing that no one else would be allowed to enter the White House that day.

As the Woolworth's ladies surrounded Marilyn, Nellie Kelly leaned close to her and fingered the FLORA name tag.

"She'll ride forever 'neath the streets of Boston," said Nellie Kelly. "But she'll have to do without me until I'm dead."

"Aunt Nellie. You're not on tour."

"And miss you bringing the silver hammer down on Nixon? We're here to help."

> *Nose of Nixon, eye of politician,*
> *Liver of blaspheming Republican*

The Woolworth's ladies tightened their circle around Marilyn, who remembered holding hands with little girls in the schoolyard, circling, orbiting to rhymes that would solve the riddle "Where is love?"

Her peaceful reverie was broken by Biddie O'Brien. "So fair and foul a day I have not seen. Cannibalism. That's what it amounts to. Emotional cannibalism. Look at them," said Biddie, who pointed to the masses packed outside the gate and across the ellipse. The pack nodded, repeating in hushed tones in deference to the seriousness of the day: "Cannibalism, cannibalism." They licked their lips.

Nellie Kelly spoke: "They've needed a good shock, something almost planetary, though you know I don't indulge in any of that blarney like reading the cards, as it can lead to excommunication."

The Woolworth's ladies laughed as loud as men. Nellie Kelly was, of course, lying.

"As I was saying," continued Nellie, "they haven't had a good shock since darling President Kennedy was shot dead in Dallas."

The tourists in the line, whom Marilyn assumed would be offended by Nellie Kelly and the ladies, the tourists who represented the badlands, the flatlands, snow and tornado country, turned to them and nodded in solemn agreement.

It was at this moment that Marilyn saw Kate and Joe Albion by the gate, surrounded by the Gunn twins, Christina Smythe-Corduroy Stuckey, Frances Bright, who was amorously attended to by Yogi Jones, Betty Bloom, Dr. Squibb, and David Marat. It was charming how the tragedy of one man and the triumph of the political system had united them. Kate and Joe Albion strained toward the commotion in the tour line, but Marilyn, unsure of their intentions, concealed herself in the warm aroma of Nights of Araby perfume mixed with magnolia blossoms.

Having terrific peripheral vision, Kate Albion saw Marilyn clearly.

"If anything happens to Marilyn," said Kate, "it's Richard Nixon's fault."

"It's Richard Nixon's fault," chanted the group, following up with "Shave his head! Shave his head!"

Blow-drying had simply come too late for the president.

The tour line inched forward and a tape-recorded voice with the distinctive rhythm and tonal qualities of a game show host addressed them from behind the magnolias:

Welcome to the White House.

Nellie Kelly and the ladies gave the tape-recorded voice their undivided attention as they moved toward the entrance to the first floor.

It is a unique privilege, for here is the only place in the world where the elected head of state regularly opens his official home to visitors.

Nellie Kelly and the Woolworth's ladies approached the threshold, Marilyn at their core, as the recording continued:

President and Mrs. Nixon are delighted to have you visit this country's most historic home. And remember: even by passing through it, you become a part of its history.

For a girl, thought Marilyn, history is just a collection of uncomfortable shoes. But being a true American fortified by Mrs. Finnegan's uniform, and wishing to exorcise her mother's demon, Marilyn crossed the threshold into the

White House, where the town guide waited for their group.

The main hallway had six marble columns and was lit by a large glass lantern that reminded Marilyn of the Revolution-era lamp posts in Boston. Marilyn entered the East Room.

"The room is eighty-seven and one-half feet long and approximately forty-five feet wide," said the tour guide, who bore a heavy resemblance to Bill Cullen.

I'll take ritual sacrifice for one hundred, Bill.

Three crystal chandeliers glittered with thousands of hanging prisms in the white-and-gold room that boasted the full-length portraits of George and Martha Washington. Marilyn paused before George, and in his features she clearly saw a resemblance across the centuries to Belle's face. The guide droned on, trying to seem at ease and in no way alarmed by the blow-dried madman upstairs in the White House.

tic toc
tic toc

Marilyn clutched her Filene's bag. Belle had said, "Now you watch for me when you pass from the East Room to the Green Room."

"President Kennedy lay in state in this room before being carried to the Capitol," said the tour guide.

The summer's gone
And all the roses dying. . . .

Marilyn stood in the center of the East Room and, her heart a little broken, imagined President Kennedy's coffin displayed there.

It's you, it's you
Must go
And I must bide.

Nellie Kelly and the Woolworth's gang surrounded the mesmerized Marilyn. "Hurry up, please, it's time," said Nellie, and she guided Marilyn past the inlaid mahogany doorways to the Green Room.

The guide said, "The Green Room is approximately thirty feet long and twenty-three feet wide and has only one window—"

Biddie O'Brien was alarmed when a long thin black arm reached out from behind a discreetly placed white servant's door and selected her like a grab bag at a church bazaar. Behind the white door, there was a horror of commotion as Belle Washington, the whites of her eyes gleaming, beheld in horror the Nights of Araby–soaked Biddie O'Brien. Biddie sniffed at Belle as if she were a dangerous exotic flower from another planet that Biddie desperately wanted for her Easter hat. Belle deposited Biddie O'Brien back into the Green Room and was more selective this time, coming up with Marilyn Albion.

Nellie Kelly and the Woolworth's ladies surrounded the white door, and the infuriated Bill Cullen–look-alike tour guide howled as if his own body were being violated. Nellie and the ladies, brazen and adventurous, decided better left unsaid that one was missing. They continued on the White House tour, proud that they had fulfilled their historical destiny.

In the servants' quarters, among the maids, butlers, and cooks, Marilyn watched the black-and-white television. President Nixon's face flashed upon the screen. The makeup men had concealed the fact that he had been

349

crying in the Cabinet Room with members of Congress. Backstairs, they knew everything about the Nixon White House. Just before the cameras went live, the president had said, "Blonds photograph better, don't they?" But now Mr. Nixon spoke to the nation not of blonds, not of high crimes and misdemeanors, not of Watergate, not of secret wars in Cambodia.

> I shall leave this office with regret at not completing my term, but with gratitude for the privilege of serving as your president for the past five and a half years. . . . I have never been a quitter. To leave office before my term is completed is abhorrent to every instinct in my body.

"Looks like he's quittin' now to save his ass," said Martha Washington. "Mm mm mm. Whatever would Mr. Washington have said if he had seen this fool at the head of his country."

Mr. Nixon did not speak to the nation of impeachment proceedings or the vileness of the press. Mr. Nixon spoke to the nation about boxing, about

> the man in the arena whose face is marred by dust and sweat and blood, who strives valiantly, who errs and comes short again and again. . . .

"Who does he think he is? The Brown Bomber?" said Franklin Finney with indignation.

"He's the Mad Bomber," said Belle Washington, who was greatly appreciated for her clarity of vision. Belle pointed to Dan Rather's image on the screen. "Look at this fool, running off at the mouth about the 'nobility' and 'touch of class' in Mr. Nixon's speech."

Strom Thurmond, the white supremacist senator, flashed up on the screen. He was not popular backstairs, but their hate slashed only casually at his image because he was too easy a target. Senator Strom Thurmond sang the praises of Richard Nixon: his beauty, his passion, his sense of fashion.

Roger Mudd said:

> Well, Senator Thurmond, if he was so wonderful, why did he have to resign?

The maids, butlers, and cooks gave each other high fives, laughed as loud as the Woolworth's counter ladies, and wondered aloud if Mr. Mudd had some soul in his family tree.

In the living rooms across America, the applause meter quivered wildly and pressed razor sharp against the president's jugular vein.

Marilyn was alone in the servants' bathroom, where she had adorned herself in her black dress and pearls. She breathed deeply and hypnotically until her whole being was alive and vibrating with Woman.

> *My lips just ache*
> *To have you take*
> *The kiss that's waiting*
> *For you.*

Oh, thought Marilyn in the servants' bathroom, I was born too early. Maybe I do have brain damage. I've never done a thing like this. What if I'm mistaken for an assassin?

But Marilyn breathed and dug deep into her courage because she knew it was her destiny to absolve the poor beast, out-Flashed by JFK. Marilyn emerged from the bathroom.

"Belle. Where is the president going to be?" she asked.

"He'll be in the Lincoln Sitting Room, carrying on, bawling and talking up at the pictures on the wall, getting all sentimental and squirrelly. You know Mr. Nixon."

"Won't he wonder who I am?"

"He wonders who he is," said Belle Washington.

In the early hours of the morning, Belle led Marilyn through the labyrinthine back corridors and stairways that led the servants to the president's private quarters, and deserted her. Marilyn panicked, but remembered her duty as an American.

Marilyn stepped up the staircase. A Secret Serviceman appeared at the top of the landing, unfriendly, a brick in his heart. Marilyn moved in her slow, liquid walk, as if she just might lose her balance maneuvering her splendid body through the world, as if getting from one place to another were an act of God. As Marilyn closed in on the Secret Serviceman, he visibly struggled with a compulsion to hold her up, to protect her.

Marilyn was surrounded by a white light. Marilyn had walked from the dark side of the moon and into the White House.

The Secret Serviceman was mesmerized. He tried to pull himself out of her trance. "Poison apple," he whispered, his mouth dry, but a smile flickered on his lips and he took a bite. Marilyn put her hand on his strong arm for balance. She took off one spike heel, shook a tiny stone out of it, and put the shoe back on her foot, never looking down, her eyes locked into his eyes.

"Are you General Haig?" she asked the Secret Serviceman.

"No, ma'am. Secret Service." He straightened and preened.

"You look like a general."

Her eyes were full of love. She looked at the Secret Serviceman as if he were the only man in the world.

"I have to see the president now, General. He's waiting for me."

She kissed the tips of her fingers and pressed them against his cheek.

The Secret Serviceman looked at this voluptuous blonde, with her parted lips and enlightened eyes, and saw the ecstatic incarnation of woman: fearless beauty in an evil and dangerous world.

Marilyn moved away and out of his sight. The Secret Serviceman was proud of the president, who was about to become a man and take his place among the great leaders of the United States of America. Not enough can be said for blow-drying, he thought.

Marilyn felt the tiny teeth of panic dig into her body, but she gathered her breath into her belly and conjured herself into a self-induced trance that allowed her to walk into the deserted Corridor of Time, named for its paintings of former presidents. At the end of the corridor was a tall and narrow, clear cathedral window. In and out of the magic-lantern slide show in Marilyn's mind slipped the Corridor of Memories, where Marilyn Monroe's body lay in its crypt in a light green dress upon champagne-colored velvet, looking as beautiful in death as she did in life.

Marilyn walked to the alcove of the Lincoln Sitting Room and saw that, although it was August, a fire blazed in the gray marble fireplace. The room was tiny, perhaps the smallest in the White House, with a few Victorian chairs and a low couch with high sleigh arms to the side. The president sat in the corner of the room on an over-stuffed brown leather chair. His suit was rumpled.

> *Little Jack Horner*
> *Sat in a corner*

His back was to the doorway. Terrified, but having gone too far to turn back, Marilyn maneuvered her splendid body through the small room and stopped before President Richard Nixon, whose eyeglasses reflected the play of the flames.

> *Dot dot dot.*
> *Dash dash dash.*
> *Dot dot dot.*

As Marilyn approached the cornered President, she saw that it was true: Richard Nixon had bad hair.

As she drew ever closer, she was taken aback by his ugliness and nervously fingered her pearl necklace. She bit on one pearl to steady her nerves. Richard Nixon looked at Marilyn the way a naughty animal who has just clawed the couch to shreds in an act of instinct looks at his angry and righteous owner.

"Poor Mr. President," said Marilyn, and Richard Nixon relaxed and basked in her pity, canonized at last.

From the shadows of the room sprung the keeper of the black box, tall and tanned, crewcut red hair, sunglasses snug upon the bridge of his nose.

"Don't!" the president said to him. "Outside! She's come for me."

The Secret Serviceman looked carefully at Marilyn, then at the black box that sat heavy and dangerous in Richard Nixon's lap.

"Out!" ordered the president.

The redheaded Secret Serviceman backed out of the room.

"Thank you, ever so," said Marilyn, and the president remained silent. Marilyn knew that no one would sing "Happy birthday, Mr. President" to this man, no one would lift a glass of milk against the sun to hail this chief, and someone who held the pawn ticket to his soul was definitely collecting.

> *No milk for the devil.*
> *Poor devil.*

Marilyn saw that Richard Nixon had come to resemble the papier-mâché effigies of him that burned throughout the world. She turned her back to the president, as if it were the most normal of things that she should be standing full-blown in the Lincoln Sitting Room. Like a charmed snake, she turned toward him, and ripe and sweet, in a small, undulating voice she said, "Talk to me, Richard Nixon. Tell me all about it."

> *Hot hot hot.*
> *Flash flash flash.*
> *Hot hot hot.*

Richard Nixon removed his eyeglasses and placed them on the table beside his chair. He liked this. A blond bombshell had never come so close to him. Perhaps this was a gift from the king of Egypt. He had just seen the king of Egypt. They had ridden through the king's country on a beautiful railroad car, and try as he might, to his dismay and to the king of Egypt's relief, no one would assassinate him.

He rested his hands upon the little black box in his lap.

Marilyn did not look directly at the box because she did not want him to be suspicious.

"Egyptian kings can do such things!" exclaimed Richard Nixon, and then with spiritual recognition, he looked more closely at Marilyn and said, "Miss Monroe! We thought you were dead."

Richard Nixon's eyes narrowed as he became defensive. "What do you want with me?" A little synapse twitched in his mind. "Ahhh. I know."

> Those little eyes, so helpless
> And appealing,
> One day will flash
> And send you crashing
> Through the ceiling.

Marilyn watched the wheels click and whir in Mr. Nixon's mind. Even in Nellie Kelly, Marilyn had never encountered so elaborate and byzantine a contraption.

"It's a mercy killing," said the president. "So I don't have to go through with this. It's a cabal. A cabal!"

> Thank heaven for little girls.
> Without them
> What would presidents do?

The president relaxed. "I was fond of Egypt," he said. "Camel caravans, you know, with all these bells. Bells of Neeta they call them. Weary trudging through the desert but making music with each step to inspire the beasts. Maybe I should hang some around my neck. Get inspired. That's what they tell me anyway, but between you and me, Marilyn— May I call you Marilyn?"

"Yes, Mr. President."

"Between you and me, Marilyn, I don't know if we can

trust the Egyptians. Without their bells, they lose interest in living. They die."

Marilyn placed a Victorian chair before President Nixon and sat opposite him. She marveled at his ugliness, which was shatteringly strange and riveting in its completeness. The president had been drinking. His face sagged miserably under the weight of intoxication. He had been raised a Quaker, and packs of conscientious objectors had come from his childhood religion, which disowned him for becoming Henry Kissinger's "mad bomber." Poor man. He would never be welcome at the Blue Lagoon because he was an unrepentant Republican. Marilyn's stomach churned. How very sad for him, and how very sad for the world that the black box was all ajumble in his lap as he reached for his drink.

Mr. President took a sip of his lowball and spilled a little on the Lincoln Sitting Room floor. "History will prove me out. Show me as a great president."

"You'll be very special," said Marilyn. "They'll say that you brought the country together with a passion usually reserved for assassinations."

The president thought about that, but his attention span was short. He forgot what he was thinking about as his mind seized the next glittering toy it thought it saw.

"A lot of strange people lived in this house, Marilyn," confided the president. "You know whose room this was? This was Lincoln's room. That's a picture of him having a reception here. That's his wife, hovering in the background. You know. Hovering."

The president demonstrated hovering with his hand, and Marilyn looked at the nineteenth-century print of Abraham Lincoln and his family that hung above the gray marble fireplace.

357

The president continued. "You know, Mary Todd Lincoln had four sons, but only one of them lived. And the one that lived put her in an asylum for what he called 'excessive grief' over her husband's death. That'll teach you to have sons, I'd say. Now I myself would be proud if my loved ones had to be put in asylums because I was assassinated. That'd be true love, especially in a woman. What do you say, Marilyn? What do you say to that?"

Marilyn said, "So long, fame. I've had you."

"If I had been killed, I would have been great," said the president. "Everyone would have said I was great, damn it! As great as him."

"Him?" asked Marilyn.

The president did not answer, and Marilyn wondered if all presidents fantasize assassination, candles held aloft by the mourning world, Blackjack straining in rage at the bridle, and the eternal flame lit at the grave site.

"Yes. Mrs. Lincoln loved him enough to go nuts. That's true love," said Mr. Nixon.

"True love, Mr. President."

Marilyn was horrified but maintained her composure. She felt she was splitting at the seams, like Miss Monroe in her dress backstage, preparing to sing at the Garden.

"You know who else lived in this house? Andrew Jackson," said the president.

He was getting excited. Marilyn did not think this was good. The president continued.

"Now he's not so memorable, but his last reception in 1837, on George Washington's birthday—you know what those pricks did? They dragged a fourteen-hundred-pound cheese they'd aged down in the basement up into the East Room."

"They were looking for love," said Marilyn.

"In the Great Hall!" shouted the president. "A fourteen-hundred-pound cheese, and they invited everybody, not just the rich bastards. They invited everybody in to try it out, and they sang:

> *'Happy birthday, Mr. President.*
> *Happy birthday to you.'*

Yeah, they all sang. All of 'em. You know the song. You've heard it, right?"

"Yes. I've heard it."

"Well, everybody came all right, everybody. But you know, they smeared the White House with sticky yellow cheese. All over the place. Everywhere!"

> *Hot hot hot.*
> *Flash flash flash.*
> *Hot hot hot.*

In his excitement, the president flung his arms and the little black box tumbled onto the carpet.

"You've never seen such a sight in your life!"

"Mr. President. The box, Mr. President."

Marilyn bent over to pick up the black box, but the president got to it first.

"Always a gentleman," said Richard Nixon. He was the ugly, awkward child preferred by his mama, loving his mama as obsessively as Freddie Finney loved his. Loving your mother, however, does not necessarily prevent you from dropping more bombs than all the bombs ever dropped in all the wars ever fought on the planet, a distinction earned by Mr. Nixon.

The president looked at the black box in his hand as if he had never seen it before. Then he began to examine it, almost sensually. He tried to open it.

"I'll show you something, Marilyn. Damn."

Mr. President couldn't get it open. He was not coordinated. He was not athletic. Mr. President had never been invited to play touch football on the white sand of Cape Cod with the Secret Service. As he struggled with the box, Marilyn was profoundly sad. Here she had believed Richard Nixon to be the Great Republican Evil, the beast, the devil at least, but he was just a guy in a suit telling a story.

"I've been thinking about the Apocalypse," said Mr. President.

"There's no need to think of that," said Marilyn, alarmed into the reality that although in boy time, this was a broken man with the power to destroy the world sitting on his drunken lap.

"I like to relax in the beautiful green-and-blue Pacific," said Marilyn, digging deep into her hypnotic skills, searching the room with her peripheral vision for the hooded creature, neither man nor woman, but seeing only the shadow of the guardian of the black box in the alcove.

"Do you know where they thought up the atomic bomb? Los Alamos! A boys' school!" said the president.

" 'The woods are lovely, dark, and deep. . . .' " said Marilyn.

"You know what they called the bombs, the bombs we dropped on Nagasaki and Hiroshima? Little Boy and Fat Man. People shouldn't have boys."

"You have promises to keep. . . ."

"Let me show you something."

It was impossible to hypnotize the president. His attention span was too short. The president rose and, taking the black box with him, walked out into the Corridor of Time, past the redheaded Secret Serviceman whose eyes were riveted upon the box.

Marilyn followed Richard Nixon past the portraits of the presidents, and they stopped before the painting of John Kennedy.

"Him and that damned hairdo. Made the women wild. Nobody chased my motorcade like that, because I was respectable. I kept my dick in my pants like a gentleman.

"You know why I hated him so much? He made fun of me. He made fun of my mother. He didn't know it, but making fun of me is making fun of my mother, and she was a saint. A saint! Rich bastards. If you got your hands dirty working for a living you were shit. Shit! You know why I hated him so much?"

"He didn't love you," said Marilyn.

Mr. President's head bowed down, and he clenched the black box in one hand like a grenade with the pin pulled. The moon glowed through the tall, clear cathedral window at the end of the hall, casting a narrow plane of moonlight across the eyes of the presidents.

"I wanted to bring peace to the world. I went to China, for Christ's sake! I went to the fucking Kremlin. You think anybody's had the decency to thank me? At the Kremlin, they kept waking me up in the middle of the night, but I didn't crack. Not me. Not Dick Nixon."

Hello good-bye. Mr. President was desperate to impress Marilyn.

"I'll show you something only presidents know about. I'll show you something." He looked at her nervously, a thin film of sweat on his upper lip. "Come on. I'll show you something." He turned, shoulders hunched, and Marilyn followed. She was not so sure she wanted to see "something," but Marilyn followed him because she was a great American. The Secret Serviceman, discreet but relentless, walked behind them at a short distance.

The president descended a staircase and quickly turned

into a small white marble room, Marilyn close behind him. Awkward but effective, the president shut and locked the door. The Secret Serviceman pounded against it, but he was abandoned. On the wall inside the marble room was a small electronic panel of numbers, and the president carefully pressed a secret combination. It was the date of his mother's death.

A rush of air was heard, and the wall opened to reveal an elevator with one button in it. The president stepped into the elevator, but Marilyn hesitated. She was feeling claustrophobic. She wanted to turn back, but she did not want the president to be alone with the black box.

She stepped into the elevator, and her fear was overtaken by an acute sensation of aliveness. The president tried to press the one elevator button, but he missed and had to try again. He made contact and smiled nervously but proudly.

"I've been faithful my whole life, so far," he said.

A soft hydraulic hiss snaked through the small space and the elevator descended deep into the ground, moving rapidly downward for several minutes. There was a stabilizing whisper of air, and the elevator door opened into the most extensive atomic fallout shelter in the world.

"Go on. Go on! Take a look. We're safe now," said the president, as he pressed a combination of numbered buttons on the wall inside the shelter. It was his wedding date.

"No one can get in or out now," he said proudly.

Marilyn realized that only Mr. President could signal for the elevator. She was alarmed.

Marilyn walked through the shelter and saw that it was set up in parallel to the Commonwealth Avenue house, with its drawing room, corridor, and library. Prominent in the library was President Kennedy's book, *Profiles in Courage,* for which he won a Pulitzer Prize. Beside it was a right-wing diatribe entitled, *The Bay of Pigs, or How the Democrats Lost Cuba.*

Marilyn descended a circular stairway and was walking through the bedrooms when Richard Nixon's voice echoed from above: "Marilyn! Come here! I want to show you something!"

Marilyn walked up the circular stairway and toward the president's voice in the kitchen, which was at the back of the shelter. Through the open doorway into the kitchen, Marilyn saw an underground, atomic-fallout-proof greenhouse. In the midst of the greenhouse, among the man-sized sunflowers, stood Richard Nixon with outstretched arms. He wanted to be embraced. That was all he wanted, but he dropped his arms and stiffened when Marilyn hesitated.

"That could cost the world," he said angrily as he walked awkwardly past her, through the kitchen and into the library.

Hello Good-bye
Hello Good-bye

Marilyn followed him. Marilyn was a great American. 'Tis a far, far better thing than I have ever done, she thought.

The president sat in a leather chair and motioned for Marilyn to sit opposite him. He put the black box on the table beside him.

"Nobody loves me. Everybody hates me," said the President.

"Let me hail the chief for you," said Marilyn.

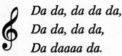

Da da, da da da,
Da da, da da,
Da daaaa da.

"I wanted to be beautiful. I wanted to be brave," said the president. "I wanted to go into the lion's cage, but I was afraid. Sheba Sheik had big teeth. If she ate me up, my parts wouldn't have grown back."

Rintrah, the MGM lion, roared above ground.

"She wouldn't have eaten him," said the president. "She would have licked his hand."
"Whose hand, Mr. President?"
"Jack Kennedy's hand."
Marilyn stood before the president. She looked to the east. She looked to the west. She looked directly at President Richard Milhous Nixon and sang in her small, undulating voice:

Happy birthday to you . . .

"I have heard Marilyn singing. I do not think that she will sing to me," said the President, his eyes flickering with hope that her song really was for him.

Happy birthday to you.
Happy birthday, Mr. President.
Happy birthday to you.

Marilyn kissed the tips of her fingers, pressed them against his cheek and asked, "Who is it that you want to be?"
The silence was dark and deep.
"John Fitzgerald Kennedy. I wanna be John Fitzgerald Kennedy," said the President.

364

"You are John Fitzgerald Kennedy. Stand up, Jack."

Richard Nixon rose slowly from his chair, being careful not to wrench his famous bad back. He smiled like a Kennedy in pain. He dazzled with beauty.

> *What style!*
> *What passion!*
> *What a sense of fashion!*

Marilyn was as pleased as Mary Shelley must have been when she created Frankenstein's monster.

"I have to have sex once a day, or I get migraines," confided the president. "And that wouldn't be good for the free world." Mr. President winked.

Marilyn wondered if there was something imminent, a hidden proposition, in his statement. The shock of that possibility brought Marilyn Albion thudding back to earth, no longer on tour, no longer inhabited by Miss Monroe. This was real. A little too real. How very solid was the world.

Marilyn Albion watched Richard Nixon roam the atomic fallout shelter, and what she saw was a man who had become the depository of the national insanity.

Marilyn Albion had been trapped inside the Monroe-esque grotesque, as trapped as Richard Nixon in his ugly presidentialisms. However, the subtle lifting of her breasts to bear the brunt of history had a motion reminiscent of Mrs. Finnegan.

The President said, "Cha cha cha?"

> *It was the best of times. It was the worst of times.*

Marilyn Albion moved toward the president. She had come this far. She would not resist history, although repulsion heaved like the great deep waves of the Atlantic. She held her breath and ran her fingers through his hair. It was as soft as any other human's hair, not beautiful but not barbed.

The president kissed her hand, absolved of sin, the sin that had brought him banishment from the White House: ugliness.

"Shall we ascend?" asked Marilyn Albion, and the dashing president rose up into his invisible back brace, brushed an imaginary Jack-like lock of hair from his brow, and punched the numbers that opened the elevator door.

Marilyn Albion lifted the little black box from the end table, and at that moment she knew that each president would want to create the sensation of profound chaos shattering the daylights out of mortality. So great will be that desire, that he will have to fight the constant urge to create a crisis—or to have himself murdered—so that he may provide the ticket for the national thrill ride.

The hooded figure, neither man nor woman, stood by Marilyn Albion and pulled from her body all the infestations of history. She heard the hooded figure speak, but she knew it was her own voice:

> *Say good-bye to Miss Monroe.*
> *To Mr. Kennedy.*
> *To Mr. Nixon.*

In the elevator with the president, Marilyn opened the black box and looked at the little amber lights that surrounded the green button. The president said, "That's something the president has to take care of." He smiled with media enlightenment, his teeth as white as the Cape Cod sand.

Marilyn Albion snapped the lid shut on the doomsday box and handed it to him.

Hot hot hot.
Flash flash flash.
Hot hot hot.

The president nodded, and the elevator door opened with a hydraulic thrust. The redheaded Secret Serviceman stood at attention. The president winked, handed him the black box, and turned down the Corridor of Time as if Marilyn were too inconsequential to merit a good-bye.

What a stud.

The president moved toward the muffled strains of "Hail to the Chief," which the military band on the White House lawn was playing for him; and Marilyn Albion, glad to be abandoned and alive in the free world, walked past the portraits of the presidents lining the corridor, the presidents basking in the August morning light that flashed across their eyes in one thick gold shaft.

Thanks, Mr. President.
Thank you, ever so.